To Gracie, Thanks for all the great Toon City memories / to love, Mike Phelan

The *Secret of Bell Island

*Spies and Intrigue.
Treasure, sabotage and murder.
A haunted mystery U-boat.
Lost and found family and yes, even romance.
You want more?
There's more ... much more ...

A novel by Mike Phelan

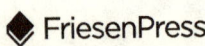 FriesenPress

One Printers Way
Altona, MB R0G 0B0
Canada

www.friesenpress.com

Copyright © 2021 Mike Phelan
First Edition — 2021

All rights reserved.

No part of this publication may be reproduced in any form, or by any means, electronic or mechanical, including photocopying, recording, or any information browsing, storage, or retrieval system, without permission in writing from FriesenPress.

This is a work of fiction. Names, characters, businesses, places, events, and incidents are either the products of the author's imagination or used in a fictitious manner.

ISBN
978-1-03-912730-2 (Hardcover)
978-1-03-912729-6 (Paperback)
978-1-03-912731-9 (eBook)

1. Fiction, Historical

Distributed to the trade by The Ingram Book Company

Table of Contents

Chapter 1 1

Chapter 2 8

Chapter 3 19

Chapter 4 27

Chapter 5 33

Chapter 6 39

Chapter 7 42

Chapter 8 50

Chapter 9 58

Chapter 10 64

Chapter 11 71

Chapter 12 76

Chapter 13 86

Chapter 14 99

Chapter 15 108

Chapter 16 116

Chapter 17 123

Chapter 18 130

Chapter 19 135

Chapter 20 144

Chapter 21...154

Chapter 22 164

Chapter 23 172

Chapter 24 182

Chapter 25 190

Chapter 26 196

Chapter 27.. 210

Chapter 28 224

Chapter 29 229

Chapter 30 272

Chapter 31..286

Chapter 32 300

Chapter 33 305

Chapter 34 319

Epilogue.. 323

Dedication

For Lieutenant Gordon F. Phelan,
Royal Canadian Navy, World War Two

As well as those who first fished and farmed on Bell Island, and the miners who lived and died in their toils on and under the red rock. To their families for their courageous spirit. For those who served their country with honour, and to the memory of all those from the ore-boat tragedies of September 5th and November 2, 1942 near Lance Cove.

And for Bell Islanders everywhere, past, present, and future.

Foreword

In 1891, Newfoundland was still part of the British Empire and remained so until 1949, when it became a province of Canada. In Conception Bay, on Belle Isle, which eventually came to be called Bell Island, there lived a small population of about seven hundred hardy souls, consisting mostly of fishermen and farmers. Although the heavy red rock had been known about for many years, and had even been used as boat ballast, its value as a commercial commodity was not realised until 1892, when applications to search for minerals were filed. By 1895, Bell Island began shipping some of the highest-grade iron ore ever discovered to steel manufacturers in Nova Scotia.

In just a few years, hundreds of men were employed as miners, and Germany had become a major customer. The steel they manufactured using raw materials from the island would most certainly have played a large roll in the stockpiling of armaments leading up to the First World War. The little island's rich resource became even more important to Germany after the Great War, and once more, they manufactured thousands of tons of steel. At the commencement of World War Two, when their supply was again cut off by Britain, the German high command began planning a response, the consequences of which could spell disaster for Bell Island.

Prologue

Bell Island, July 1955

The day was warm, bright, and sunny with a light wind from the south. In the morning light, the high cliffs of Bell Island shone brightly, displaying bands of slate grey shale layered with lighter sandy-coloured rock and just a hint of the rich iron ore deposits being mined on the other side of the island as the small car and passenger ferry *Kipawo* slowly approached its mooring at the bottom of Beach Hill.

Standing close to the back of the boat, behind his father and a half dozen other passengers, the five-year-old boy stumbled forward and then back as the docking vessel came to an abrupt stop. On the previous trip, a crewman had forgotten to secure the light safety chain meant to bridge the open gap at the boat's stern.

The boy felt suddenly weightless for a moment and then shockingly cold as his thin body landed in the cold, greasy water. As he slid under, he could smell diesel fumes and feel a gentle tug toward the large, discoloured bronze screw still slowly churning the water near him. The sharp intake of breath he had taken instinctively as he landed in the water began to escape, and he felt a hot pain in his chest. His green eyes were wide open, and he could see sharp, white barnacles on the boat's hull. Then came a sweet silence from the muffled thunder of the engine as it was shut down, and the propellor stopped rotating, the last of its swirling vortex of bubbles rising lazily to the surface. As if in a dream, he sank in slow motion, arms above his head, unable to move. Above, the twinkling surface receded, and the picture began to dim. The last image he remembered was of a beautiful angel reaching out her hand. . . .

Chapter 1

Over St. John's, Saturday, July 14, 2018

The WestJet flight from Vancouver had been fairly pleasant for the most part but became steadily more turbulent as the Boeing 737-800 headed into a thunderstorm over Eastern Newfoundland, and the air pockets near St. John's turned the seventy-ton beast into an airborne roller coaster in a driving rain.

Touchdown brought an obligatory round of applause from some passengers, while others, including Matt, slowly unclenched their death grips on the armrests and breathed a sigh of relief. He didn't mind the height or bucking-bronco effect, and for that matter, he would rather be free climbing a steep rock wall in a stiff breeze than pretty much anything else. In fact, the grey hair and calendar age of sixty-seven notwithstanding, he was still fit and trim, running several miles a day and staying toned with weights in his home gym. No, it was being over the open ocean on final approach that had frightened him, although intellectually, he knew that falling out of the sky would make no difference whether over land or sea. After all, dead is dead. But for Matt, the deep had always been both an irresistible attraction and a source of terror.

As the plane came to a gentle stop, the passengers began standing to retrieve belongings from the overhead compartments. A young boy who had been sitting several seats behind him, when he wasn't racing up and down the aisle, darted around them and bumped hard into Matt. The boy's haggard mother apologised to him, and everyone around them, as they worked their way toward the exit at the front. Soon they met again at the baggage carousel inside the terminal.

"Sorry about the boy," she said, embarrassed. "Honestly, he's like a little savage!"

Matt smiled. "No problem. He's been cooped up on the plane since Calgary. I noticed that's where you got on."

"Yes," she said. "I was visiting friends there while my husband is working up north on the oil rigs, and now I'm here for my sister's wedding. I've got to say, I wasn't sure we'd make it that last little while. I was some scared."

Her son sped past and yelled back, "Mom, you were shit baked!"

"Jesus help me." She laughed. "Do you see what I got to put up with? Tell me now," she continued, "you don't sound like a Newfoundlander. Who do you belong to?"

Matt smiled again as his memory of the colloquialisms commonly known as '*Newfounese*' came flooding back.

"You're right," he confessed. "I'm Matt McCarty. My folks were from Nova Scotia, but we moved to Bell Island when I was five after my father was hired to supervise electrical work in the iron-ore mines. I had a bit of an accent once, but I've been away almost fifty years, so it's pretty much gone now unless I get excited."

Shaking hands with him, she said, "Nice to meet you, Matt. I'm Mary Walsh, and that little devil there is Gerald."

They both finished collecting their luggage, and with laden carts, began heading toward the terminal exit.

"So, I suppose this will be some fun visit you'll be having after fifty years away. Do you still have people here?"

"It will be a bit mixed actually," he replied. "I'm here to bury my father and to visit with some old memories."

"Oh no!" she exclaimed. "I'm sorry to hear that."

"It's all right," Matt said. "My father was in his late nineties and still living on his own, so I guess that's a win in anybody's book. I hadn't spoken to him since I left in 1968. Apparently, he just went to sleep one night and didn't wake up. I'm really only here because there's no one else except for an old family friend who gave me the news. Dad's being put to rest in the Mount Pleasant Field of Honour as a World War Two navy veteran."

"Well," she said as they parted ways, "sorry again about your trouble, but I do hope you find some enjoyment while you visit home after so many years."

"I'm sure everything will work out the way it's supposed to. Looks like Gerald has burned off some energy," he said, noting that the boy now lay across the luggage on their cart, seemingly fast asleep. "So long for now."

"'Bye. All the best now," she replied and disappeared in the crowd.

The rain had let up, but it was still grey, wet, and windy as Matt went to the car-rental counter and checked in. Then he made the long trek from the terminal down an outside semi-covered walkway to the rental lot. Checking the key fob against license plates, he located a new white Chevy Tahoe SUV. Throwing two large duffel bags and his carry-on backpack into the rear cargo area, he climbed into the cab. After adjusting the seat for his lanky six-foot frame, Matt drove out of the airport parking lot. At the World Parkway traffic light, he could choose to turn right for a few miles toward the Portugal Cove ferry to Bell Island or left to downtown

St. John's. For now, his childhood home would have to wait, but that visit would come soon enough. He turned left, and speeding up, began the short drive to the city and the long overdue reunion with his father.

○ ○ ○

Much of St. John's had changed in the past fifty years. Love it or hate it, there was now a modern-looking box of a building, housing the new museum, standing in sharp contrast next to the Romanesque Basilica Cathedral on Military Road. The large Catholic church was a familiar and unchanging edifice, standing high on a hill overlooking the water, where it had greeted sailors entering the narrows of St. John's harbour for almost one hundred and sixty years. There was also a shiny new city hall, convention centre, and stadium built on the crumbling bones of old tenement dwellings and failing small businesses.

However, the heart and soul of downtown near the waterfront remained. Many of the older Second Empire style row houses that were built after the Great Fire of 1892, which destroyed much of the city, had been renovated and painted in bright, contrasting jelly-bean colours. There were also more drinking establishments block for block downtown than ever before. And for St. John's, purported to be the oldest city in North America, that was saying something.

To Matt, it made little difference, for although he could likely have a drink or two without it being a problem, he chose not to. In the now-distant past, a few drinks had usually led to a few lines of cocaine, and that had definitely been a problem—a problem that had left a trail of broken relationships and lost opportunities in its wake, a problem that, after a quick rise toward the top of a promising music career, had seen him work his way down to the bottom and then lower still as addiction took control of his life. The last straw had been when the woman who loved him said with tears in her eyes as she left, *"I thought we were going to be a family."* A sweet girl who deserved better.

The first NA meeting was tough. Standing up and admitting to the others in the circle that he was an addict and needed help was the hardest thing he had ever done. It took that admission, and then several months of rehab hell, but eventually he began to feel again. In the clean and sober years that followed, there had been other women, but it was never for long, and it had never felt quite right. There was never again "the one." Eventually, he just stopped thinking about it. Life was good for the most part, and in time the loss faded.

○ ○ ○

Fran Kavanagh was standing in the doorway when Matt pulled into the drive of her beautiful home, west of downtown on Waterford Bridge Road. It was an older two-story house with a huge semi-circular bay window on the main floor. She wore patched and faded blue jeans, an old red-checkered flannel shirt, and had a garden claw in her hand. She was obviously enjoying her retirement from Memorial University and still had the devilish smile he remembered.

"Jesus, Mary, and Joseph!" she bellowed as he emerged from the vehicle. "Is that young Matty McCarty I see all grown up now?"

"Fran Kavanagh!" he yelled back. "You're still the same sexy-looking girl I used to dream about!"

"You lovely, lying bastard," she laughed. "Come in! We'll have a cup of tea and talk about your dad."

Fran was four years older than Matt and had been his sister's best friend up until the day Heather died. It was no secret that he'd had a crush on Fran as a thirteen-year-old, until he had met his first serious girlfriend at Topsail Beach two years later. When he left after Heather died, Fran had kept in touch off and on, though more so in recent years, and remained Matt's touchstone to his Newfoundland past. She seemed to know everyone in the city, or knew someone who went to school with someone who did. If you were from away and had heard the often-joked-about belief that every Newfoundlander knew every other Newfoundlander, you would be close to the truth if you were talking about Fran Kavanagh.

"I only saw your father a few times over all those years," Fran said as they sat at the kitchen table drinking a mug of Red Rose that she had poured from a steaming brown ceramic teapot. "He was a quiet man," she continued, "and we both know he liked a drink. At the end, he was just on his pension and living in a bed sitting room down there on Duckworth Street."

"He was an alcoholic," said Matt. "That's just a fact. I used to judge him for it, but I know better now; although I can't help but wonder what demons drove him there. He was a lousy father. Not for what he did but for what he didn't do. Probably just not cut out for it, I suppose. I didn't realise it until now, but I'm not angry anymore. I was young when Mom died. He wasn't very present to start with, but after that, he became a ghost. If Heather hadn't been there to take care of me, I don't know what would have happened."

"Your sister was an angel," Fran said. "She loved you so much. When she got the cancer so young, it nearly killed all of us who knew her."

Matt was quiet for a moment, realising she didn't know why he'd actually left the island so suddenly way back then. "I got kind of hard after she was gone. Dad was drunk all the time, and there was nothing to keep me here. I took some money from his wallet one night when he was passed out and just left. I wound up in Vancouver, and things were really good after that for a long while, until they weren't. Once I found cocaine, it was pretty much all over. By anyone's guess, I should probably be dead several times over after what I did to myself. Going through that made me look at Dad a bit differently."

"Well, Heather would be as proud as I am if she could see you now and how you turned your life around," Fran said. "How long has it been since you got cured of your addiction?"

"There's no cure, Fran," he answered, smiling. "It's been over twenty years since I had a drink or a drug. But that's only from being grateful and living one day at a time."

"Okay, now," she said mysteriously, "let's have another cuppa. There's something I need to show you."

After pouring more tea in the cosy kitchen, Fran opened a cupboard door, reached up, and took down a large wooden cigar box. It looked old. Handing it to him, she said, "I haven't opened it, but I believe this is everything your father thought was important enough to keep."

Chapter 2

Bell Island, Saturday, July 14, 2018

Just off Compressor Hill, a new-looking sign attached to a rusty, old iron-ore car advertised, *"Tour Bell Island's Historic #2 Mine and Museum."* The small, dented, and well-used relic of the past was displayed on a short section of rail track, and a painted arrow directed one up a short curving drive toward the attraction. In a large open field behind the museum, thousands of tons of waste rock, left over from the heyday of mining, created a miniature mountain. Here and there, it showed patches of greenery and wild purple lupin flowers as the mound was slowly reclaimed by mother nature. Even so, almost seventy years after the No. 2 mine shut down in 1950, the scene still bore silent testimony to the fact that, once upon a time, this area had been one of the four thriving, noisy, and dusty mining operations dotting the north side of the island, where hundreds of honourable men with strong backs tore the unyielding, heavy red rock out of the earth and from under the sea. One by one, the other mines had shut down, beginning ten years later. First No. 6, and then No. 4, and finally, in 1966, the end came, as No. 3 brought its last load to the surface, leaving only the ghosts of the past to roam the now-empty submarine slopes.

In the building's souvenir shop, Cassie Clarke gave change from a twenty-dollar bill to the leering forty-something tourist standing next to his unhappy-looking wife. His eyes were on Cassie's chest and not the change. She rolled her eyes, the way only a young teenage girl can, shut the till, and moved on to the next customer. The shop and the cafe beside it, where her best friend Bev Adams worked, were part of the mine-museum experience, which was doing a thriving business, even laying on extra underground tours as the warm weather brought the tourists over from St. John's and beyond. She loved the part-time summer job and had learned a lot about the workings of the No. 2 mine, often exploring with her friend all the way down to where a greenish pool of ground water had welled up from below once the powerful pumps had been shut off, flooding all the mines up to where the water had sought its own level.

Long-time tour guide Tom Crane would gently correct those who thought the flooding came from the waters of Conception Bay, pressing down from above. Wide-eyed children and parents alike stared at the cloudy ground water while he asked them to imagine donning scuba gear and following the submerged maze farther and farther down the slope, finally reaching a depth of sixteen hundred feet below the Atlantic Ocean floor. Crane would continue, saying they would then be three miles from shore, seeing hundreds of sunken artefacts along the way from a bygone era. Still present, but unseen from above the water, were empty ore cars, boilers, wheelbarrows, tools, horseshoes, steam and water pipe, and even an occasional old lunchbox, along with rusted, crumbling, and gnarled wiring ready to trap any unwary diver.

The four submarine mines on Bell Island had entrances or "collars" that gently sloped down long tunnels from the surface, with rooms being carved out of a number of thick, solid slabs of iron ore that were stacked one upon the other like giant fallen dominoes tilting down under the sea.

From the beginning until the later 1940s, horses were used in the mines, fed and groomed mostly by older children. The animals hauled ore carts from the side tunnels for transfer to the main slopes of each mine, where the rail lines would take the raw ore from the many offshoots up to the surface in multi-car trains that clamped to a moving cable. Rock would then be sorted from the ore by hand, again often by children, or by those too old or unable for other reasons to still labour below. After modernisation, the horses were retired and their duties—as well as the separation of ore from rock—fell to more practical machinery.

The entrances to the abandoned workings of No. 3 and No. 6 submarine mines had been sealed up after they closed. Their collars were crushed into the ground and back-filled, with barely a sign now of where they had once been. That left the No. 2 mine museum nearer Town Square, and No. 4, farthest to the west, sitting alone by itself now in an empty field, its original, slightly crumbling concrete collar still intact, proudly showing the year it had been poured over its rebar form in 1916. The No. 4 collar was now used as a venue for mini plays about island history and legend, providing summer jobs for talented local students. About two hundred and fifty feet inside, however, there was a solidly erected wall with a heavy locked door to keep people from the possible danger beyond of falling rock or unwittingly becoming a victim of the inevitable groundwater hazard farther in where it was pitch black.

There were much older, separate mine workings accessible on the north side of the island, where more than a dozen large cave-like tunnels opened onto the beach at the bottom of the cliffs and Cassie had explored most of them. This honeycomb maze was an extension of the long-exhausted No. 1 and No. 5 surface mines that began in the 1890s.

Cassie was born with a curious mind and loved poking around in the old remains from the past. There was still an occasional surprise too, like the time she and Bev had found an opening in the cliff, which was uncovered after a small collapse from the constant wave action had dislodged some rock near her favourite spot on the beach at Grebes Nest. It led into a tunnel unlike any of the others she had seen.

After picking Tom Crane's brain, as she did most days anyway about mining history, she'd found out that her discovery was likely a naturally occurring cave. In his youth, he had heard of one that spies were rumoured to have used during the war, and as a boy, he and his friends had tried to find the "lost tunnel" many times without success.

Cassie was determined to follow the cave as far in as she could this summer, but that would require planning and gathering more supplies. Up to now, she and Bev had only explored the first fifty feet to where the natural daylight began to dim. Lying here and there, farther back, were what looked like old empty packing crates with some kind of foreign writing on them. No one else except her best friend knew about the mystery tunnel.

Cassie was a tall, slim, pretty girl with bright-green, intelligent eyes and long, straight red hair that fell halfway down her back. She didn't really look much older than her fifteen years and had only ever been as far as St. John's, but somehow, she appeared worldly wise and had learned at an early age how to take care of herself. Cassie's mom, Elizabeth, had been taken suddenly by illness when Cassie was four, and she had never known her father. Elizabeth had met him while she was visiting in St. John's, and after a brief romance, he had disappeared, never knowing that he had a daughter.

She'd been raised by her grandparents until Granddad had passed on, shortly before her ninth birthday. Now it was just Cassie and her grandmother, Evelyn, living in their comfortable, old, former-mining cottage down on the Green—an area to the island's northeast that had once had a much larger population, when the mines were still in operation.

In 1961, Evelyn's own mother, Lorraine Sparkes, had left five-year-old Evelyn in the care of her widowed friend Peggy Clarke while she travelled to the mainland for a job interview, but mysteriously, Lorraine was never heard from again. Evelyn had been lovingly cared for by the family and eventually married Peggy's son, Henry.

o o o

Arriving home after work, Cassie was greeted at the back door with a slobbery head bonk from Kip, Evelyn's ageing Newfoundland dog. Kip was a gentle, sad-eyed beast, and at almost the same age as Cassie, he was slowing down, older now than most for such a large breed. One of the few memories she had of her mom was being held by the hand as a child and riding on Kip's powerful back, holding tightly with her other hand to his thick, curly black ruff. She looked at a framed picture of Elizabeth on the mantle above the fireplace and smiled wistfully. Next to it was a similarly framed picture of her great-grandmother, Lorraine. Both pictures showed them smiling, with their waist-long hair down—both so beautiful and so unknowable.

"Hey, Cass," her grandmother said, greeting her. "How are all the tourists doing today? We're having meatloaf for supper."

Evelyn had a habit of asking a question and then plowing on with another topic before getting an answer. It was one of her endearing quirks and always drew a smile from Cassie, who had learned to wait before answering.

"Tourists are good," she replied as she helped set the table. "Had a bunch in from the States who used to have people from here, name of Parsons."

"Oh yes," said her grandmother, "there used to be bushels of Parsons here. I think one of them even died down in No. 3. Crushed by an ore car, I believe. What did they think of the mine tour?"

"They didn't mention any crushing, but they loved the tour. Of course, Tom has a lot to do with that."

"Yes, yes," Evelyn sighed. "Tom Crane is the best guide they got alright, and so handsome too. I'd give him a go, if I was still after a bit."

"Thank you for that visual, Gram, and on that note, I'm going to go clean up for supper." Cassie headed down the hallway with Kip lumbering after her, while Evelyn put the meatloaf on the old yellow formica and chrome kitchen table.

After supper, with dishes cleaned and put away, Cassie took her violin and went out on the back porch. The only thing between her and the ocean was a grassy strip of land that led to the cliff and the older mine tunnels that broke out onto the shore below.

"Okay, Kip. What do you want to hear tonight?" she asked. Kip had been named by her grandfather after the *Kipawo,* an old, long-retired ferry boat that had run between the island and Portugal Cove on the mainland. It was said that the name befitted the dog because he was a powerful swimmer, and according to her grandfather, he was so strong that he could probably haul a couple of cars across the stretch of water called the 'Tickle' from the mainland as good as the boat, if he put his mind to it. Kip thumped his heavy tail twice on the wooden porch in answer to her question and then dozed as she began to play.

St. John's, Saturday, July 14, 2018

"It's kind of sad, you know," Fran said, "but your dad must have really treasured whatever few mementos he kept in that box. He had so little left to show for such a long life, I guess he wanted to guard it from getting stolen by anyone in that old rooming house. It was only after a few days that the manager found it behind the dresser and passed it on to me."

His father had never smoked cigars, to his knowledge, but had been a chronic cigarette smoker. Players Plain, two packs a day. That plus the alcoholism should have led his father to an early grave, but there you are. Never can tell. A bit nervously, he lifted the little latch and slowly opened the lid. He was so removed from his father's world after all these years that he felt a bit like a voyeur, looking at the private belongings of a familiar stranger. Opening the lid released the pungent smell of stale cigarette smoke.

Pushing aside for a moment an old letter on top of the box's contents, he saw the bone-handled pocket knife he had given his father when he was twelve. He had forgotten buying it for Father's Day so many years ago, but now, he could see himself walking into the Patrick Curran Hardware Store on Water Street, counting out his money, and looking up at old Mr. Curran when he realised he was short of the tax on the four-dollar price tag. The man had taken the money Matt held and just handed him the knife with what might have passed for a smile. Seeing it here, after so many years, triggered a feeling stored safely away long ago as he remembered how proud he had been to see the rare look of genuine pleasure on his father's face when he'd opened the gift. He was both surprised and happy that his father had thought it important enough to keep all these years. Scraping the blade's edge across the top of a fingernail, it was obvious that his father had kept it sharp too.

In the bottom of the box were a few small items, including two Bell Island brass miner's tokens. These were small, round, numbered tags registered to each miner and placed on a nail board when they checked in for work at the mine entrance. More intriguing were two other brass items: Spent casings from a .45 calibre pistol. He had never known his father to have any interest in firearms. Most puzzling, though, was the heavy gold ring depicting an imperial eagle, with wings spread wide, clutching a Nazi swastika. Below that was the embossed image of a submarine with U-184 on its bow in relief. Looking on the inside of the ring, he saw that it was stamped "22k" and engraved with "*GD 29-05-42.*" Matt thought that, perhaps, his father had come across the ring while serving in the navy during World War Two. But to his knowledge, his father had been assigned as a lieutenant to a small corvette and never went far beyond Halifax harbour while on patrol. *Also, this ring must be pretty valuable.* Curious.

All thought of the ring disappeared when Matt picked up the letter. The creased and stained envelope, with faded but neat handwriting, was addressed to his father, "*Mr. William McCarty, Tessier's Lane, St. John's, Nfld.*" and marked "*Personal.*" The return address stated that it had come from "*L. Sparkes, Grammer Street, Bell Island.*" The postmark was dated August 11, 1961. He looked the letter over very carefully. It had definitely never been opened. He set it down on the table and looked at Fran.

"I don't know why, but I feel nervous about opening this. If he didn't, I don't know if *I* even have any right to. Suppose he didn't open it because he knew it was going to be something bad. Maybe something that I don't want to know."

"That's going to be up to you, Matty," Fran replied. "You have to decide. But if you don't open it because of fear of the unknown, well . . . that doesn't sound like you, and you might regret it someday. I think that might be what kept your father from breaking the seal on that envelope. Regret is a terrible thing."

"You're right as usual," Matt said, as he made his decision.

It was apropos that he used his father's knife, carefully inserting the tip of the blade under the flap of the envelope. For a moment, he felt some kind of approval, maybe even a kinship with his father, as he sliced it open, and the letter dropped out onto the kitchen table. He began to read.

> *"My Dearest Bill, I am back on Bell Island. This will come as a shock, and I hope you can forgive me as I tell you now why I left so suddenly without saying anything. When you came back, and we met again here after so many years, I was so happy that we could spend some time together. With no regrets, I became pregnant with your child, a sweet little girl named Evelyn. I knew it wouldn't have been right for me to be the cause of a breakup with your family, so I went away to have her.*
>
> *I love you, Bill. You know I have since the first day I saw you when you came to stay with us here during the war, and I know you loved me. If things had only been different! Sparky always liked you, and he would have been so happy if you and I could*

have been together, but it's no one's fault that you had promised yourself to another before we met. It is so unfair that your loyalty is one of the things that attracts me to you the most, and also the very reason why my heart broke.

I was sorry to read in the paper that your wife has passed away. This may be wrong for me to say, but Bill, you have denied your own happiness for so long, isn't it time you realise that you deserve some? You mustn't still blame yourself for what you had to do during the war, and what happened with 'Operation Red Iron' was not your fault. Please come back to me! Bring Heather and little Matty, and with Evelyn, we can become a family. The house on Grammer Street is big enough for all of us, and I know it could be a place of happiness.

I will wait for one month, Bill, but if I don't hear from you by then, I will be selling the house and leaving Bell Island to interview for a good job on the mainland. I am leaving little Evelyn with my friend Peggy Clarke, who lives down on the Green, until I get settled. Again, I'm sorry I waited so long to tell you, but you deserve to know.

Evelyn is five years old now and a very happy little girl, except she does have my red hair, so she can be a bit stubborn sometimes, ha-ha. I hope you and the children are well, and I want you to know how much you mean to me, and that I do not regret what we did. I will always treasure our time together, no matter what you decide. Please give Matty a hug for me. I feel such a special connection to him."

The letter was signed simply *"Love always, Lorraine"* and that was it. Nothing more.

Matt's mind was working in slow motion. Too much to process. Why was his father on Bell Island during the war, and what was it that he blamed himself for? Why did this woman feel a "special connection" to him? His father and this woman? They— The penny dropped.

"Jesus H. Christ," he announced quietly. "I have a half sister."

Chapter 3

Germany, May 1941

Kurt Becher, twenty-eight, came from the seaport city of Emden in northwest Germany. On March 31, 1940, the RAF dropped a four-thousand-pound "blockbuster" bomb on the shipyards there. The device had little effect on them, but the accompanying clusters of incendiary bombs torched a number of nearby civilian houses, including Becher's, killing his entire family. Becher had a brilliant mind and had studied structural engineering before the war, but his hatred now for the British turned him dark inside. He wished with all his heart to see the West and all it stood for destroyed, and he would do anything for an opportunity to help make that happen.

A chance meeting with twenty-four-year-old August Kahr, who had been educated abroad in the United Sates, set the stage for them to work together as spies in an operation that could deliver a major blow to Germany's enemies. Kahr's specialty was chemistry, and he was well versed in the manufacture and use of high explosives. Since his return to Germany, he had helped develop a new highly efficient method of delivering an almost pure, undiluted charge of nitroglycerine in a stable package no larger than a regular stick of dynamite but with ten times the explosive power.

Kahr was handsome, outgoing, and got along well with everyone he met. While he might be a perfect candidate for espionage, he was not a diehard patriot of the fatherland, and he was not confident that Germany would win the war. He realised that it would not be long before the United States got involved. If that happened, he believed it would just be a matter of time before the massive resources of the West eventually led them to victory. For his own well being, however, he kept his opinions to himself, and on the surface, appeared to be a loyal, blond-haired blue-eyed, shining example of the superior race.

When he was approached by the Abwehr, who knew of his talents, which included an excellent command of the English language, he was quick to join the powerful intelligence organisation. *Better to be on the inside,* he'd thought, *and knowledge is power.* After being assigned his first mission, he recommended recruiting a talented structural engineer he had recently met for certain parts of the job. Kurt Becher was secretly investigated and considered to be an excellent choice to join him for the deadly operation that was being planned.

Bell Island, September 1941

Becher and Kahr arrived by submarine under cover of darkness just offshore of the Vichy controlled, French owned island of St. Pierre. They were then transported by motorboat to Newfoundland's Point May, and from there, overland to St. John's and finally to Bell Island on the small passenger ferry *Maneco*.

Once they reached Bell Island, Becher and Kahr found food and lodging in a comfortable boarding house run by Mrs. Emeline Dawe. Next door was the island headquarters for the St. John's based Avalon Telephone Company, and nearby, the small town boasted a surgery and a number of shops, including a pharmacy, restaurants, grocery stores, taverns, and dry goods and hardware retailers.

The German agents reported to the iron-ore company office on Bennett Street shortly after they settled in. They presented their excellent forged documents, showing identification as well as letters of reference, attesting to their skills in both structural engineering—important for mine expansion—and chemistry, which would assist the company by fine-tuning their method of room and pillar mining, using newer specialised explosives. The decision was made to hire them right away, and because there was a shortage of office personnel, their credentials were not checked immediately. The two new men began working, and no actual follow up ever took place.

o o o

In 1942, German U-boats continued to wreak havoc on allied shipping, causing death and destruction. On March third, a German submarine had fired several torpedoes at the cliffs near the narrow opening to St. John's harbour, in an unsuccessful attempt to see them topple and block the entrance. Then on September fifth, a U-boat had entered Newfoundland's Conception Bay and sank the SS *Saganaga* and the *Lord Strathcona,* two iron-ore carriers anchored just off Bell Island, with the loss of twenty-nine lives.

In the aftermath of the sinkings, the recently formed Canadian Intelligence Corps in Ottawa received a report from the British admiralty that a U-boat would be leaving the German submarine pens at Kiel soon, with orders to sink more ore carriers off Bell Island. It was confirmed that the sub would also drop off specialised nitroglycerin explosives to saboteurs already in place among the island's local population, so that they could complete a mission to destroy the actual mines and infrastructure. With that news, the CIC realised that the spies had probably been involved, likely as spotters, with the previous ore-carrier attack. The information was passed along to the Royal Canadian Navy Special Operations Section in Halifax, who set to work drawing up plans for a secret mission.

o o o

According to the official navy records, from April 1942, newly commissioned twenty-two-year-old RCN Lieutenant William McCarty was to be assigned to HMCS *Cobalt*, a small corvette warship patrolling the waters outside Halifax harbour, providing escort service for merchant-marine convoys preparing to cross the Atlantic. However, McCarty never set foot on the ship. In reality, he was now the newest member of the RCN SOS. He was chosen as a likely candidate for clandestine services, along with several others recruited from the sixty Canadian Officer Training Corps graduates of St. Mary's University in Halifax that year, where he had achieved high marks, earning a degree in electrical engineering in addition to being a top athlete. When he was approached by the navy and asked if he would use his talents to covertly assist in the war effort, the choice for him was obvious. He sensed that there would be intrigue, romance, danger, and adventure. Naively, he saw himself winning the war singlehanded, saving the girl, and signing autographs at the premiere of the movie they would make about his daring exploits.

In October, six months later, through freezing cold and blistering heat, he was battered and bruised from hiking, climbing, and learning the use of explosives and small arms, as well as training in close-quarters combat, not to mention the many hours of theory and practice with cyphers, code books, and wireless telegraphy radio operation. He was definitely cured of any romantic notions of heroism under fire, and he would happily have settled for a good night's rest. Right at this moment though, he felt a slight thrill of excitement, having just been told he was being given his first assignment.

McCarty reported as instructed, in civilian clothing, to a mansion at number 16 Barrington Street in Halifax, where he was admitted and checked closely before being ushered into a large smoky drawing room. It held a long, carved wooden conference table surrounded by a dozen richly upholstered straight-backed chairs, at which were seated a number of people dressed in civilian attire but all with a military bearing. At the head of the table stood one of his former campus professors, whom he had known simply as Mr. Warford. Rather than his usual threadbare suit and crooked tie, he was wearing an immaculately clean and pressed senior naval officer's uniform, with the insignia of a lieutenant commander.

"McCarty," he began, "welcome to our little planning session. You have been observed closely by myself and others over the past several years and have proven your worth academically as well as in character and athletic ability. That is why you are standing here this evening. Let me introduce you to our other guests, and then we'll get down to business."

The meeting then proceeded to lay out the detailed plans for "Operation Red Iron." It began at eight twenty p.m. and continued until midnight.

Bell Island, Monday, 2:00 a.m. November 1, 1942

The Kreigsmarine U-boat, water pouring from the conning tower and deck, surfaced at two a.m., on a cold, cloudy night close to the north side of Bell Island. Two men in a small boat rowed out under cover of darkness to meet it. The submarine crew quickly handed them the last of a number of shipments of special explosives, detonators, blasting caps, and other supplies. Lastly, as in the other shipments, they were passed several smaller but heavy, sealed, wooden shipping crates emblazoned with an imperial eagle's head clutching a swastika. The spies then reported that there were several likely shipping targets at the usual anchorage on the other side of the island, and that they would be fully loaded by the following day.

"Very well," the submarine's first officer said, stiffly. "We will stay on station, and in one day, at zero three hundred, we will strike. You will illuminate and confuse the navy boats with your spotlight, as before, as they try to locate us. Remain strong, do your duty, and make the fatherland proud!"

The two Abwehr agents raised their right arms and saluted him. "Heil Hitler!" One of them turned to his partner and in his broken English said, "I will cast off, and you set the oars."

"Right," the other said, grinning, "just be careful with those explosives." Then more quietly, he added, "And watch out that the stick up the first officer's arse doesn't hit you when he turns around."

"*Jawohl,*" his partner replied. "Save us from these new officers, so full of themselves." He usually joined in when his partner joked about their superior officers, but he felt uncomfortable doing so. Underneath the forced camaraderie, he was a fanatical Nazi and would remove with prejudice any obstacle that stood in his way when it came time to strike their blow for Germany. However, when it came to his charismatic and handsome fellow saboteur, his feelings became confused.

As they grasped the oars, the submarine quietly slipped into the depths and rounded the western end of Bell Island, just off shore of a sea stack called the "Bell" to lie in wait until the next night.

The saboteurs rowed through the icy water toward the shore near Grebes Nest. The weight of the shipment made the little boat sit low in the water, but the sea was calm. In the year since they'd first been employed by the ore company, they had kept pretty much to themselves. The project was meant to be a longer-term undertaking, and there was very little oversight. They had free run of the mines, coming and going as they pleased, which suited their plans perfectly. The irony of them being hired to make things safer was poetic.

A little more than twenty-four hours later, near three-thirty a.m. on November second, the newly commissioned German submarine, U-518, rose ninety feet from the bottom of Conception Bay near the wrecks from September fifth of the *Saganaga* and *Lord Strathcona* to periscope depth. The first torpedo was fired at the coal boat SS Anna T, anchored off Scotia Pier, but it missed. The ton and a half device, carrying seven hundred and fifty pounds of explosive hexanite, then passed near the *Flyingdale* and detonated on the shore, shaking the island, frightening residents, and causing heavy damage to the loading facilities.

The captain then acquired the nearest ore-boat target and ordered more torpedoes to be fired. Ripping through the hull of the anchored, fully loaded iron ore carrier *SS Rose Castle*, they exploded, killing twenty-nine. The boat soon began to go down, and U-518 registered her first ever kill. Quickly reloading the tubes and firing again, the free French ore vessel

Paris, Lyon, Marseilles 27 was struck a mortal blow and sank next, killing twelve. Her other crew members, and Rose Castle survivors, managed to get through the freezing waters to shore with the assistance of local residents, where they were cared for at Lance Cove. Some suffered from hypothermia and others died after rescue, but many would survive.

Bell Island, Tuesday, 4:00 a.m., November 2, 1942

As of October thirtieth, Lieutenant William McCarty had been in the field, working undercover on Bell Island, posing as a visiting electrical engineer from the company's Cape Breton, Nova Scotia operation. He was staying as a houseguest on Grammer Street with company employee Jack Sparkes and his eighteen-year-old daughter, Lorraine. Sparkes would act as his guide and assist him with the mission. McCarty had just that day received what was supposed to be the latest, updated intelligence information, indicating that the next planned U-boat attack on ore carriers anchoring at Bell Island would not take place until the middle of November. The information was wrong, like a lot of the outdated and incorrect information he received. He had been there days before the submarine attack but been powerless to do anything about it. When he'd heard the explosions from the torpedoes, and felt the ground shake, he'd closed his eyes, knowing what must have happened and cursing the helpless feeling.

Chapter 4

St. John's, Saturday, July 14, 2018

Matt handed the letter to Fran. "Is this real? Can he actually have fathered another kid? And look at this other stuff. I don't get it! Who was this guy? What did he blame himself for? And what was *Operation Red Iron?*"

A pause. "Matt, God knows this doesn't happen often, but I am almost at a loss for words. In all the years I have known your father, he has always been a quiet, gentle soul who kept to himself."

"Well," Matt replied with a wry smile, "if I have a half sister, there was definitely at least one thing he didn't keep to himself. I've got a lot of questions, and I'm pretty sure some of the answers are over on Bell Island. I was going to visit anyway, but now this?" He shook his head. "Now there's a mystery, and one way or another, I'm going to get to the bottom of it."

"Okay," Fran said. "Let's get you settled away in the spare room. That was a long flight, and you could probably use a little rest before supper. See if you can relax a bit, and tomorrow, we'll bury your mystery man, then do some digging of our own . . . into the past."

○ ○ ○

The next morning, there was no rain, but it was still overcast. *Fitting for a funeral,* Matt thought. However, by the time the casket was lowered, the sky had brightened and a touch of sunlight shone through. A number of beret-wearing veterans from the Canadian Legion, attired in spotless navy-blue blazers, sharply creased grey-flannel pants, and sporting row upon row of shiny medals, were on hand to honour one of their own. The grey granite military headstone marking his father's grave was one of several hundred exactly the same, and all were aligned perfectly at attention, it seemed.

Rather than thinking it condemned his father to obscurity, by being just another forgotten soldier among the hundreds, Matt was hopeful that he might finally find some peace among those who could perhaps understand him better than his own son. The honour guard finished the ceremony, Matt was handed a crisply folded Canadian flag, and then it was over. After perfunctory goodbyes with the assemblage, and as he and Fran turned to leave, they were approached by a distinguished-looking man in his forties, wearing a dark three-piece suit.

"Excuse me," the man said, in a slight British accent, giving them a friendly smile. "I wish to offer my condolences on your father's passing. I am Peter Farrell, a liaison officer with the Department of Veterans Affairs and I am here to make sure that his remains are being laid to rest respectfully.

"Thank you," Matt replied, "but I thought the arrangements and costs were being borne by the Canadian Legion through their own funding."

"Oh yes, yes," Farrell agreed. "I just thought a personal touch would be in order, given the importance of your father's devotion to duty. You do know he did a lot to assist in the war effort so long ago, don't you?"

He looked closely at Matt, as if expecting some sort of agreement or reaction. Something told Matt that this person was not quite all they appeared to be on the surface. Glancing at Fran, he carefully replied.

"Well, Mr. Farrell, I know Dad served on a small warship doing convoy duty out of Halifax, but I don't think he saw any action, and while I'm proud that he joined the navy, he probably didn't do any more than most of the other brave individuals doing the same job."

"Of course," said Farrell. "All the men did a tremendous service for the country."

"And women," Matt added.

"Yes, women too," Farrell agreed flatly as his smile began to fade. "I am happy to have met you. I won't intrude further on this sad day."

He started to walk away but then quickly turned back. "I hope this is not indelicate, but may I just ask that you consider, as many surviving relatives do, the donation to our war museum of any unwanted items that Lieutenant McCarty may have acquired during his time in the service? Perhaps a souvenir he might have come across or any old papers? He might have wanted to have any such items shared by everyone instead of winding up tucked away, collecting dust, or being thrown out. Again, I know this is soon, but I will only be here another day and feel obligated on behalf of Canada to ask."

Matt looked back at the man. "Mr. Farrell, I hadn't seen my father in fifty years, and we were never close. If he left anything from that time, I would happily share it with the museum. The fact is that he was a destitute alcoholic and left nothing."

"Well, again, I am sorry for your loss, Matthew," Farrell replied. "We'll leave it at that then." He walked away.

When the man was out of sight, and they'd reached Fran's car, she looked at Matt. "Well, that was odd."

Matt looked back at her. "It was more than odd, Fran. That was downright weird. Thanks for not saying anything when I told that guy Dad didn't leave anything. Something's not right about any of this, and I don't trust him."

"I wonder if he's even who he says he is?" she replied.

"Wow. I didn't even think of that." Matt frowned and glanced back toward where they'd last seen him. "I hope your Wi-Fi is good; I've got some research to do."

○ ○ ○

Across from the graveyard and a short way down the street, Farrell got in the passenger side of the car that was waiting there for him.

"What do you think?" asked Hunt. "Did you find out if the old man talked to him or left anything?"

"I'm not sure what to think yet, but he was a bit too quick to say there was nothing. We might never know now, since you held that pillow over the old man's face too long, but I think he's a sly one and knows more than he's saying. Follow them back to her place and keep an eye out. Call me if he makes a move, and see if you can do it without killing anyone else."

Farrell got out and walked a bit further down James Lane to his own rental vehicle. *Probably going to need to have a less-cordial chat with Matthew McCarty before long,* he thought.

○ ○ ○

When Matt got back to Fran's place, the first thing he did was take a long, hot shower. It relaxed him and helped him think. After he got out, he threw on some sweats and dragged out his laptop. As Fran made them some tea, he brought up a search engine. After looking again at the letter from Lorraine Sparkes, he typed "Operation Red Iron," and with a little flash of insight, added, "World War Two, Bell Island."

What showed on the screen was a series of articles about the history of iron-ore mining on Bell Island but nothing further. However, in a certain nondescript building in Ottawa, near Parliament Hill, the search raised a virtual flag and notice was taken.

When Fran pulled into the driveway on Waterford Bridge Road, Hunt continued on past her, eventually turning around and parking across the street a few doors down in front of a blue duplex. He now had a clear view of Fran's house and was positioned to see if anyone came through the front door. He was low man on the totem pole and not happy to always get the shit jobs. *Not my fault that old fuck couldn't take it,* he thought. *It was almost like I was doing the old man a favour. Where's the fun in that?*

He'd probably have to stay here for hours until they went to bed. He was getting angry, which could be bad news for anyone around him. Well, except for Farrell. Nobody messed with Farrell; it just wasn't healthy. Hunt was strong and beefy, but while Farrell wasn't a big man, what he lacked in size he made up for in mean. Hunt fit the stereotype of a schoolyard bully, and in fact, he had been until getting expelled at fifteen. The boys were easy to intimidate, but before long, that became so routine that it didn't satisfy his need to dominate. He soon discovered that girls were a lot more fun, because the more they feared him, the more he became aware of other feelings.

Trapping a girl up against the back wall of the school and copping a feel was his favourite, and the more fearful they were, the more exciting it became. That had all come to an end though when a classmate of one of his favourite victims tried to intervene, and Hunt had given the boy a severe beating. He'd been expelled, and though the police had investigated, no charges were ever laid—even though he had beaten the boy so badly he'd had to undergo surgery for a broken cheekbone. The girl was so traumatised by the ordeal that she'd been unable to say what happened.

It was his favourite memory, even though there had been many others like it and many more young girls over the years. *Maybe tonight,* he thought, *after this bullshit stakeout, I'll cruise downtown and find one. Something racked and ripe.* Fourteen or fifteen was prime. Exciting. Old enough to understand what was happening to them but too young to do anything about it.

Chapter 5

Bell Island, Sunday, July 15, 2018

The day was still grey after the rain, but there was a promise of sun as Cassie did her morning chores and then got ready for a day of adventuring around the cliffs with Bev. As usual, they would pack a small lunch for eating later, either in their tunnel or maybe on the clifftop overlooking the ocean and Grebes Nest.

Evelyn was off to church near Town Square, but she didn't ask Cassie to come along anymore as her granddaughter explained that her spiritual connection came from the outdoors. The low clinging fir trees, the fields of wild roses and beautiful lupin flowers, the ocean, and the very red rock itself were enough to keep her in touch with her version of a higher power.

"Sorry, Kip, I'd take you along if I could, but we're going to be doing lots of climbing, and you know it's getting harder for you now, little puppy," she said, explaining as best as she could while scratching him in a favourite spot behind the ear.

Kip was not happy but resignedly flopped down on the living-room rug and rested his huge head on his paws, watching balefully as she went out the door. Cassie slipped her backpack over her shoulders, mounted her bicycle, and headed west along the small well-travelled paths that hugged the rugged cliffs by the ocean to meet up with her friend. Sometimes they were joined by a couple of boys they knew from school, but lately, Doug Butler was hanging out with some people who just smoked dope and drank most of the time, and Bev had heard he was getting into some heavier drugs too.

It was becoming a bigger problem on the island lately, and parents were really upset that nothing seemed to be working to try and stop what was now being termed an "opioid crisis." Fentanyl had already claimed one of their friends, and it kept getting worse instead of better. Cassie couldn't understand why the death wouldn't shock people into staying away from that crap. She had smoked a bit of weed and tried some of the wine that Evelyn kept for special occasions, but it really didn't do anything for her. Poor old Bev had just got super sick when she'd tried smoking a joint and that was that.

The other boy, Evan King, was the first and only boy Cassie had ever seriously kissed, and that was nice, but he'd gotten kind of weird the last time they were together. He'd said he wanted to have sex, but she told him she just wasn't ready for that. Now he was going out with a girl from the other side of the island who was more accommodating, and that was fine with her. *"His friggin' loss,"* Bev had said.

Bev was a little shorter than Cassie and had jet-black, shoulder-length hair, with a small natural shot of grey on the right side that she constantly tucked behind her ear. At school, when Bev walked down the hallway, heads turned, and there was no shortage of island boys who would be happy to spend their time staring into her huge brown eyes.

Cassie caught up to Bev by Grebes Nest, named for the diving birds who made their seasonal home in this area, near the cliffs that extended around much of the six-mile-long and two-mile-wide island. Both girls laid their bikes down near the edge and began to descend one of the accessible paths down to the rocky beach. It wasn't too difficult getting down, but there were some sharp rock projections and care was needed. Reaching bottom, they could see a fabulous sea stack, one of a number of rough pillars of rock left standing after the cliff around it had weathered and crumbled over time to the ocean below.

This one stood alone, a hundred feet high, and was joined to the shore by a narrow rock walkway. One of Cassie's wishes was to climb it someday, but the reality was that once in a while chunks of rock would fall off, and so without having the proper climbing equipment, common sense prevailed—at least for the time being. Strewn around the base of the cliffs throughout the area, up and down this side of the island, large squarish boulders lay scattered here and there amid smaller piles of fallen rubble. Sooner or later, this entire area would be reclaimed by the sea, as evidenced by the many long horizontal cracks along the clifftop.

The never-ending wave action gradually undercut the softer rock, and the overhanging weight would eventually become too much to hold up. Then the face would shear away. It had happened many times in the past over the island's long history and would happen again, but even as the cracks in the rock above widened a little bit each year, it was impossible to predict exactly when the next rockslide would occur. Every foray along the bottom of the cliffs, and every exploration into the multitude of old mining tunnels accessible from the beach came with risk, and while not prohibited, the healthiest choice would be to stay clear. Curiosity, however, has always been a companion of discretion, young or old, and both girls were prime examples of the saying.

Cassie and Bev kept walking a little farther west along the beach until they came to a small tunnel entrance. Unlike the larger rough and rounded beach mine openings, this one was smaller and squared with supporting beams on the top and sides. It went through a cliff outcropping and came out after about two hundred and fifty feet on the opposite side. The tunnel had been blasted through by a former mine explosives man named Reid, who'd turned fisherman after the shutdown. He had created an opening to a previously inaccessible area of the beach that was more forgiving to the keel of dory boats landing their catch. For some local families who chose to stay after the demise of the mining era, the return to fishing showed the spirit and stoicism of Bell Islanders, bringing them back full circle to an earlier age. The girls began walking through as it got a bit dark in the middle.

"Cass, what do you want to do after next year?" Bev asked as their footfalls echoed in the dim light.

"After the last year of high school? I love it here, and it'll always be home, but there's so much out there I want to experience. I would love to go to university somewhere to study, but there's no way me and Gram can afford it."

"I'd like to go to uni," Bev replied, "and I would dearly love to get out there and do some adventuring. At least get across Canada, all the way to the Pacific. I've even thought about joining the air force, so I could see everything from way up there," she said, pointing at a jet leaving a contrail high in the sky as they exited the tunnel.

"Never can tell," Cassie replied. "Who knows where we'll be in a few years?"

"Not with that fucker Evan King!" Bev answered, making a face.

"No, not with Evan," laughed Cassie, giving her friend a quick hug.

They were now on the west side of the fisherman's passage. Up ahead on the left was the entrance to their secret tunnel, hidden by some strategically placed scrub brush that was held there by a few rocks. As they approached the opening, Bev glanced up and saw a clean-shaven man with short blond hair standing near the cliff's edge, wearing a suit and looking straight down at them. Probably in his thirties, he seemed like a statue, unmoving and expressionless. She knew most of the people from around this area, and there was nothing familiar about him. Cassie followed her friend's frozen gaze and saw him too. They both looked at each other, and not wanting to give away their secret, turned and walked quickly back the other way. Cassie gave a backward glance, but the man was gone.

o o o

Jurgen Meyer had arrived on Bell Island two days before from Germany. He had been in a meeting there, and at his own request, he had been chosen by the group for this mission. He descended the path and walked along the beach after waiting for the two girls to leave. Meyer scanned the area in both directions for about a hundred yards, finally having to retreat when the tide began coming in. He knew from looking through the old Abwehr records over the previous week that two saboteur spies had worked near this area in 1942, with the aim of destroying the entire mine operation. For some reason, the explosion they'd planned had never occurred. Both spies had gone missing, along with all of the concentrated nitroglycerin they had received by submarine, as well as two hundred and eighty-eight kilograms of Nazi gold that today was worth twenty-five million dollars. His assignment was to find the gold before certain others, who might already have a credible lead regarding its whereabouts.

As for the explosives, Meyer couldn't see it, but directly in front of him, out under the Atlantic and far down in the flooded mines, there was a two-and-a-half-ton time-bomb, dormant for seventy-six years, that could go off at any moment.

Chapter 6

Ottawa, March, 2018

Peter Farrell had never been employed by Canada's Department of Veterans Affairs, but he had worked for the government. His job with the Canadian Intelligence Corps was to review and electronically scan older hard-copy government documents, and in particular, those from World War Two. It was a trusted position, because he was privy to the often-sensitive details of various secret operations carried out by the military during those turbulent times.

Farrell worked in a subbasement of the clandestine headquarters of the CIC, an unimposing, older but very modernised three-story brick building near Parliament Hill in Ottawa. He enjoyed the job for his own reasons, and it gave him great pleasure to open a long-sealed file to examine the contents and see how badly an operation had been mishandled. Some very obvious immediate and urgent matters had been reported by agents in the field only to be stamped by their superiors as "no action necessary," as if the report had not even been read.

Peter Farrell was in his late forties, and he'd been at the job for almost twenty-five years. As he picked up one particular dossier, his whole life had changed in the space of thirty minutes. The file before him was sealed and labelled

"Operation Red Iron' - Bell Island, Nfld. November 1942." Opening it, he began to read. Soon, his years of experience, not to mention a near-genius IQ, caused him to make certain mental cross-file references. He had access to German files from the same time period, and one file in particular seemed to connect to the Canadian dossier. By the time he finished, he had committed the details of both entire files to his eidetic memory. *They should have taken the report in this file, from Lieutenant William McCarty, seriously,* he thought, smiling wider now. It was time to retire and become very rich.

Farrell was cruel. Guilt and remorse were unfamiliar constructs to him. He easily fit the definition of sociopathy, but his maladaptive behaviour went much deeper. Peter Farrell was a psychopath. On the surface, he was seemingly a distinguished, charming, and witty gentleman. Cross him though and he could easily become enraged and violent, even kill, and then continue on as if nothing was amiss. It had happened recently and not for the first time. A stranger had bumped into him on the street and not apologised—a sign of disrespect he would not tolerate. He'd followed the victim home and knocked on his door. The man had no time to react as Farrell jabbed him with the hypodermic. Then Peter Farrell's calm demeanour changed, as a switch in his brain clicked to the on position, resulting in a surge of high-voltage rage. The crime would never be solved. Too random. Nothing to tie it to. No reason. Just a mutilated corpse left behind and a lot of unanswered questions for the authorities and the man's grieving family.

THE SECRET OF BELL ISLAND

Ottawa, Monday, July 16, 2018

Near Parliament Hill, in the same nondescript brick building that Peter Farrell had now retired from, computers using next-generation pattern-and-keyword-recognition software had raised a flag within seconds of Matt McCarty's search the day before. The junior officer who'd glanced at it assumed it was a false positive. With millions of people doing millions of internet searches twenty-four hours a day, it was to be expected that someone would occasionally type a sequence of words and numbers that corresponded to a confidential government file, triggering a low-level blue flag. *A thousand monkeys with a thousand typewriters,* he thought, amused. It was not common, but it happened a few times each month. Usually, it was with older files like this one that did not yet have thirty-digit-long encrypted file numbers, and there was almost always a quick resolve. However, as policy dictated, he looked deeper, typing a series of commands.

In less than a second, the IP address of the computer doing the search was checked and a basic profile of the registered owner generated. In this case, a connection was made between a former naval intelligence officer running an operation called "Red Iron" and one of that officer's relatives. With the familial connection lessening the likelihood of the search being random, the program automatically upgraded the flag from blue to yellow. He meant to kick the file upstairs to a senior officer for further analysis, but there were other matters that drew his attention, and it was two weeks before it finally reached Colonel Robert Bowdring. When it did, the proverbial shit hit the fan.

Chapter 7

St. John's, Monday, July 16, 2018

Matt woke up the next morning at six-thirty to the delicious aroma of bacon wafting up from Fran's kitchen and the sound of an old Eagles song playing on her vintage radio. After a quick shower and shave, he put on a pair of faded blue Levis and a black t-shirt. A pair of old, once-white Reebok runners completed his standard ensemble. Combing his now-short grey hair, he smiled at the mirror. There was a time when it had been shoulder length and brown, but that was a long time ago.

Matt wasn't religious by any stretch, but as he had every morning for the past clean-and-sober twenty years, he whispered the Serenity Prayer: *"God grant me the serenity to accept the things I cannot change, the courage to change the things I can, and the wisdom to know the difference."*

○ ○ ○

"Good morning, Mister Matt," Fran said as he arrived in the kitchen. "Did you sleep well?"

For a moment, the fleeting memory of being underwater and an angel reaching for him flashed randomly, as often happened shortly after waking, as though he'd revisited the traumatic event in his sleep, but as always, it faded quickly.

"Great," he said, smiling at her. "Not used to something that comfortable. I'll get spoiled."

Fran looked at the cigar box, still on the table where they'd left it. "Well, my young friend, what's the plan?"

Matt gave the box a little pat. "I made reservations before I left Vancouver for a stay in a nice rental cottage over on Bell Island. I'm going to go there and see if I can track down someone related to this Lorraine Sparkes. If the 'Sparky' she referred to was her father, I'm sure someone will remember the name, even after all this time, and maybe Lorraine's daughter is still around. Who knows? I'm not going to get caught up in hoping for any particular outcome, but after the first shock of that letter, I'm getting pretty curious. I guess there could have been a lot more to the old man than I ever knew."

"Do you remember much from when you lived there as a boy?" Fran asked.

"Yes," Matt said. "Even though we moved from there to St. John's when I was ten, I remember a lot from that time, good and bad. Dad was always either at work or drinking at the tavern, and Mom was sick a lot and couldn't leave her room, but Heather was always there for me, even when she was still a kid herself.

"Sorry about your mom, Matty; you got a rough break there. It's a shame we didn't treat people with mental illness better back then."

"That's why we had to come to St. John's," Matt said. "There was supposed to be professional treatment for the mentally ill, but all Mom got was shock treatments, and in the end, she killed herself. I can't dwell on that though . . .

and at least now there's better treatment for the poor souls afflicted with the disease."

"After all you've been through over the years, with your own troubles, it would be nice if you could locate some other family," Fran said.

"Are you kidding?" he replied in an exaggerated accent. "Sure Jaysus you're the only family I needs, b'y."

"Well, just in case," she said, laughing, "my friend and former colleague at MUN, Stewart Luffman, is still the head of the Centre for Newfoundland Studies, so if you need any research information about Bell Island history, here's his number. I'll let him know you might call." She gave him a big hug, and then he walked out the door with his duffel bags for an adventure over on Bell Island.

Matt loaded up the Tahoe and headed to the ferry in Portugal Cove. The day was sunny, and with the windows down, he was enjoying the warm breeze. He felt excited about the chance to visit his childhood haunts and do some exploring of the old mine workings. One of his duffel bags held ropes, anchors, pulleys, carabiners, ascenders, climbing harnesses, and pretty much anything he would need to do some rappelling and climbing around the steep cliffs. Noting from his research that there was some rockfall from time to time he would need to be careful, sure, but it was nothing he hadn't dealt with before.

o o o

After reaching Portugal Cove and waiting in line a short while, he got to the little pay booth and then proceeded onto the ferry. It was the MV *Legionnaire,* but even on a forty-four-hundred-ton vessel, this would not be easy. *The boat is solid, but for Christ's sake, it's still anywhere from three to six hundred feet deep in the Tickle—*

He snapped out of that thought, forcing himself out of the car, as the ferry rule stipulated, and climbed the stairs to the waiting area above. He sat inside, and feeling the shudder of the boat leaving the dock, closed his eyes. The trip was short, just a few miles across, and when the announcement that they were about to dock again was given, he got up and pushed the button that opened the passenger cabin door. Stepping over the sill, he saw the sun shining on the high cliffs, triggering once again a memory long buried but often visited in his dreams.

Getting up from where he had been sitting in the lounge several tables away, Hunt followed Matt back to the car deck. He had called Farrell when Matt began loading luggage into the SUV. Hunt was instructed to stick with him and not to be surprised if he headed to Bell Island. Farrell had called it all right; this fucker knew something, and Hunt would sit on him until he either led them to whatever the prize was that his secretive boss was after or until Farrell gave the word to beat the information out of him. Hunt was ornery at the best of times, but today he was feeling especially frustrated. Having cruised George Street downtown the night before, where a lot of younger teenagers congregated outside the numerous bars, he had seen a couple of likely candidates, but in this hick town, it seemed like there was a cop walking on every block. He couldn't take a chance on getting busted picking up an underage girl, so he'd gone back to the hotel instead and settled in with the kind of internet porn that could also get him arrested.

o o o

When Matt left the ferry, he didn't follow the line of cars heading up the curving Beach Hill Road right away. He drove straight ahead, letting the regular island traffic get past him, and parked in the little lot in front of Dicks beachfront restaurant, a revered institution that continued to serve the best fish and chips known to man since 1950. The town of Wabana had been incorporated that same year and encompassed a number of areas from West Mines to the Green in the northeast and down to the Front on the south side of the island, where the ferries to Portugal Cove docked and where the nearby long-abandoned ore-loading piers continued to disintegrate.

He walked down near the water's edge and recalled the time a seven-foot-long shark had been caught in the restaurant owner's salmon net by mistake. He'd been six at the time and a local news reporter arranged with his father to have Matt's picture taken next to the carcass for size contrast. The memory from that day was still razor sharp. The photographer had told him to put his hand on the shark's back by the dorsal fin. The skin was dry and felt like sandpaper. The animal's eyes were large black buttons, and he could remember seeing his father standing behind the photographer, his dark eyes as expressionless and alien as the shark's.

As he continued walking, the wet beach rocks sounded almost like glass, squeaking and crunching beneath his feet. He looked over to where the *Kipawo* had docked so many years earlier. The old pier was long gone now, having been replaced to accommodate the new larger vessels. Matt noticed another vehicle in the small parking lot. The driver seemed to be making a point of not looking in his direction. Something seemed vaguely familiar about the car. *Getting spooked,* he thought, *with all this family mystery shit.*

THE SECRET OF BELL ISLAND

○ ○ ○

As Hunt waited by the restaurant for the next ferry from St. John's to arrive with Farrell on it, he thought for a moment that McCarty might have noticed him, but the target just got back in the SUV and headed up Beach Hill. Hunt noticed a young teenage girl, maybe thirteen, wearing jean shorts and a little halter top get out of her parents' car and go to the restaurant take-out window. *Just starting,* he thought. *Nice.* He smiled and licked his lips.

At the top of the hill, Matt saw a sign with an arrow pointing to the Bell Island Cottages and turned in. He parked by the little green cabin with white trim. The area was dotted with a few others of various sizes and colours, with plenty of space between each. There was a picnic table in the front of his and a little white-latticework fence. A small outdoor table and chairs on the porch in front of a sliding glass door completed the outward appearance. A friendly looking woman in her fifties came out of the small office on the other side of the driveway and greeted him.

"You must be Mr. McCarty," she said, smiling. "I'm Sharyn, and welcome to Bell Island."

"Hi, Sharyn," he replied. "Please call me Matt, and I am very happy to be here. I've been wanting to visit home for a long time."

"Home? Are you from Bell Island?"

"That's funny," he said. "That just came out. I lived here as a child when my father worked with the mines, but I was born a mainlander, and I've been out West in Vancouver for about fifty years."

"No matter," she said. "You're a Bell Islander. I can tell. Welcome home." She handed him the keys, and they went inside.

"This is exactly what I was hoping for," Matt said, looking at the cosy kitchen and comfortable couch in the living room.

"Bedroom's got a double, so it's big enough if you get lucky while you're here," she said, with a twinkle in her eye.

Matt laughed. "I know the island is magic," he said, "but I don't know if I believe in miracles."

"Miracles do happen," she said, laughing back at him. "My husband still has one nearly every couple of weeks! Anyway, all your pots and pans, dishes, and cutlery are in the cupboards, and there's the toaster, coffee maker, and pretty much everything you need to enjoy your stay. There's a good grocery store if you keep going down this road until you get to Quigley's Line. Then just follow it all the way 'round till you see Clover Farm's Grocery on your right. Got a green roof; can't miss it."

"Will do," Matt said.

"Oh, by the way, for your bread, go to the end of the street past the grocery store and look on your left for the Rolling Pin Bakery. Best bread and buns around. They also serve a nice breakfast, if you don't want to cook for yourself."

"That's great," he replied. "I'll go pick up a few things after I get unpacked."

Sharyn said goodbye, turned to leave, and then stopped. "Oh, nearly forgot. The community museum with the No. 2 mine tour is right across the street from there too, on Compressor Hill Road. If your father worked with the mines, you have to do the tour," she said. "There's nothing like it."

"It's on my list," Matt replied. "I suppose there will be a knowledgeable guide conducting the tour? I'd like to ask some questions, and hopefully they would know some of the history."

"Make sure you do the tour when Tom Crane is on," she said. "All the guides are good, but he worked in the mines until they closed in '66. What he doesn't remember isn't worth knowing."

o o o

Matt walked into the Clover Farm's Grocery and picked up enough food to last him a few days. He noticed there was fresh-caught cod for sale. One time, when he was almost eight, a fisherman had come into the dock and was giving out a few codfish to the local boys for free, as they were still plentiful and he had been very successful that day. From his dory, he'd tossed a ten-pounder up to Matt, and he'd tried his best to carry it all the way up Beach Hill to his house, thinking it might get his mother to come down from her bedroom. He'd gotten almost halfway when he realised there was no chance that he would make it. He just wasn't strong enough. He'd left the fish on the side of the road in the bushes. He'd given up. He had always given up. . . .

o o o

. . . sliding slowly under the water, the smell of diesel, watching the sharp white barnacles on the boat hull as the twinkling lights above faded, and the angel reached down to him. . . .

Chapter 8

Bell Island, Thursday, November 5, 1942

Lieutenant William McCarty got dressed and went downstairs for breakfast. His host—a big red-haired man who looked as though he had known his way around a bar-room brawl or two in his youth—was forty-seven-year-old Jack "Sparky" Sparkes, his local contact. Jack was an electrician who worked for the mine company and had been chosen as the best-suited candidate, after careful vetting, to assist the young navy lieutenant and be his guide for any field work that needed to be done in connection with the undercover operation. Sparkes was a widower and lived with his attractive daughter, Lorraine, who had recently finished training as an operator and now worked for the Avalon Telephone Company in their Bell Island offices.

Lorraine had been introduced to McCarty when he came to their two-story gabled house on Grammer Street directly from the ferry with her father. Jack sensed right away that she had an interest in the handsome stranger that seemed beyond just being just friendly. It might be that the man returned that interest, but he was here to do a difficult job and certainly seemed to be quite serious about it.

"Here you go, Bill," Jack said when the navy man sat. "Scarf 'er down."

Jack clattered a large plate of sausage, beans, and bread down in front of him on the kitchen table. Then he put out some Crosby's molasses and a large pot of tea, and even a can of Carnation evaporated milk. There was no white sugar, but they were doing pretty well, considering.

"Thank you, sir," McCarty replied.

"None of that now, my son," Jack said quickly. "It's Jack or Sparky, your choice, but none of that 'sir' business, right?"

"Okay, Jack it is then," he said, surrendering. "Do they call you Sparky because of the hair or your last name?"

"Well, Bill, I've got a few versions of that story depending on the audience, and whether or not I've a drop of rum in me," he admitted wryly. "Let's just say for now that, if you do see me drunk at some point, don't let me near any live wires for the love of Jesus!"

"Fair enough," said McCarty, smiling.

As he mopped up the last of his beans with his bread, he considered his next steps. "Jack, what do you say we go by the main company office this morning. I want to look through some personnel files."

Jack nodded. "All right, skipper. We'll be off here in a tick."

Bill went back upstairs and took the gun out of his small, brown-leather suitcase. He pushed a full seven-round magazine into the opening at the bottom of the pistol's grip until it clicked. Pulling the spring-loaded slide fully back, he then let it go, and a .45 calibre round was peeled off the top of the magazine, travelling forward and putting the pistol into battery position with the hammer cocked. Clicking the safety on, he secured the semi-automatic Colt in the shoulder holster under his left arm. He left his backup, a Colt Detective Special revolver, out of sight under his navy uniform in the suitcase.

After pulling on a bulky sweater over his shirt, he combed his short, jet-black hair straight back and went downstairs, where he saw Lorraine getting ready to walk over to work in Town Square. She smiled warmly at him as she pulled her long red hair back into a ponytail and then walked out the door, saying goodbye. Jack noticed Bill's eyes linger on her as she left.

○   ○   ○

The company's 1936 Ford panel delivery truck had seen better days. Newfoundland winters had taken a toll, and there was an old towel stuffed in the rust hole around the floor shifter. The cab was spartan, and the flat banjo-spoked steering wheel had spider-web cracks from heat and cold. The rubber pads were worn off both the brake and clutch pedals, but the vehicle was mechanically sound and started up right away. The wheel wells, running boards, and front and back bumpers were outlined in white, and the headlights had louvered shades over them as mandated during wartime. Bill looked behind into the cargo area and saw side-mounted shelves, neatly stocked with various electrical supplies.

The day was sunny and mild, so Jack didn't have to scrape any ice from the windshield. There was very little snow on the ground, and what little there was quickly melted in the warm sun. When they arrived at the main office on Bennett Street, the frenzied activity of three days before had died down. The sinking of the two ore carriers had taken many lives, and the mood was sombre.

A woman in the back was sitting and just staring at a typewriter. She wore a black armband. Jack looked at Doris, the receptionist who walked over to greet them, and raised his eyebrow towards the other woman.

THE SECRET OF BELL ISLAND

"Hello, Jack," she said. Quietly she added, "Brenda's fiancé from Nova Scotia was on the *Rose Castle* that got torpedoed. He's gone. She came in this morning and just sits there. Mr. Delaney tried to get her to leave with pay, but she won't go."

Jack introduced McCarty to Doris and Richard Delaney, the senior manager, who had joined the group and knew why McCarty was there. Several other staff looked up at them from their work.

Bill asked if it would be okay for him to offer his condolences to the woman still staring blankly at her desk. Without waiting for an answer, he walked over and got down on one knee beside her. He said something quietly, and she turned toward him and nodded. Then he stood up and reached out his hand. She took it and walked with him to the front counter.

"Brenda is going to go home for today," he said. "Would it be possible for one of the staff to escort her please?"

Looking at McCarty with an expression of wonder, Doris said slowly, "I can take her. Someone else can watch the front for a little while."

Brenda looked at McCarty and reached out to touch his arm on her way out the door.

"What did you say to her?" asked Delaney, with an incredulous look on his face. "She wouldn't budge for me."

McCarty looked at him and then Jack Sparkes.

"I told her I was going to kill those responsible," he replied matter-of-factly. Then to Delaney, he said, "I'm going to need to look over your personnel files. I believe the people I was sent here to find probably work for the company. Can we go to your office to talk?"

McCarty discussed the details of his mission to root out two enemy saboteurs sent by Germany to try and destroy ore production on the island. When Delaney asked why the local troops, trained to defend the island, couldn't be used to help, McCarty explained that they must not do anything to alert the spies and risk them doing something drastic before he had a chance to find out where they may have either hidden, or perhaps already planted, the explosives that he knew they had received.

"I know you have a good force here," Bill said, "but these people are ruthless and could be deadly to anyone they may regard as a threat. I think they are hiding in plain sight as mine staff, but they could even be posing as part of your coastal defence."

At that same time, in their lodgings not a half-mile away, Kurt Becher and August Kahr were still celebrating their part in helping U-518 sink the enemy shipping, and how foolish the Canadian Navy had looked, rushing around, up and down the length of the island, chasing after the killer submarine to no avail. Kahr had a brief thought that maybe Germany might have a chance after all. Either way, it wouldn't change his plans. Around noon, they both dressed for the outside to visit the tavern and try to stomach some of what the local's called beer.

"Ihr Bier ist pisse," came from Becher, stepping into the street.

"No German!" hissed Kahr. "Only English." A pause. "But you are right," he admitted, laughing. "There is no denying their beer is piss. When we win the war, you can have all the German beer you want. But for now, you have to try to fit in with these swine."

They didn't notice Lorraine Sparkes, who had just started to open the front door of the phone company next door on her way home for lunch. Hearing the exchange, she quickly ducked back inside without seeing their faces or realising they had just come from the boarding house.

THE SECRET OF BELL ISLAND

"Lorraine, are you alright?" asked Hanna Martin. "You look pale."

Recovering quickly, Lorraine said, "No, I'm fine. I just felt a little faint for a moment. I didn't eat any breakfast this morning, and I guess I'm still thinking about those poor people who were on the boats."

"Damn Nazis. Come with me to the lunchroom," Hanna said. "I have extra, and we can relax for a while. Eat here with me instead of walking home for lunch today."

Hanna had recently come from St. John's, where she had worked for the phone company part time. She had transferred to Bell Island when a full-time opportunity arose. She seemed to be rather shy but got along well with Lorraine, as most did.

"All right, Hanna, thank you; that's very generous. I'll bring something for both of us tomorrow."

o o o

Back at the main office, McCarty pored over dozens of personnel files going back six months. At the intelligence meeting in Halifax, he had been told that the spies had not been here any longer than that. He had no way of knowing that they had actually arrived a full year earlier, and so, would not show up on the employee list in front of him. By the end of the day, he had no likely suspects and was ready to call it quits. Jack was doing a shift of his regular electrical work, so he walked the short distance from the main office to the house on Grammer Street.

The door was unlocked, as was usual on the island. He went in and took off his heavy coat and boots before putting on the kettle for tea. Going upstairs, he pulled the heavy sweater over his head and was standing there when Lorraine came out of her room directly across the hall.

"Oh, I didn't know you were home," he said, surprised.

"That's okay. I didn't know you were here either," she replied, a little flustered, her face reddening.

Without Jack home as a buffer, they were both a little tongue tied and at a loss for what to say or do next.

"Uh, would you like some tea?" Bill finally asked, after an awkward silence. "I put the kettle on already."

"Sure, that would be nice," she replied. "I'll get the cups down. Did you want to maybe . . . ?"

He looked into her piercing green eyes, a little bewildered, and for a moment felt like he was fourteen again.

"The gun," she said, "could you . . . ?"

"Oh, I'm sorry," he said, taking it off and breathing for the first time in about a minute. "Yes, of course. You weren't actually supposed to see that, so . . . I . . . uh. . . ."

"It's alright," she said with a musical little laugh. "I didn't see a thing."

It was at that moment that twenty-two-year-old Lieutenant William "Bill" McCarty realised that he was in love for the first time.

Before he'd been approached by naval intelligence, he had been seeing a girl in Halifax who was the sister of a friend. It was quite common for promises of marriage to be made in the moment during those times by young people entering the services, unsure if they would even survive the war. Although they didn't know each other very well and hadn't consummated their relationship, he'd felt pressure from his friend and a misguided obligation, so one night, he had asked her to marry him. She'd accepted, and her family began making grand plans for a large wedding. Pretty soon, he'd realised he had made a terrible mistake. However, he was an officer and would not go back on his word. Maybe this was how things were supposed to be, he'd told himself, but he didn't really believe it.

As Bill and Lorraine sat across from each other at the kitchen table drinking their tea, more comfortably now, Jack arrived. "Well now," he said with a grin, "how are you two getting along?"

Lorraine had been smiling, but now that her father was home, she looked serious.

"Bill," she began, "I know I'm not supposed to know why you're really here, but I've got a pretty good idea, and I have to tell you both something important!"

Chapter 9

Bell Island, Tuesday, July 17, 2018

The weather gods were smiling on Bell Island. It was expected to be sunny and warm for the next week or so. Matt's kind of weather. Not too hot, with a bit of a breeze and a cloud or two here and there for contrast. He'd had a restful sleep and what little bit of lingering jet lag he'd had was gone. It was hard not to feel relaxed here on the island. Matt thought he would try the breakfast special at the bakery that Sharyn had mentioned. He washed up and brushed his teeth, got dressed, and headed out the door.

The sign out front proclaimed, in yellow script, that it was *"The Rolling Pin Bakery,"* operated by the Bell Island Co-op. Going in, he sat and ordered his preferred breakfast of sausage, eggs, hash browns, and toast. Here at the bakery, it was all that, and want it or not, brown beans added on. He acquiesced to the young waiter's recommendation of not having his bread toasted. It came still warm from the oven with homemade local blueberry preserves. Afterwards, as he lingered over coffee, an older woman came out from the kitchen on a break.

"How was your breakfast, my dear?" she asked.

"So good I may not eat until tomorrow," Matt replied.

"Sure, that's no good. Young man like yourself, you'll be needing a nice feed of Newfie steak later."

"Oh, I do like a nice feed of thick-cut fried baloney, don't get me wrong," he replied, playing along, "but I'm planning on having my next meal down at Dicks on the beach, scarfing down a big plate of fish and chips with stuffing and gravy."

Giving him a studied look, she sat, and with her elbows on the arms of the chair, tapped her chin with an index finger and smiled. "Ah now, my son, it's a puzzle you're after giving me. Your accent doesn't sound like you're from here, but at the same time, you do talk like local. It's like one of those, what do you call it, paradoxes. So, what's the deal?"

Matt started to reply.

"Wait!" she yelled, pointing at him with the same index finger. "Don't tell me! I've got it! I'll bet you were from here once, but you've been away for a long time, like maybe since you were a teenager. Because you got the lingo, not like a tourist trying to fit in but more real-like. I'm not hearing the States or the wannabe-like-the-States Ontario crowd in your accent. You're from out West, right? You look all mellow too. Vancouver?"

"Jesus Christ!" Matt exclaimed. "Pardon my French. How did you do that?"

The baker got up from her chair and said simply, "Easy b'y. Sharyn over to the Cottages called me up and told me you were on your way over for breakfast. Welcome home, my son." Then she gave him a pat on the shoulder as the rest of the staff and a few customers clapped and roared with laughter.

"Don't forget to tip your waiter now, buddy," was her parting comment as she headed back into the kitchen.

For Matt, there was nothing left to say. He got up, paid the bill—tipping the waiter generously—and left, chuckling good-naturedly along with the rest of them.

Matt left the Tahoe parked where it was and walked across Compressor Hill Road. Down a little way on the left was the Bell Island Community Museum, where they offered the underground mine-experience tour. Matt entered the small building and asked a woman at reception if Tom Crane was in. She said that he was around, but as the next tour wouldn't start for about a half hour, he was likely in the coffee shop.

Walking into the small café, he saw a man who had to be Crane sitting at a table, looking out the window and absently stirring his tea. He was tall and lean with a handsome, rugged face that looked as if it had experienced and laughed a lot over what Matt estimated to be about seventy or so years.

"Excuse me, are you Tom Crane?" Matt asked.

"Yessir, that's me in the flesh," Crane said with a smile that seemed to light up the room. "We'll get started here pretty soon. Just waiting for the tour bus to get here from the ferry before we go down below."

"I'm looking forward to taking the tour but not today," Matt said. "I'm hoping I can ask you a few questions, if you don't mind. I used to live here when I was a child, and Sharyn over at the Cottages said you were the man with the answers for all things historical."

"Sharyn!" he exclaimed. "Known her forever. Fire away, my son. What's on your mind?"

Just then, a young teenage girl came over to take Matt's order.

"I'll just have some coffee please, Bev," Matt said, noticing her name tag, "and another tea for Tom."

"Okay." She paused. "You're not wearing a name tag," she prompted.

"Oh." He stood up, extending his hand. "Matt McCarty."

"Right," she said. "Down from the mainland for a visit then I s'pose?" Before he could answer, she looked at Crane with a pretend scowl, "and a gentleman too, unlike some others," she finished, walking toward the coffee pot. Then she turned around and flashed a big smile while tucking a lock of her grey-streaked hair behind her right ear as Crane slowly shook his head.

"McCarty." Tom repeated. "You say you lived here? Was your dad Bill McCarty, the mines' electrical supervisor back in the fifties, by any chance?"

"Yes, that's him," Matt said. "Did you know him?"

"Afraid of him, more like," said Crane, laughing. "I remember you now as a little kid, tagging around everywhere after your sister. I had a crush on Heather, and your dad used to give me the evil eye whenever I got within ten feet of her. Anyway, we were only nine or ten, and I believe your family soon moved away. How is she? Got married, I s'pose, had lots of kids?"

"No, Tom," Matt said. "Wasn't meant to be. She got cancer and died way back when she was twenty-three over in St. John's."

"Matt, I'm sorry. That's terrible, so young."

"Yes, well, my father passed just this past week, and I came out from Vancouver for that, but I'm on a bit of a quest now." Matt leaned in a bit. "I'm hoping you can help out. If she's still living, I might have another sister. A half sister I didn't know about. Did you know of a man from back probably in the forties or fifties, name of Sparkes? I believe his nickname was Sparky. He would have had a daughter named Lorraine and a granddaughter called Evelyn."

Tom Crane appeared deep in thought for a moment and then looked straight at Matt. "No," he said, "none of those names ring a bell." His manner changed abruptly as he got up. "You'll have to excuse me now," he continued. "The bus is arriving, and I better prepare to start the next tour. Thanks for the tea." With that, he quickly left.

Over behind the counter, refilling the coffee pot, Bev Adams overheard parts of their conversation. She was about to say something to Tom as he walked past but held off. Of course, he would know those names. They both knew who those people were.

Matt approached the front counter and reached for his wallet.

"On the house," she said, waving it away. "Because you're an islander and a gentleman. Where are you staying to while you're having your visit?"

Matt liked her straight-forward manner, inquisitive and probably not much of a filter when it came to speaking her mind.

"I'm staying over at the Cottages; probably see you again when I do the tour."

"Make sure you wear your name tag next time."

"Okay, you got it," he said, smiling, and then slipped a five back on his table for a tip as he left the building.

o o o

"Okay, Mr. Matt McCarty," Bev Adams said quietly to herself. "Why is Tom Crane playing cute?" *Can it be he knows something is wrong about the man,* she thought, *or what? I do believe we've got a mystery on our hands. Too bad Cassie is off today, because I think the summer just picked up a bit for the both of us.*

o o o

Matt walked slowly back up Compressor Road to the bakery, digesting what had just happened. It was clear that Tom Crane knew more than he was letting on, the way he'd gone from being friendly to shutting down like that. Whether he had some nefarious reason for not being more forthright or was simply being protective of someone's privacy, Matt wasn't sure, but he was determined to find out a lot more.

Before driving back to the Cottages, he went inside to buy some fresh bread. The staff smiled as he walked up to the counter. The story of the baker and the breakfast would become the stuff of island legend before long and was already well on its way.

Chapter 10

Bell Island, Wednesday, July 18, 2018

Matt woke to another day of sunshine at seven a.m. After his morning run, thinking he would let the bakery calm down a bit before providing them with another round of entertainment, he made toast, spreading some peanut butter on it while having his morning coffee.

As Matt left the cottage, he saw Sharyn watering her garden.

"Hello, Matt," she said, lifting the brim of her straw hat. "What are you at today?"

"A little exploring today, I believe," Matt said. "I enjoyed my breakfast over at the bakery yesterday."

"Did you now?" she replied with a smile. "I suppose you met Joanne?"

"Ah, Joanne the baker. Yes, indeed I did. Lovely woman and very good with her accents. She could pretty much tell where I came from, where I'd been, and what colour underwear I had on."

Sharyn roared with laughter. "Fair enough," she said. "Tell you what, you're a good sport, so let's go over tomorrow morning, and I'll buy."

"Okay," Matt said, "but I've got to warn you, I'll probably be ordering the expensive Newfie steak."

He waved goodbye and drove to Main Street. Heading north for about a half mile, he saw an old, battered, once-yellow building on his left. The green trim had mostly flaked off, and many of the clapboards were loose and falling down. Once upon a time, it had been the Prince's Theatre, where Heather had taken him to see *Jailhouse Rock*, starring Elvis Presley, when he was just seven years old.

The structure had obviously fallen on very hard times. Matt had been prepared to have a realistic view of his childhood memories and knew that time might have taken its toll on the places he remembered, but this was sad to see.

Driving west now, he came to Ten Commandments Road and stopped for a moment on the street that had been named for the ten company houses built there around 1900. The grassy field beyond, with two lazily grazing Newfoundland breed ponies, had once been a hive of activity with a tall deckhead building, crushers, conveyers, and other machinery, with men and ore cars coming and going though the collar of the No. 3 mine shaft. A high chain-link fence topped with barbed wire had run around the perimeter to keep trespassers out and curious children like him safe.

At the south end of the field, he had lived on the ironically named Wall Street, which had run parallel to the old ice arena. The street was gone now, along with its five houses. It was hard to imagine that they'd ever existed. The street, the houses, the fence, the mine, and the people . . . gone. All gone. All that remained now were the ponies, an occasional remnant of broken concrete foundation poking up through the long grass, and hundreds of beautiful pink and purple lupin flowers like those covering much of the island, waving in the ever-present breeze. While Matt had not thought of this place for many years, he now realised that he desperately needed to be here on Bell Island . . . and to understand why.

○ ○ ○

At the north end of the field, parked on the shoulder of West Mines Road, Peter Farrell observed Matt's movements through a pair of powerful binoculars. Hunt, sitting in the driver's seat, asked him what was happening.

"I still don't understand why you won't just tell me what we're actually looking for. Can't we just go say hello and beat the answers out of him?" Hunt offered.

Farrell lowered the binoculars and looked over at Hunt for a moment, thinking, *If I didn't need the muscle once in a while.* . . . Then, raising the binoculars again, he said, "We'll get to that, but for now, we're going to take a more subtle approach. Just trust me that, when the time is right, I will tell you more, and I promise you will be happy."

○ ○ ○

Matt got back in the SUV and turned around, driving almost in a straight line past Farrell and Hunt toward the north side of the island. He stopped near another small mountain of overburden signalling where No. 6 mine used to be. It was a little chilling to see the overgrown remains of a set of railroad tracks leading down through the nettles and weeds toward a grassy mound and then just disappearing into the earth.

He walked beyond the mound along a rutted grassy track, and reaching the cliff's edge, he could see that large squarish blocks of the cliff wall were strewn along the beach about a hundred feet below, having succumbed to undercutting from relentless wave action. He enjoyed watching the water crashing into the cliff and over the large partially submerged rocks a little farther off shore. The sound was both soothing and a little bit scary. He had brought his Canon SLR along, with a

250mm lens attached, so he sat down and took pictures of the rock formations with water cascading over them, sending twenty-foot-high sprays of foaming ocean into the air.

After an hour or so, Matt got up and was starting back for the Tahoe when something caught his eye. Looking up, he could see another vehicle stopped near his. It seemed familiar somehow. Squinting a bit, he thought he could see a man shading his eyes while peering into the SUV. Matt lifted his camera and looked through the viewfinder, zooming in. The man was large, bald headed, and clean shaven. Then the passenger door of the other car opened, and in the viewfinder, he could see quite plainly the face of Peter Farrell, the man from the cemetery. Matt clicked off a couple of quick photos and continued walking slowly toward the SUV. In a moment, both driver and passenger got in their dark blue vehicle without seeing him and drove away.

Matt was no detective, but he didn't think it was coincidence that Farrell was right there, right now. And the man with him certainly looked like classic "muscle," straight out of a bad movie. It seemed obvious that Farrell, if that was his name, had lied about having anything to do with war veterans and was more likely interested in something his father had been in possession of. Mentally going through the contents of the cigar box, the only thing that stood out except for the letter was that gold Nazi ring. He knew it was probably worth something. Could that have some connection?

Matt realised that, in keeping with the relaxed island attitude, he had left his cottage door unlocked. Maybe he'd better get back there quick in case they knew where he was staying and decided to go through his belongings, looking for who knows what. Doubling his pace, he arrived at the Tahoe, got in, and headed home.

○ ○ ○

When he arrived, everything was still as he had left it. Going through the box's contents, he read the letter again and then folded it and put it in his wallet. As an afterthought, he took his father's knife and made a small slit in the lining of one of his duffel bags and put the rest of the contents inside. Matt made something to eat, and at about nine p.m., was about to review his notes when there was a knock on the door. He closed his notebook and computer and felt for the knife in his pocket. He didn't know why, but it was reassuring to know it was there. Before him, when he opened the door, was a sheepish-looking Tom Crane.

"Tom?" said Matt, a question mark clearly hovering between them.

"I know the Sparkes family," Crane began. "I lied about that, and I'm a friggin' arsehole."

"Come in and grab a seat," Matt said. "I'm not buying that you're an arsehole, but I knew there was something you weren't telling me. Now that I know what, the question is why? But hold that thought a minute while I go put on the kettle."

With tea in hand, they settled in the living room, and Tom Crane began to talk.

"I have to go back a bit here, Matt," Tom said, "so bear with me. First of all, I'm sorry about yesterday. It's just that, when you talked about having another sister and then mentioned the Sparkes, well . . . I sort of panicked, and I'll tell you why."

Matt leaned forward attentively as Tom explained.

"Back in 1961, Lorraine Sparkes came back to Bell Island after being away for about five years or so. She had a little girl with her, and it was obvious from the hair and the green eyes that it must be her daughter. All the Sparkes girls have the long red hair and those eyes. Nobody knew who the father was, and she wasn't saying. After being here for a few months, Lorraine left little Evelyn with a friend, saying she would be back to get her when she could, and that's all I know about that part. She left the island, never to be heard from again. Now Evelyn did all right, was raised proper and then had a daughter named Elizabeth. Poor Elizabeth died about four years after having her own child, a daughter as well.

"Young Cassandra was left with her grandma Evelyn and grandpa Henry. Well now, Henry passed about six years ago when Cassie was nine, and since then, it's just been Evelyn and Cassie and that huge old dog of theirs. I've known the kid since she was a baby. She's as smart as a whip and sweet as they come. For the summer break, she works part time over at the museum with her best friend, Beverly, who you met yesterday, both of them pestering me every five minutes with their questions about the mines and the old days," he said proudly.

"So, now we come to it. I love Evelyn and Cassie as if they were my own family, and I don't want to see everything get all stirred up for them and then maybe having to go through more heartache and disappointment when you leave. God knows they've had more than their fair share of hurt already."

Matt let that settle for a little while and then replied.

"Tom, I can see why you would be protective about their feelings. Stirring up the past can bring things to the surface that have been comfortably buried for a long time, and sometimes are maybe even better left alone. But I think you know they deserve to be offered the opportunity to decide that for themselves, otherwise you wouldn't be here, right? Especially since I may be able to shed some light on things."

Tom nodded.

"I'll tell you what," Matt continued, "since you seem to be almost like family, I'll go to Evelyn and give her some information I have about where I believe she came from, and then she can decide whether to tell young Cassandra. Here's what I know so far." With that, he took out his wallet and produced the folded letter in its envelope.

After Tom read the contents, he nodded, saying, "Yes, Evelyn needs to see this. Might be more questions than answers for her now, but it's up to her to figure that out, I s'pose. Do you want me to come along?"

"No," Matt said, kindly but firmly. "This is something I have to do on my own. But I promise, I will be respectful and very careful in how I talk with her."

"I have no doubt of that, Matt. I think I can say for sure that you're a good man. If you go see Evelyn tomorrow, Cassie will be working the morning shift at the museum, around nine, so you can do your one on one. Here's where she lives." He wrote the address down on a piece of notepaper.

"Okay," Matt said, "I'll go visit sometime after breakfast."

"Oh, and Matt," Crane said, hesitating by the cottage door, "if I'm wrong about you. . . ."

"I know," Matt said, nodding. "You don't need to say it."

Chapter 11

Bell Island, Friday, November 6, 1942

Bill McCarty ate his breakfast and made plans. There were several leads to run down, and as another mild day unfolded outside, Jack Sparkes would drive with him to various locations on the island to do it. The dirt roadways were wet but clear. Thankfully, the serious weather with the heavy snow was still a month or more away.

Lorraine was already at work when Bill and Jack left the house. After telling them the night before about the conversation she'd overheard, she knew that Bill was concerned. The two men got in the truck and started off for their first destination on the south side of the island: Scotia Pier. If the spies had been spotting for submarine targets, the top of the cliff there would be a good choice. Mines Manager Richard Delaney told him that one of the buildings, formerly a staff boarding house, was no longer used except for storage and could make a good vantage point for the spies.

As they drove, Jack took a quick look over at Matt.

"Well?" he asked. "Do you think that what Lorraine heard was real or just a couple of the boys friggin' around?"

"I don't know for sure, but it seems suspicious," Matt replied. "It's too bad Lorraine didn't get a look at them, but I'm glad she played it safe and stayed inside. I didn't want to worry her, but if those two are the saboteurs, they're playing for keeps."

They drove south down towards the beach until a right-hand fork put them on Lance Cove Road, heading west. It was little more than a rutted track, but the Ford truck had heavy-duty springs, and the tires gripped the road well. Along the bumpy ride, McCarty explained his theory to Jack of how the spies might be going about their business. He said he was sure that they would be in higher positions than the miners but below management. They were probably skilled technicians, and such a position would give them some independence to go about their nefarious activities and not draw too much attention to themselves. They probably even had access to a company vehicle.

"Jaysus, that sounds like me," Jack said. "Okay, I give up."

Gallows humour was a Newfoundland tradition—a result of the many hardships they had endured over the centuries.

"I suppose you're safe for now, Sparky, but I'm keeping an eye on you," McCarty returned with a laugh.

They stopped at the top of Scotia Pier next to the old staff boarding house, which overlooked the cliff where ore was dumped far below, after its cross-island rail journey from the mines. Two men were struggling in the doorway with a wooden box labelled "Deck Chain." Bill and Jack jumped in to lend a hand. They each took a corner with the other men, and the four of them lifted the heavy box up onto a cart waiting there.

"Thanks, b'ys," one man said with a wink and a nod. This was a gesture particular to Newfoundlanders. It could be a sign of anything from a greeting to a thank you.

"No problem sure," Jack responded in kind. "Anytime, b'y."

"Are ye here to fix those lights in the building that stopped working?" the other man asked, noticing the panel truck that said Electrical Department on its side.

"Yes," Bill broke in before Jack could answer, taking advantage of the opportunity to be in the building without arousing curiosity. "It was reported that it might have been caused by some people who weren't supposed to be here. Have you seen anyone around who looked like they didn't work for the company, or maybe seemed like they were in the wrong place?"

"What do you mean? Like a thief or that?" asked the first man. "No. No one like that. Just the regular ranger patrol, but we knows those fellas."

"And the night watchmen we saw who were here on the night the boats went down," said the other. "Maybe you could ask them."

"No, b'y," said Jack quickly, looking at McCarty. "We're just going to take a look at the lights. The rest of it's somebody else's job."

With that, Bill and Jack went inside, and the two men pushed the cart with the deck chain away.

"I know one thing," Jack said.

"No night watchmen?" asked McCarty.

"No friggin' night watchmen," Jack replied. "They only have them at the mines."

They walked through the building to where some windows looked out over the bay on the first floor and saw nothing suspicious. Going upstairs, they walked toward the windows and noticed two thick electrical wires hanging down. They looked slightly melted and both had a sooty coating.

Jack took a look. "Well, I can see why there's a problem with the lights. These two wires must have overloaded and taken out the main fuse."

"Yes," agreed McCarty, "and here's how." He reached into a dark corner and dragged out a tripod stand with a lighting fixture attached.

"That's a carbon arc spot lamp," Jack said. "Powerful light in a portable package. I think it heated up too much trying to draw more current than the wiring could handle."

"Yes," agreed Bill, "the lamp would be just the thing for signalling a submarine out in the bay or interfering with a navy ship trying to find it, and anyone who saw it would think it was one of the regular searchlights the coastal defence force are using."

Putting the light back in the corner where they'd found it, they went back downstairs. From the truck, Jack grabbed a replacement sixty-amp fuse. Before they left, McCarty talked to the men they had helped earlier and got them to agree to leave a message at the main office for him if they saw the "night watchmen" return.

August Kahr and Kurt Becher had nearly completed their plan to destroy all four of the Bell Island submarine mines using Kahr's special-formula nitroglycerin. Beginning nearly a year before, in their legitimate cover jobs as structural engineer and explosives expert, the spies had directed various drillers and labourers to take core samples of over two hundred support pillars near the one-mile depth of submarine mine No. 4, ostensibly to check for structural integrity. When no workers were around, the spies had placed two sticks of explosive in each of the pillars, then plugged each of the drilled holes with bits of the loose ore found in abundance throughout the mine complex. The explosives were unnoticeable and didn't need to be wired. They would all be triggered at once by the concussive force of a smaller wired explosion, causing the collapse of over two hundred pillars almost at once and setting off a catastrophic chain reaction far beyond even the spies' imagination.

o o o

Later that evening, on Grammer Street, Jack Sparkes and Bill McCarty sat before the living-room fireplace and talked about plans for the next day. The rest of the afternoon had been unproductive, with McCarty going to a number of locations and inquiring about several of the staff that could be possible leads. Nothing seemed out of the ordinary, however, and except for the mysterious conversation that Lorraine had overheard, it began to feel like they were chasing ghosts.

"Would you like a drop of rum, Bill?" Jack asked.

"Not for me thanks," McCarty replied. "I never developed a taste for spirits."

"Ah well," countered Jack, "my condolences and all the more for me then, my son."

Just then, from upstairs, came the haunting sound of a violin playing. They both stopped talking for a moment, and Bill looked straight ahead without seeing.

"Ah, Jaysus," said Jack, "wouldn't that sound just break your heart now."

McCarty didn't hear him, but he heard Lorraine when she began to sing in a sweet voice:

> *"Take nothing for granted, honour your friends,*
> *Rejoice every morning,*
> *When you're wrong, make amends.*
> *Be honest and faithful, to your own self be true,*
> *And don't be afraid to say,*
> *'I love you'."*

Chapter 12

Bell Island, Thursday, July 19, 2018

Matt was up, showered, and dressed by eight o'clock. He met Sharyn outside, and she drove them over to the Rolling Pin Bakery where (true to his word) Matt ordered Newfie steak. Things were quiet, and the sit-down area was empty except for themselves and a couple of tourists. Nothing was mentioned about the previous encounter. Joanne, busy, popped out from the kitchen just to say hello, then disappeared again.

"So, what are you at today, Matt?" Sharyn asked.

"Just going to play it by ear, I guess," he replied, but inside, he was planning on how he was going to approach calling on Evelyn Clarke, and feeling quite nervous. Continuing, he said, "I might wander the cliffs and then catch up on a little reading later."

"Sounds good," she said. "Be careful around the cliffs, though. There's been a few rock falls lately, and it seems like there's more of them every year."

"I'll be careful," he replied. "Don't worry."

Then he wondered how much she might worry if she saw the contents of his rigging bag, with everything he was going to need to jump off a cliff and rappel to the rocks below. Some of the best areas of the island were only accessible by boat unless you dropped in from above, and considering how he felt about boats, especially small ones, he'd rather take his chances with the cliff, rock fall or not. Then again, given a choice of a small boat on the ocean and meeting Evelyn Clarke, today he might just choose the boat.

After breakfast, back at the little cottage, Matt prepared himself for the visit to the woman who might be his half sister. He drove to Main Street and then continued north until he arrived at Hibbs Road, stopping in front of the house just before the address that Tom Crane had given him. He got out and started walking towards the door but then hesitated, about halfway there, and slowly walked back toward the SUV. After standing there a minute, he steeled his nerve and started again toward the little house. Once again, he stopped and turned around.

Then he heard a bell-like but clear voice say, "Well? Are you going to stand there all day or go over and knock? The suspense is killing me."

Turning around, he walked to the passenger side of the Tahoe and saw a woman standing in the front yard of the house where he had parked. She was in her fifties and had a tanned athletic build, as evidenced by the cut-off jean shorts and sleeveless t-shirt she wore. She was of medium height and had dark reddish-brown hair in a long pageboy cut, with bangs above her electric blue eyes. Completing the picture were full sensual lips and a sprinkle of freckles across her high cheekbones and the bridge of her perfect nose. She was smiling slightly and looking directly at him in a frank, appraising manner. Something about her made him feel like he had just been caught with his hand in the cookie jar. He also knew, in that moment, that he would be helpless to stop himself from trying if she casually suggested that he flap his arms and start flying.

To his credit, Matt didn't stammer. He calmly said that he was just double checking the address and would now proceed to the Clarke residence and knock, thank you very much. She continued to smile. His stomach felt funny, but he didn't know why. He turned again toward number 23 and walked straight into the wide SUV mirror. Composing himself once more, he proceeded. Glancing back, he saw that her smile had grown even wider. Matt could see a row of perfect white teeth and hear what he knew was a laugh but sounded like music. *Oh, that's what it is,* he said to himself, recognising the long-forgotten funny feeling. *Butterflies. Great.*

o o o

Evelyn answered the door about ten seconds after he knocked. She had a youthful look and was quite slim. She wore her sixty-three years well, and while her long pony-tailed hair was mostly grey, he could see it would have been a striking red at one time. She took his measure with a neutral expression, cocking her head slightly to one side.

As he opened his mouth to speak, she said, "You must be Matthew McCarty." A statement, not a question. "Why is Kathleen staring at you? Come in."

While he was trying, nonplussed, to figure out who Kathleen was, he found himself being led inside. A glimmer of understanding had him turn around just before the door closed to see the woman next door still standing in her yard. Still looking directly at him—or maybe through him—and smiling.

He was led into a cosy kitchen where a kettle was boiling on the stove. As she poured the water into a large teapot, Matt said, "Obviously you must be Evelyn Clarke, and I'm guessing Tom called you?"

She smiled for the first time. "Did you think he wouldn't call me with something like this? For Tom, this is like winning the lottery. He gets to show you who's boss and then be the knight in shining armour as well. Gotta love him, though, and he's still a good looker for an older man. How do you want your tea? I think Kathleen likes you. Now start at the beginning and don't stop unless I stop you."

There was a long pause while he tried to reconstruct the jumble of words he had just heard and make some sense out of them.

Finally, he said, "Tom seems like a good guy, even if he can't keep a secret, and I'll have my tea with just a drop of milk please."

Without further comment, she poured his tea into a large mug, and put it in front of him on the kitchen table, as he began his story. An old electric clock, its little motor humming on the wall beside the ancient fridge, said it was ten-thirty in the morning. Toward noon, he finished the story of where he came from, his Bell Island childhood, St. John's, and then Vancouver—minus some details for now—his or maybe *their* father's passing, the letter, Fran Kavanagh, and even the concern about someone who might be following him. Evelyn now had a pretty good sense of what was going on, only stopping him a couple of times for a clarification.

She looked at him for almost a full minute without speaking or changing her expression. Then she said, "Give me Fran Kavanagh's phone number. Phone too." He just handed it over. She called, and when someone answered, Evelyn asked, "Is this Fran Kavanagh? Yes? Just a minute." To Matt she said, "Out back," pointing to the door leading from the kitchen. "This will take a few minutes. Mind the dog. Do you want more tea?"

Beginning to get the rhythm of how Evelyn operated, Matt just said no thanks, opened the back door, and walked out. There was either a medium-sized black bear or a giant dog lying down on the back porch next to a comfortable-looking chair. Eyeing Matt, who sat down (thinking it was the safest course), the massive animal got up slowly and walked toward him. After meeting each other's eyes for a moment, the dog laid its huge head on Matt's knee. He wasn't sure if the beast was being friendly or perhaps preparing for battle. He reached out tentatively and gently scratched it behind the ear. The animal shuffled around closer to him, and Matt got both ears going. He wasn't sure, but he thought he might have heard a baritone groan of pleasure. After about twenty minutes, the back door opened and Evelyn appeared, handing him back his phone.

"I see you met Kip," she said. "You're in trouble. You were supposed to call Fran yesterday. Call her by tonight or she says I'm supposed to kick your skinny butt. And when I asked her about your sanity, she said that you probably *are* crazy but that doesn't mean someone's not following you. Now come here."

Matt got up, and she put both of her arms around him and hugged. He returned the hug, and then Kip walked heavily over and head-bonked him, depositing a little drool and nearly buckling Matt's knee.

Back inside, they began exchanging stories, slowly at first and then faster, bits of information here and there, jumbles of words in the moment they would only half remember later. More tea and then snacks, and before long, it was after four-thirty, and they heard the front door open.

"I'm home, Gram!" came a girl's voice. "Bev's with me."

"In the kitchen," Evelyn returned. "Come and meet someone."

Both girls walked into the room. Bev's eyes went wide as she exclaimed, "Jaysus, Cassie, it's the guy I told you about from the museum!"

Evelyn said, "Cassandra, I want you to meet my half-brother, Matthew."

As Matt stood up, Bev exclaimed, "Fuck me, he's your half-grandpa!"

"Language, Beverly," said Evelyn, "and he's Cassie's great uncle. I think. Half anyway, I guess."

As Matt and Cassie looked at each other, Bev's eyes kept darting back and forth between them, waiting. A lifetime passed as Cassie's eyes slowly welled up.

Bev said, "Okay, now I'm gonna fuckin' cry." She looked at Evelyn. "Sorry."

As a tear rolled down Cassie's cheek, she asked, "What do you want? Why did you have to come here and ruin everything?" Then she turned and ran down the hall to her room.

The look Bev gave Matt was one of sympathy, with a touch of murder added, as she walked down the hall after Cassie.

"I'm sorry, Evelyn. I should probably go," Matt said, confused but somehow understanding. This was all overwhelming even for him, and he'd had a lot of life experience. For a young teenager, having her whole world take a sudden turn?

"No," replied Evelyn. "I'm going to start supper. In about twenty minutes, you go and ask her through the door if Bev is staying and if they want to come help set the table."

Matt sweated the next twenty minutes with some small talk as Evelyn bustled around the kitchen. Then he reluctantly walked down the hall.

"Well?" Evelyn asked, as he returned.

"There was a kind of muffled grunt, and then I'm pretty sure Bev said a word I won't repeat."

"Ah, sure we'll be okay then," she said, taking a pot off the stove.

Cassie was quiet and avoided looking at Matt during supper. Bev started out trying to look stern but couldn't keep it up. Naturally inquisitive, she asked where he came from, why he was here, and after his polite but brief answers, she began to describe what she would do if he hurt her friend in any way. Cassie held up her hand and stopped her, just before she could describe how his testicles would be removed under such circumstances.

Whether Evelyn was letting the scene play out this way on purpose or not, it worked.

"Look, I'm sorry," Cassie said, finally looking at him. "It's just been me and Grandma for a long time, and it seems like everybody we care about either leaves or dies and. . . ." Her voice trailed off.

"And letting someone else in is taking a chance. It's a risk. A big one," Matt finished.

"Yeah," Cassie agreed.

Avoiding Evelyn's look, Bev said, "This'd be a lot easier if you were an asshole."

"Tell you what," said Evelyn. "Let's take things slow and easy. We can start by doing the dishes. I'll wash, and Cassie and Matthew can dry. Bev?"

"Yes," said Bev, "time for me to go."

They all got up. Bev gave Cassie a hug and a raised-eyebrow look. Then she walked over to Matt, gave him a little hug, said, "Bye, Half-Grandpa," and left.

"Uncle," said Cassie quietly. Whether correcting her friend or surrendering, she wasn't sure.

After the dishes were done and put away, Evelyn put the kettle on the stove to make tea while Cassie and Matt walked

THE SECRET OF BELL ISLAND

into the living room. Cassie pointed at the two large framed pictures on the mantle.

"That's my mom," she said, pointing to the vivacious smiling redhead on the right.

"Beautiful," Matt murmured.

"And that's my great-grandmother."

As Matt looked to the left, he saw a black and white portrait of a strikingly good-looking woman with long flowing hair. *A chill ran up his spine as he looked into the eyes of the angel he had seen as he was drowning when he was five years old.*

"Are you okay?" Cassie asked as he froze in place.

"Yes, I'm alright. Your great-grandmother had red hair too, right?"

"All the Sparkes girls do," Evelyn answered, coming out of the kitchen. "It's been a running joke I guess for generations."

"Okay," Matt said. "A lot of things are becoming clearer by the minute." He looked at Evelyn. "I believe your mother saved my life when I was five years old."

He explained the traumatic event, really for the first time ever out loud, then began several hours of more stories, discussions, and history trading. By midnight, they had barely scratched the surface when it was time for Matt to leave. They agreed to meet up the next day and have supper together at a restaurant. Evelyn would choose a place for them to go.

"Maybe Tom would like to join us," suggested Cassie. "Should I ask him tomorrow when I'm at work?"

"Sure," said Evelyn.

"Yes," added Matt, looking at Evelyn. "Tell him I insist."

Cassie looked puzzled but just shrugged. "Okie dokie."

At the door, they said goodbye, but as he turned to go, Cassie ran up and threw her arms around his waist, burying her head in his chest. He could tell she was crying. He held her and looking over her head at Evelyn, and surprising even himself, he said softly, "It's okay. No matter what, I'll be there for you."

As he walked back to the SUV, he saw the woman from next door sitting in a lawn chair near her front door.

"Been out here the whole time waiting for me, right?" Matt said, more statement than question.

"Ooh," she responded. "Mr. Confident now, are we?"

"Well, you caught me off guard before."

"Oh? Not used to talking to women?" she asked with a raised eyebrow.

"Not one like you," Matt replied. Then he heard that sound again that he knew was laughter but sounded like music.

"Goodnight, Kathleen," he said, thinking she would be impressed that he knew her name.

"Goodnight, Mr. Matthew McCarty from Vancouver who used to live on Bell Island."

Acknowledging defeat with a nod, he got in the Tahoe and left.

Bell Island, July 1955

Lorraine waved at her friend arriving on the boat from St. John's, and as she stood on the wharf she looked at the other passengers standing on deck as the *Kipawo* was about to dock. She thought she saw a familiar face for a moment, but it couldn't be. He would be older, sure, but . . . ? Could it be? It had been . . . what? Thirteen years. Here for her maybe? No, he would have married years ago because of that promise made before they'd even met. She didn't know why she still felt this way after so long, but there was no one else for her. Never would be.

As the ferry docked with a bump, a young boy standing just behind the man stumbled forward and then back. The safety chain was not in place, and she screamed, "Look out!"

As the boy stepped back into space, the man's eyes swung around toward her, and they both recognised each other. He seemed to freeze for a moment looking at her, and then as he started to look behind toward the empty spot where his son had been, she was already diving into the water, long red hair streaming behind her, reaching out her hand to the boy as he sank toward the bottom.

Chapter 13

Bell Island, Friday, July 20, 2018

Jurgen Meyer was ready to order soft-boiled eggs and dry toast in the restaurant of the Bell Island Inn on Memorial Street where he was staying. The inn was a hundred-year-old former convent, converted now into a lovely hotel, preserving its original heritage look but with all the modern amenities. Meyer was soft spoken, with a slight German accent, tall and gangly at six-foot-four, all elbows and knees. He was clean shaven, with close-cropped blond hair and bright hazel eyes. He retained a youthful, pink-skinned, innocent look even in his late thirties. Meyer looked over the top of the menu at two individuals several tables away, who were also staying at the hotel, and considered various termination options for the pair should it become necessary to kill them.

One was thin and wiry looking with a cruel mouth and dark furtive eyes. That would be Peter Farrell. The other was bald and powerfully built but starting to lose the battle of the midsection. His clinical assessment was that the big man called Hunt wouldn't be a problem. Farrell would be the more dangerous of the two. He had the look of a man who would not stop, no matter what kind of injuries he sustained and no matter what sort of pain was inflicted on him. If it came to it, Meyer would take him first.

Long before Matt McCarty had been flagged by the Canadian Intelligence Corps after his search for information about Operation Red Iron, a certain organisation based in Germany had become aware of a related but separate matter when Peter Farrell had begun showing interest in Nazi gold hidden in North America during the Second World War.

When it appeared that Farrell had a possible lead on the whereabouts of a particular cache of gold, which they suspected had been secreted somewhere on a certain island in Newfoundland, Jurgen Meyer, at his own request, was assigned the task of finding it.

o o o

On Friday morning, when Cassie woke up, she reflected on what had happened the day before. She had known disappointment in her young life, but despite her natural reluctance, she was slowly yielding to other possibilities. She dressed quickly, had some cereal, and then put down some food for Kip, giving him a quick ear scratch before heading off to work. On the way up Compressor Hill, she thought about how she had almost started to laugh at the interaction between Bev and Matt, even when she felt like crying. Bev was a lot like a golden lab pup most of the time but could quickly become a guard dog in attack mode when it came to looking out for Cassie or anyone else she considered family.

After the hours of exchanging stories with Matt the night before, Evelyn slept in until eight o'clock and then got up to put the kettle on the stove for the first of many times during the day. Looking out the kitchen window, she saw Kathleen out in her garden, as expected, and after pouring a mug of Red Rose, she headed out back. Kathleen Ryan and Evelyn were "fence neighbours" and best friends. Kathleen was fifty-two and had moved here after her husband died eleven years before. Until recently, she had owned a little knick-knack shop on Lance Cove Road that catered mostly to tourists but had sold the business to a long-time employee. Her small house was paid for, and she lived on a modest income.

Evelyn's house had been in the Clarke family forever. Since Henry's death, she lived on a pension and small annuity. Before leaving Evelyn with the Clarke family in 1961, her mother had sold the house on Grammer Street. There wasn't much, but eventually, when Lorraine never returned, the proceeds helped with Evelyn's upbringing. Besides losing her mother, Evelyn had also never known her grandmother or grandfather, Jack Sparkes, who'd both died before she was born.

All that was left now were a few boxes of old belongings stored in the basement that Evelyn had never been able to bring herself to look at. She had put on a brave face all these years, but she'd been devastated as a child when her mother left. Now, with Matt in the picture, maybe it was time. Maybe it would be easier if he could help her come to grips with the relics of the past.

"So," said Evelyn across the fence to Kathleen, "the tall handsome stranger. What do you think?"

"Do you want a verdict now or after you spill your guts?"

"First impression," returned Evelyn, "then you get the whole ball of yarn."

"Okay. Funny, fit, witty, and transparent in a good way. Seems honest enough, a little intimidated by a strong, good-looking woman like myself, but comes back strong too, and not bad-looking for an old fella."

"So pretty much perfect?"

"Yeah, pretty much," Kathleen sighed, nodding her head slowly, "but that's not your fault."

Nodding sympathetically, Evelyn proceeded to fill her in on the details of the night before.

o o o

Matt had toast with homemade preserves from island-picked blueberries and some orange juice for breakfast in his cottage, and of course, a small pot of coffee to round things out. He opened his waterproof rigging bag and pulled everything out. Checking and rechecking the equipment, he made sure everything was in order.

His plan was to investigate the possibility of climbing the sea stack which rose a little over a hundred feet high near Grebes Nest and was accessible via a short rock bridge from the beach. He parked the SUV near the east end of the Bell Island airstrip and then began hiking through a grassy field toward the cliffs. To his right, he could see the arched portal entrance to the old No. 4 mine.

Soon he skirted around a low mound—one of many that usually signified remnants left over after the very early surface mining. He would have kept walking except for the partially exposed concrete corner that had no business being there. His natural curiosity aroused, Matt reached down and tugged at a clump of sod, exposing a rusted, hinged metal grill about four feet square with a pull handle. He was able to raise the handle from its recess, but pulling hard did not budge the hatch. Shading his eyes, he tried to peer through the grill to no avail. He pulled a flashlight out of his rigging bag and could see metal ladder rungs leading into the darkness but nothing more.

o o o

Hunt followed McCarty after he left the cottage. Shortly after they parked, Hunt saw that McCarty was quite engrossed with something on the ground and shining a flashlight at it. After a few minutes, McCarty moved on toward the cliff. Looking through the binoculars, Hunt said out loud to no one, "What the fuck was that asshole looking at?" He waited until McCarty was out of sight, then traced the man's steps until he saw what Matt had uncovered. Hunt thought maybe it had something to do with sewage and shook his head, not for the first time thinking that McCarty was off his rocker.

Matt descended the path down to the beach. He walked along the short rock bridge to the base of the sea stack and set his gear down as the waves came in and sent salt-spray showers up the side. After a visual inspection, he decided to free climb at least partway and test the rock higher up. The wide band of iron ore at the base was solid, and the rock above it looked pretty good up to about the sixty-foot mark.

He didn't usually wear gloves, but these rocks were sharp. He compromised with fingerless gloves and changed into his high-ankle rock-climbing shoes. Finally, he donned a Petzl helmet and attached a Go-Pro high-definition camera. Publicly, he would say it was for reviewing his technique, but most of his friends in the climbing community who did the same thing knew it was for someone else to review in case of the unthinkable. It was noon, and Matt was in his element.

As he began to free climb, there were some good hand and footholds, and higher up even more; progress was quick up to the thirty-foot level when they became a little sparse. Looking to his right, he saw a crack that might provide a good hand-hold, but the rock proved brittle, and a small fist-sized chunk pulled away, falling below with a clatter. He managed to climb another ten feet to just before the halfway mark when the rock changed to cracked and broken interlocking layers, like a loose deck of playing cards, and he could go no further.

Reluctantly, he began to make his way back down. Looking behind him, he caught a glimpse of a large figure crouched by a bush at the cliff's edge. He realised in that moment that it was the same person who had been down by the beach when he'd gotten off the ferry, and also looking in the Tahoe two days earlier. There was no doubt now that there was a connection between this rough-looking individual, Farrell, and his father. Matt briefly considered contacting the local island RCMP detachment, but what would he say? Suspicious activity? What kind? No, they would peg him as paranoid and send him away with a standard "We'll look into it" reply. By the time he descended and packed his gear, the man was long gone. He retraced his route back to the SUV.

o o o

Matt got back to the cottage at three o'clock. He showered and then dressed in his "formal" evening attire, which meant putting on some clean jeans, regular shoes, and an actual shirt with buttons. He had time before his dinner engagement, so he gave Fran Kavanaugh a call. After giving him a good-natured hard time about not keeping in touch, she spoke in a more serious tone.

"Matt," she said, "something was bothering me about that ring with your dad's stuff. I called my friend Stewart at the university and asked him if he could make any sense of it, and of what Lorraine said in that letter, especially if your dad was supposed to be on a navy ship around Halifax during the war."

"Did your friend have any clue how those things might be connected?"

Taking a deep breath, Fran said, "He had an idea, and it makes sense, but it's going to seem far-fetched."

"Fran, a lot of things seem far-fetched to me these days, so at this point, I could almost believe that pigs might start flying over this cottage any moment. Let me have it."

"Okay," she said, "he needs to see the ring before he will commit to his opinion on that, but he thinks your father could have been a naval intelligence agent sent to Bell Island in the winter of 1942 to find two German spies."

There was a considerable silence on Matt's end.

"Matty? Are you still there?"

Finally, he said, "Remember a moment ago when I talked about those pigs? Well, a couple of them just flew past the friggin' window."

Fran continued. "Stewart says he checked with a colleague who's familiar with wartime Bell Island. The man told him it was not a well-kept secret that a Canadian Navy operative was sent there in 1942, almost two months after the first submarine attack on the ore carriers. The navy was sure there were spies living on the island, spotting targets for the U-boats and maybe even working for the mine company as their cover."

Silence again.

"And another thing, Matty," she said. "Those two brass miner's tokens?"

"Yes?"

"They weren't your dad's. According to mining-company records, they were registered to two of the mine staff, Kurt Becher and August Kahr.

"Is that it? Are you sure there are no flying saucers involved, or maybe my old band wants to get back together?"

"Well," she said hesitantly, "there could also be a hidden fortune in stolen Nazi gold, but that's not for sure."

"Of course," said Matt, this time without a pause, "how foolish of me not to think about buried treasure to round out the story."

Wouldn't it be something if his father, with whom he had never exchanged more than a few words, actually had a whole other life—a secret one. He had always been an enigma, and this just deepened the mystery. After his conversation with Fran, Matt called Evelyn about their supper plans and was informed that Kathleen would be joining them, and that Tom would meet them at the restaurant.

∘ ∘ ∘

When Matt pulled up in front of Evelyn's house, he got out and saw Kathleen by her front door wearing a little summer dress and the barest hint of makeup, looking breathtakingly beautiful.

"Do you actually live in that house," he asked, "or do you just hang out in front of it waiting for defenceless men to be smitten by your gardening talents?" She smiled that smile and he was careful not to trip over anything as he walked over to her.

"Kathleen Ryan, homeless waif," she confessed, officially introducing herself.

"Matt McCarty, klutz," he returned, shaking her hand and noticing that her touch caused something to start gently punching him in the stomach from the inside.

Evelyn and Cassie came out of their house just then, and they both turned toward the new arrivals.

"Where should I sit?" Kathleen asked Matt.

"In the back," he answered. "I don't think I trust you."

"Ah," she said, laughing, "so you *are* smart."

Ignoring the music as best as he could, Matt opened front and back doors.

"Hi, Cassie," Matt said. "Hop up front with me, and the old gals can sit in the back." He gave a sidelong look at Kathleen, which she returned, raising an eyebrow that spoke volumes.

"Hi," Cassie replied, now seeming a bit shy.

"Alright, Matthew," said Evelyn, "head up Compressor Hill and turn left at Quigleys Line, we're going to the Keeper's Cafe down at the lighthouse."

Following her directions, they wound up going east on Lighthouse Road. Once Matt parked, they all took a stroll down past the restaurant near the cliff's edge, which was even higher than Grebes Nest. Sea gulls nested on a tall sea stack just off shore of the lighthouse, and the waves boomed loudly as they crashed into the pinnacle's weathered hollows. Seeing a sign that cautioned them to be careful because of unstable conditions near the cliff's edge, Matt asked if they knew whether he needed permission to do any cliff climbing in this area. Evelyn and Kathleen had no idea, but Cassie said that it was probably more of an "ask for forgiveness rather than permission" kind of situation.

"Have you been climbing for a long time?" Cassie asked. "I really want to climb the sea stack by Grebes Nest, but I guess I'd need equipment, and probably some lessons wouldn't hurt." She laughed and her face lit up. It made Matt smile to see her enthusiasm.

"Would you believe I was there today?" he asked. "I got up about halfway, but it's trickier than it might seem, and there are some unstable rock ledges. Even with full climbing gear, it would be a challenge."

Evelyn and Kathleen exchanged looks as Cassie stared at Matt without speaking.

"Uh-oh," said Evelyn, noticing the way Cassie was looking at him.

"Yup," agreed Kathleen, smiling. "You can almost see his halo."

Going inside, they saw Tom Crane at a long table he'd reserved. He looked sheepishly at Matt and shrugged his shoulders. After a meal of homemade fishcakes and fresh salad, the entertainment started with local musicians playing accordion and guitar, along with some bodhran Irish drumming. During a lull in the music, Matt spoke to Tom and asked about the grate opening he had seen by the airstrip.

"Oh yes," said Tom, "back in the twenties, the company was going to drill a tunnel all the way to the piers for underground ore delivery, but it didn't work out. You must have found an old ventilator shaft. I thought they were all filled in years ago."

"Could be it's blocked further down, but I think maybe they missed this one," Matt said. "Do you think it would be stable, if I decided to have a closer look?"

"If I had my tour guide hat on, I'd say stay the frig away from it," Tom replied. "But between you and me, if my knee was in better shape, and I had a chance to do it safely, I'd be in there like a shot. I don't know what it might be like below, but the air shaft is probably safe enough, and there are likely rebar rungs going down. Just have to be careful it isn't flooded or lacking a proper air supply."

"I saw some ladder rungs, and I'd like to maybe check it out," said Matt.

"How about if I come along," Tom said, "and if that shaft isn't blocked, I'll be your spotter while you drop down and have a gander?"

Evelyn, Kathleen, and Cassie noticed Matt and Tom deep in conversation, and as the two men huddled together, the three women exchanged quizzical looks.

Evelyn smiled. "The boys look like they're up to no good."

Cassie and Kathleen nodded in silent agreement.

Soon, Peter Doyle—the evenings master of ceremonies—called out to Cassie.

"Miss Cassandra Clarke," he announced loudly in the microphone, "your presence is requested up here on the stage." Cassie hesitated, looking a little embarrassed at Matt, who had no idea what was coming and just looked back at her, nodding toward the stage.

"Young Cassie," the impatient emcee bellowed, seeing her reluctance, "get yer arse up here now!"

She rose then and strode to the stage, shaking her fist at the emcee, who roared with laughter, along with everyone else. Cassie might not know much about her family history, but there weren't many Bell Islanders who didn't know about her and her violin playing. On Friday evenings after the tourists departed from the lighthouse area for the day, it was mainly locals who showed up and jammed at the Keeper's Cafe, eating delicious homemade food and enjoying a drink or two.

Taking the instrument that was offered to her, she said thank you and then stepped up to the microphone, and in a clear voice, said, "My great-grandmother Lorraine Sparkes wrote this song." She began playing, and after a few bars, began to sing.

> 'Take nothing for granted, honour your friends,
> Rejoice every morning,
> When you're wrong, make amends.
> Be honest and faithful, to your own self be true,
> And don't be afraid to say,
> 'I love you'."

By the time Cassie finished the touching ballad, there were more than a few tears shed, including a few from Matt. Later, Doyle the emcee announced to a curious crowd that Bill McCarty's son was the newcomer in attendance, which drew a smattering of applause from some old timers who remembered Matt's father from the old ninteen-fifties mining days.

Later, Matt dropped everyone off around eleven-thirty and promised to check in with Evelyn the next day. She asked if he would come by, as she was hoping to get his help with something. He agreed and then left for the cottage.

As Kathleen walked toward her house, Evelyn said to her, "So, would that be the Tom Crane syndrome I'm seein' when you look at my big brother?"

Kathleen Ryan grinned wickedly as Cassie said, "Oh God, please not another one of those visuals for my poor virgin mind,". . . but she was smiling as she said it.

Later, as Matt was drifting off to sleep, he considered the far-fetched idea that his father could have been involved with finding German spies back in the war. And who the hell were Kurt Becher and August Kahr? The names sounded . . . German.

o o o

That night, after telling Farrell about the grating at the end of the runway, and how the crazy fucker McCarty was climbing around the cliffs like a goddam monkey, Hunt finally confronted Farrell, demanding to know exactly what they were doing here.

Farrell saw the writing on the wall and knew it was time to give the dimwit the full picture, since he had every intention of killing Hunt eventually anyway. He poured a drink and began a story about spies and Nazi treasure. Hunt's eyes grew wider as the story unfolded, and while Farrell found it amusing that Hunt thought the object in the field had something to do with sewage, he had no doubt it actually led to something quite the opposite. However, he kept that to himself for now.

Chapter 14

Bell Island, Saturday, November 07, 1942

August Kahr kick-started the three hundred and forty-six cc Royal Enfield motorcycle that was parked behind the boarding house in Town Square, and got ready to start out for Grebes Nest. It was cold, and a light snow was falling as he adjusted the scarf under his thick woollen coat, but with sheepskin-lined gloves, leather helmet, and goggles, it was bearable as he sped along West Mines Road. Once he reached an area close to the cliff, he parked the bike in some bushes out of sight, carefully making his way down a passage to the beach and then walking a little further west. There was no direct access to the secluded Grebes Nest cove, but if the tide was out, it was possible to get around the point in relative safety.

The cave entrance was difficult to see if you weren't looking closely, and even then, it would just look like a darker spot in the shadows. He had found the opening while scouring this area for a likely place to cache their explosives and small boat. At first, he had considered the older mine-tunnel openings a bit further east on the beach, which were no longer in use, but they were too exposed for their purposes, and people still walked in that area. Scrambling over the slippery rock and into the almost invisible entrance, Kahr cursed fluently in German until he reached a dry area about twenty feet in.

The saboteurs kept their small boat hidden inside the entrance, and even after a half dozen late-night U-boat supply meetings just offshore, it had not been discovered. Further in were the now-empty wooden boxes stamped *"Gefaehrliche - Reine Nitroglycerine."* ("Dangerous - Pure Nitroglycerin")

Clicking on a heavy oversized flashlight, he walked further into the gloom, carefully skirting a large void on his right and also the occasional muddy sink hole scattered here and there. About a thousand feet in, the natural cave ended where it intersected with the now-disused side shaft, drilled by the company from the No. 4 submarine slope. That opening was now boarded over and signs had been placed on the mine side that said *"Danger - Do Not Enter - Unstable Area."* No miner would consider disobeying the sign, as the company did not do such things lightly. Kahr and Becher had counted on it, as this had been the route that they used to transport the nitroglycerin to the support pillars in the depths of the mine on Sunday evenings, when no one was on shift.

The man-made shaft continued on into the inky darkness, curving gently southeast toward Scotia Pier on the other side of the island. There were evenly spaced air shafts leading to the surface, seventy feet above. At the two-thousand-foot mark, on the right side, a side shaft had been blasted for future machinery placement, and it had been fitted with a strong metal safety door. Kahr stopped in front of it and keyed open his own heavy-duty padlock.

Sitting on a few rough wooden shelves were twelve heavy boxes, each bearing the stamp of the imperial eagle clutching a Nazi swastika in its talons. Not for the first time in the year he and Becher had been on this God-forsaken island, he picked up a small pry bar and opened the lid of the first case in front of him, shining his lamp on the contents. Laying in a bed of straw was a roughly shaped, gleaming ingot of pure gold, weighing one kilogram. Twenty-three of its brothers and sisters lay shining brightly beside and underneath it. There were no foundry markings, which in itself gave a chilling indication as to where this gold may have originated.

Kahr was smiling broadly, because he had no intention of seeing this gold go toward Germany's plan to secretly continue the Third Reich in the event the war went badly . . . or to anyone other than himself. Becher, on the other hand, was a zealot and unlikely to share his view—not that it would matter in the end. Kahr planned to quietly sit out the war and then come back for the gold, rich beyond imagination instead of being an imbecilic pawn in Hitler's impossible fantasy.

Carefully tapping the lid back onto the box, he went to a far corner and moved several strategically placed rocks to reveal a thirteenth wooden case, unmarked and smaller than the rest, unknown to Becher or anyone except himself. Inside was a very carefully cushioned and tightly sealed glass bottle. It contained a clear, colourless liquid labeled only *"Achtung,"* over a skull and crossbones.

It contained a German discovery made in 1938 by Gerhard Schrader, a mixture of phosphorus, cyanide, and other agents. It was originally meant to be a pesticide, but it was too powerful to use in the fields. Not content with its already deadly properties, Schrader had made it even more powerful before it was proudly offered as the lethal nerve-gas agent "*Sarin*." Kahr had a use planned for the mixture, a use he had thought of the day he had been given the full details of this mission.

MIKE PHELAN

Bell Island, Sunday, November 08, 1942

Kurt Becher was not happy. As far as he was concerned, Kahr did not take their mission seriously. In the beginning, it appeared that they both put Germany first and were working toward destroying iron-ore production on Bell Island. Lately, however, Kahr was drinking a lot and going off by himself. He said he was checking to make sure no one had discovered the cave opening and their boat, but Becher was now doubting his loyalty to the cause. He did not let on that he was suspicious but watched carefully to make sure Kahr did his part to fulfil their objective.

When Becher had told him he was willing to die for Germany, a drunk Kahr had joked that, if he was lucky, maybe he would get that opportunity; however, Becher was not all that sure he was joking. What made things even more difficult was that his confused personal feelings for Kahr were interfering with his own ability to do his job. Nazi party policy was very clear about homosexuality, but whereas some might have the conflicted situation become an opportunity for growth, it only served to drive Becher ever closer to the brink of madness.

o o o

Bill McCarty woke early Sunday morning and dressed. It had snowed a little the day before, but now it was clear and sunny, in sad contrast to the fact that later this morning there would be memorial services at both the Catholic and Protestant churches for the victims of Tuesday's U-boat attacks. The victims had already been laid to rest, but today being Sunday, there would be many attending services to pay their respects.

As he came downstairs, Jack was in the kitchen humming a tune while frying some eggs and getting toast buttered.

"Good morning, Bill," said Jack. "Have some grub, and we'll get you set for the day." Then, winking at McCarty, he yelled up the stairs, "Come on down, darlin'! Young Bill here wants to eat, and he won't start without you."

As if on cue, Lorraine appeared, coming down the stairs just as her father finished talking.

"Dad!" Lorraine said, reddening.

"Go on, love, I'm only after kidding you," Jack said, grinning as he noticed Bill gazing at Lorraine. "Besides, I don't think Bill's that hungry now anyway."

Lorraine was in a dark dress befitting the solemn occasion, and with her hair up and a little bit of make-up, she had gone from pretty to stunning. It was plain now that McCarty was trying not to show he was smitten. As she sat, he pulled himself together.

"Good morning, Lorraine," he said. "I really enjoyed your playing and singing last night. Did you write those words?"

"Funny," Jack interjected, "I never heard that one before."

"That's because it is new, dearest father," Lorraine said to Jack while looking at McCarty.

"Ahh," said Jack, smiling slyly. "Now look," he continued, "I need you both to do something for me. The company gave me this new camera for photographing repairs, and I need to try 'er out. Just sit there for a minute, Lorraine, next to the young skipper. That's it. Now for God's sake, Bill, don't look too happy, will you?"

McCarty made a face and said, "Okay, Sparky, you're the boss."

Lorraine turned toward him, laughing, and without thinking, reached out her hand and put it over his as the shutter clicked.

"Jack," he said, recovering, "I have an idea that I need to discuss, and reluctantly, I'm going to ask your permission to involve Lorraine. I think she could be helpful for the purpose of identifying certain parties."

"Bill, Lorraine is old enough to decide for herself. I know you wouldn't expose her to any harm on purpose, and I pity anyone I see who ever tried to hurt her."

"Before either of you go any further," she said, "yes, I will help in any way I can. Bill, I'm sure I know why you're really here, so let's hear your plan."

"Lorraine, I'm sorry to drag you into this," McCarty said, "but we're in desperate times, otherwise I wouldn't ask. As your father already knows, I am an intelligence officer in the Canadian Navy, and Jack is working with me. I'm here on a mission to find two foreign agents, who we know have plans to sabotage the mine workings. I am also convinced that they took part in helping to sink the ore carriers last week, *and* the two in September. I don't mean to sound dramatic, but there could be danger if I unmask these spies, so you can't speak about this to anyone outside our circle. Agreed?"

"I promise," she said, and then he outlined an idea for today that he hoped would help reveal the identity of the spies.

o o o

After McCarty explained the plan, Jack and Lorraine Sparkes walked to the Catholic Church of St. James in Town Square while McCarty took up a position at St. Cyprian's Anglican Church. They were to carefully observe the mourners for certain signs. Bill said to watch for men in pairs who did not seem to belong, perhaps standing by themselves and looking either unconcerned with the proceedings or even seeming to enjoy the pain of those around them. McCarty went on to say that people show their grief in different ways, and to not necessarily be suspicious of everyone, but to observe and take note. He also said that, if they did become convinced something was out of the ordinary, and *if* they could do it safely, maybe Lorraine could position herself to try and overhear them, in case the men engaged in conversation, and Jack could take a picture of them with his new camera.

Kurt Becher and August Kahr dressed appropriately for the occasion. Wearing solemn faces to go with their dark clothing, they exited the boarding house and made their way to the church. It would not only be in keeping with their cover to join the mourners to grieve for the dead but it could be quite enjoyable too.

As the service began, there were so many attendees at both churches that they overflowed to the outside. At St. James, after the service, Lorraine walked outside with her father. She saw two men engaged deeply in a hush-toned conversation. They looked out of place and were standing apart from the crowd. She gestured to Jack, and they began walking until they were close behind the men.

As Lorraine got closer, she could see that one of the men was quite emotional. The other, sensing her presence, turned around and asked, "Did you know Jim Fillier?"

"No, I'm sorry," she said. "Was he on one of the boats that sank?"

"Yes," replied the first, "a good friend, and he was only twenty-two. It was his first day on the *Rose Castle*. Henry King was on there too, another good Bell Islander."

Jack spoke up. "We're very sorry for your loss." Turning to Lorraine, he said, "We have to be going now." They both walked away.

MIKE PHELAN

○ ○ ○

Searching through the crowd in grid-pattern style, from a higher vantage point, as he had been trained, McCarty watched with interest as two men regarded the service with a quiet intensity. He was being unobtrusive but decided to move a little closer, looking for a clue as to who they might be. One of them, the smaller man, was lighting a cigarette. McCarty didn't smoke but had borrowed one of Jack's just in case an opportunity such as this arose.

"Excuse me, do you have a light?" he asked the nearer of the two.

The man simply stared at him without responding.

"I am sorry for my friend," said the other easily in a non-local accent. "He is a little hard of hearing. Please, allow me." The man struck a match, cupping the flame as McCarty bent forward. Lifting his head and looking into the other's eyes, McCarty realised he was looking into the cold eyes of one of the saboteurs. There was no doubt.

"Thank you," Matt said.

"Not at all, my friend," the man replied. "You are with the company?"

"Yes," McCarty answered. "I'm doing electrical consulting in connection with the expansion project. You and your colleague?"

"Ah! We will become well acquainted, I am sure," he said. "We are attached to the structural engineering aspects of the undertaking."

"My name is William McCarty," Bill said, nodding toward him.

"I am August Kahr, and my quiet friend and colleague is Kurt Becher," he said, returning the greeting. "I hope we meet again soon on a less sad occasion."

"Yes, I'm certain we will meet again," finished McCarty.

McCarty hadn't missed seeing the watch, which Kahr was in the habit of checking often. It was a black-dial Stowa, used exclusively by the German Wehrmacht. He thought it was no accident that August Kahr was displaying it. It almost felt like an open challenge from a person who thought that nothing or no one could touch him.

As Kahr and Becher left the church area, McCarty followed unseen at a discrete distance. He saw them enter the boarding house next to the phone company and recalled the conversation Lorraine had overheard, confirming what he already knew. Jack's new camera would soon be put to good use by capturing images of the two.

When he arrived at Grammer Street twenty minutes later, Jack asked him, "Did you see anything suspicious?"

Lorraine brought her hand up to her mouth as McCarty answered: "I saw everything. Today I looked into the face of evil."

Chapter 15

Bell Island, Saturday, July 21, 2018

After breakfast and an early morning run, Matt pulled up in front of number 23 Hibbs Road, but he didn't see Kathleen standing outside her house next door. Feeling disappointed, he got out and began walking toward Evelyn's. He now understood his feelings toward her; he was just surprised that he was having them despite so many years of being content to do his work, play his music, and enjoy his hobbies. This thing with Kathleen had come out of the blue, spontaneously and totally unexpected. Their banter and subtext humour were exciting and somehow familiar.

He kept getting the urge to just walk up and kiss her. He saw himself for a moment as a gangly, sweaty teenage boy at a high school sock hop, trying to get the courage up to ask a pretty girl to dance. That made him laugh out loud. He hadn't really thought about it that much for a very long time—the idea of romance. Over the years, it had simply seemed to slowly drift out of his life's picture.

He knocked on Evelyn's door. Kathleen answered. Caught off guard and without a chance for his brain to shout *"NO!"* he stepped forward and kissed her lightly on the lips. Then he quickly stepped back and croaked, "Good morning."

Slightly dazed, she said, "Good morning. Won't you come in?"

"Yes, thank you," he responded, somewhat formally. "I believe I will."

Walking inside, he was greeted by Kip who, surprising everyone, actually broke into a slow gallop toward him. Matt got down on his knees quickly instead of being knocked down and braced for impact. Slowing down, the dog only skidded a short distance on the linoleum, so the collision was minimal. After a quick ear scratch, Matt was able to navigate toward the kitchen with Kip on his heels.

"Tea? How are you? Sleep well?" Evelyn asked in quick gunshot succession.

Matt was catching on, and after waiting a moment, he answered: "Yes, please. I'm fine, and I had a good sleep."

Kathleen smiled. "Thanks for the tea, Ev. I'll talk to you later." Looking at Matt, she added, "As for you. . . ." She let the sentence hang there as she turned and left.

"Cassie's out with friends this morning," Evelyn said, ushering Kip out the back door, "and I'm wondering if you can help me with some boxes I have in the basement, left over from when Lorraine left. They've been stored down there ever since, and I might have never looked at them, but now that you're here, maybe it will be easier and shed some more light on. . . ."

Matt could see a glisten in her eye. "Let's go find out," he said.

Evelyn dabbed at her eyes with a tissue and led Matt toward the basement. Clicking a switch inside the small door at the top of a narrow flight of stairs, several bare bulbs cut through the dark basement shadows. Against the far wall, several shelves held a couple of suitcases and some medium-sized cardboard boxes labelled on the outside in thick pencil.

"Okay," Matt said, smiling at her, "we're goin' in."

He reached up and took down a cardboard box labelled "Lorraine." Opening it, Evelyn saw some of her mother's clothing, looking as if it could have been from the 1940s. There was a dark dress, some scarves, and a couple of hats, and as Evelyn felt around the bottom of the box, her hand closed on a small book. It was bound in green leather, and in gold lettering on the cover, it read *"Five-Year Diary."* On the inside cover, there was an inscription: *"To Lorraine, Merry Christmas, Love, Dad."* The first entry, in blue ink from a fountain pen, was dated *"January 1, 1940."*

"She would have been nearly sixteen," Evelyn murmured, "about the same age as Cassandra." She quickly flipped through the pages. "Matthew!" she exclaimed, "it looks like almost half of this book is filled!"

There were two photographs, bookmarking the last entry. Evelyn opened it to that page. A date on the back of one photo said Sunday, November 8, 1942. Skimming over a couple of earlier pages, she looked at Matt, who was waiting, hardly breathing.

"Oh, Matthew," she said. "He was here in 1942. Your father. Look at them! I'm sure now that what Lorraine said in the letter is true, and that William McCarty must be my father too."

She passed him the first black and white photograph. It showed a very pretty young woman in a dark dress, with her hair up, sitting at a table next to his youthful-looking father, who appeared to be making an unsuccessful effort to look serious. Her hand was covering his. The other photo was of his father and Evelyn's grandfather, Jack Sparkes, standing together outside in front of an old truck.

Evelyn and Matt both sat there for a moment, looking at each other, speechless, and then they began to read from the diary together.

It was a story of love seen through a young woman's eyes, and also one of pain and sacrifice during the time of a world at war. It was difficult for Matt to fathom his father in the role of a brave and duty-bound hero, but that was what was unfolding before him. Lorraine was careful not to be specific in what she wrote about McCarty's undercover work, but Matt got the general idea. Evelyn began to see her mother as a real, three-dimensional person instead of just a lonely, painful childhood memory.

One passage, dated October 30, 1942, referred to the day Bill McCarty had shown up with her father for the first time after being picked up from the ferry. Lorraine described a tall, handsome, serious-looking man with black hair combed straight back, carrying a small, dark-brown leather valise, and her instant attraction to him. At the same time, both Evelyn's and Matt's eyes went to the top shelf in the basement, where they could see the leather suitcase referenced in the diary.

"Your turn, Matthew," Evelyn said.

Taking down the suitcase, Matt said, "I don't understand. If it's his, then why would it be here? Seems like every time we find an answer, we wind up with twice as many questions."

Matt placed the suitcase on a small table and opened the lid all the way. The aroma of mothballs greeted him as he saw his father's naval lieutenant's uniform, with two stripes and curl on the sleeves, neatly folded with his officer's hat on top. Seeing a slight bulge in the suitcase's side pocket, he withdrew a small leather folder. Inside it was an identification card with a sharp black and white image of his father. It was embossed with the seal of the Royal Canadian Navy and read,

"Lieutenant William McCarty, RCN 2940M, CIC Special Operations Section." There was a handwritten note in the folder too. On one side, it said, *"Kahr and Becher - saboteurs - nitroglycerin explosives."* On the other, *"GN Cave?"*

Lifting up his father's uniform, he saw a leather shoulder holster containing a Colt semi-auto pistol with a deep-blue mirror finish. Having some knowledge of firearms, Matt pressed the magazine release, and the seven-round mag dropped into his hand. He could see it still had ammunition in it, but two rounds were missing. Looking at the headstamp of the remaining cartridges, he could see that they matched the two empty casings in his father's cigar box. Two rounds had been fired from this pistol a very long time ago, and his father had saved the empty casings. Why? What had he shot at? Or who?

"This is such a lot to take in," Evelyn said. "It seems like the whole world changed in the last few days."

"I never really knew how much I'd been missing until now," replied Matt. "Did you ever try to find out what happened to Lorraine?"

"Years ago, I tried to find her, but I think the authorities assumed I'd been abandoned, so they didn't go very far with any investigation. All I know is that she was supposed to be going to the mainland for a job interview, but I don't know if that meant St. John's, all of Newfoundland, or maybe even out of the province. I kept at it on my own for a while, but eventually, with having to care for my own child and then raising Cassie, I just stopped."

She sighed. "Even though I've had a pretty easy life, and of course, Cassandra has been my constant joy, I think what I've been missing is the inner peace that comes from some kind of closure, and one thing is crystal clear to me now."

"Yes," he said, "I think I know what you're going to say. We need to know where Lorraine went, and the rest of her story, no matter what."

"Yes, we need to know." She nodded. "No matter what."

"I don't know exactly where to begin, but we will get to the bottom of things," Matt said. "I promise."

They heard a door open upstairs, and then Cassie's voice as she yelled, "Hey, anybody home?"

"Yes, we're in the basement," replied Evelyn.

"Who? You and Uncle Matt?"

"Yup, it's me," he yelled back.

"Okay," Cassie said. "I'll throw on the kettle. What's for supper?"

As they headed upstairs, Evelyn looked over her shoulder at Matt. "So, it's 'Uncle Matt' now, is it?" she teased.

"I like it," he answered, "and it's better than Bev's 'Half-Grandpa,' but even that's starting to grow on me."

"Beverly is a force unto herself," Evelyn said, smiling. "No use in trying to fight it, but don't tell her I'm actually laughing inside when she drops the 'F' bomb."

Cassie and her friends had spent the day down at the beach where the ferries arrived, driven there by Selby Gosse, a boy who was fond of Bev. They spent the day jumping and diving off the wharf next to the ferry dock. Ironically, it was close to where Matt had fallen in so many years before. All of them loved the water, and on a hot day like today, they found the clear, cold ocean water refreshing.

Later, after supper dishes were done and put away, and a fresh kettle put on the stove for tea, Matt and Evelyn told Cassie—still with her long red hair damp from swimming—about the diary they had discovered. Evelyn handed it to her, and the girl hugged it tightly to her chest like it was a person. They could tell it would probably be memorised by morning.

Something had been nagging at Matt for the last day or two. It was bizarre to think he had been followed to the island, but after seeing Farrell and the big man, it was impossible to deny. He realised he might have been observed near Evelyn's house.

"Ev," Matt said, "I need to tell you all something. I think Kathleen should be here for this too. Cassie, can you go next door and see if she can drop over?"

Once the group was sitting comfortably in the living room, and with Cassie still clutching the diary, Matt began. He told them about the man at the funeral and how he had seen the same person and an accomplice here on Bell Island too. Matt went on to describe his phone call with Fran and that the man who called himself Farrell might think that he knew about a fortune in stolen Nazi gold.

"I know this all sounds crazy," he said, "and I wouldn't blame you for thinking it, but I care for all of you, and I just want you to be extra careful until this all gets sorted out. I'd go to the police, but there's really nothing to report. From now on though, please keep an eye out for anything unusual, and while *I* don't believe in some secret horde of gold, there could be trouble if *they* do. Some people will stop at nothing once it gets in their blood."

Kathleen nodded. "We'll be careful. I don't believe in taking chances. Well," she looked at Matt, "not usually anyway. So what now?"

"I don't think we need to drastically change any routines, just be aware," said Matt. "I'm going to see if I can find out more, maybe enough to take to the authorities. In the meantime, I want to show you the men I'm talking about. I have a few photos and even a bit of video footage of one of them from when I was climbing the other day."

Using Cassie's laptop, Matt showed them the pictures he had taken when the men were looking in his SUV, and also some accidental video Matt had gotten when he had turned around and seen the big man while on the sea stack near Grebes Nest.

"So," Matt said, "if you see either of these people hanging around your houses, or if you're confronted, then it would be time to call the RCMP and report it."

"Understood. Now, I have an important question," Cassie said, staring intently at the screen as she replayed the video.

"Yes?" he said, as the rest leaned forward, waiting for her to speak.

"Uncle Matt, will you take me climbing?"

Silence.

"Yes, Uncle Matt," Kathleen said, smiling sweetly. "Will you take Cassie climbing?"

Evelyn shook her head slowly and got up to refill tea mugs.

"Tell you what, Cass," Matt said, looking at Kathleen through narrowed eyes, "if you want to go out tomorrow, I can show you some safety basics, and then we can decide. But only if your grandma agrees. Do you want Bev to join us?"

"Yes! Thank you!" She got up and gave Matt a hug, while Kathleen gave him her best Mona Lisa smile.

Chapter 16

Bell Island, Sunday, July 22, 2018

Hunt was pissed off. Farrell had told him to go to the cottage where Matt McCarty was staying and keep an eye on his movements. They were supposed to alternate, but as usual, Hunt was getting stuck with the majority of the boring jobs.

The SUV was still there, and Hunt was once again tempted to just go kick the door in and beat the information they wanted out of McCarty. Sometimes Farrell was too goddamn cautious for his own good. Hunt had gold fever now, and it might not be too long before his desire overcame his fear of Farrell. He didn't know that Farrell was already certain where the gold was.

When Hunt finally drove away, he didn't notice the little car following at a discrete distance.

o o o

After Matt explained his idea to Evelyn, she had loaned him her vehicle. He correctly assumed that the pair would know where he was staying and keep an eye on him, likely thinking he knew where the so-called fabulous long-lost treasure was. As he ate lunch, Matt had seen the big man's rental vehicle across the street and slipped out the back door to Evelyn's car.

Matt followed Hunt when he finally left until he saw him stop at the Bell Island Inn, then slowed and pulled into the circular driveway of St. Michael's High School just beyond it. He saw the driver get out and enter the hotel.

In his room on the second floor, Jurgen Meyer saw Hunt get out of his car down below and noticed a little car pull into the high school just beyond. Was it following Hunt? *Yes, certainly*, he thought, *and not driven by a professional*. If the big man had been less dull-witted, he would have noticed the tail. Meyer quickly grabbed his camera and snapped several shots of the car, getting one of the driver before he drove back the other way. He had his ways of finding out who the car belonged to and opened his laptop. Going to a dark site and using the licence plate number, Meyer could see the registration of the car, along with a screen capture of the owner's driver's license. The driver was obviously not the older woman in the picture, but he now had a good lead to follow up on.

o o o

Good, Matt thought. *Now I know where they are.* He would add the information to the running list of notes he had been keeping since the odd meeting with Farrell at his father's funeral. His overriding concern was for the safety of what he now considered to be his family. He would let nothing endanger them. Period.

Back at the cottage, Matt changed vehicles. He would bring Evelyn back later to get her car, but right now, he had an appointment with two young persons who wanted to try some climbing. After calling ahead to let them know he was on his way, he tossed the gear into the SUV and headed to Hibbs Road. Once he arrived, he saw Kathleen tending to her garden.

"Hi," he said warily. "Um. . . about yesterday. . ."

"Bit of advice," she interrupted, walking toward him, expressionless.

"Uh huh?" he said, with some slight trepidation.

"If you're going to kiss me," she said, reaching him, "then, dammit, kiss me."

She wrapped her arms around him and pressed her lips to his. The next thing he remembered was hearing a wolf whistle and a girl's voice shouting, "Hey there, Half-Grandpa, don't be havin' no heart attack now, buddy!"

Bev and Cassie were standing just outside Evelyn's door, both wearing big grins.

Released from Kathleen's embrace, Matt stumbled only a little bit before finding his way back to the SUV. Kathleen nodded at the girls and walked back to her garden, intuitively knowing that he was looking at her and that balance had been restored to the universe.

○ ○ ○

"Okay," Matt said, once the girls were in the Tahoe, "we're going over to the steep path that leads down to the sea stack by Grebes Nest. Before you can climb, I need to know you can descend, so I'm going to teach you both the basics of rappelling, which means wearing a harness and lowering yourself from a height using a rope attached to it through a device called a 'figure eight.' To start with, you're going to show me you can walk backward down the path using the device. Follow so far?"

Both girls nodded in the affirmative. Matt parked the SUV near the airstrip as before, and the three hiked toward Grebes Nest. On the way, Cassie told Bev about the news from the night before and showed her the pictures of Hunt and Farrell that Matt had put on his phone.

"And what about that guy in the suit we saw?" Bev asked Cassie.

"Oh, I forgot about that," she replied. "No, that's someone else."

They explained to Matt what they were talking about.

"So," he said, "there may be a third person involved. If there is, I don't think he's with the other two."

"Do you think we should tell him about the thing?" Bev asked Cassie.

Matt gave Bev and then Cassie a questioning look.

"When we saw the guy in the suit," Cassie explained, "we were just about to go into a cave we discovered at Grebes Nest. It isn't part of the mine workings, and someone did their best to keep it hidden. Inside there are some old, empty wooden crates with writing on them we couldn't read. Anyway, we didn't go in that day, because we didn't want give away the secret."

She related the story as she knew it from Tom Clarke, and Matt recalled the entry *"GN Cave?"* in his father's notebook. Could it mean Grebes Nest?

"It's possible the cave *could* be connected to what's going on," he said. "So, how about if we get you both doing some rappelling, and then if you're okay with it, we can have a look."

○ ○ ○

Once they neared the cliff, he chose a hundred-and-fifty-foot dynamic rope, secured it to a small sturdy tree trunk back about twenty feet from the steep path, and threw the rest of it over the edge. He explained how to use the figure-eight device and went over climbing protocols. Cassie and Bev took turns using both of Matt's adjustable climbing harnesses, and they got the hang of things pretty quickly. When Matt was confident they were completely familiar with the basics, he suggested they stop for the day, and that next time, if they had permission, he would let them actually suspend and lower themselves from a secure rock face. Their excitement at the prospect made Matt smile. He seemed to be doing a lot more of that lately.

Matt secured the gear, put the duffel bag on his shoulders, and they walked through the fisherman's pass to Grebes Nest. Looking up, they didn't see anyone above as Bev led the way to the cave. They scrambled up a few feet to an overhanging ledge where a low six-foot-wide, shadowed opening in the undercut cliff was covered with dead, dry brush held in place with a few medium-sized rocks. Pushing it aside, Cassie, Matt, and Bev entered and pulled the covering back in place. Just inside the cave, it opened up, and they could easily stand.

"Crap," said Bev, "we didn't bring a flashlight."

"Hang on a sec," Matt replied. "I keep a few with my gear."

Reaching into the duffel, Matt pulled out two small handheld Pelican flashlights and also a Fenix headlamp meant to attach to his climbing helmet when the need arose. The lights were powerful and able to focus both wide and narrow beams of high-intensity light. They walked further in as Cassie explained how they had originally come across the cave.

"There are those crates I told you about," she said, pointing to a corner where Matt could see some wooden boxes.

Walking farther into the cave, it was easy to see why they hadn't been able to distinguish the writing. It was in a foreign language, and the flashlight the girls had used was not very powerful. Focusing his light on the box, Matt read, "*Halton Sie Trocken-Gewichet 8.125Kg.*" Turning it over, there was more writing on the other side: "*Gefaehrliche - Reine Nitroglycerine.*"

There was no wi-fi service available for him to look up the other words, but he was damn sure they were German, and the last word was one that needed no translation. He had the girls stand back for a minute while he checked every box carefully. There were an even dozen, and they were all empty.

"Do you think there is any way these could be left over mine explosive boxes?" Bev asked.

"Very doubtful, especially with the German printing," Matt replied. "You've found something pretty important here, and I'm sure this is connected to the war and the saboteurs my father was apparently trying to track down all those years ago. I think a thorough exploration is in order, but it's a bit late to begin that now. I'd also like to ask Tom Crane if he could join us. Is that okay with the both of you? It's your secret, so it's up to you."

"There's no way we're going to keep this a secret forever, and exploring is what we want to do. Tom is a natural to ask along," replied Cassie, with Bev nodding in agreement.

"Okay," Matt replied. "Let's pack up, and we'll come back soon."

Retracing their steps, they were soon back on the clifftop. Matt dropped Bev off at her home on Backview Street and met her parents, who were friends of Evelyn and knew about their recently discovered relationship. Bev told them how much fun it had been learning some climbing basics. After exchanging phone numbers, they determined to get together soon, and in the meantime, they were both appreciative that Matt had taken an interest.

Matt and Cassie carried on and parked around the corner on Hibbs Road. Before they got out of the car, Cassie said, "Uncle Matt, today was one of the best days I ever had in my whole life." She wasn't quite crying, but it was close.

"One of the best for me too, Cass," he said, and they both just sat there for a while.

Evelyn, hearing the vehicle, looked at them from the side window for a moment, nodded once, and then put the kettle on. Going inside, they ate a classic corned beef and cabbage supper together. Kathleen came over for tea after, and stories were exchanged back and forth. During it all, Kip kept an eye on the proceedings and occasionally dropped by each of them for an ear scratch. At age sixty-seven, Matt felt like he was home for the first time in his life.

When it was finally time to call it a night, Matt walked Kathleen to her door. She looked up at him. "Been eleven years for me," she said simply.

"That all?" he replied, smiling. "Got you beat."

"Slow?" asked Kathleen.

"Slow is good," he responded. They hugged for a long time, and then he got in the SUV and drove back to the cottage.

Chapter 17

Sunday, November 15, 1942

In the boarding house, Kurt Becher was impatient. The plan called for them to be picked up the following Sunday by submarine and returned to Germany, but he was restless, wanting to finish the mission. Kahr seemed to be quite happy to drink and sit around their room.

"Relax, my friend," said Kahr. "We will be back in Germany soon enough. You have done a fine job with this mission, and I am sure Adolf himself will pin a medal on your chest. Maybe two!"

"I do not want your jokes about this!" Becher said angrily. "You do not take our work seriously, and you even tempt fate with your foolish cat-and-mouse conversations with these swine. We cannot afford to take chances this close to achieving our goal."

Kahr looked contrite. "I understand, my dear colleague," he replied. "I admit, I do appear over confident sometimes, but it is really just to hide my anxiety. I promise I will be more careful and keep my drinking under control. *Ja?*"

Kahr's mastery of manipulation continued to work its magic on Becher. He had suspected for a long time that Becher had feelings for him that went beyond friendship, and the man's perversion was very useful for keeping him in line.

Just then, the boarding house phone in the hallway outside their door rang. Kahr opened the door and picked up the receiver. He listened for a minute and then asked several questions. When he hung up, he was smiling broadly.

"August was that the report?" Becher inquired.

"Yes, Kurt, our friend has all but confirmed what I suspected. There is just one more thing to do, and then we will know for sure."

o o o

It had been over a week since Bill McCarty had discovered the identities of the spies, coming face to face with August Kahr and Kurt Becher. Rather than arrest them immediately, he continued to monitor their activities. The last thing he wanted was for the two to panic and detonate the explosives before he could find out where the cache was hidden. In the meantime, the saboteurs continued to go about their business as usual without exhibiting any suspicious activity. McCarty decided that a tour of the mine where Kahr and Becher had spent most of their time was in order.

After making his decision, McCarty said, "Jack, let's fire up the truck. I want to go visit the No. 4 mine."

"Now?" Jack asked. "There won't be a shift on today, being Sunday."

"Yes, but there will still be someone to let us have a look around, won't there?"

"Sure," Jack replied, "there'll be one or two of us doing repairs and that," Jack said. "Sundays are good for getting things done, when we can run tests and get things fixed that need the power turned off, like lighting and so on."

"Perfect," Bill said. "Do you think we could maybe get them to let us take a little run down inside the slope? At least partway?

"That's right; you haven't been inside the red beast yet, have you?" Jack said, grinning.

"That doesn't sound very inviting, Sparky, but let's go have a look."

Laughing, Jack said, "Okay, skipper, let's go."

McCarty went upstairs, got his pistol, and put on a sweater. Back downstairs, he then said goodbye to Lorraine. She got up from the living room and walked towards him at the kitchen door. Her hair was down, and her emerald eyes were mesmerising. She put her hand on his arm and told him to be careful. The last thing he wanted to do just then was be careful, but instead of following his desire, he got on his boots and coat and went outside.

Jack had the truck started, and soon they were driving along West Mines Road toward No. 4 and turning north onto a narrow, rutted path that led to the entrance, with its "1916" date above the collar. Once there, they got out and went into the dryhouse—a structure where miners could get ready for work, and also where there was a repair shop for the electricians to fix headlamps, charge batteries, and take care of regular day-to-day electrical and other tasks.

Introductions were made between McCarty, in his role as a visiting electrical engineer, and Harvey Pendergast, the electrician on duty. As the man put on the kettle for some tea, Bill questioned him carefully about Becher and Kahr. Harvey volunteered that one of them was a bit strange but that they both seemed to know their business. There were people working for the company not only from the island and around Conception Bay but from many other places too. No one suspected that they were anything other than what they appeared to be: a couple of hard-working foreigners.

"I wonder if there's a chance I could go down the slope a ways while there's no shift on?" McCarty asked.

"Not a problem, sir. We'll have you down there in a tick," said Harvey.

"Thanks, Harvey, and please just call me Bill."

"Alright then, my son, let's get at 'er. Reach over there and get yourself a hat and lamp. Those ones are all charged up," he said, pointing to a rack of batteried headlamps.

Going over to a shed near the mine entrance and opening the doors, Jack revealed a maintenance shuttle sitting on a curved track siding. They pushed the car onto the main rail line and then pulled back on a long mechanical lever on the shuttle, which activated a grab clamp similar to a pair of locking pliers. The clamp attached the car to a loop of endless cable that ran down into the mine. They could pause at any level they wanted simply by releasing the lever, disengaging the clamp and applying a brake. When they were all set, Harvey threw a large switch, which started a fifteen hundred horsepower electric motor, and the endless loop of cable began to move.

The car squeaked loudly before settling into a quiet rumble as it began its descent into the earth. As the light began to fade behind them, Bill and Jack switched on their headlamps to supplement the electric light bulbs strung along the main slope and side-tunnel rooms, which gave off a dim yellowish light. These off-shoots were all numbered in white paint with even numbers on the west side and odd on the east. By the time the slope reached the end of the line, there were close to two hundred and fifty numbers indicating the different levels.

When the two men reached the six-hundred-foot mark at level twenty-two, McCarty had Jack stop the shuttle. He had seen a "Danger" sign in the distance on his left, and naturally curious, he asked Jack if he knew anything about it. Jack told him about the ill-conceived plan to run an underground ore-car system all the way through the island to the south side piers, and that the plan had been abandoned years before.

Walking toward the sign, Bill could see rail tracks leading into the proposed shaft, curving around, and sure enough, heading inland to the south. Close up, he could read the rest of the sign: "Danger - Do Not Enter - Unstable Area." Meant to be a barrier to entry, the sign was pushed slightly to one side, and boot prints in the mud told him that at least two people had disregarded it.

Moving past the barrier himself, McCarty could see there were footprints going inland to the south, in the company-drilled shaft, and also north through what looked like a natural cave leading toward the cliffs.

"Would it be unusual for men to just ignore that sign and take a chance on going into an unstable area?" McCarty asked.

"Very unusual," Jack replied. "Anyone caught disobeying an order like that could get fired, and I don't know anyone who would want to take that chance, especially for no good reason."

They went back to the shuttle car and proceeded deeper into the mine. Now nearly a mile out and far under the bay, Jack stopped the car and pointed out a small dryhouse to Bill, so called because it was one of a number of areas at different levels where there was a separate room kept somewhat clean, dry, and warm where miners would go to eat their lunch or to have minor injuries tended to.

Before getting back in the shuttle, Bill spoke up. "Jack, I've seen a few little white crosses painted on the ribs of the walls. Are they memorial crosses?"

"Yes, b'y," he answered. "Many a fine man and boy have met their end down here, and that's just a way of remembering them. Some men don't want to work near the crosses, and the company tries to paint them over when they see them, but the crosses always come back." Then he winked as if maybe he knew how.

As McCarty looked around, he couldn't have known that he was standing next to enough explosives to finish mining on Bell Island perhaps forever. Every support pillar around him and Jack Sparkes was packed with concentrated nitroglycerin, so cleverly disguised as to be almost impossible to find.

They continued their journey down the main slope until they were over two miles from shore and nearly sixteen hundred feet below Conception Bay. McCarty saw a curtained-off area to one side and inquired about it.

"What's that, Jack?" he asked. "I've seen a few areas like that on the way down. And what is that big concrete bin with the heavy lid?"

"That bin will be your feed for the horses, and it's concrete to try and keep the rats out," said Jack. "And this," he continued, drawing back a large canvas tarpaulin, "is the lovely Lucy, sweetest girl you will ever find down in the mine."

He walked over to a stall, where a large draft horse stood, and stroked her muzzle. The small corralled area was relatively clean and had whitewashed walls, which helped to reflect light from the one dim bulb. The tarp helped to keep warmth generated by the horse's body heat in. Jack explained that the animals were used to haul ore from the side tunnel rooms to the main slope, where the electric cable hoist would take over, pulling ore cars up to the surface.

Reluctantly, McCarty called a halt to their investigation. Getting back in the shuttle, Jack pulled the lever, clamping onto the return cable, and they began to ascend.

"Well, Bill, what do you think? Most people either love or hate their first trip down."

"Sparky, I have to tell you, I love it down here. Knowing that I am so far out under the ocean? It's pretty exciting."

"That's what I thought. Even with your business face on, I could tell you liked it," Jack said, smiling.

"I'll go you one better," McCarty replied. "I've already been offered a job with the company for after the war, and I'm pretty sure someday I'm going to take them up on it."

"Jaysus, that does my heart good, Bill. They say if you like it here in the winter, summer will be a piece of cake. I remember we had one here only a few years back." He laughed. "Summer that is."

Bill laughed with him, and they traded stories back and forth all the way to the surface. Back on top, they put the shuttle car away and thanked Harvey for his help. Then it was back to Grammer Street, where Lorraine was preparing a nice supper. She introduced them to her friend from work, Hanna, whom she had invited over, and afterwards, the four played cards and drank tea. Later, after Hanna left, Jack banked the fire while Lorraine and Bill headed upstairs. Before he could react, Lorraine leaned close and kissed him on the cheek. Then she said goodnight and quickly went into her room, shutting the door. McCarty just stood there for a moment before going into his room. Unable to sleep right away, he played the events of the day over in his head, reliving several times the very last part: the way her kiss had lingered on his skin.

Chapter 18

St. John's, Monday, July 23, 2018

While Cassie worked at the souvenir shop, and Evelyn read from her mother's diary, Matt headed to the ferry and drove to St. John's. He felt a bit reluctant going to the city, because even though he had only been on Bell Island for a week, he was now feeling a strong connection to his long-lost home.

In the semi-circular drive in front of Fran's house, there was a gorgeous Willow Green 1957 Ford Thunderbird convertible with wide whitewall tires. He was still looking at it five minutes later when Fran opened the front door. Standing a little behind her was a diminutive man wearing round horn-rimmed glasses, a rumpled tweed three-piece suit, and a bow tie.

"Matty!" Fran exclaimed, coming down the steps. "Do you like my new car?"

"You never drove a car like this one, Fran," he replied, laughing. Fran had only ever had one car in her life: an old Volkswagen Beetle that had been on its last legs for thirty years. "I'm guessing it belongs to the gentleman behind you."

"All right, fair enough," she confessed. "Matt, this is Stewart Luffman. What he doesn't know about Newfoundland in general and Bell Island in particular isn't worth a cod's arse."

"It's a pleasure to meet you, Matthew," Luffman said.

"Well, it's good to meet you too, and thank you for being so helpful as I try to make some sense out my father's involvement in the war." Looking at the car, Matt added, "That is one beautiful factory-fresh-looking T-Bird."

Stewart replied, "My dear father bought that car new after a windfall many years ago. He barely ever drove it, and I only take it out in summer. There are six thousand original miles on the odometer."

After Matt ogled the car a while longer, they went inside and had the ever-present Red Rose tea, as well as homemade cookies. Matt and Stewart were having a great time talking cars and trading stories. Then Luffman disclosed that he had some news to share.

"The ring you found among your father's effects. You brought it?" Matt reached into his pocket and handed it to him. Looking at it closely, an excited Luffman said, "This ring is quite the anomaly and confirms what I thought. It is supposed to be on the finger of a U-boat captain who died with his full crew in a submarine presumed lost and lying crushed by water pressure over a mile deep below the Atlantic Ocean."

An involuntary shudder went through Matt as Luffman went on to explain that the engraved inscription was from Kapitanleutnant Gunther Dangschat of U-boat 184. It bore his initials and the date the boat was commissioned and put under his command, on May 29, 1942.

"Many people," Luffman said, "especially Bell Islanders know the tragic stories of the U-boat attacks on ore carriers there during World War Two," he said, "but U-184 was not involved in those. She was only ever on one combat patrol, and after sinking one ship, she was presumed lost with all hands on November 22, 1942, when attempts to contact her failed, supposedly in deep water just north of the underwater rise called the Flemish Cap several hundred miles directly east of Newfoundland. There was a rumour of her involvement on a secret mission, but nothing was ever confirmed, and it isn't mentioned in any of the very detailed official German war records."

"I can't explain how it ended up with my father," Matt said, looking at the ring with renewed interest. "It looks genuine, but I'm no expert."

"I am convinced of its authenticity, Matthew," Stewart said. "My curiosity is aroused now, and I'm not going to let this go. Any of the resources I have available are at your disposal, if you have other questions."

The other reason Matt had come to town was farther west, where a store that sold climbing equipment and accessories was located. He could tell that Cassie was a natural when it came to climbing, and Bev was a close second. Wanting to support both of them in the sport, which by all accounts they were going to get involved in anyway, he was going to make sure they did it safely and with the appropriate equipment. On the way back to the ferry, Matt gave a lot of thought to the ring in his pocket. Was it possible that, even though it wasn't documented, this other submarine U-184 had visited the island?

By the time Matt got back to the cottage, it was nearly suppertime. He called Evelyn, who said that he was invited over for a pasta feast being prepared by the master-chef team of Beverly and Cassandra, and that Kathleen was already there and joining them to eat.

Bev walked from the kitchen where she was stirring sauce over to where Evelyn was talking to Matt on the phone, and he heard her say loudly, "Tell half-Grandpa his girlfriend wants another kiss off him." She then made loud smacking sounds.

Muffled, from the kitchen, he could hear Cassie say, "I'll get the defibrillator ready!"

A mile and a half apart, both Matt and Kathleen slowly shook their heads.

The pasta was a success, and the evening went well. After eating, Matt went to the SUV and brought in the equipment he had picked up earlier. Uncharacteristically, Bev went silent over the gift, while Cassie just beamed and then spoke up.

"Grandma, we discovered a cave over by Grebes, and I bet it would be safe for us to have a look inside if we use these helmets, especially with the lights attached."

Matt had been wondering how to get around to letting the girls know he would need permission from Evelyn, and also Bev's parents, before they could do any further exploring there. Cassie had made a reasonable argument though, and seeing Matt nod, Evelyn agreed—as long as they were careful. Bev would ask her parents and report back.

o o o

Jurgen Meyer was patient and relaxed. He'd found a good spot where he could observe the little green house on Hibbs Road and soon noted Matt's arrival and identified him as the person who had followed Hunt to the inn. Taking a stroll, he saw that there was no security in place on the premises except for a large benign-looking dog. After several hours, he decided he had enough to go on for now and started his rental car. Heading back to the inn, he passed in front of number 23 just as Matt was leaving, with everyone standing by the front door. Matt and Meyer locked eyes for just a moment, but it was Bev who let out a yelp.

"That's him! That's him!" she cried, pointing. "That's the guy from up on the cliff!"

While Meyer mentally kicked himself for the lapse of professionalism, Matt reached into the centre console of the SUV for a pen and paper. He wrote down the make, model, and plate number of the car, wondering if this new player was staying at the Bell Island Inn too, and had an idea.

"Evelyn, do you know anyone connected to the inn over on Memorial?" he asked.

"No, not me," she said, "but Kathleen, don't you?"

"Yes," she replied. "My sister-in-law, Kitty Fitzpatrick, works there on the front desk."

"Do you think she'd do you a big favour without asking too many questions?" Matt asked.

"We're very good friends," she said, which was an answer.

By noon the next day, Matt knew the names and room numbers of Peter Farrell, Delbert Hunt, and Jurgen Meyer, all with open-ended checkout dates.

Around that same time, Jurgen Meyer was becoming acquainted with Matthew McCarty and his family's history, especially his father's.

Chapter 19

Bell Island, Monday, November 16, 1942

Bill McCarty woke to bright winter sunlight streaming through the small window next to his bed. The aroma of sausage, eggs, and toast wafted up the stairs and into his room. Remembering the peck on the cheek the night before from Lorraine, the young man usually so reserved in his manner and movements jumped out of bed, dressed quickly, and started bounding down the stairs, stopping in his tracks when he saw Jack and not Lorraine in the kitchen. Jack, holding a frying pan, stopped and looked at him, head cocked to one side, just as Lorraine's bedroom door opened. McCarty quickly turned around, and seeing her, nearly lost his balance, stumbling backwards the rest of the way down the stairs.

"Ah sure, she has that effect on all the boys, Bill" Jack said. "No need to be embarrassed now, my son."

Face burning, McCarty walked meekly to the table and sat down.

Lorraine joined him at the table, giving her father a look on the way that would have killed an ordinary man.

"What's on the docket today, your honour?" Jack asked, looking at McCarty and smiling innocently.

Happy to have an excuse to change the focus of attention, Bill said, "You know, Jack, we should go around to the other mines and poke around. Even though it looks like No. 4 is probably their target, those two may have been down the other slopes as well. We can talk to a few of the workers and see if they can add anything to what we already know."

"Good idea, skipper," Jack said, turning businesslike. "We'll start just down the way at No. 2 and then on to No. 3 just over off West Mines Road. That should take most of the day, but if we have time, No. 6 is in a straight line north over toward the cliffs from No. 3."

"Okay, I just have to grab something upstairs before we go," Bill replied.

"It's okay, Bill, you can say it," said Jack, smiling again and lifting his sweater slightly on the right side. "I'm carrying one too, just for luck." Bill could see a holstered Webley .455 calibre revolver on Jack's hip.

On the way to the mine, they dropped Lorraine off at the telephone company on Main Street. From a window of the boarding house next door, August Kahr observed her being let out of the electrical-department truck by a certain individual he had recently become acquainted with. Soon it would be time to pay a visit to the house where he was staying on Grammer Street.

o o o

The No. 2 mine began at the north end of the East Dominion tramway track. In the opposite direction, the track ended at Dominion Pier to the south. Jack parked the truck near the Deckhead, and he and McCarty walked into the shack beside it, where the timekeeper informed them that Kahr and Becher had not been in the mine for at least six months.

The entrance collar for the No. 3 mine was about a half mile west near the corner of West Mines and Ten Commandments Roads. McCarty noticed a wooden board peppered with small finishing nails in a little booth next to the tunnel entrance. There were dozens of little round brass medallions hanging on it, each one stamped with its own number and the mine-company name.

"Is that how you identify each miner who's down below?" McCarty asked.

Sam Peach—the older gent who was manning the booth—nodded. "Aye, young fella. Nobody goes down without they comes a'past me, and I gets their brass."

After further small talk, Bill and Jack determined it was unlikely that Kahr and Becher had ever set foot in No. 3. The same proved true for No. 6 when they checked there.

McCarty looked thoughtful for a moment and then said, "Jack, those men were hired to do a structural survey of all the mines, not just No. 4 where they seem to spend all of their time. I've got an uncomfortable feeling that I missed something down there. I'm afraid they may have already planted the explosives, and we just don't have enough time or resources to find them before something really bad happens."

From the beginning, Jack had waited patiently as McCarty revealed his investigative plans one by one. He was mindful of the young man's businesslike attitude and respected his authority, but it was time now to contribute his two cents.

"Bill, I know the operation is supposed to be kept confidential, but you can't do this all by yourself. I'll do anything to help, but we've got some other good resources right here in front of us. You might just have to say the hell with it and let Bell Islanders fight for Bell Island."

McCarty considered what Jack had said for a long moment before answering. "You're right, Jack," he finally agreed. "I've been too caught up in the damn rules to see it before. Let's talk tonight, and tomorrow, I've got an important telephone call to make."

Bell Island, Tuesday, November 17, 1942

Tuesday was clear and unusually warm with little wind. McCarty walked over from Grammer Street to the telephone-company switchboard offices after breakfast with Lorraine. Once there, he spoke with the manager in charge and identified himself, explaining what he needed. He was shown into a room where he knew no one could listen in. He gave Lorraine the confidential number of his commanding officer in Halifax, and she connected him. Then she left the room as he began to speak to Commander Charles Petten.

"McCarty, I wasn't expecting to hear from you for several more days. Is everything alright there?"

"Sir, I believe things are coming to a head. I have two specific individuals in mind whom I am sure are the spies. I need authorisation to shut down one of the mines for up to several days, if necessary, to prove it and to find the explosives we were warned about. It would be a short-term inconvenience while we do a thorough search with a larger group of men."

"Lieutenant McCarty," the commander responded, "what you are asking isn't possible. We need every bit of ore we can get, especially with losing four shiploads in the last two months, and we can't have every Tom, Dick, and Harry knowing what we're doing. It could cause panic and who knows what else. You carry on with what you're doing now. You have my permission to identify yourself to Captain Walter Dwyer with the Newfoundland Militia's Coastal Defence Command on the island. He'll assign you a man or two to keep watch on the pair. I'll even requisition a small plane for you to do a little aerial surveillance if you need it."

"Yes sir," said McCarty, knowing there was nothing more to be done.

"Lieutenant," the commander finished, "you were picked for this assignment because you're a smart, independent thinker. Just do it within the parameters you've been given. That is all."

"Yes, sir, thank you, sir," McCarty said, ringing off and wondering how a person was supposed to think independently while being constrained by those parameters. He had seen first hand that Bell Islanders don't panic. Every hardship they had ever endured simply made them stronger, and while they would never ask, they were owed. Smiling grimly, he left the room, knowing now what he had to do.

Petten's suggestion to reach out for formal assistance wouldn't work. August Kahr would be clever enough to see through any attempt to try covert surveillance on him by someone from the military. No, this would require a solution no one would suspect. Independent thinking. Something sneaky. After Jack Sparkes' suggestion sank in, his natural instincts took over from his military training and its obsession with secrecy. It had taken a while for it to connect, but now it was obvious. They would use Bell Islanders to defend the island from the saboteurs. Simple, really. Who knew the island better?

It was nearing lunch by the time McCarty and Jack set up a confidential meeting on Grammer Street with Telephone Company Manager Hayward George, Mines Manager Richard Delaney and Lorraine about his idea. For the rest of the afternoon, Bill McCarty laid out a three-point plan and invited discussion on how to improve it.

<u>First</u>: the phone company would listen in on any phone conversations made from the boarding-house phone next door. Hayward George would let the operators know it was important and to make sure that they kept the knowledge to themselves. Next, under the guise of repairing a faulty phone line, McCarty and Jack would gain entry to Becher and Kahr's room when they were out and install a small listening device, connecting it to the house phone just outside their door. A monitoring post would be set up next door with two of Jack's trusted work friends from the electrical department.

Jack would install the device, and McCarty would search the room carefully while it was planted. Afterwards, if it appeared that either or both men were leaving the boarding house, one of the two persons on listening-post duty would follow them. If both went out, they would both leave the post and watch the men in case they split up. Being local men, it was very unlikely that they would be noticed.

<u>Second</u>: Richard Delaney would recruit a trusted No. 4 mine supervisor to have each shift conduct what they termed a "safety sweep," whereby every employee would be on the lookout for safety hazards and unusual items, including blasting paraphernalia, wiring, and signs of unauthorised activity all the way from the mine-entrance collar down to the lowest level. McCarty and Jack would never have been able to accomplish the momentous task by themselves. While efforts would be made to keep the real reason confidential, there might be suspicions there was more to the sweep than a simple safety exercise, as there were already rumours of saboteurs being whispered.

<u>Third</u>: McCarty would contact Captain Dwyer with the Coastal Defence Command, and with Commander Petten's

authority, he would requisition the small single-engine patrol plane on the island to do a full air reconnaissance, checking both pier areas, the north side of the island, and even over by the lighthouse that had been constructed at the east end two years before. Even though McCarty was convinced the main area of concern was the No. 4 mine, he didn't believe in taking chances, and as long as the plane was available, he might as well use it. The final part of the plan would have him and Jack travel the length of the island by boat, looking for any signs of where the saboteurs might have a base of operations.

o o o

That same day, Kahr and Becher left the boarding house at three p.m. Becher had been complaining of an earache and walked to the office of Dr. Templeman, ironically the same doctor who had issued death certificates for victims of the torpedo attacks that Becher had helped to cause. Kahr told him he was going to visit St. Cyprian's Church, but Becher knew that meant he would be going to Basha's tavern in Town Square to drink. As the two men assigned to watch the pair shadowed them discretely, Hayward George called the Sparkes residence. Soon McCarty and Jack arrived at the phone-company office, got the supplies they needed, and went next door.

Outside Becher and Kahr's room on the second floor, Jack opened the telephone's hinged wooden front, drilling a small hole in the oak cabinet, and through the plaster and lathe wall into the spies' room on the other side. Bill used a skeleton key to open the door and threaded a wire back to Jack, gently pushing a tiny microphone flush with the busy wallpaper where it was nearly invisible. Jack spliced the microphone to extra wires in the phone, connecting it back to the listening post next door.

McCarty cleaned up some loose plaster dust from the floor and then searched the room discretely but thoroughly. On the bureau between the two beds, there were two brass miner's tags, a small amount of change, and various grooming products. After looking behind the mirror for hidden paperwork, he pulled out dresser drawers and checked the underside of each. The closet held nothing but a couple of British make suitcases. The only thing in the room left to check was the beds. Lifting the first mattress, he saw a file folder containing two cardboard cards, each about three by five inches. Under the symbol of a swastika, in German and English, one of them announced:

"My name is August Kahr, and I am a soldier in the German Army with the rank of private. My serial number is RK296485. I demand to be treated as a prisoner of war.

The other card held the same information for Kurt Becher. Additionally, there were some photos of the mines, piers, and tramways, as well as the ferry dock, shore gun battery, and even the local militia barracks down near the Front. One piece of paper had a list of numbers, probably relating to how many troops were guarding the island or how many miners were on each shift. McCarty carefully put the folder back exactly as he had found it and smiled grimly. *Jackpot.*

o o o

Much later, after midnight, Kahr was awoken from his usual light sleep by a tapping sound on his second-floor window.

Someone was throwing pebbles at the glass panes. He slipped out of bed and looked down below, where a person he recognised was waving him down. Dressing quickly, he descended the stairs and quietly exited the front door. He went around the corner and spoke quietly with the other person for several minutes. Re-entering the house, he took pencil and paper and wrote a note by candlelight. Then he shook Becher, who panicked at first, thinking there might be a fire, but then he saw Kahr, finger to his lips, pointing at a note he had written:

"Do not speak. They are listening and on to us. Get dressed quietly - do not pack. Quickly!"

Chapter 20

Bell Island, Tuesday, July 24, 2018

Matt's phone rang at nine a.m., just as he was about to make a small pot of coffee after his morning run and shower. It was Beverly Adams' dad, Pat, asking Matt if he could join them later that afternoon for a barbecue at their home on Backview Street. They had been moved by his generous gift of the climbing equipment for Bev, and since Matt had refused any reimbursement of the cost, Pat said that this was the least they could do to show their appreciation. Cassie, Evelyn, and Kathleen, as well as some of the Adams' other friends would be attending. Matt said that he would be happy to come along, as requested, around five p.m.

Before Matt could continue with his coffee, he heard a light rapping on his door—a classic "shave and a haircut" knock. Looking through the side window, he began to smile at the pleasant surprise, and after responding with the obligatory two answering knocks, he opened the door. Kathleen stood there with her flashing blue eyes, smiling mischievously and looking fabulous in a pair of blue jeans and a white t-shirt. She wore a pair of runners and had a light sweater over one arm.

"Breakfast?" she asked.

"Rolling Pin Bakery?" he asked in response.

"Yup," she answered, stepping inside, looking at him, and pushing the door closed with her foot.

"Now?" he asked. "Or . . . ?"

"Later," she finished, and reached for him.

They arrived at the bakery around eleven a.m. for more of a brunch than breakfast. After they were seated, Joanne came out from the kitchen to say hello.

"Well," she said, "I see the Vancouver guy is here bothering our local women."

"Other way around, Jo," Kathleen replied. "The poor boy can't resist my charms."

"Oh, is that what they're calling them these days?" she replied, laughing.

"Hey," Matt interjected, "how about some grub? I've had a very strenuous morning."

Joanne looked at them, first one, then the other, and said to him, "Ah, my son, if you're going to go out with a Bell Island girl, you'll be needing more than that to build up your strength." Then she headed back to the kitchen, winking at Kathleen.

After brunch, they walked over to the Community Museum. Matt still hadn't done the mine tour, and they both decided to take the hour-long adventure together. Tom Crane was the tour guide for their group, and they looked around while waiting for the tour to begin. In the museum, Matt saw artefacts from the beginning era of surface mining and down through the decades until the closure happened in 1966. Among the items on display were carbide bits used to drill holes for dynamite, a methane-gas detector, log books of ore shipments, various types of lamps, and hundreds of other bits of interesting bric-a-brac.

There were also some framed sepia-toned photographs on the wall, and two of them caught his eye. One was a candid shot of a man climbing out of a small single-engine plane sporting an RCAF roundel. The plane was in a field, with a large barn nearby, and showed a cliff edge in the background overlooking a large body of water. There could be no doubt the man was his father. A caption read, *"Mine Reconnaissance November 1942."*

A second, uncaptioned photo was posed in the backyard of a company house. Standing was a group of purposeful-looking men, and in front of them, three more were kneeling, each on one knee. Before them on the ground was a torn and muddy-looking red, white, and black flag with a swastika in the centre. Remembering the photo he had seen in Lorraine's diary, it was easy to see that the man on the left was Jack "Sparky" Sparkes and that the man on the right was his father. The man in the middle was wearing an RCAF uniform with pilot's wings. Taking out his seldom-used mobile phone, he took pictures of both images.

To his credit or detriment, Matt was becoming more accepting of the weird and absurd these days. Matt doubted the airplane picture had anything to do with mine reconnaissance. With what he had learned so far, it was more likely that it was looking for spies. He was reminded of the old Winston Churchill saying, *"It is a riddle wrapped in a mystery inside an enigma."*

The tour began downstairs, where Tom Crane had a model of No. 2 mine that showed the room and pillar system of extracting the ore. A brick-sized chunk of hematite was on display, and picking it up, Matt was amazed that it was so much heavier than an equivalent-sized ordinary rock. Donning hardhats, they went through a doorway and descended some stairs into the mine proper. The tunnel was well lit and cool.

The tour group of twelve walked slowly down the gentle slope, and Kathleen slipped on her sweater while Tom narrated a pre-arranged script with an occasional ad-lib comment thrown in. They descended about six hundred and fifty feet before coming to a place where the ground water had welled up to impede any further progress. The water had a greenish tint and beckoned to Matt. He couldn't help imagining himself stepping over the barrier and slowly walking in until the water closed over his head, and he began to be pulled down, deeper and deeper into the tunnel.

A hand on his arm brought him back to the present. "Are you okay?" Kathleen asked. "It looked like you were somewhere else for a moment."

"I've got a thing about water," he said. "Especially something like this. It's not rational but it's real to me, and one of the reasons I never learned to swim. I imagine myself walking into the water until something pulls me all the way to the bottom."

"Evelyn told me about you falling off the ferry when you were a child," Kathleen said, "and about Lorraine pulling you out, but I don't think she knows how traumatised you were by it." She squeezed his arm.

"I told her about falling in, but this is the first time I ever talked about that part," he replied, looking at her.

She put her arm around him, and they continued on as Tom described the old underground horse barns to the group. The rest of the tour was enjoyable, and Matt gained some appreciation for what the miners had to endure over the years. Even though Bell Island's mines were safe in comparison to many others, between 1895 and 1966, there were still over a hundred killed on the job, both above and below ground, not to mention the everyday accidents that left many unable to work and provide for their families. The tour finished around three p.m., and after saying goodbye to Tom, Matt and Kathleen drove back to the cottage so she could pick up her car.

"See you over at the Adams?" Matt asked.

She kissed him lightly and walked to her car, blue jeans doing what they do best when they fit a woman properly. Then she looked back for a moment, smiled, and said, "Bring your toothbrush." Then she drove away.

Matt took his second shower that day and put on some fresh clothes. Soon he was driving toward the Adams house on Backview Street.

Matt was greeted by Bev's mom, Bernadette, at the front door. They joined Pat, and the rest of the guests who were out back, and introductions were made. By now, they all knew that he was Evelyn's half-brother.

When Bev saw him, she sang out, "Hey, there's my half-grandpa!"

A number of guests raised their glasses, looked his way, and yelled, "Half-Grandpa!"

"I'm *your* half-grandpa?" Matt asked Bev.

"Yes, b'y; didn't you already know that?" she replied. "I'm sharing you with Cassie."

As Bev walked off, her mother looked at Matt. "Looks like you've been claimed, my son. All of Beverly's grandparents have passed, so you better get used to it. Once her mind is made up. . . ."

"Understood. I hope I measure up," Matt said.

"Oh, I s'pose you'll do," she replied, laughing. "You know she latched onto Cassie when they were two years old and never left her side since."

A number of older people were attending the Adams' barbecue, and Matt showed a number of them the flag photo, asking if any of the men in the picture looked familiar. One older woman named Emma Rees said she had seen a copy of the same picture before where she worked as an aide at the Bell Island Senior's Complex. She said it was in the room of one of their long-term-care patients from Bell Island named Patrick Kelly, a former RCAF pilot. She said that he was ninety-eight years old, with another birthday coming up soon, and still pretty sharp of mind.

Pointing at the uniformed man kneeling in front, Matt asked, "Could that be him when he was a lot younger?"

"It might be," she replied. "Handsome man, but he is quite elderly now, so it's hard to say."

Matt asked if he would be able to visit with him, and she thought the old man would probably enjoy it.

The barbecue was a great success, and Matt made some new friends among the group. The story of Evelyn's mother's lost love was discussed in detail by all and sundry, and Matt could only smile, taking it all in. There was no guile with Bell Islanders, and they spoke their minds, like it or not. Although no one had any direct knowledge, everyone at the party was happy to express their opinion about the love affair. The topic eventually moved on to the mines—as any conversation on the island eventually does. Why did the enterprise fail? Could they get the mines opened again? Did anyone really even want to see that happen? Debate on the island had been elevated to an art form, and there was no end to the speculation. Matt felt included. He felt accepted. He again had the feeling of being home.

"Hello Mr. Popular," said Kathleen. "Got your toothbrush?"

"Yes, ma'am," he replied. "I wonder what these good people would think if they knew what we were up to this morning?"

"Do you really think there's anyone here that doesn't already know we're 'doing it?' Don't forget where you are, my son," she said with a laugh. "Now I'm going to mingle."

"Wait a minute," he said. "I meant to ask you before, but I got a little distracted when you took your clothes off. What happened to 'slow'?"

Walking back to him, she leaned forward and whispered softly in his ear, "Didn't you know that time is relative?" Then she kissed him on the cheek and walked away.

Surrendering in the face of overwhelming odds is nothing to be ashamed of, he thought philosophically, and tore his eyes away from her retreating form.

Later, Matt went inside to wash his hands after eating some excellent barbecued ribs and saw Evelyn in the kitchen having tea with Bernadette. He joined them, and after being asked, he told them about some of his adventures out west. Cassie and Bev were in the living room but listening intently to every word. Eventually most of the guests went on their way, and they all agreed to have another bash before Matt went back to Vancouver.

After the party, walking back with Kathleen to her place, Matt excused himself as she went inside, saying he would join her in a minute. He then turned around and backtracked to the corner. The car was nondescript, but Matt had seen it before. He walked up and stood by the driver's door, waiting. Still looking straight ahead, the driver finally lowered his window.

"Hello, Jurgen," Matt said. "You missed a great barbecue."

Meyer turned toward Matt and cracked the slightest smile. When he spoke, his accent placed him from somewhere in Germany.

"I still can't believe I made eye contact with you like that yesterday. That was clumsy, but I suppose the young girl had

THE SECRET OF BELL ISLAND

already told you she saw me before. There is something disarming about this island," Meyer said, furrowing his brow. "It's most disconcerting."

"Yes, but the place is kind of relaxing too. Don't you agree?"

"I do, Mr. McCarty. But I cannot allow myself to become distracted from my assignment."

"Call me, Matt. I think it's time we talked about that assignment. Don't you? Which I'm guessing would be something to do with gold. Why don't you come in and have some tea?"

"This is most unusual, Mr. . . . Matt. But I suppose, in light of recent developments, it might be time for us both to put the cards on the table."

"Agreed," Matt said. "Let me make a quick call, and we can meet over at my sister's house."

"That would be Evelyn," Meyer said, "not Ms. Ryan, whose company you have been keeping." They were statements, not questions.

"Correct," Matt replied, and then he made the call.

Within twenty minutes, Evelyn, Kathleen, Cassie, and even Bev were gathered at the little green house on Hibbs Road. Jurgen Meyer introduced himself as an investigator for a European not-for-profit group, whose mission was to repatriate some of the ill-gotten spoils of war taken by Nazi Germany. The public face of the parent group was well known, and they did not doubt Meyer's authenticity. How the group achieved their goals, however, was definitely not well known. To add his tentative approval to Meyer's presence, Kip lumbered by and gave the man's leg a small bonk.

Meyer went on to relate how his presence on Bell Island had come to be. According to certain German war records, there was supposed to be a cache of gold hidden by Nazi spies somewhere on the island—part of a Reich plan to hide resources in case the war went badly.

Meyer had it on good authority that Peter Farrell, a former Canadian government employee, had used his privileged access to confidential documents to try and find those valuables for his own selfish purposes.

He further explained that he'd noticed Evelyn's car following Hunt, and after discovering the identity of the driver, he'd made the connection between Matt and the unfolding events, aware of the role Matt's father had played during the war. That set off an explanation from Matt about his previous interaction with Farrell—how he'd misrepresented himself at his father's funeral and even followed him to Bell Island. He told Meyer that, until the previous week, he'd had no idea that his father had even been on Bell Island during the war.

Meyer began to see the wisdom in perhaps joining forces, at least temporarily. He and Matt agreed to keep in touch and discuss doing a little exploring around the island in search of the hidden gold that even Matt had begun to believe might be more than just a fairy tale. Matt even had the beginnings of an idea about the supposed cache, but he wasn't ready to share that yet.

After Meyer left, the living room was still buzzing with the excitement of the discussion. For Cassie and Bev especially, this was not what they had been expecting. They were used to slow-paced summer vacations on the island and were beside themselves at the prospect of searching for hidden treasure. As the room eventually grew quiet and introspective, Matt stood up and looked around the room.

"So, I just need to know something," he said very seriously, looking at each person in turn and letting the words hang in the air for several seconds. "How do you like me so far?"

He was bombarded with couch cushions, lace doilies, at least one newspaper, and roars of laughter. Even Kip contributed a low, volcano rumble of a bark.

Matt and Kathleen walked Bev home, and then took a stroll in the moonlit night past some of the well-kept little cottage houses on Backview Street, eventually winding up back at her place. They sat and talked for a while, and everything just seemed comfortable and easy. When it came time for bed, Kathleen took Matt's hand, and they walked to her bedroom.

As they started to undress, Kathleen said, "Been a pretty long day; do you mind if we don't . . . ?"

"Of course, I don't mind," he replied. "Besides, I'm ancient, and any more of what happened this morning might just finish me off."

"I don't think so, Matt," she said, kissing him and turning out the light. For Matt, it was the first night he could remember that he didn't have the dream.

Chapter 21

Bell Island, Wednesday, November 18, 1942

McCarty had incontrovertible proof now of the spies' existence and knew who they were. However, until they showed their hand by leading him to where the explosives were, he would have to remain patient. He didn't yet know that they were already on the run.

Shortly after breakfast, the phone rang. It was RCAF pilot Lieutenant Patrick Kelly, calling in response to McCarty's request to Captain Dwyer for a plane and pilot. When McCarty mentioned Commander Petten's name to Dwyer, he couldn't do enough for him with no questions asked. McCarty told the pilot he would meet him at the airstrip in thirty minutes. Kelly replied that he would have the plane warmed up by then.

Jack dropped Bill off at the airstrip just west of No. 4 at about ten a.m. He would go over to the mine again and nose around until he heard the plane coming back. After introductions, McCarty boarded the 1941 Fairchild military model as Lieutenant Kelly asked Bill what he wanted to do. Kelly was a native of Bell Island and seemed like an easy-going chap who clearly loved his job. He had already served overseas before being reassigned after many missions to do patrol work at home. McCarty decided to tell him what the real plan was.

"Lieutenant," McCarty began, raising his voice to be heard over the idling motor, "you've been told that we're doing some scouting for a mine-expansion project—"

"Yep," broke in Kelly, "and we both know that's bullshit. So, let's see now, we got an officer, I'm guessing navy, trying to look civilian. That's you. Don't deny it. Some ore carriers getting ambushed and sunk by U-boats, and rumours about spies hiding out on the island. So, I'm guessing you're doing a little hunting." He paused. "That pretty much cover it?"

"Yes, pretty much," McCarty said, smiling. "So, for now, let's just be a couple of fellows out for a cruise around the island, slow as you can, and we'll keep an eye out for anything suspicious, and Pat, can you not—"

"Got it, McCarty. This is our show and mum's the word. If the brass here got wind of what you're really up to, they'd fuck it up in thirty seconds. But later on, we're gonna drink, and you're going to tell me where I sign up to have some more of this. I'll stay a bit above stall speed, and let's see what we can spot. In that locker next to you is a Thompson machine gun. Just push the drum mag in, if you see anything worth shootin'." Kelly was smiling, and his bright-blue eyes were twinkling as he said it, but McCarty could tell he was serious.

The takeoff on the grass into a prevailing westerly wind was bumpy, but with a roar, they cleared the end of the runway. The ground dropped away, and then they were flying over the cliff at Ochre Pit Cove. Although Kelly had already gotten flight clearance, he radioed in again and identified himself, letting the ground know he might be doing some manoeuvres that would take him down close to the ground, and to tell the shore battery to please not try to kill him. They heard a metallic sounding *"Roger"* on the other end, along with a laugh as he was obviously well known to those below.

They continued west past a tall rugged sea stack just offshore that Kelly called the "Bell" and circled back, flying over Freshwater Cove and bringing them near Lance Cove on the south side of Bell Island. As a sign of respect, Lieutenant Kelly dipped his wings as he flew past the area where the four iron-ore carriers had recently been sunk and where the rescued, injured, and the bodies of the dead had come ashore with the help of the men and women who lived there.

Still on the south side of the island, flying in an easterly direction, they came first to Scotia Pier, which McCarty had seen with Jack from the clifftop. Next, they came to Dominion Pier as it was in the process of loading an ore boat, with clouds of reddish-brown dust rising all around as the cargo was dropped into the hold. Just past the pier was the ferry landing, and McCarty could see the *Maneco* ferry in mid-crossing, on its way from the island to Portugal Cove. Above the cliff to his left were the two 4.7-inch quick-firing Mark IV shore battery guns manned by the Newfoundland Militia. The gunners waved, and McCarty was grateful that Kelly had let everyone know they were friend and not foe. Again, the pilot dipped his wings, this time in greeting, before moving on.

Besides the high rocky cliffs, McCarty had seen low dense bush, small evergreen trees, and a few ponds, but nothing of a suspicious nature from the air. He was positive that Kahr and Becher had some kind of hiding place where they had stored the explosives, but it would most likely be in closer proximity to the No. 4 mine and near the water. McCarty figured the plane ride was not going to be productive directly, but it was affording him an opportunity to relax and see the whole picture from a fresh perspective. Continuing on towards the eastern tip of the island, McCarty could see another tall, roughly pie-shaped sea stack just offshore of the cliff where a lighthouse stood.

"That lighthouse is new," Kelly yelled above the noise of the engine, pointing at the beacon, "just a couple of years old."

Back on the north side of the island, after nearly completing their roughly sixteen-mile oval flight, McCarty could see wide open patches of bare ground and rock where there had once been a low forest. It was said that, in the early days before large-scale surface mining began, you would need a compass to find your way through it.

"All right, Pat, we're done. Let's head home," McCarty said, and Kelly gave him a thumbs up.

o o o

Jack Sparkes heard the drone of the single-engine plane returning to the field and arrived as it taxied back toward him after landing. He picked up his camera just as McCarty was alighting from the plane and took a picture for posterity.

When McCarty got close to Jack, they both heard a loud boom and felt the ground tremble slightly. To the south, they could see a rising cloud of smoke and dust near the centre of the island. In a moment, he heard a yell over the sound of the still-idling Fairchild. Patrick Kelly came running across the field, waving for him to stop.

"I just heard over the radio that it looks like there was an explosion over by the west tramway at Kent's Bridge!" Kelly exclaimed breathlessly. "Can it be connected to your business?"

"I believe it is," McCarty replied. "How's your gas situation?"

"I topped off the tank earlier, so we're good for a while yet," Kelly said hopefully.

"Okay. Jack, you go and check in with our friends at the phone company to see if there has been any movement at the boarding house, but I'm guessing neither one of the spies is there."

"Got it," Jack replied. "And you?"

"Me?" McCarty answered, remembering the plane's machine gun. "Lieutenant Kelly, 'Mr. Thompson' and I are going hunting."

As Jack ran to the truck, Kelly and Bill got back in their still-warm seats, bumped back down the field, and took off. McCarty reached down behind his seat and opened the small storage locker. Taking out the military-issue Thompson machine gun, he opened the breech and checked it. Then he reached back and grasped a full hundred-round drum magazine and inserted it by sliding it sideways underneath until he heard the unmistakable click. He gave the drum's spring-winding mechanism a couple of extra turns until it was tight. The plane was now in a steep left banking turn and heading over the middle of the island toward the dust cloud rising near the bridge, where one railroad track crossed over the other.

"Jesus Christ!" Kelly exclaimed. "They got both tracks! The bridge is down, and there's a bunch of cars derailed."

"Okay, Pat, let's get close. Real close. Is that . . . someone on a motorcycle? There! Crossing that field going towards the woods!"

"Yes," Kelly replied, "and he's not wasting any fucking time either!"

"Even if we could land in this field, there's no way we'll catch him in time before he gets to the trees. Line me up behind him and get ready for some cold air and noise."

"Okay, but make sure you don't shoot through the prop, for Christ's sake."

McCarty didn't answer, but Kelly could hear the sound of the charging bolt on the heavy .45 calibre machine gun being pulled back. Bill had no doubt it was August Kahr driving away from the scene, and that he had caused the explosion below, but could this really have been their plan? It was going to be inconvenient, but it would get rebuilt quickly, with the system only down for a few days at most. *Must be a diversion to throw me off,* he thought.

McCarty saw a flash from the woods, and a second later, a bullet ripped through the fuselage of the plane and out through the roof.

"Becher!" McCarty yelled, and as Kelly banked left, he thrust the machine gun out through the window. Squeezing the trigger, he sent a wild spray of slugs earthward, countering the machine guns recoil. It would be a miracle if he hit Kahr, but he was sending a message. He saw clumps of dirt kick up around the motorcycle as he led it, letting the spy drive into the line of fire. The barrel began to get very hot as he expended the last of the ammunition. The motorcycle appeared to wobble a bit as it entered the line of trees, but he was sure he hadn't connected.

"You didn't tell me they'd be shooting at us! Now look at what they've done to my pretty plane!" Kelly was talking to Bill but looking at the one-inch hole that had appeared down between their seats, and then raised his eyes to the one above their heads where the bullet had exited. After rolling the window back up, McCarty detached the drum magazine from the gun and checked the breech.

"Sorry, Pat, you had the general picture right but not how deadly this pair is. I'm going to ask you not to report this, at least not until we've got them."

"We?" Kelly queried. "Them?"

"Okay," Bill replied. "Short version. Two spies, enough explosives to do a hundred or more of what we just saw . . . going off all at once inside one of the mines. We just witnessed what I think is a diversion, but it would be hard to convince the people I report to of that. The 'we' part is a trusted group that are helping track down the saboteurs."

"Well, I guess you'd better add me to the group," Kelly replied. "I've already paid my admission fee, and a little payback would be nice."

"You're cool under fire; that's for sure. I'm proud to have you in the club," Bill said.

"Cool? Are you kidding? If you smell something awful it's because I think I shit myself back there. You must be older than you look to be in this game and doing what I just saw you do," Kelly continued. "How many of these operations have you done?"

McCarty just looked at him and started laughing. It was the first time he could remember laughing in a very long time. *Probably nerves,* he thought, which made him laugh even harder.

They circled around for a while, hoping to catch sight of the saboteurs, but they were nowhere to be seen, and according to the fuel gauge, it was time to head back to the field. The pilot radioed in and had a message relayed to Jack Sparkes at his house. He was waiting for McCarty when they rolled to a stop.

Kelly received permission to remain available for more "mine reconnaissance" should the need arise, while McCarty filled Jack in on what had just happened.

After a low whistle, Jack said, "Well that figures in with what I was going to tell you. It looks like Kahr and Becher have cleared out of their lodgings. Mrs. Dawe at the boarding house was woken up by them leaving in quite a hurry around two in the morning. She thought maybe they had some late mine shift."

"No," McCarty replied. "They had some other work in mind. Somehow, I think they must have known we were on to them and closing in. But how could they have known?"

"I'll vouch for the men who followed them yesterday," said Jack. "They're regular townspeople you'd see any day of the week around here, and you'd never notice them."

"Okay, Sparky. First, we'll drop by the main office and talk to Delaney about the explosion. Then we're going to go over to the boarding house to have another look around."

o o o

By the time they reached the office, plans were already being discussed about how to deal with repairing the bridge and tracks, so that ore transport to the piers could resume. In the meantime, the ore pockets at both piers were full and any boats arriving would still be able to be loaded from the large stockpiles. McCarty let Delaney know that it was definitely the two suspects, Kahr and Becher, who had sabotaged the bridge and tracks. He said that it would be best to keep the information between them for now. Agreeing, the manager expressed regret over not having fully checked their references, and McCarty let him know that it wouldn't have made any difference. Those two were going to carry out their plans no matter what.

Bill and Jack went to the boarding house and spoke with Mrs. Dawe. She reiterated that the two lodgers had left the building in a hurry at about two a.m.

"Did they have their suitcases or were they carrying anything with them?" Jack asked.

"I don't believe so," she said, "but I haven't been in their room to check. I was still a bit awake from earlier, so that's the only reason I even noticed they'd left. Why is everyone in such a hurry these days?"

"Sorry to interrupt ma'am," McCarty said, "but you said you were already awake. Why was that?"

"Ah," she replied, "I thought I heard something tapping on one of the windows, like maybe a tree branch in the wind, but I didn't pay much attention to it. One of the lodgers must have gotten up to check on it though, because I heard one coming down the stairs. He soon went back up though. I didn't see any point in getting up myself until I heard both of them coming downstairs, and that's when I realised that they were leaving the house. Funny though, I don't recall it being very windy today. Would you boys like a nice cup of tea?"

"Thank you, no, Mrs. Dawe, but we're going to have a look in their room, if you don't mind," said McCarty. "I think they've left for good, and we'll make sure anything they left gets forwarded to them. Is their lodging all paid up?"

"Oh, my yes," she said. "They paid up for the whole month. How will I give them what they're owed?"

"Don't worry about that, my dear," Jack replied, looking at Bill. "You keep the balance, and my young friend here and I will see they get everything that's coming to them."

Upstairs, both men went through everything the saboteurs had left behind. Jack used his knife to cut the linings in both suitcases, and inside the second one, he found a neatly folded red, white, and black flag with a large swastika in the centre. There was no folder under either mattress, but on the floor between the bed and the dresser was a crumpled piece of paper—the note that Kahr had shown to Becher. They were gone and weren't coming back.

From the top of the dresser, McCarty looked at the two brass miner's tags. He pocketed them and also stuffed in the flag. Then he and Jack left the house.

"Bill, what do you think about that tapping business that Emeline mentioned?"

"Could have been wind in the branches of a tree, I suppose, except. . . ." Looking up, they could both see that there were no tree branches anywhere near the boarding-house windows.

"So?" queried Jack.

McCarty showed Jack the note he had picked up, and said, "One of them came downstairs shortly before they left. I think a third person came by to warn them we were closing in."

Chapter 22

Bell Island, Wednesday, July 25, 2018

Matt McCarty woke from one of the most restful sleeps he could ever remember having. There was sunshine streaming in the open bedroom window, and lifting his head a bit, he could see and smell the ocean just beyond a narrow strip of land, dotted here and there with low grassy mounds, the remains of waste rock overburden from the surface mining of a hundred years before. Kathleen walked into the room and announced that there was breakfast waiting in the oven warmer. Her hair was damp from the shower she had just taken, and she was wearing a white towel wrapped around her tanned, athletic body.

"Hungry?" she asked, smiling that smile.

"Oh, I'm developing an appetite alright," he replied. "C'm'ere a sec. I want to ask you something."

"Uh huh? And what might that be, sir?" she asked, coming close to the bed, her electric-blue eyes never leaving his.

Reaching up and taking her hand, he looked at her and said tenderly, "Do you have any orange juice?"

Giggling like a teenager, she jumped on the bed and said, "Okay, now you're gonna get it!"

Funny, he thought, pulling her toward him, *I never thought of myself as a morning person.*

○ ○ ○

Matt parked at the community museum where he had taken the mine tour and then walked next door to the Bell Island Senior's Complex. He was greeted at the front desk by Emma Rees, the same woman who had been at the barbecue and told him about the pilot, Patrick Kelly.

"Hello, Matt," she said, shaking his hand. "I'm terribly sorry, but Mr. Kelly suffered a small stroke yesterday. He's partially paralysed, and I'm afraid he's having some difficulty when he tries to talk."

"Does he have anyone here with him?" Matt asked. "Family or friends?"

"No, he came back to Bell Island about thirty years ago after a long career in the military up on the mainland. He's been with us for a long time, but except for the staff, who all love him, he doesn't get any visitors."

"Is he well enough for me to go and say hello? Maybe if I mention my father's name, it might help."

"If you want to try, that's fine. It won't hurt, but he may not be very coherent. We're all sad, especially the women staff he flirted with. He seems to have lost that sharpness that made him such a joy to be around."

Emma led Matt down a hallway and into a room that had a nameplate for "Patrick Kelly."

"Patrick," she said, "this is Mr. McCarty; he'd like to have a visit with you. Is that okay?"

Kelly looked up at them from the bed where he was reclining. His eyes were a cloudy cataract blue. He nodded briefly, which Emma took as a sign that Matt could talk with him. She left the room, saying she would be down the hall by the front desk.

MIKE PHELAN

Matt and Kelly looked at each other for a moment, and then Kelly motioned for him to come closer.

"McCarty? Bill?" He strained forward for a closer look. His words were a little slurred, but Matt definitely understood him.

Matt decided to address him by his former military title, thinking it might help somehow.

"Lieutenant Kelly, I'm Matt, Bill's son. Do you remember him?"

"Bill McCarty?" he responded, clearing his throat. His face lit up, and took on a faraway look. He began to chuckle, and it was clear that he was looking into the distant past for a moment. He seemed to be having some trouble with his left side, but with his right hand, he pointed to a dresser drawer and said, "Open."

"You want me to open that drawer?" Matt asked.

Kelly nodded.

Matt crossed the room and opened the dresser drawer. Inside was a cardboard box, which he removed and brought over to the bed where Patrick Kelly lay. The man nodded toward the box, and Matt opened it. Inside was a crumpled red, white, and black cloth. Matt shook it out and saw the swastika. There were still the remnants of what looked like muddy prints all over it, as if from many boots. Kelly nodded toward the framed picture on the wall at the foot of his bed.

"This is the same flag, isn't it?" Matt asked. "The one that you and my father and Jack Sparkes stood on when that picture was taken."

Kelly nodded and managed to say, "Yours now."

Matt took a chance. "And the mission?"

His brow furrowed and labouring to speak, the former pilot forced out a loud warning: "Not finished. Still danger in No. 4!"

Knowing that all the mines were now flooded, and wondering if perhaps Kelly was confused, Matt moved on. "And the spies?"

"Those fuckers?" Kelly croaked, with what might have been a rasping laugh. "Ask Bill or Sparky. . . ."

The effort to speak must have taken a lot out of him. Kelly nodded off, and while Matt had a burning desire to know more about the spies, he didn't want to push the man any further. He started to fold the flag, but after pausing for a moment, he just crumpled it back up and shoved it into his jacket pocket. It felt good, and it felt right. For a moment, he could imagine being with his father and Kelly, flying above the island, looking for nefarious saboteurs from World War Two. Those men had really done it!

But what had happened to the spies? Or the gold, if that really existed? Suddenly, he thought of Farrell and Hunt. If they found out about Patrick Kelly, they probably wouldn't hesitate to come and harass him about hidden gold. That led to another thought: Had they gone to his father? Did they have anything to do with his death? He walked down the hall and asked Emma Rees to call him right away if anyone else came around asking about the pilot. Leaving the building, he headed next door to say hello to Tom Crane and the girls.

o o o

Matt was greeted by Crane as soon as he walked in the door. He was talking with Bev Adams, who came over and gave Matt a hug. "Hi, Half-Grandpa! When can we go back and explore the cave?"

"Let's see," Matt said. "Tom, what are the chances that you, Cassie, and Bev can take the day off from work tomorrow?"

"Well, the girls filled me in on what's happening," Tom replied, "and I've been speaking with Evelyn on the phone. A horde of Nazi gold? Unbelievable! But to answer your question, I make my own hours, so count me in, and because they're both working part-time, I can see the girls' schedules are adjusted, so they can have the day off too."

"Okay, Bev," Matt said, "there's your answer. We're going in tomorrow. Tom, bring one of your mine hardhats for yourself if you decide to join in. The girls and I have our climbing helmets. I'll go tell Cassie."

As Matt walked into the souvenir shop, he could see Cassie serving a customer. When the man turned around, he was looking into the face of Peter Farrell.

"Mr. McCarty!" he exclaimed. "What a pleasant surprise! Imagine seeing you here. How are you? It looks like you have recovered from your parental loss, and I've noticed you have been enjoying the company of a beautiful lady."

"I'm doing just fine, Peter," Matt responded without hesitation. "How are you and Delbert getting along over at the Bell Island Inn?"

"Ah, you are clever, aren't you? I could tell the moment I met you that we had that in common," Farrell replied. "You know, Hunt doesn't give you half the credit you deserve. It is unfortunate that you are being uncooperative. The elderly lieutenant was uncooperative too, I'm afraid."

After a long pause, Matt said quietly, "So either directly or indirectly, you killed my father."

"A gross oversimplification, my dear fellow. Let's not forget his advanced years, and of course, the alcohol—"

"I guess that made it pretty easy for your trained gorilla to control him. I've got a feeling that Delbert couldn't really handle much more than a helpless old man," Matt said, looking Hunt up and down.

THE SECRET OF BELL ISLAND

"Not true," Farrell responded. "He also likes to handle young teenage girls."

Matt looked around and saw Hunt holding a gift-shop adolescent-size t-shirt in his massive hand, smiling at Cassie. Matt casually walked to where Hunt was standing, and with a quick move, pulled the shirt from his hand.

"This isn't right for you," Matt said. "Too small. It'd cut off your circulation. You wouldn't be able to breathe."

"You're dead." Hunt said matter-of-factly.

"What do you think not being able to breathe means?" Matt replied.

Farrell joined them as they stood facing each other. "Gentlemen, please. No need for ruffled feathers. I'm sure we can come to some sort of agreement on this."

Matt laughed. "Farrell, you're a walking cliche. You present as a sophisticated gentleman thief, but you're really just a cheap, two-bit crook. And Delbert, you're the wannabe flabby muscle with a fear of women."

Farrell now dropped all pretence of sophistication and was nearly apoplectic, shaking slightly with anger.

Matt looked at him and smiled. "Time to go now, boys. Stay away from my family if you want to live."

The threat was lost on Farrell. Hunt, however, being a coward at heart, saw a look on Matt's face that he recognised—the look of a man who had the capacity to kill if pushed. He felt fear, despite his size and strength.

As the men moved to leave, Matt stood his ground, and Hunt had to move around him to exit. It was a small victory, but Matt found it very telling that Hunt hadn't simply walked through him.

"Cassie, are you okay?" Matt asked.

"Uncle Matt, it would take more than those two creeps to scare me. They're just lucky Bev wasn't in here."

Her look told him otherwise, but he could sense that she was being brave in spite of her fear, which was the mark of true courage and made him feel very proud.

That evening, the whole group drove down Beach Hill Road and ate at Dicks restaurant. The low split-level white building backed onto the cliff and faced the ocean within a stone's throw of the ferry terminal. They ordered their meals at the counter and then found a large table covered with a checkered cloth while the food was prepared. The clean red, green, and yellow tile floor looked as if it could be original from 1950, and the walls were covered with photographs depicting local scenes from every decade going back over a hundred years.

Matt and Kathleen walked around, looking at the pictures, and one of them caught his eye. There he was, just as he remembered, photographed in a newspaper article kneeling next to the shark that had been caught in Walter Dicks' salmon net. Kathleen noticed the faraway look in his eyes and poked him.

"Hey! Earth to Matt," she said. "Where are you?"

Matt pointed. "Right there actually. That handsome little kid in the picture," he replied, looking at her and letting his statement hang in the air.

She looked at him, and then at the photo, and then back at him. "Oh my," she said. "Oh no! Were you scared? Who made you do that?"

"My father, and it was frightening at the time, but in hindsight, I think he might have been trying to bond with me. At least, that's how I like to think of it. He just didn't know how."

"I'm sorry you had to go through that," Kathleen said.

"Oh well, the nightmares didn't last that long, and the intense therapy helped," he quipped.

Looking at him, she said, "I see you, you know. Past the jokes that hide the hurt, I see you, and I like what I see. All of it." Then she reached for his hand and squeezed it tightly.

Cassie and Bev crowded around to look at the focus of their attention.

"Are you shitting me?" This from Bev. "Ahh, Half-Grandpa, you were some f'ing cute."

"I know, kid," he said, looking through the front window at the beach rocks where he had knelt down more than sixty years before. "I can't help it. It's just my nature."

They all laughed and then sat down to eat, malt vinegar causing steam to rise from the piping hot fries and fish so fresh that Tom said he was sure his tried to jump off the plate and make for the sea.

After supper, it was decided that they would make the next day a picnic, with Evelyn and Kathleen joining them while Matt and the girls did their cave exploration. It looked as though Tom's knee problem meant he would have to be content to stay up top as well. Matt called Jurgen Meyer and told him about their plans, as well as what had happened with Farrell and Hunt. Meyer said that he would be around to keep an eye on things, but that if he was doing his job properly, he would be out of sight.

Not for the first time, Matt thought about his father's pistol, which was now in a lockbox in Evelyn's basement. It would be easy to have it at the ready in case of trouble, but he wasn't going to buy into that kind of fear. That would be giving in, and he was damned if he was going to let that happen. If and when the time came for action, he would trust in reason and instinct. Smiling, he pragmatically thought that, in addition to those two attributes, maybe a healthy chunk of two-by-four might also be in order.

Chapter 23

Bell Island, Wednesday, November 18, 1942

As August Kahr crouched under Kent's Bridge near the centre of the island, he now had confirmation from their confederate that his identity had been discovered by a government intelligence agent: the man Kahr now knew as William McCarty, whom he had met the previous Sunday. The authorities had set a trap to catch them, but luckily, they had been warned in time. Hopefully, McCarty would think that this blast was Kahr and Becher's objective, and when the remains of two bodies were discovered, blown to bits and badly burned, they would close the case, thinking the spies had accidentally blown themselves up. Meanwhile, their ultimate plan would be brought to fruition: a mine explosion like no one here had ever seen. It was *wunderschonen* that the spy catcher would celebrate the death of two innocent civilians.

Kahr laughed as the two men he and Becher had lured here struggled against their bonds, looking wide eyed when they saw the dynamite. He enjoyed seeing the look in their eyes as he spoke to them soothingly in German, and they realised what was about to happen. He looked from the open space where he had gotten off the motorcycle toward the tree line and waved his arm overhead from side to side. Becher stepped out of the trees, where he was set up with a scoped rifle as protection, and waved back.

Taking no chances on having a dud, Kahr pushed blasting caps into each of the five dynamite sticks that were wrapped together and screwed down the wires to the terminals on a portable detonator. He pulled the plunger up and gave it a half twist, smiling at the wide-eyed desperation of the men looking at him. Then he set the package on the tracks, with the plunger propped so that the next ore car to come down the track would push the plunger in, triggering the explosion.

His last act before getting on the motorcycle and riding toward the tree line was to look at the two men, who were frantic now, knowing the end was near, and say, "Heil Hitler!" while giving the straight-arm Nazi salute. Even though he considered Hitler to be a crackpot, he liked seeing the men's pathetic angry-yet-fearful reaction.

o o o

Kahr was just partway to the tree line and safety when a six-car string of ore carriers set off the explosion. As a small mercy, the two bound men were killed instantly by concussive force. Kahr had underestimated the blast and was knocked off the motorcycle, which fell over and stalled. He lay there for a minute, gathering his wits as fist sized chunks of iron ore rained down narrowly missing him while Becher came out of the trees to see if he was all right. Before Becher could reach him, Kahr got up and stopped him with a wave of his hand. He slowly righted the motorcycle, trying to kick-start it several times before the motor finally coughed and then caught. As he looked up, he saw Becher point up into the sky and then start running back toward the trees.

Kahr, his head still ringing from the blast, turned and saw a low-flying small plane in the sky heading straight toward the cloud of smoke and dust in the air behind him. This was unexpected. He had thought it would be an hour or more before anyone could get here to investigate what had happened. Panicking, he stalled the cycle again before revving the motor and bumpily driving toward the trees.

As the plane got closer, Kahr could hear its radial engine over the sound of the motorcycle. Then he saw a flash from the trees and heard a loud crack as the sound of Becher's rifle reached his ears. Chancing a look, he saw the small plane bank left, and then all hell broke loose. Small mounds of dirt and tufts of grass exploded all around him as the staccato sound of a machine gun firing reached his ears. All the way to the tree line, he had to zig zag left and right to avoid driving straight into the hail of bullets.

Reaching cover, after what seemed like hours but was only seconds, he and Becher crouched down while the plane circled and then turned back in the direction from which it had come. Kahr had no idea how he had been discovered so quickly. His first thought was that McCarty had been the one in the plane. He didn't know how, but he was sure of it. He checked himself carefully and found flecks of metal and droplets of blood on his face and coat where a bullet had ripped through the front fender, showering him with small hot shards.

"August, are you alright? We are safe now," Becher said, concern showing as he reached out and picked several small metallic particles from his compatriot's face. Kahr realised then that his own hands were shaking and he had tears in his eyes. Angry that Becher had seen him in a moment of weakness, a deep, quiet rage toward the government agent set in.

The fact that two innocent lives had just been lost did not even cross his mind.

"August, what will we do now?" Becher whined. "Where will we go? We can't leave until we complete our mission, but the boat doesn't come to pick us up until Sunday night!"

"Quiet! I have planned for this. We are going to hide until things calm down," Kahr responded. "By Sunday, it will be safe to go down into the mine and set the detonator to trigger the explosion when the first shift goes to work on Monday morning."

They sat there for a while to make sure the plane wasn't coming back and started slowly to relax. Soon, before the authorities could arrive, Becher slung the Mauser rifle over his head, resting it against the canvas rucksack on his back, while Kahr reached into an inside pocket and took a healthy pull from his silver flask of cheap whisky, before starting the cycle.

With Becher sitting behind him, they set off on a bumpy ride alongside the Scotia track to the road, which led to Lance Cove on the south side of the island. They took refuge in an abandoned cabin that Kahr had found, which was within sight of the water where several small boats were tied up. When the time came, Kahr and Becher would get back to their cave at Grebes Nest to perform the final act of sabotage. However, besides McCarty, who he would be happy to kill on sight, Kahr had a couple of other loose ends left to deal with. He would take care of one of them tonight, long after most people went to bed and when militia patrols were less likely to be vigilant.

"August, this place is perfect!" Becher exclaimed. "How ever did you find it?"

"Kurt, I know you think I spent all my free time drinking in the tavern, but no, that is not correct. The company motorcycle and I have explored most of this little island, and I chose several places like this just in case the need arose. Don't forget, my friend, above all else, I am a planner and like to prepare for every situation."

Becher's admiration for Kahr was obvious, and any concern he'd had about Kahr's loyalty or sincerity now evaporated. He had long since realised that his feelings towards Kahr went far beyond mere friendship. He was angry and conflicted about it, but also filled with yearning and forbidden desire for the man he had been sleeping in the same room with for the past year.

"August, I am truly sorry I ever had any doubt about you, and I hope you will forgive me."

"Nothing to forgive, Kurt. We are living in a stressful time, but soon, everything we have been working for will be accomplished, and we will be back in the fatherland. And Kurt?" Kahr looking meekly at the floor. "I really do appreciate your friendship."

His performance was flawless, and while Becher's feelings of love for his friend deepened, Kahr was deciding when the best time would be to shoot the degenerate homosexual. Becher slept soundly as Kahr looked at his Stowa wristwatch and saw that the time was now two a.m. It would be safe enough to take Lance Cove Road back toward town.

o o o

He rode carefully, his vision reduced because of the mandatory wartime light louvers that shaded the motorcycle's beam, and he kept an eye out for any militia patrols. His contact lived in a tiny house at the west end of Fourth Street, and answered immediately to his soft knock on the wooden storm door. Telephone operator Hanna Martin fell into his arms and kissed him.

"Oh, August, I was so worried," she said breathlessly. "I thought that something terrible must have happened when I didn't hear from you sooner! Oh! Look at your poor face!"

"I am fine, my darling. Has there been any word about the explosion?" he asked. "Did anyone talk about it at work?"

"They are pretending the explosion was an accident—that a worker mishandled some dynamite while preparing for repairs to the bridge. But I listened in on a conversation between Lorraine Sparkes and her father. They know it was caused by you and Kurt, and that you weren't the ones killed in the blast. They will be hunting you, and August . . . they think there may be someone locally who is providing you with information! I am so afraid that I will be found out! If I am discovered as an accomplice, I would be put in jail or maybe even hanged! What will we do?"

Kahr was disappointed that McCarty hadn't bought his plan, which would have relieved the worry of being caught, but in the end, it changed nothing.

"Hanna! Look at me. Be calm. I promise none of those swine will harm you. I have planned for this, and before you know it, you will have nothing to worry about."

Hanna looked at the man she had fallen in love with. What she'd thought had been an accidental meeting at Lawton's Drug Store soda fountain had been carefully orchestrated. He'd followed several of the women, including Lorraine, for weeks until he learned that Hanna was the only candidate both alone and vulnerable. Their "chance" meeting had resulted in her having dreams of a life with this handsome, charming gentleman who said he would marry her and take her to his home in the United States, but he told her that she must keep their relationship secret for a while.

The sex was just part of the job, as he did not really care for such things, although unbeknownst to either of them at this early date, she was carrying his child. When he'd showed interest in her job, Hanna had provided him with a few innocent bits of information, just some local gossip, and they had laughed. Soon she began to listen to specific individuals for him, at his request, as she fell deeper in love with the man. By the time she began to suspect who and what he really was, it was too late. She loved him but also sensed that he had a cruel streak and worried about ever defying him. She was in too deep, and no one would ever understand, especially after the submarine attacks. She was lost and could turn to no one except Kahr.

He held her in his arms and then took her hand, leading her to the tiny bedroom. Later, after making love and telling her how wonderful life would be after the war, when they were living in the United States, and she lay sleeping, he got up quietly from the bed and took a 9mm Luger from his jacket. In courting this woman, he'd told her quite a bit about himself, knowing that this time would have to come eventually. As he placed the pillow against her head, she woke and struggled for breath against the pressure. He held her head down until she fully realised what he was doing. He smiled as she flailed, grabbing uselessly at his arm, and then the muffled shot made her go limp.

"I promised I wouldn't let any of them hurt you," he said aloud. "No need to thank me, my darling."

They probably wouldn't look for her for a day or two, but he wasn't going to chance it. Wrapping her body up in the sheets and blanket from the bed, along with the bloody pillow, he dragged her outside into the still, cold winter night. Stars were shining down from a cloudless sky, as he opened the lid to the old dry cistern and unceremoniously dumped her in.

Checking back inside, he cleaned up a few spots of blood, turned the mattress over, and put another blanket on it. Kahr packed up her meager belongings, put them in the girl's cheap suitcase, and took it out back where it joined her in the cistern. In all likelihood, anyone who put two and two together would think she had simply fled. The road back to Lance Cove was clear, and as he arrived back at the abandoned cabin, the sun began to rise. *All is well,* he thought, smiling again as he looked at the other loose end: the still sleeping form of Kurt Becher.

North Atlantic Ocean, Thursday, November 19, 1942

The German U-184, with its crew of fifty, had been travelling on the surface in calm seas for most of the two days that followed her torpedoing and recording of her first ever kill—the British merchant cargo ship SS *Widestone*—some five hundred nautical miles south of Greenland. One of the three lookouts on the conning-tower bridge spotted an airplane through his Zeiss binoculars, and yelled, "*Alarm!*" They quickly descended the ladder, and the last man pulled down the spring-loaded hatch, spinning the wheel and dogging it closed against the tons of water that would be pressing down on it.

Overhead, a Canadian PBY Catalina submarine-patrol seaplane circled back for another look after the waist gunner yelled that he'd spotted something through the port-side gun blister.

Below, Kapitanleutnant Gunther Dangschat cried, "*Tauchen! Tauchen!*" Every crew member not directly involved with another task ran as far forward as possible to add their weight to the crash dive as the bow-plane wheels were turned, cold sea water flooded the ballast tanks, and the boat plunged below the surface. Twenty-five of the crew's complement were crammed into the tight space by the forward torpedo tubes, sitting and lying on the unfired ordnance. The U-boat levelled off at one hundred feet, changed heading, and made its escape.

After circling for twenty minutes, the Catalina put the sighting down in the log as a probable whale breaching, and the plane headed back west toward Newfoundland.

U-184 stayed submerged for the rest of the day and surfaced only after dark. Switching to the two powerful diesel motors that ran the twin propellers, generators began to recharge the banks of lead acid batteries, which were the only means of propulsion while under water. The boat could stay down for about twenty-four hours but had to surface eventually to power up.

While they were on the surface, the radio operator received a radio telegraph communication. He handed Dangschat a coded message marked *"Captain only,"* which he had to decode himself on the Enigma cipher machine. The message was unusual and also the first they had received since sending news that they had sunk their first kill near midnight on the seventeenth. Congratulations were brief, and the captain puzzled over a new order: They were to rendezvous with two German agents at coordinates that would bring them within sight of land near Bell Island, Newfoundland.

The spies were to be picked up and transported back to Germany under the utmost secrecy. The submarine was not to engage any enemy shipping in the meantime, except to defend itself if they came under attack. It was imperative that they arrive by Sunday, November twenty-second and rise to periscope depth at twenty-three hundred hours. Then they were to wait for a signal from shore, at which time they should surface and retrieve the two men, who would row out to meet them. They were to send no more transmissions except to acknowledge and transmit their current location.

It was early Friday morning, November twentieth, when the captain complied. They were just north of the Flemish Cap, an undersea mount about three hundred and fifty miles east of Newfoundland. In order to maintain a cloak of secrecy, the German Kreigsmarine would issue a notice that U-184 was missing and presumed lost near the position they presently occupied. The captain told the first officer what they were doing, but to the rest of the crew, they were simply slowly patrolling while looking for a convoy to attack.

The new course was laid in, and toward first light, he had the first officer signal the engine room to switch back from diesel motors to electric and for the helm to take the boat down to eighty feet at four knots. The bow planes dipped slightly, and the boat slid under the cold waters. As he always did for luck when diving, he touched the heavy gold ring on his right hand, which his wife had given him the day he took command of U-184. It was engraved with his initials and that day's date, *GD 29-05-42*.

Chapter 24

Bell Island, Thursday, July 26, 2018

It was another beautiful Bell Island morning with just an occasional cloud and a slight breeze to add contrast to the warm sunny day. Tom's pickup truck and Matt's SUV had no trouble negotiating what became a narrow dirt pathway at the western end of the road known as "Crane's Lanes." The pathway ended at Big Cove, close to the cliff overlooking Grebes Nest. Tom Crane and Evelyn got out of the cab of Tom's pickup and proceeded to set up a little day camp for their picnic, complete with a portable shade canopy.

"Okay!" Matt said. "I don't want to take the long way to the cave like we did last time. Who wants to jump off a cliff?"

"I do! I do!" came an excited chorus from Cassie and Bev.

Kathleen looked at him sideways and raised an eyebrow.

Matt looked at her. "What?" he said. "You never wanted to invite teenagers to go jump off a cliff?"

She nodded slowly. "Well, when you put it like that...."

"Okay, girls," he continued, "harness check please, and then check each other while I set an anchor for us to rappel from."

Matt set a three-point self-equalising anchor, using three strongly rooted trees back from the cliff. If any one or even two anchors failed, the remaining one was more than sufficient to hold their weight. With both girls double-checked, Cassie went first, attaching the "dead" end of her rope to the anchor. For her first descent, Matt also attached his own rope to her harness as backup and was prepared to belay her if she slipped or lost control of her own rope. As the girl stood near the edge, Matt spoke to her quietly.

"Cassie, I've got your back. I can hold your weight easily with the second rope. Okay?"

Without hesitation, she said, "Uncle Matt, I'm ready to go."

Looking in her eyes, he noted that she was excited but calm. Her hands were steady and in the right place to start the descent.

"Yes, you are," he agreed, smiling. "Now, lean back slowly and let the rope take your weight until you're at about forty-five degrees to the rock wall. That's it, now slack the rope a little to begin descending and then go at your own pace."

She started carefully walking backwards down the side, experiencing a slight thrill of fear with the first step, as she placed her trust in the equipment, herself, and Matt. By the time she was halfway down, Cassie was pushing off a bit from the cliff with her legs and allowing herself to drop a few feet at a time. The dynamic rope stretched just enough to absorb any shock. Reaching bottom, she came off the line and looked up.

"How was that?" Matt yelled down.

The girl raised both arms high in the air and let out a scream of joy, easily heard over the low waves rolling in to the shore.

Then it was Bev's turn. Like Cassie, she was a natural, and when she reached the bottom, both girls took turns yelling as loud as they could. Evelyn looked at Matt as he prepared to join them.

"A week," she said simply.

Matt looked at her quizzically.

"You've been here barely a week, and our whole world has changed. Since you arrived, Cassandra has been the happiest I've ever seen her." She paused. "I wish we could have connected all those years ago."

"Yes," said Matt, "and I wish you could have met Heather. You would have gotten along great together. And as for me," he said, smiling and squeezing her hand, "well, I would have had a little sister to pick on."

From far below, they heard Bev yell, "Hey, Grandpa! Let's get going!"

Looking at Tom, Matt said, "Keep an eye on these two. Especially this one," he said, pointing to Evelyn.

"Never known him not to," quipped Kathleen. "Now go join the other teenagers and take a flying leap."

"Nice way to treat your boyfriend," he said.

"Boyfriend?"

"Don't blame me; you started it."

"Me? How?" she asked, batting her eyes at him and laughing.

No answer was necessary as he pecked her on the cheek and then walked toward the cliff. Pushing off in a wide arc, he rappelled fifteen feet at a time and was soon standing next to the girls, who stared open-mouthed.

Looking at Bev, Matt said, "You called me 'Grandpa'."

"Yeah, I guess you've been upgraded from half," she said, still looking at him in amazement.

"Okay," Matt said. "Let's go in and do a little exploring. We'll stop by the wooden boxes to check helmet lights and handhelds before going further."

The three explorers made their way into the cave, and after a short walk to where the old wooden explosives crates were, they switched on their helmet lamps, the powerful beams

THE SECRET OF BELL ISLAND

illuminating the way ahead. They all carried backpacks with water, snacks, and a small first-aid kit, in addition to backup flashlights and multi-tools.

The tunnel wound slightly back to the east as they walked, and it widened to about twenty-five feet. The ceiling was almost twelve feet high and showed a smooth ripple effect, as if at some very distant time it had been under water. The floor of the cave was mostly clear, but in places, there had been some rockfall.

Stepping over one such pile, Matt yelled, "Stop!"

A few feet further in, there was a void in the surface. It was about ten feet across and roughly circular. Carefully stepping up to the edge, he shone his flashlight down and heard distant running water but could not see bottom.

"Bev, hand me one of those rocks by your foot," he said. Tossing it over the edge, they waited. After a moment, they heard a distant splash.

"Cassie," Bev said, "you're the math whiz. How far down is that?"

"It took about three seconds," she replied, calculating quickly. "At thirty-two feet per second/per second I'd say it's near a hundred and fifty feet to the water."

"Okay," Matt said, "there could be other pits like this. Do you both feel comfortable moving on or do you think we should go back?"

Both girls pointed ahead.

"All right, but we're going to be extra careful going forward. I'm not a fan of deep water."

"Don't worry," Cassie said, quoting a favourite old movie, "the fall would probably kill you."

"Hell, yeah," Bev agreed, straight-faced.

Matt nodded, and they continued on. By now, the three were about five hundred feet into the cave. A large rockfall ahead had them scrambling up and over the debris pile to within six feet of the roof.

"Hey, look, there's a fossil," said Cassie pointing at the rippled roof.

"It's a trilobite! Holy crap, that thing is about 500 million years old," said Bev. "I've seen fern fossils around before that are even older but not this. These guys actually crawled around."

"Let's not wake them up," Matt said. "They look kind of mean."

Bev groaned, and with that, they climbed down the other side and came to what looked like a dead end.

"Is that it?" asked Cassie. "I thought the cave was supposed to meet up with the shaft they started to dig for that old underground rail system."

"Wait a minute; the cave just narrows, and we can get around here to the left," Matt replied. "Look," he said, shining his helmet lamp forward. "It opens up again around this corner for a long way."

They eventually reached a point where, once again, the cave narrowed some more and appeared to come to an end at a large rock-fall blockage. This one went all the way to the roof, and there would be no getting past it.

"I can feel a little breeze. It's coming from over there," Bev said, pointing to a small opening on the left.

"Too small to climb through even for me," said Cassie, sounding disappointed.

"Let's have a look," Matt said, getting close to the opening and shining his handheld flashlight through. "I can see something, and it looks like the cave continues on past this blockage. There's a sign, but I can't read what it says. It looks like it's partly facing towards another shaft that looks different than this one."

"Lemme have a look," said Cassie, excitedly. "Wow!" she yelled. "That's iron ore over there! That has to be the No. 4 shaft! There's a big locked door on the surface, in behind where they do the mine plays, so we must be the first people to see inside it in over fifty years!"

Next, Bev had to have a long look, and finally Matt went back for seconds. Now he could see that there were rail tracks coming out of the No. 4 mine and curving off in the distance toward the old ore piers to the south.

In a few moments, he turned to them and said with a grin, "I wonder if they back-filled the No. 4 shaft before putting up that inner door or if it's clear on the other side?"

"Well, gee, I don't know, Grandpa," said Bev innocently. "I wonder how a person might be able to find out?"

"Funny, that," remarked Cassie looking angelic. "I actually have a friend who acts in the mine plays, and they might have a key to the outer front door—"

"Wait a minute," interrupted Matt, "would Tom Crane have access to No. 4 or know someone who could let us in without having you both lead me into a life of crime?"

"Not as much fun," said Bev, "but probably for the best, I s'pose."

They sat down and had a snack before heading back toward the beach. After hiking to the entrance, being careful to avoid the muddy spots and the pit, they turned right, walking past the place they had rappelled down from, and went through the fisherman's shortcut to the pathway next to the sea stack. Once they were back at the clifftop, they were greeted by Tom, Evelyn, Kathleen, and even Jurgen Meyer who had been viewing the proceedings from a distance while watching for any sign of Farrell or Hunt.

After stories were told about their adventure in the cave and how they could see the No. 4 mine, Tom told them that the sign they couldn't read was actually a danger sign, which he had seen himself more than fifty years earlier. With his connections, he could get them into the mine entrance, and even past the inner steel door, but he didn't know if it had been backfilled to prevent entering any further. To his knowledge, no one had gone through the steel door since 1961, when that particular mine closed for good.

As they began packing up, Matt told Meyer and Tom about the warning he had been given by Patrick Kelly, that there was still danger in the No. 4 mine, and informed Meyer of his exchange with Farrell and Hunt in the souvenir shop.

"I could eliminate the threat from them quickly," said Meyer, "but I do have certain protocols to follow. It may be better for you to withdraw from this whole operation and keep your family safe."

"There's only one way to keep my family safe, Jurgen," Matt countered, "and it isn't by running away. I don't do that."

"Me either," said Tom. "I might have one bad knee, but I've still got two good hands." He showed them two huge scarred- and-bony-knuckled fists.

"Good," said Meyer, "it is agreed then. We will go into the No. 4 mine. Matt, I think you and I have the same idea. What I am seeking—"

"Is probably somewhere along the shaft they dug for the underground ore-delivery system," Matt finished.

"There is another more delicate matter that could be a bigger problem for you, besides those two would-be criminals," Tom said.

"I know." Matt nodded. "But even if there is no substance to that old pilot's warning, safety has to be the first priority. They won't like it, but Cassie and Bev can't come in there with us."

It wasn't easy. Both girls displayed an innate ability to argue their point eloquently, but in the end, it was to no avail. Eventually they capitulated and agreed to act in a support role, which somehow ended with Matt agreeing to let them be on site with Tom Crane while Matt and Jurgen entered No. 4 through the steel door inside the old concrete mine collar.

Back at Evelyn's house, plans for the following day were discussed and finalised.

As they left Evelyn's later, Kathleen looked at Matt. "So," she started, "now what?"

"Well," he answered. "You've had your way with me, so now I'm a ruined man and my reputation's shot. What are you going to do about it?"

"Hmm," she said, "I might have an extra empty drawer that none of my current stable of gentlemen friends are using."

"So, is that an invitation to live with you in sin while I'm here?"

"While you're here I guess, and then—"

She didn't get the chance to finish before he took her in his arms and kissed her, ending any further discussion.

Behind them, in Evelyn's doorway, she and Cassie and Bev all watched.

"Fish in a barrel," said Evelyn.

"Yup," replied both girls in unison, nodding their heads sagely, wise beyond their years.

Chapter 25

Bell Island, Friday, November 20, 1942

Hanna Martin was supposed to report for work at eight a.m. When she didn't arrive by nine, there was concern, because she had never been late since transferring from St. John's to take the job. Lorraine knew that the saboteurs had likely been warned to flee by a third party, and recalling Hanna telling her about a mystery man she was seeing, as well as considering Hanna's position of trust with confidential information, a dark thought occurred to her. At first, she had assumed the young woman might be seeing a married man, but now she wondered. After speaking with her manager, she walked next door to the boarding house with a sinking feeling. Knocking on the door, it opened after a minute.

"Good morning, Mrs. Dawe, I'm Lorraine from next door at the phone company."

"Oh yes, you're Jack Sparkes daughter, aren't you?"

"Yes, ma'am. I'm helping with trying to locate the two lodgers you had here. Did they by any chance get any phone calls lately?"

"Oh my, yes," Mrs. Dawe answered. "Mr. Kahr was always getting calls from that young woman. I think she was his sweetheart," she confided. "You must know her. I saw them talking several times together down by St. Cyprian's."

"Mrs. Dawe, why do you think I know her?" Lorraine asked.

"Why, because she works next door with you at the telephone company. You mean you didn't know?"

Lorraine's blood ran cold as she thanked the woman and went back next door. She quickly called and spoke with her father as he and McCarty were getting ready to begin a sweep of the areas of the island where they suspected the two spies might be hiding.

After Jack told Matt what Lorraine had said, they decided to go to the young woman's house to confront her with their suspicions, unless perhaps she had already joined the spies in an attempt to escape. Putting on their heavy winter coats, McCarty and Jack got in the company truck and drove until they reached a little grey house on Fourth Street, the last one before a field that led to the Scotia ore track. Just in case the saboteurs were hiding out here, both men checked their guns before proceeding. There had been a light dusting of snow the previous night, and they could see footprints on the frozen ground going to and from the house.

"Jack," Bill whispered, "can you go around back, just in case, while I go knock on the front door?"

"Okay, skipper," he replied, "but no getting shot. If you get hurt, Lorraine would have me for dinner."

Jack walked along the right side of the house and peeked around the back. There was a small window but no back door. An outhouse and what appeared to be an old cistern completed the picture. McCarty called to him through the back window, and Jack went to the front, entering the house.

"The door wasn't locked," McCarty said. "I called out, but no answer. It looks like she packed up and left. Only thing is, she left her purse here, and there's some money in it. What woman leaves without her purse?"

"Bill, it looks like something has been dragged along the side of the house, and I can see some footprints by an old cistern out back."

"You think it's—?" McCarty asked.

"I don't want to think that," the big man answered. "Jesus, I don't want to."

"C'mon, we have to look," said McCarty, heading out and toward the back of the house.

"Look, Bill, here's the drag mark," Jack said, pointing to the ground. "You can see it leads around the corner toward the cistern where the footprints are. And the lid has been disturbed."

He looked at Jack, who already had tears welling up in his eyes, remembering the shy, delicate creature who had shared supper with them in his home, sure now of what he was about to see. McCarty walked to the cistern and lifted the hinged lid.

The covering Kahr had used to drag her had fallen open, exposing the young woman's naked porcelain-white body. She was lying on her side, knees drawn slightly up. She looked almost like a sleeping statue. There was a dark spot near her temple, visible where her long blonde hair had fallen back, and a frozen trickle of blackish blood traced a path along her left cheek. Next to her was an old, battered brown suitcase that had opened and strewn its contents along one wall. McCarty realised he also had tears in his eyes as he gently lowered the lid back down.

Jack stayed at the scene while McCarty took the company truck and went to the main office on Bennett Street. Once there, he spoke with Manager Richard Delaney, and arranged to use the meeting room. Then he called the phone company where Lorraine was on duty and told her that Hanna had been killed. He asked that Lorraine stay at the office there until he came to pick her up after work, as a safety precaution. Then he was put through to Captain Dwyer of the militia. McCarty asked if he could come and meet him at the main office on an urgent matter regarding island security.

o o o

Dwyer arrived within the hour, and in the meantime, McCarty arranged for a man to go with him, to keep the murder scene secure, while he brought Jack back to the office. Once back, they were offered food from the staff cafeteria, but neither man had any appetite. For the first time in his life, Bill McCarty had a desire to have a drink of alcohol.

When everyone was seated in the main office boardroom, McCarty told them about finding the young woman's body and briefly explained his mission, expressing the need for absolute secrecy.

"Lieutenant," Dwyer said to McCarty, "I'll have to run this up the chain soon. How long do you need it kept quiet?"

"Gentlemen," he said, "I need forty-eight hours. After that, you can make a report to your superiors. The spies have had an easy time of it so far, and I feel responsible for my part in that, but I swear that I shall confront and deal with these Nazi bastards within two days."

When the meeting broke up, McCarty walked toward the front door and saw Brenda, the woman who had lost her fiancé in the submarine attack. She gave him a tiny smile as he walked by. *I haven't forgotten my promise,* he said silently as he added Hanna Martin's name and the still unidentified victims of the bridge explosion to August Kahr and Kurt Becher's death list—a list that the spies were going to pay for.

McCarty and Jack went back to Hanna's house to make sure the body removal was carried out with the proper respect and dignity. McCarty descended into the dry cistern himself and covered the woman's body before hoisting it up to Jack and the man who had been securing the site. He then retrieved her belongings and put them in the suitcase. The mood was sombre, and no one spoke as they carried out the grim task.

A green military ambulance with a red cross painted on the side arrived, and the body was placed carefully inside by two attendants, who were given instructions to deliver the remains to the mortuary behind Dr. Templeman's office.

By the time Jack and McCarty left the little house on Fourth Street, it was time to pick Lorraine up from work. McCarty asked to be dropped off at the telephone company, and Jack drove home. Lorraine's eyes were red, and she had obviously been crying. As they left the office, she took hold of McCarty's arm with both hands while they walked and didn't let go until they arrived at Grammer Street.

There wasn't much said during the evening, but they did manage to eat a little. It was agreed that Bill and Jack would resume their plan to patrol the island the following day in any likely areas where they might spot the saboteurs. Around ten o'clock, Jack retired to his bedroom at the back of the house on the ground floor, and after banking the fireplace embers, Lorraine and Bill walked upstairs to their rooms. McCarty was reading by the light of his oil lamp when he heard a very light knock at his door.

"Jack?" he asked. The door opened slowly and quietly. Lorraine stood there in her long white cotton nightgown for a moment without speaking. Bill's heart was in his mouth and every thought and feeling he'd had about her hit him all at once.

Closing the door, she said sadly, "I don't want to be alone tonight." She walked to the bed. He drew back the covers and she got in beside him.

"Your father?"

"He'd understand," she said, turning toward him. There was an aroma of wild rose petals as her beautiful long red hair fell over him. He put his arms around her soft form, and they kissed.

Chapter 26

Bell Island, Friday, July 26, 2018

Bev Adams woke up when her alarm went off at seven a.m. At the same time, Cassie Clarke was getting dressed over at Evelyn's. She tip-toed past a sleeping Tom Crane, who had spent the night on the living-room couch, and went quietly out the back door. She and Kip walked through the low dew-covered grass down toward a large, squarish rust-coloured rock, a leftover from the first surface mining days in the late 1800s. Soon she saw Bev coming across the field to their usual meeting spot.

"Hey there, Kipawoof," she said to the huge Newfoundland. "Hauled any cars across the Tickle lately?"

Kip wagged his tail, raised his massive head, and emitted a sound that was a cross between a foghorn and a bark.

"Shhh, little puppy!" said Cassie. "No waking anyone up, okay? This is supposed to be a secret meeting."

Bev snickered as usual at Cassie's incongruous term of endearment for the huge animal and gave him his favourite rub behind the ears.

"Okay," Cassie said conspiratorially, "so I'm not crazy about the idea of sitting around knitting while Uncle Matt and Mr. Meyer go in the mine and have all the fun."

"Me neither, but I don't want to piss off Grandpa," countered Bev.

"I don't see him getting angry," Cassie said. "Maybe more like disappointed."

"Shit, that's even worse! I'd rather jump off that cliff with no rope than do that!" Bev said, pointing towards the Number Two Cove in the distance.

"Yeah, I know what you mean. How about if we stay by the entrance with Tom but have our backpacks and gear ready, and if they take too long or we start to 'worry,' we go in?"

"That could work. No direct going against orders but standing by and maybe an 'oops we thought you were in trouble' excuse."

"Ask for forgiveness instead of permission," offered Cassie.

Bev laughed. "And all those people who think you're sweet and innocent, when you're really a secret badass."

"Who, me?" said Cassie, smiling angelically as she leaned down to give Kip a kiss on his massive head.

When they walked up to the house, Evelyn was standing by the back door. Kip was now being accompanied by one of their other neighbour's three cats, who all seemed to be drawn to the gentle beast. The dog turned around on the porch until he was satisfied and then hunkered down. The cat wormed its way in between the dog's warm front paws and began to purr.

"Were you having a confidential meeting with the neighbourhood cats, Kip?" Evelyn asked him. The dog looked up but didn't answer. "I hope you're being careful out there," she continued, still looking at him.

"I'm sure Kip is being very careful, Grandma," Cassie said, looking down at the ground.

Bev just nodded vigorously while looking anywhere but at Evelyn.

"Good. I'd hate to see him get in any trouble. Okay, let's have some breakfast before all you adventurers head over to the No. 4 mine," the older woman finished.

o o o

The plan for the day was to look for a fortune in hidden Nazi gold. Whether or not it existed, Jurgen Meyer appeared very serious about it, while Matt and company were looking forward to an exciting adventure more than having any real expectation of finding something more valuable than a great day exploring.

After breakfast at Evelyn's, which included bacon, eggs, pancakes, and homemade blueberry jam, Tom, Matt, and the girls left the house and drove towards the No. 4 mine to meet up with Jurgen Meyer. Tom led the way in his pickup truck, showing Matt a back way along a rough dirt track across the fields to the mine. As they approached it from the side, Matt could see the long half-round tube of moss-and-lichen-covered concrete, looking like a huge water main, slanting downwards before diving beneath the ground toward the ocean beyond. The collar's old-fashioned arched facade at the opening was debossed with the date "1916" and was crumbling in places from age, having weathered over a hundred years of harsh Atlantic winters. In contrast, a new-looking sign at the entrance announced, "Theatre of the Mine."

Meyer was already there, and after a greeting, he looked at Tom. "I haven't seen either Farrell or Hunt around the hotel. If they should show up, will you be alright?"

As Tom Crane unlocked the red wooden door at the mine entrance, he pointed to a four-foot-long toolbox mounted on the side of his truck. "Winchester Model 12 made in 1953.

Five rounds of 12-gauge double-ought buck as fast as I can work the pump."

A rare smile crossed Meyer's features as he adjusted his backpack, nodded approvingly, and prepared to enter the mine with Matt.

"Umm, Grandpa, are you sure me and Cassie shouldn't stand by near that danger sign, just in case something happens and we need to go get help? After all, it's been a lot of years. The mine is probably going to be safe enough, but who knows what sort of condition that tunnel might be in?" Bev asked, looking waif-like.

"Uncle Matt," Cassie sighed dramatically, "that sign even *says* 'danger.' I'd be really worried the whole time you're gone, but I think that, if we could just go part way, to keep an eye out in case of an accident, we'd feel a lot better."

Bev looked up at him, and Matt could swear her big brown eyes were even larger than before, and . . . was that an actual tear in one of them?

Meyer remained impassive, but the girls could sense that Matt was weakening.

"Think of Evelyn," said Cassie quietly.

"And Kathleen," Bev added, sadly.

Matt broke. "Just to where the sign is and no farther. Understand? And if I don't like the lay of the land while we go down, you both march right back here, no questions asked. Got it?"

"Yes, Uncle Matt," Cassie replied softly.

"Yes, Grandpa," Bev added meekly.

They both kept a straight face, but Matt saw the low-five they gave each other as they went to get their gear.

"Didn't need to use the old 'forgiveness instead of permission' routine," Bev said.

"We'll keep it in reserve as a backup just in case," Cassie returned, as they both grinned from ear to ear.

A modern light-switch just inside the outer door illuminated the interior as far back as the four-foot-wide, seven-foot-high, solid-steel door that was inset into a heavy reinforced frame. The door and hinges were rusty, but Tom had some penetrating oil in his tool box, which he applied liberally and let seep in for a few minutes. He had a key for the large modern padlock securing the door, and after removing it, all three men had to pull together before it reluctantly screeched open. The air on the other side was heavy, damp, and still, but there was no blockage. The light behind them didn't penetrate more than twenty feet, and beyond that, it was pitch black. There was evidence that strings of lights had once been mounted on the roof, and a few naked bulbs still hung down, but their power source had long since been removed.

Meyer took a powerful flashlight from his small backpack and turned it on. Matt and the girls switched on the lights attached to the front of their climbing helmets. The scene was similar but ruggedly different from the No. 2 mine tour. The walls were narrower and the roof or "back" was lower. Instead of having an even gravelled surface underfoot, the terrain was rocky and red like the walls and ceiling. Warped and rusted railway tracks ran from the steel door back down as far as they could see.

They began their descent. The lights, bouncing as they walked, created eerie shadows on the rock walls, made even weirder because of the way the iron ore cleaved as it had been blasted, leaving sharp vertical lines looking like the bellows of an accordion.

"Are you guys, okay?" Matt asked the girls as they crunched along the uneven surface.

"All good, Uncle Matt," answered Cassie cheerfully.

"Cool, Grandpa," Bev chimed in. "How about you, Mr. Meyer?

"We are past the formal stage now, Beverly and Cassandra. You may both call me Jurgen," he responded stiffly in his German-accented English. "I know I can seem sometimes a little bit like what you call a stuffed shirt, but I am really quite a lovely fellow."

The other three laughed out loud as Meyer looked puzzled. "What?" This made them laugh more.

About a hundred feet in, they came to the first side tunnels on the left and right of the main shaft. They could see the white painted numbers identifying east from west, still contrasting quite clearly against the rust-red walls. Rail tracks curved off the main line at each intersection they came to, and in several such offshoots, empty, rusted ore cars could be seen, still waiting to be filled after almost sixty years. One car still had a sprag inserted, a three-foot-long steel rod that was thrust through the spokes of a wheel to keep it from rolling away while unattended.

It was cool in the mines, and they all wore light fleece jackets against the chill as they descended further. The hollow echoes of their footsteps were the only sounds that broke the heavy stillness of their surroundings. They had travelled eight hundred feet when Matt judged they were nearly in line with how far they had come from in the opposite way, from the beach, through the natural cave that ran parallel to the mine shaft. About one hundred more feet ahead, the next side shaft on the left was the one that joined the two like the letter 'H' where the danger sign was. The only problem was that, fifty feet in front of them, their lights reflected brightly off of a smooth surface. Water. The main shaft continued to slope downward beyond that to a point in the distance where the water reached the roof.

"Fifty feet," said Meyer. "We have to go through the water about fifty feet before we can get into that side tunnel to the danger sign. Maybe there will not be much water in there."

Matt couldn't speak as they continued walking forward, fixated on the cloudy green expanse of beckoning still water. Fifty feet. How deep would it get? Would the side tunnel be dry or—?

"Uncle Matt, are you okay?" Cassie asked.

"Yes, I'm fine. I just don't like that water."

"Maybe we could get a little boat?" Bev offered.

Meyer was already wading into the water. "I will check."

"Wait!" Matt yelled. "Take this just in case."

Grabbing a rope from his pack, he quickly looped an end around Meyer's waist and tied a bowline knot.

"I'll feel better about you walking into the water, just in case." he said. "We don't know how deep it is or what might be under there."

"I can swim, Matthew, but if it makes you feel better, okay," Meyer responded, and continued wading toward the next side tunnel. By the time he reached it, he was almost up to his waist. Then he disappeared through the opening on his left.

"It's dry in here," Meyer's voice echoed back. "There's a little rise, and the water ends a few feet in. I'll hold the rope at this end now, while you come to me."

Meyer took up the slack on the rope until it was taut and kept it that way as Matt started wading into the cold emerald water. Looking back for a moment, he said, "Cassie and Bev, this is as far as you go. Stay here if you want to, but you can go back up any time. We'll be fine, okay?"

They looked at each other. "We'll wait here. Be careful please."

Looking more confident than he felt, Matt waded along the side, his heart beating faster until he was up to his waist at the level-twenty-two turn off. If he had just followed Meyer, it would have been fine, but noticing one of the little white crosses indicating a long-ago death at a spot a few feet farther down, he took one more step in that direction than Meyer had.

In a second, as if pulled down from below, he dropped and the water closed over his head. He had stepped into a space excavated for a large vertical compressor, which had resided there years before, and the weight of his gear sent him nearly twenty feet to the bottom. His foot became entangled in loops of rusted wiring that had been tossed in when the mine shut down, after the machinery that had provided air for the large drills had been removed.

Meyer felt the rope run through his hands before he could stop it, as Matt dropped into the void. Both girls saw Matt disappear from sight, and without a second thought, they both dropped their backpacks and started splashing toward the spot where they had seen him go under, their helmet lights dancing crazily along the walls and roof.

Meyer came into sight. "Halt!" he yelled. "No further. There could be more voids under the surface!"

They stood there helplessly as he discarded his own backpack, throwing it onto dry ground, untied the rope from himself, and fearlessly dove beneath the surface where Matt had disappeared from view.

Matt tugged against whatever was holding his foot fast below. The rope had also tangled and caught on a small metal bracket fastened to the rock wall above his head. He felt no panic in the moment and was actually quite calm as his recurring nightmare became a reality. There was no going to the surface with his foot caught, and no reaching down to try and free it with the rope jammed. He could almost have seen the humour in the situation, if he wasn't about to drown.

Time slowed down as it had so many years before, and what took only seconds seemed like hours. Strong hands grabbed his arms then and pulled hard. After several tugs, the rusted and rotten wiring disintegrated enough to free his foot. Thinking quickly while still underwater, he reached into his right-hand pocket and pulled out his father's bone-handled knife. He sliced at the rope, and with only two passes, the old knife—kept razor sharp by his father all those years—cut through, and he was released. The last of his air trailed small bubbles as he rose to the surface, being towed by Meyer.

The girls had continued wading toward the area where Matt had disappeared in spite of Meyer's warning. It was taking so long! Bev Adams finally said, "Fuck this," and along with Cassie, was about to dive below the water just as Matt's head and Meyer's both broke the surface. The men waded back to where the girls were standing, just past their knees in water that had gone from benign to deadly in seconds.

"Thanks, Jurgen," Matt said, coughing several times and catching his breath. "That was very brave."

Meyer pointed at Cassie and Bev as they swarmed Matt. "These two were just about to dive in and follow you down. I only stopped them and jumped in because the report I would have to file if you all drowned would be very long and tedious, not to mention the explanations to the local authorities."

"Oh. Well, thanks anyway, I guess," Matt said, exchanging a look with the girls. Cassie and Bev both looked at Meyer with narrowed eyes.

"Ha!" shouted Meyer. "Got you! You all think I am a cold fish, but not only am I a lovely fellow, I am also very humorous. What I said was a joke. A German joke. The best kind," he said, looking innocent.

This time, they all laughed, and that was when Jurgen Meyer became part of the family.

"Okay," Matt said, "I know we're all wet and getting cold, but I have to at least take a quick look by that old danger sign to see if the way beyond is clear. As long as I stick to the route Jurgen took, I'll be fine, so you girls should start heading back up top to dry out. We'll be along shortly."

"No," said Cassie.

"But you're cold and wet. You should—"

"No," said Bev, "and we're not waiting here either. You said yourself the route is safe, as long as we just take the same steps Jurgen did. We're going with you to the danger sign."

Cassie picked up her backpack and slipped it over her slim shoulders. "Let's go," she said.

"They have shown character and courage," Meyer said.

"With a touch of crazy," Matt added proudly, looking at them.

"Not such a bad combination," Meyer finished, as the four waded back into the milky green water.

Bev was the shortest, so Matt kept an extra close eye on her as the water rose a bit above her waist. They entered the side shaft very carefully, avoiding even one more step down the main slope. They began walking toward where it intersected the old company tunnel that had been abandoned in the 1920s. A little way in, they came to the danger sign from so long ago. The ore seam ended abruptly as they squeezed past it and entered the excavated area, following the track that curved back to the left, heading inland.

The walls widened a bit and the roof rose to about fifteen feet. Any suggestion that the girls wait at the danger sign was abandoned without question, and the four began walking forward. The area seemed stable enough, and while they were cold and a bit uncomfortable from being wet, they weren't worried about safety. After a moment, Cassie saw something on the rocky ground.

"What's that?" she asked, pointing to a small object.

Meyer stepped forward. "That's a detonator," he said. "A German military one from the World War Two era."

"The wires are still attached, but the plunger is depressed, either in safe mode or after firing," Matt added.

Meyer reached down and carefully unscrewed the wing nut terminals, disconnecting the wires and rendering the device safe.

"Let's be extra careful anyway," Matt said. "If there is unexploded ordnance, it could be unstable."

Following the wires up ahead around a slight bend, they could see what the detonator had been for. They ran under a pile of rubble that went from floor to ceiling, where an explosion had left tons of rock and dirt, which they had no hope of getting past.

Fatigue and hunger began to set in as they reversed course and headed back down the tunnel, past the danger sign and toward the surface.

"They were here," Meyer voiced. "I know it. They blew that tunnel for a reason."

Matt looked at his watch as they trudged the last hundred feet toward the surface and the bright light that was shining through the big steel door.

"Three o'clock," he said as they emerged.

"Time flies when you're havin' fun," quipped Bev.

"Let's eat," said Cassie.

"*Ja,*" Meyer agreed.

"What the hell happened to you?" contributed Tom Crane as the four wet explorers emerged from the mine collar.

o o o

Matt went back to the Cottages to put on dry clothes and pack up his few belongings in preparation to move into Kathleen's place, while Meyer went to his hotel to shower and change. On his way back to Hibbs Road, he saw Farrell and Hunt having a meal in the hotel restaurant.

They all met back at Evelyn's after supper to discuss the day's events and to decide what to do next. A somewhat less-dramatic version of the water incident was reported for the sake of Evelyn and Kathleen's peace of mind. More emphasis was placed on the fact that it appeared undisputable that the saboteurs from World War Two had intentionally blasted and collapsed the old tunnel. Jurgen Meyer was more convinced than ever that they had done so to cover the hiding place of the cache of gold they had been instructed to hide for Germany. But if they had done that, and the tunnel was collapsed, how would they retrieve it after the war? Tom Crane was quietly thoughtful for a long time, as a second pot of tea and more biscuits was passed around, and then stood up.

"Matt," he said, "I have an idea."

Everyone stopped talking. When Tom Crane had an idea, it was usually a good one and people listened.

"A while ago, when we were at the Keeper's Cafe, you told me about your first walk when you got to Bell Island, down toward the beach near Grebes Nest. Do you remember?"

"Yes," said Matt slowly, "I asked you if you knew anything about that old rusty grating I found while walking."

"Remember what I said?"

"You said it might be from—"

"An old air-ventilator shaft," Tom continued, "and from where you said you saw it, near the end of the airstrip, I think it might be beyond the point in the tunnel where you say that big collapse is. So, if that shaft isn't blocked—"

"We might have a way to get farther into that tunnel!" A wide smile now replaced Meyer's usually impassive expression. "That is indeed very exciting news, Tom."

o o o

By ten o'clock that night, everyone who had been to the mine was exhausted and in need of a good night's sleep. Meyer headed back to the hotel still smiling, and Bev said she thought that maybe they had broken him. Tom headed home but would be available for a further adventure at a moment's notice. Cassie and Evelyn bedded down for the night as a light, cooling rain began to fall, which meant that Kip would spend a rare night inside, his massive bulk hunkered down on the hallway floor at the back of the house, just past Cassie's room, where his indoor bed was a child's size mattress.

Matt had already put his suitcase contents away in two drawers at Kathleen's house, having been upgraded from only one, as she described it, "for good behaviour." Lastly, he put his toothbrush in the holder next to hers. They both laughed as he performed the ceremonial placement.

"Whatever is this world coming to?" she asked rhetorically.

"Don't know," he replied, "but something good, I reckon."

"Yup," Kathleen agreed. "So, about your little water adventure. Now tell me what really happened."

Matt reflected for a moment on the near tragedy, and the knife his father had kept all those years. In a roundabout way, the man he'd never really known had reached out from the past and helped to save his life. Then he recounted every detail of the entire ordeal, leaving nothing out.

"I'm no shrink," she said, "but you don't seem any more traumatised for having this horrific nightmare from the past come true. Why?"

"I don't know for sure," he answered, "but I've faced the worst now and come through okay. I think my fear of water is gone, so it might actually be the best thing that ever happened to me."

"The best?" she asked, raising an eyebrow.

"Well," he clarified, reaching for her, "maybe the second best."

Later, he got up for a glass of water. In the small kitchen, he looked out the window, north toward Conception Bay. The rain had stopped, and he could see clouds scudding across a full moon. He thought about this whole incredible, unexpected adventure, his relationship with his old family, as well as his attachment to this new one. Now, with this freedom from a lifetime of fear, on so many levels, he knew he was finally becoming the best version of himself. He headed back to the warm bed and the woman he had only met the week before but had known for a thousand years.

Chapter 27

Bell Island, Saturday, November 21, 1942

Kurt Becher was hungry. The events of the past days had made him anxious and fearful of being caught. The drinking water was all but gone now, and they had no food supplies left. He had seen fishermen coming and going near their boats down by the water, close to the cabin they were hiding in, and Kahr had joked that Kurt should go ask them if they could spare a fish or two. Becher didn't know what to make of August Kahr anymore. One day, he would seem so open and caring, but the next, he would be cold and distant. When Becher asked what had happened with Hanna Martin, he'd said everything was fine and that the girl had promised to keep quiet about her involvement with the two. Although he didn't question it, Becher thought he was not telling the whole truth.

From their vantage point, Kahr could see a grand-looking house at the east end of Lance Cove. For a while, he had considered stealing in during the night to take some food but abandoned the idea after seeing a large dog seemingly guarding the premises and trailing after a woman any time she came outside the dwelling. With a touch of irony, and unknown to the spies, the dog had been a pet of the radio operator on the ore ship *PLM 27*, which Kahr had helped the submarine U-518 torpedo. The animal had managed to swim to shore after the sinking, even helping its owner to safety through burning oil and debris. When the sailor moved on, he had been unable to take the dog with him. The animal had unofficially adopted the woman who had cared for it, applying salve and comfort for the burns it had suffered.

August Kahr looked at Becher, noting that he would likely not last another day without food or drink. Meanwhile, through it all, Kahr kept his eye on the prize. Another day and a half, and it would all be over. The submarine would arrive to pick them up, and the final part of his plan would play out. He still needed Becher for now, so there was nothing else to do except go and find some supplies.

"Kurt," Kahr began, "we have to eat if we are going to make it through to tomorrow night. There is still work to do, getting down into the mine to set the detonator. It's time for us to leave here."

"But it's broad daylight, August. Won't we be seen?" Becher replied, afraid.

"Possibly, my dear fellow," he answered, "but there are other company motorcycles out there, and I don't think the whole island is looking for us just yet. Anyone who might see us will probably think nothing of it."

Kahr actually knew it was a serious gamble, but there was no need to frighten this rabbit any more that it already was.

Continuing, he said, "We passed a small store on our way here, and I think we should pay it a visit."

"You mean just walk in and—"

"And buy some food and drink, of course. What else? Be bold, my friend, and no one will think twice about us."

There was nothing really to pack up, so the two put on their now almost-empty rucksacks and left the cabin. The motorcycle was pulled back out of the bushes where it had been stashed, and both men mounted up to leave. At the top of Lance Cove Beach Road, there was a crossroads and a little house with a small storefront. A sign over the door announced it simply as "Kelly's." In smaller letters underneath, it said, "B. Kelly, prop."

o o o

As Kahr and Becher entered the store, a little bell hung over the door chimed, and they caught the flavourful aroma of some kind of stew coming from the back. A tiny old woman walked out, slowly wiping her hands on a flowered apron and smiling pleasantly.

"Hello, b'ys," she said in a strong voice that belied her eighty-plus years." Seeing Becher's rifle, she said, "Ye must be from the barracks, are ye?" referring to the building where the Coastal Defence Force militia personnel were housed.

"No, ma'am," Kahr replied. "We're from the mines, out doing some survey work for the company. That smells like a nice pot of stew you've got going back there."

"You're not a Newfoundlander," she stated categorically. "You must be from up in Canada, or is it over in the States you're after coming from? All kinds comes here to work in the mines," she said, not waiting for an answer. "Would ye be wanting a drop of stew now, along with a nice dumpling?"

"Yes, please, ma'am, if it's not too much trouble."

"No trouble, sure, but I have to charge you fifteen cents a plate. It's not easy getting by since my Raymond died. Of course, that was thirty year ago, so I s'pose I'll be alright," she finished with a wan smile.

Becher and Kahr ate well, sitting back in her kitchen, and had hot tea to finish it off, along with some sweet biscuits the old woman had made—her husband's favourite she said.

Later, Kahr figured that Becher probably did it to impress him, or maybe it had something to do with how his family had been bombed in Germany, but as the old woman reached out to take away his empty plate, Kurt Becher produced a knife, and with a quick thrust, it entered the woman's abdomen up to the hilt. She grabbed his hand in both of hers and looked at him, uncomprehending. She opened her mouth to say something but nothing came out, and then she collapsed, her wrinkled face turning parchment white as her life slipped away. The hooked rug under the table soaked up her blood.

Kurt Becher looked in disbelief at his own hand, still holding the knife, as Kahr finally asked casually, "Was that your first?"

Becher could only nod.

"Alright," said Kahr. "It's okay; don't worry. I don't think it was necessary, but you just did what you thought you needed to do, right?"

No answer. He just kept staring at the body.

"Kurt! Pay attention. We have to put her somewhere so no one will miss her for a while."

Woodenly, Becher obeyed. They dragged the old woman's body, on the hooked rug, across the linoleum to the basement door and all the way down the stairs. By the time they put her in the coal bin and closed up the shop, they thought no one would know they were ever there. Both of their rucksacks felt warm on their backs from the stew they had put in canning jars, along with an assortment of treats and bottled drinks from the shelves. As a bonus, Kahr had found the old woman's near-full bottle of rum and taken it along, but not before they each took a long pull.

As Becher began to feel a warm glow in his belly, he started to feel good, marvellous in fact, and held onto Kahr tightly as they roared away up the hill to Lance Cove Pond, and from there, on back trails towards the north side of the island.

The remains of small rough-built shacks called "tilts," where workers commuting from outport communities had slept during the week in the early days of mining, still dotted the landscape under the cover of spruce and fir trees here and there. The two spies holed up in one of them, waiting for nightfall, when they would take a calculated risk to ride east toward Grebes Nest and their secret cave, where the final part of August Kahr's deadly plan would unfold.

o o o

Saturday morning on Grammer Street found Lorraine Sparkes and Bill McCarty still holding each other. For both Lorraine and McCarty, though he was twenty-two, it had been their first time. As they woke up, a look passed between them that was both a loving greeting and a sad farewell. As she got up unselfconsciously and stood before him to put on her nightgown, he couldn't help reaching for her. She gave a tiny smile, shook her head, and silently opened his door, going back to her own room.

Jack was cooking a large breakfast by the time they came downstairs, and McCarty was ravenous.

"Nothing wrong with your appetite this morning," Jack observed as McCarty reached for more toast. And you," he said, pointing at Lorraine and pausing, "eat up for Christ's sake or you'll waste away. Now, what fun are we going to get up to this morning?"

Anxious to change the subject, McCarty tore his eyes from Lorraine. "We need a boat. We're going to take a look along the coastline. They received shipments of explosives and other supplies by submarine, and they would have had to store it all somewhere. They also must have had a small boat to rendezvous with it. I know there must be some place close to the water that they used to help set this all up.

"Okay, skipper, I'll give a call over to Joseph Bunce. He's got a nice little twenty-foot motor dory we can use to run around the island and have a look-see, and I trust him all the way."

Jack got on the telephone and spoke with Bunce, who lived down near the beach in the area known as the "Front" on the south side of the island, facing Portugal Cove. Although McCarty was sure the saboteurs had their base of operations on the north side, they would cruise that way around the island from the south where Bunce's boat was located.

As McCarty and Jack prepared to leave, Lorraine walked straight up to Bill and took both his hands in hers.

"Be careful." She kissed him lightly on the mouth.

As she stepped back, all three exchanged looks, and after a slightly uncomfortable silence, Jack said, "What about me?"

"You," she said, raising a little fist at her father, "you just watch out for him." Then she hugged her father fiercely and walked away.

The mild weather was holding, and the old truck started right away. As Jack turned onto East Track Road toward the Front, he broke the silence.

"I'm not going to ask what happened last night, because you're so friggin' honest, you'd probably tell me."

Silence. A mile passed.

"You love her," Jack stated. It wasn't a question.

There was a long pause. "It's difficult, Sparky. I promised myself to someone already," he continued, "for no other reason than I felt obligated. I was a damn fool and now. . . ."

"And now," Jack said quietly, "because you're a gentleman, you'll deny your own happiness, because that's what men like you do. But you're in love with my Lorraine. I can see it plain as day."

"Yes."

It was quiet for a while.

Jack eventually held out his big right hand. "Alright then, b'y, no more to be said, I s'pose."

McCarty grasped Jack's hand and squeezed it tight.

The dirt road down Beach Hill was a steep S-curve and very narrow. At the bottom of the hill, Jack turned right and parked the truck. Looking up, they could see the two guns of the First Coastal Defence Battery standing guard high above on the cliff.

Jack did the introductions, and Bunce said simply, "I knew the Fillier and the King families," speaking of the Bell Island men who had been killed on the torpedoed SS *Rose Castle*.

No further explanation was necessary for Bunce's willingness to help in the search for the two saboteurs who had been complicit in the Bell Islander's deaths and the deaths of so many others.

Bunce primed the dory's little three-horsepower Acadia motor and cranked the flywheel over by hand. It caught on the second try and soon the classic low-revolution putt, putt, putt sound could be heard. Even though the weather was holding mild, all three men were dressed warmly against the breeze as they motored west toward Dominion Pier. McCarty hadn't seen this close view of the island from the water until now, and he marvelled at the rugged beauty of the high cliffs, with their bands of red hematite layered with sandstone and shale.

As the three men followed the coastline, it became apparent that no submarine would dare to surface on this side of the island except to attack quickly and then submerge.

Dropping off supplies to the saboteurs would not have happened anywhere near here.

A short distance farther west, past the Dominion, they slowed down at Scotia Pier and McCarty could see where a torpedo had missed the boat it was targeting and destroyed a portion of the beach and part of the support structure for the ore-delivery system. Men were working to repair the damage, and McCarty did not envy them the task. A building close to shore had all its windows blown out from the concussive force of the blast, which had shaken the earth, waking up a large portion of the island's population. Jack signalled Bunce and they continued on. As they approached Lance Cove, they saw two men there tending to their boat, a larger one with heavy-looking nets on its deck.

"Hello, Sparky," hailed one of them, and McCarty wondered, not for the first time, if there was anyone on the island that the man did not know.

o o o

Jack introduced Bill to Gerald Shea and Harold Dean. They exchanged nods of greeting to him and Joe Bunce, who they were already acquainted with. It became apparent that McCarty's mission on the island might be the worst-kept secret of the war, as Harold Dean stated, matter-of-factly, "You're that navy man from up in Canada. Are ye lookin' for them German fellas s'posed to be hidin' out on the island?"

Bill and Jack looked at each other, and Jack shrugged his shoulders as if to say, *Well, it wasn't me who told them.*

McCarty just nodded. "Yes, have you seen anything unusual or suspicious?"

"Seen a couple of fellas hunkered down in that little cabin up there," Gerald answered, pointing with his pipe up the hill a ways toward a run-down-looking dwelling. "Didn't think nothing of it till now. Left this morning on a company motorcycle, they did."

"And you're sure it was two men?" Jack asked.

"Aye, and one of them had a rifle strapped on his back," Harold replied. "Pulled that motorcycle out of them bushes and went on up there," he continued, indicating north up from the beach toward Lance Cove Road.

"Joe, can you stay here with the boat for a bit while we go have a look at that cabin?" McCarty asked.

"Yes, sir," said Joe Bunce. "I'll just sit here and tell a few lies with the b'ys. What's in that little flask you got there, Gerald?"

Jack and McCarty walked quickly up the hill toward the run-down cabin, which was little more than a shack. They could see where the bushes on the side had been pushed down by the motorcycle. The door had no lock, and they entered warily just in case any surprises had been left behind. There were boot prints in the dust, and an empty bean tin was lying on the floor.

"Food," said McCarty. "They've been on the run now for days, and they'll be needing some supplies. We should cut this short and go get the truck. We'll come back this way and check any shops to see if they've bought anything."

"Okay," Jack agreed, "but if they're on a motorcycle, we're probably better off on them too."

McCarty agreed. The trip back to the ferry dock didn't take long. Joe Bunce ran the little Acadia "make and break" motor (so called because the one-cylinder design was so simple it was said that you could make any part that might break yourself) flat out. McCarty thanked Joe for his help and knew better than to insult him by offering any money for his fuel and his time. Joe agreed to meet them Sunday morning with his boat over by the Number Two Cove on the north side of the island, where they would patrol west down the shore, hoping to find where the spies might be hiding out, perhaps in one of the earlier-era abandoned-mine-tunnel openings on the beach that stretched from there all the way down to the sea stack near Grebes Nest.

Bill and Jack first drove home to Grammer Street to have lunch before continuing. Lorraine happily cooked up some sausages and left-over potatoes for the two men, and they all sat at the kitchen table to eat. Heartache, on the surface at least, seemed to have given way to acceptance as both she and McCarty talked easily while Jack looked on.

After their meal, Bill and Jack washed the dishes and then headed over to the corner of Ten Commandments and West Mines Roads, where the company transport was kept. Jack signed out two powerful Royal Enfields, like the one McCarty had seen August Kahr riding. It was not Jack Sparkes' favourite mode of transport, but he was capable enough on the two-wheeled "contraption," as he called it.

o o o

The men rode past the little house where Hanna Martin's body had been found. They continued on past it and into the field beyond, driving south alongside the Scotia tramway, taking the same bumpy route Becher and Kahr had taken down to Lance Cove Road. There they turned west again until reaching the turn-off down to Lance Cove itself. On the right, at the crossroads, was a little corner store called "Kelly's," where the saboteurs would most likely have gone for supplies, being the closest shop to the cabin where they had stayed. Bill and Jack pulled up in front of the shop and noticed motorcycle tracks in the mud outside, which then continued on up the hill that led to Lance Cove Pond.

Dismounting their motorcycles, they walked up to the front door, which was closed but not locked, meaning the shop should be open for business. Walking inside, the little bell rang, letting the owner know someone was entering.

Jack waited a moment and called out, "Mrs. Kelly, it's Jack Sparkes! Are you back in the kitchen?"

No answer.

"Hello, Bridget? Are you there?"

Still nothing.

"I don't like it," McCarty said and started cautiously toward the kitchen, drawing his Colt .45 from its holster.

Jack backed him up, Webley revolver in hand. They went past the front counter and into the kitchen beyond, where they smelled the aroma of beef stew. On the worn and cracked blue-linoleum floor, they noticed a few drops of blood leading toward the coal-cellar door. Unspoken, Jack kept an eye on the door while McCarty had a thorough look around the small single-story building. Finding no other sign of life, he then opened the cellar door while Jack kept his Webley at the ready. The stairs creaked as Jack then preceded him, while he covered the rear.

She was on her back and looked almost childlike, so small and frail in death. Jack reached down and gently closed her watery blue, unseeing eyes. McCarty went back upstairs, pulled a cover from the day bed in one corner of the kitchen, and brought it back downstairs to cover the woman.

"Bill, there was no point at all to that," Jack said in disbelief. "I know we're enemies and that, but Jesus Almighty, she was just an old woman. What could she have done to hurt them?"

"Nothing," McCarty replied. "Absolutely nothing. Look at the plates and the mugs on the table. She even fed them. There is no kind of excuse for this, war or not."

Silence followed. They took the front door key from a hook in the kitchen and locked up as they left, putting the key under a rock out front for the authorities. The old woman had no telephone, so they would report the murder later, but in the meantime, the cellar was cool enough, and they had work to do. Getting back on the motorcycles, the two men rode up Clement's Hill, following the saboteurs' tire tracks in the mud.

As they rode past Lance Cove Pond, there was a slight depression in the muddy path for at least a hundred yards, and about two inches of water had collected. They lost the track and could not see it again on the other side. Somewhere within this area, they were sure the spies were holed up. The low trees provided excellent cover, and it was getting dark.

"Tomorrow," Jack said. "We'll come back tomorrow, Bill. Those fuckers could be anywhere, and it won't do us any good to stay out here tonight."

"How many more dead before we get them, Jack? How many more?"

Fifty yards away in the deep, wet grass, Kurt Becher had the crosshairs of his scoped Mauser pointed at Bill McCarty's back. One gentle squeeze of the trigger would remove a fist-sized portion of his spinal column.

"No," whispered Kahr. "If you take one, the other will be warned and know exactly where we are. Tomorrow is too important, even if it would be almost worth it. Put the rifle down."

Reluctantly, Becher lowered the weapon as they heard the motorcycles rev and watched as the men rode away north along the muddy track.

When McCarty and Jack reached Middleton Avenue, they stopped.

"Jack, I want you to do a quick swing by here tomorrow morning and check for more tracks." He pointed at the ground where it joined the main road. "If you see another set besides ours, we'll know they got this far and won't need to waste time searching back that way. Joe Bunce and I will scour the shore from the Number Two Cove down to Grebes Nest."

"Good plan," Jack replied. "How about if I ask that pilot Patrick Kelly if he wants to join me? I know he wants to help, and he knows what we're after."

"Okay, let's give him a call tonight and—Wait a minute. You don't think he's related to Bridget Kelly, do you?"

"No, it's a different Kelly," Jack said. "Her husband died years ago. Bridget was all alone, b'y," he said sadly.

After dropping off the motorcycles and driving home in Jack's company truck, the two men were nearly exhausted. Lorraine put on the tea, and Jack had a large rum. He looked at Bill, who shook his head as usual, declining the offer. Phone calls were made, arranging for the disposition of Mrs. Kelly's remains and for the police to open a file, but the investigation would be held in abeyance for the time being, as Hanna Martin's had been. McCarty called Patrick Kelly, who said he would be happy to volunteer for the next day in whatever capacity they needed him.

Lorraine and Bill stayed up for a long time after Jack went to bed, just enjoying each other's company. After the embers from the fireplace were reduced to a soft red glow, they both went upstairs to their respective rooms after one last kiss. Sunday was going to be a very eventful day for all.

Much later, after they were sure no one was lying in wait for them, Kahr and Becher emerged from their hiding place.

The motorcycle roared to life, and they followed the same path their enemies had. With the dim louvered light, they reached Middleton Avenue, looking carefully for any sign of a patrol. Seeing none, Kahr turned east, back toward the area of the No. 4 mine. Just before they reached it, he rode down almost to the cliff and hid the motorcycle in the bushes. Then they scaled down the steep path to the beach, carefully made their way around the point to Grebes Nest and entered their secret tunnel. It was now five a.m., Sunday morning.

Conception Bay, Sunday, November 22, 1942

U-184 slipped silently into Conception Bay on Sunday morning at six thirty a.m. local time. Her huge banks of lead acid batteries were fully charged, and she had easily avoided the Corvette HMCS *Drumheller* that was patrolling the waters of the bay. Kapitanleutnant Gunther Dangschat would like nothing better than to send the warship to the bottom, but that was not his mission. Nor were the fat ore boats sitting at anchor still unprotected. Their mission was only to pick up the two agents, who were likely a part of the vast operation that his fellow senior officers quietly discussed amongst themselves when no lesser ranks were listening. There were rumours of vast resources of valuables being cached by trusted agents in places known only to them, and then being escorted back to Germany, with their maps showing the location of the hidden wealth. The submarine rounded the west end of Bell Island where the depths were shallow, settling down quietly on the sandy bottom near the "Bell" sea stack and waiting patiently for the night.

Chapter 28

Bell Island, Saturday, July 27, 2018

Hunt had reported to Farrell that Matt McCarty was no longer staying at the Bell Island Cottages and was now with Kathleen Ryan at the house next door to the older woman and the young red-haired girl. Right now, he was tasked with watching both houses from a half block away on Backview Street.

After breakfast at Evelyn's, attended by all, Cassie went to the usual place out back by the big rock to meet with Bev. As he watched number 23 Hibbs Road, Hunt was surprised to see a man arrive that he recognised from the hotel: a fellow guest that Farrell had said looked like a cop.

Then he saw Beverly Adams walking through the field and heading toward the place where the red-haired girl was waiting. Hunt was so tired of being told what to do. It seemed like all he ever did was wait. For what? A bunch of gold to suddenly materialise out of thin air? That guy from the hotel probably *was* a cop.

His twisted mind began imagining the worst. It seemed like everything was falling apart. Almost everything. Maybe the dream of gold was fading, but those girls . . . they were right there in front of him. As he watched them huddled close together, he made up his mind.

THE SECRET OF BELL ISLAND

Hunt put the binoculars down and drove right out into the field beyond Hibbs Road—driven now by paranoia and twisted desire. He called Farrell's number, and it went to voicemail.

"Hey, Farrell!" Hunt yelled at the mobile device. "I quit! So you and your imaginary gold can go fuck yourselves! By the way, that asshole at the hotel you thought looked like a cop? Well, he just showed up here for a visit with your pal McCarty!" With that, Hunt hung up, dropped his phone on the front seat, got out of the car, and turned toward the girls.

Cassie saw the man walking quickly toward them, with one hand behind his back. It took a moment for her to remember where she had seen him before. He was closer now. At the museum? The gift shop maybe? Then realisation hit!

Seeing the change in Cassie's expression, Bev turned and saw the big man now lumbering toward them. With no hesitation, she bent down and grabbed a fist-sized chunk of iron ore, as Cassie yelled, and they both saw the long-bladed hunting knife in his hand.

As he reached Cassie and grabbed her wrist, Hunt wondered what she was yelling. It didn't make sense. *She's panic stricken,* he thought, even more excited now. *What is she screaming? Trip? Slip?*

The dog weighed an easy hundred and sixty-five pounds—heavy even for a Newfoundland. Coming up behind Cassie at a full gallop, as if in his prime, Kip launched into the air and struck Hunt dead centre. The result was shocking. The collision was the last thing Hunt remembered for some time.

After a while, through a blurry haze, he felt pain and pressure on his chest and thought he had perhaps suffered a heart attack or maybe tripped and collided with that big square boulder.

The sound of Cassie yelling Kip's name had carried to the house, and soon everyone was standing by the girls, who were looking down at Hunt, with Bev still holding her rock aimed at his head. The man appeared to be breathing, but shallowly, since Kip refused to get off him. When the man moaned, the dog made a low foghorn growl.

Soon, an ambulance arrived on scene, and it took both Cassie and Bev using their most soothing voices and scratching Kip behind the ears before he reluctantly gave up his prize and let the paramedics take Hunt away. The RCMP had also been called and were attending as well. Kip seemed none the worse for wear as he escorted the gurney to the ambulance and gave one good loud bellow as it drove away. Inside, the semi-conscious man shivered fearfully at the sound.

Matt and the girls gave statements, but Matt refrained from telling the whole story. Cassie mentioned that she and her uncle Matt had seen Hunt at the mine museum in the company of another man, but left it at that. The authorities would soon connect Hunt to Farrell.

One officer had accompanied the ambulance to the hospital where Hunt would be treated, to make sure he was unable to leave while criminal charges were prepared. The other officer who had taken their statements and secured the knife as evidence took photos of Cassie's wrist before leaving. It was fine but a bit red from being grabbed.

Bev's parents were contacted and told what happened. Her father came by Evelyn's house to satisfy himself that his daughter was all right, but he had enough trust in Tom, Matt, and the rest to let her stay there for the rest of the day.

Matt looked at Meyer. "Today has been crazy, Jurgen. I don't think we should do any exploring now. The girls have been through a big shock, so let's regroup and see about going back at it tomorrow."

"Agreed," said Meyer. "We have to let the authorities connect things for themselves, rather than have them wonder why we know so much, but no doubt the police will be on their way to the hotel soon."

As Meyer left, Matt walked back into the living room and told the group it would be a good idea to relax for the rest of the day and leave any more exploring until Sunday, if they felt up to it. Reluctantly, Tom and the girls agreed.

Matt continued, "Today could have gone bad, real bad, and if anything ever happened to you—"

"We're okay, Uncle Matt, honest," Cassie replied. "Between the little puppy and Bev with her pet rock, I knew we'd be fine."

"Yeah, don't worry, Grandpa. We got *your* back too. Me and that there little puppy."

○ ○ ○

Later, there was a gentle knock on Jurgen Meyer's door, and he made an uncharacteristic mistake by assuming it was the daily cleaning service. As he opened the door, the attack was swift, and the jab of the hypodermic quickly made him go limp. Farrell's search of the room was thorough but yielded nothing. He wasn't sure how this man fit in with McCarty's ragtag army of misfits, and unfortunately, he didn't have the time to do a proper interrogation. Now that Hunt had given up. it meant that Farrell had to move up his timeline for getting the gold, but at least he was pretty sure now where it was.

He dragged Farrell's unconscious form to the closet, bound his wrists and ankles with heavy-duty zip ties, and placed duct tape over his mouth. He considered killing him, but the man had not directly given him reason to. Reaching into his pocket and tossing a coin, he let fate decide. Meyer would live. With that, he left the room, placing a Do Not Disturb sign on the door handle.

Chapter 29

Bell Island, Sunday, November 22, 1942

Morning broke clear in the bright winter sunshine, while the shadowed cliffs on the north side of the island and its abandoned ore shafts revealed a layer of frost. As the sun rose, the frost would dissipate rapidly, bringing another day of reprieve from the real winter yet to come. Soon there would be ice in the bay, and the North Atlantic winds would drive deep snow drifts into tiny crystals that cut the air like specks of glass. When the conditions were right, sleet storms would cripple the island, layering ice everywhere, the weight of it bringing down power lines, turning fir trees and juniper bushes into ice sculptures, and making walking anywhere treacherous.

"Here, skipper," Jack said, "have another hotcake or two; there's still plenty left."

"I'm stuffed, Sparky. Another one and I won't be able to walk."

"Well, you won't soon be gettin' fat, that's for friggin' sure," Jack joked.

Lorraine smiled, being intimately acquainted now with McCarty's tall, slim, wiry frame, knowing there was little likelihood that Bill McCarty would ever be overweight. She looked lovingly at his handsome face, with his jet-black hair combed straight back, and knew there would be no other for her. She accepted that fact. She had no regrets about what they had done and for McCarty's part, he did not view their love making as a betrayal of his bride to be. How could anything so perfect be wrong? It was a moment in time that was fated, separate from the world and every other good and bad thing in it. Another lifetime compressed into one glorious night, and it would always be so.

"Jack, you're going to pick up Pat Kelly and check for motorcycle tracks, right? I'm meeting up with Joe Bunce to check the cliffs and shore for any sign of Kahr and Becher by those old ore tunnels. Then we meet up at the beach by the sea stack near Grebes Nest."

"Right, skipper," said Jack. "I'll drop you off at the Number Two Cove and carry on from there."

"Is there anything I can do to help?" asked Lorraine. "I feel like I'm doing nothing here."

"We need you here by the phone," McCarty replied. "I don't know what's going to happen today, and we may need to call and have you relay information, or even get help if needed. So, you can be valuable to the mission by staying right where you are. Okay?"

"All right," she responded, "as long as you're not just trying to protect me."

"I am," he said, "but not by keeping you at home. You'd probably be safer over at the telephone company, but if something happens, I don't want you distracted by anything else. I don't want to frighten you, but those men are animals, and I have no idea what they might do next. So, you stay here, lock the doors, and hold onto this."

Reaching into a pocket, he took out his backup two-inch snub-nosed Colt Detective Special revolver. He thumbed the latch back and swung open the cylinder to reveal six .38

Special cartridges, then closed it gently until it latched with an audible click. "Hold the gun in your right hand like this," he said, demonstrating. "Steady it and support the weight with your left." He quickly explained about how to use the sight, and then handed the gun to her butt first.

"It's loaded and will fire if you squeeze the trigger all the way. You don't need to cock the hammer back first. Finger never on the trigger unless you're ready to fire, and never point it at anything you aren't prepared to shoot."

She took the gun without saying anything and put it in her apron pocket. "Anything else?"

"Yes," he said. "Thanks to Jack and his camera, you know what those two look like. If either one of them shows up here and tries to get in, take out the gun, point it at them, and shoot to kill. Don't argue. Don't reason. Don't say anything. Just start shooting at the biggest part of their body, in the centre, and don't stop until the gun is empty."

At nine a.m., McCarty and Jack left the house and drove to the Number Two Cove. Both men had full rucksacks with food, water, and flashlights, along with extra ammunition if it came to that. Bunce's motor dory was pulled nose up on the beach as McCarty got out of the truck and greetings were exchanged.

While U-184 sat quietly on the ocean's shallow, sandy bottom off the western end of Bell Island, and Bill McCarty prepared to scout the north side of the island along the cliffs, August Kahr was in the final stages of his own plan to make good his escape from both the island and the war. The last detail would fall into place tonight when the submarine arrived to pick them up at eleven p.m.

"Kurt, it's time to set the detonator for the big surprise tomorrow morning," Kahr said.

The two spies had made it safely into the natural cave opening on the beach. They hiked deep inside, past their boat, carefully avoiding the ten-foot-wide open void that dropped deeply to an underground river that ran toward the sea. They arrived at the tool and machinery room, surrounded by the crates of gold and other supplies, including more firearms and two complete German military uniforms to show the authorities should they be caught, hopefully to save them from being hanged as spies. At this stage, Kahr thought there was very little chance of that happening. He only had to make it through this one more night.

August Kahr placed a portable detonator, blasting caps, and wiring into his rucksack. Then they made their way back, avoiding the muddy-looking sinkholes, and crossed over to the No. 4 mine shaft just beyond the danger sign. The area had been stable for a long time, but the sign fortunately continued to keep people out. It wouldn't do for anyone to discover the old steel-doored room and get curious about what might be on the other side. Being Sunday, the spies didn't need to worry about being disturbed as they went about their business.

When the men reached the main shaft, they turned left, past a large compressor standing upright in a newly excavated twenty-foot-deep hole. The installation had cost the life of a miner, crushed by the piece of machinery when a holding strap broke. In keeping with tradition, a little white cross on the ribbed wall above it marked the spot where he had died.

The regular strings of bare light bulbs were not on, but they both wore mining hats with a headlamp, and wore ten-hour battery packs on their belts. Kahr took out the rum bottle he had taken from the store where Becher had killed the woman. He offered it to Becher, who although unaccustomed to alcohol, took a long pull. They hadn't talked about it, and Becher hadn't volunteered anything. In fact, both had barely said anything at all, but now Kahr spoke as a more recent idea he had been toying with solidified. He made a decision.

"Kurt, why did you kill the old woman?" Kahr asked. "She seemed so harmless and was being quite helpful."

"I could tell she was going to report us to the authorities. She was the enemy and had to die, and besides, you always get to do the killing," blurted Becher. "Those two by the bridge were yours, and I know you killed Hanna Martin too."

"I am glad that you could see what I could not, and kept us safe," Kahr replied. "Here. Have another drink."

Becher was mollified then, and taking another big swallow, began to feel more like an equal. He had gained some power.

The loud echoes of their boots on the rocky ground did nothing to scare the rats. They were used to people and even followed the men for long stretches, hoping for a handout, as the miners often gave them the corner of a slice of their bread that was too dirty to eat. Kahr wasn't bothered by them, but Becher was uncomfortable when he saw them in his light beam. He picked up rocks and threw them, but the rats either did not understand or did not care what he was doing. Once when he reached down for a rock, he'd nearly picked a rat up by mistake. After that, he just tried not to think about them.

When the men were a half mile down, Kahr stopped suddenly and faced Becher.

"Kurt," he said, "I have been thinking. I am noticing a difference in you, a big difference, and I must say I am quite impressed. You seem more sure of yourself, very confident, and I have to tell you . . . I think it's a very attractive quality."

Becher felt pride at the compliment and his heart beat a little faster, thinking that Kahr might have some feelings for him after all.

"Thank you, August," he replied humbly, although positively preening inside. "I am just trying to do my duty."

"I have an idea," Becher said, "but I would have to place my complete trust in you to do something that I think you are now ready for. I would not blame you though, if you did not feel up to the task."

"August," Becher replied, "I would do anything for you, and for the fatherland. Just tell me. I think you know how I feel."

"I do, Kurt, and when we finish our mission, I think we should discuss these feelings more fully. But right now, how would you like to go and put a bullet into those two swine who have been trying to find us? Why don't we let the hunters become the hunted?"

Becher began to nod even before Kahr finished speaking.

"I need to complete this part of the plan," Kahr continued, pointing at the rucksack with the dynamite, "but you may have the honour of taking care of that big responsibility. I think they are close to discovering where we are, and unless we deal with them now, I don't think we will be able to rendezvous with our friends tonight."

Becher was nearly in tears at having Kahr place that much trust in him, and while he was nervous about the prospect, the alcohol, which he was not used to, was having the effect Kahr had been hoping for. He choked out his answer in the affirmative, and Kahr gave him details on how he should accomplish the goal. Kahr was a master of manipulation, but of course, it was easy to dupe a man in love, especially one not wise in the ways of the world.

After one more long pull from the rum bottle, with his heart soaring, Becher fairly ran back towards the tunnel they had come from and back to the beach where he would climb the path to the clifftop. From there, he would take the motorcycle to Grammer Street, along with the Wehrmacht Model P08 Luger and several magazines of 9x19mm Parabellum ammunition, which was already in his rucksack. He would kill anyone he found at the little house on Grammer Street. If he was lucky, maybe both men and the girl too.

○ ○ ○

Kahr continued downslope, whistling as he crunched along in the echoing darkness, lit only by his small dancing beam of light. Reaching level 126, he took five sticks of regular dynamite from his rucksack and placed them on a small overhead rock shelf. He took out the blasting caps and pushed them into the soft sticks, running the wires down the rock wall and along the ground to the rail tracks. He arranged several chunks of iron ore to act as an anchor to steady the detonator, and as he had done with the previous blast, he slowly pulled back the charging piston on the detonator and gave it a half turn.

August Kahr stood back to admire his work. On Monday morning, the car carrying the first shift of miners down to this level would run into the device, pushing the piston into the detonator. The resulting explosion would trigger every other stick of pure nitro they had hidden in the support pillars over the past year.

Satisfied now, Kahr began the long hike back to prepare for the meeting with U-184. Unfortunately for the submarine captain, officers, and crew, they would not be heading back to Germany tonight. It would be interesting to see if Becher returned. If he met up with the enemy, the fool would either be extremely lucky and survive the encounter, maybe even killing one or more, or they would shoot him on sight, saving Kahr the trouble of killing Becher himself later.

o o o

After Jack dropped off McCarty, he drove west until he reached the pilot's house near the little airfield. He greeted Kelly as he got in the truck, and they were off, with Jack explaining the game plan to him. Kelly was carrying a bulky rucksack.

Jack raised an eyebrow. "Is that what I think it is?" he asked.

Patrick Kelly just grinned and opened the top flap of the canvas bag to show the beautifully polished dark-walnut stock of the Thompson machine gun that usually resided in his plane.

"Got two fresh hundred-round drums just lookin' for trouble," he said.

"Jesus Christ," replied Jack. "Just don't get mad at me, b'y."

They bounced along the dirt road until Jack saw the turn off from Lance Cove Pond that he and McCarty had taken the night before. He turned the truck around and stopped on the shoulder of the road.

"Look," he said to Kelly. "Another motorcycle came out here and went onto the road back the way we came. It must be them."

They drove back slowly, looking for a place where the motorcycle might have left the road. Eventually, they reached a point where Middleton Avenue passed the West Track tramway without seeing any further trace of the motorcycle.

o o o

Bill McCarty and Joseph Bunce rounded the point jutting out from the Number Two Cove, carefully avoiding the sharp rocks hiding just below the surface, ready to cut the bottom out of any boat that ventured too near. The only hint they lay in wait was the foam that burst upward seemingly from nowhere as the waves travelled on their never-ending journey to the shore.

"Joseph, have you been fishing for a long time?" asked McCarty above the noise of the motor.

"Aye," Bunce replied, a man of few words.

"Did your father fish or work in the mines?"

That loosened him up, and he began to talk. "My father came from over Harbour Grace," he said, pointing northwest toward the other arm of Conception Bay. "He started working here with the mines in the early days, when the seam was still on the surface, you see. Then they dug pits and tunnelled after it towards the beach. You can see the remains of the first surface digging right there, where all those shafts break out onto the shore. Then later on, they started the newer shafts with the concrete collars farther back from the cliffs on a more-gentle slope, and by the Jesus, those ones went down deep, a lot deeper, with them chasing the red rock out under the bay, doing the submarine mining. I was just thirteen when I started, pickin' rock out of the ore with some other boys and a couple of old duffers who didn't have the strength left to be down below anymore."

"Did you ever go down in the mines?" McCarty asked.

Here, Bunce paused to light his pipe. "When I was fourteen," he answered with a faraway look, "on a Sunday just like today, they were doing some extra runs on the Scotia tramway to the pier, and I thought it would be a laugh to catch a ride, jumping on an ore car from the mine all the way there for an adventure. I got to the pier, but I left something behind on the tracks."

As the man lifted his right pant leg, McCarty now saw that the man had an artificial limb.

"Jesus Christ!" he exclaimed. "How did you not bleed to death? That trip is near two miles!"

"Well," Bunce replied, "she cut off pretty clean below the knee, and I wrapped my belt around my leg quick like. I don't remember much of the rest. When I could get around again, I knew I wouldn't be able to hold my own down below, and I didn't have it in me to go back and pick rocks forever like the old timers, so I started doing this. I got this boat, and I catch a few fish here and there, and I gets by."

The dory carrying the two men continued west, its little motor putt-putting slowly along the shore while McCarty kept a sharp eye on the tunnel openings for any sign of activity. By the time he and Bunce reached Gravel Head, it became apparent that it would be quite difficult to ascertain which opening, if any, was being used by the saboteurs without getting out of the boat and looking closer. It was much more likely that they were somewhere closer to the No. 4 mine, but first he had to eliminate the possibility that they were somewhere in these old shafts.

Up ahead, there was a spot where Bunce could beach the boat, and McCarty disembarked. Where he splashed ashore, there were large square boulders of iron ore and slabs of slate strewn on the rocky beach. It was obvious that the cliffs were eroding and had suffered partial collapses from time to time. McCarty removed a flashlight from his rucksack and walked carefully toward an old mine opening a hundred feet below the Gravel Head cliff.

Inside, rusted rail tracks stretched in every direction and he could see that the beach openings were interconnected.

Further in, where the slope's upward elevation now came within fifteen feet of the surface, he could see where the many original pit openings from above had been fenced by dozens of timbers and then backfilled with rock overburden to safely and effectively plug as many as thirty-five of the old open pits that had stretched along the cliffs above.

McCarty watched and listened carefully for any sign of the saboteurs, but there was none. The only sound he heard was the gurgle of a couple of little rivulets of fresh water going toward the beach. It was getting on in the afternoon as he headed back toward the boat, having gone as far as he dared and finding nothing. There was really only one area left to investigate now—an area of interest he had seen from the air with Patrick Kelly, near the shore at Grebes Nest.

o o o

Kurt Becher was not adept at riding a motorcycle. He stalled it several times bumping across the field as he drove from the cliff area. A watchman coming out of the No. 4 dryhouse had been told to be on the lookout and to call Jack Sparkes if he should see anything suspicious.

Nothing was going to stop Becher from fulfilling his promise to Kahr and doing his duty for the fatherland. He aimed straight for the man standing in front of him, who had to scramble quickly out of the way. As Becher gunned the motor and drove on, the man went back into the dryhouse, where there was a telephone, and spoke to Lorraine, explaining what he had seen and that the motorcyclist was heading toward town in her direction. She promised to pass the information along to her father as soon as possible.

Lorraine wasn't sure what to do. Neither Bill nor Jack could be reached right now. Her only option, barring leaving the house to try and find them, was to sit tight and wait until one of them called or came home. She put her hand into the pocket of the apron she was still wearing and went to a corner of the living room, next to the stone fireplace, and waited.

Becher felt elated as the man in front of him jumped for dear life out of the way. He found it amusing, and as the alcohol coursed through his veins, his confidence grew stronger by the minute. Soon he passed Ten Commandments Road and approached Grammer Street, where he would make his mark. He pulled to the side one block before the target house and checked the Luger. Magazine inserted. A round in the chamber. Safety off. Ready to kill.

o o o

Back at the No. 4 mine, Jack Sparkes and Patrick Kelly pulled up near the dryhouse to call home, check on Lorraine, and find out whether she had heard from McCarty. The man there quickly told them what had happened just ten minutes earlier, and that he had already called Jack's house. He also told then that it seemed like the motorcyclist was heading that way. Jack and Kelly looked at each other and ran back to the truck, mud and gravel flying as Jack floored the accelerator. As they drove, Kelly reached into his rucksack and took out the Thompson. He inserted a drum magazine and made sure the spring was fully wound. Then he reached on top, pulling the charging bolt loudly back, and lastly, checked to make sure the machine gun was set to full auto.

Just before Grammer Street, there was a grassy path on the right. It would bring Becher up behind the house, the second one in on the street's west side. He turned in and cut the motor just before the wooden-gate entrance. Getting off the motorcycle, Becher crept up to the back door and tried the handle, the Luger heavy in his right hand. The door was locked, but the alcohol was still having the desired effect and without another thought, he used his left elbow to smash one of the door's small panes of glass and reached in to turn the knob of the Yale lock.

Lorraine could have stayed in the corner next to the fireplace, but instinctively, she knew she had a better chance if she went on the offensive instead of waiting for them to come for her. She crept out, reaching into her apron pocket for the Colt.

Looking around the corner, she could see into the kitchen. There was broken glass on the floor and a hand was reaching inside the back door. The distance between them was less than ten feet as she took the gun in both hands and aligned the front with the rear sight, using her dominant right eye but with both eyes open, just like she'd been told. The first shot went through Becher's left wrist, rendering the hand useless. He quickly yanked it back out, and a shard of glass still embedded in the frame sliced deeply into his palm and fingers.

Not even noticing the noise, Lorraine continued to fire, one round after another, until the gun clicked on an empty chamber. Becher had jerked back off the porch in panic, but she'd still scored with one other round, smashing his left elbow. He screamed loudly as the arm now dangled uselessly by his side. He could see blood running down and a bone protruding from his wrist as he began running back the way he came, still screaming, the gun in his other hand having yet to fire a shot.

The motorcycle was forgotten, though he could not have ridden it now anyway. Running down the path as fast as possible, he nearly ran into Jack's company truck as it screeched to a halt where the path met West Mines Road. Jack and

Kelly jumped out of the truck, and Becher made his last of many mistakes. Remembering that he was holding a Luger in his right hand, he raised it toward the men and fired several rounds wildly, harmlessly striking the truck twice before the third bullet entered Jack Sparkes on his left side, just above his heart.

As Jack was hit, Kelly brought the Thompson to bear and began firing from the hip. The first twenty-round burst stitched Becher up the middle, from the groin to his left clavicle, as recoil caused the gun to climb a bit in his hands. The saboteur's legs stiffened in muscle-spasm shock, but he did not drop yet. Just before Jack fell, he raised the Webley .455 and fired one round, striking Becher in the forehead, the squat lead bullet entering his brain at an upward angle and removing part of his skullcap. Kelly sent a second spray towards the man, and although the headshot had already done so, the additional twenty rounds left no doubt about Becher's demise. The pilot compensated for recoil by pulling the barrel down slightly, sending every slug to centre mass, cutting Becher nearly in two. With his spine now severed, every muscle relaxed, and the spy folded forward from the waist, dropping to the ground, every hope of love and glory left unfulfilled.

Lorraine, meanwhile, had cautiously looked out when the gunfire ceased, and seeing her father, ran down the pathway. She ripped off her apron and knelt down beside him, cradling his head in her lap. She pressed the apron against his wound to staunch the flow of blood, while Patrick Kelly ran to the house and called for the doctor.

The doctor arrived with the island ambulance, but it was determined that they should not move Jack very far over the bumpy roads, as the bullet had lodged inside his body and further damage was possible if they tried to transport him to the surgery. A cover was placed over the remains of Kurt Becher as Jack was rolled carefully onto a stretcher, and they carried the mercifully unconscious man into the house. Soon, four of Jake and McCarty's group showed up to stand guard in case of any further assault, having also been called by Kelly.

As the doctor attended to Jack Sparkes, with Lorraine assisting, Patrick Kelly got back in Jack's company truck and went in search of McCarty, while the ambulance took away Kurt Becher's body. Kelly figured that Bill would be in the vicinity of Grebes Nest, having had time to search along the rest of the shoreline by now.

o o o

The truck bounded along the back road behind the No. 4 mine entrance until it reached the area by the sea stack just before Grebes Nest. As Kelly got out of the truck, he could see McCarty and Joseph Bunce heading toward him along the shore far below. Looking up, McCarty could see Kelly franticly waving from the top of the cliff. Bunce shut off the motor, and above the noise of the waves, they could hear what Kelly was shouting. Scarcely believing his ears, McCarty disembarked and scrambled up the steep pathway, reaching the top in record time. On the way back to Grammer Street, Kelly filled him in on what had transpired.

"Pat," McCarty asked, "is he going to make it?"

"I honestly don't know, Bill," Kelly replied. "It's a bad one, but it missed his heart. The doc is going to have to remove the bullet but doesn't want to chance moving him, so he's got to operate at the house. We'll know when we get there."

"Jesus Christ," McCarty said, "if that man dies...."

It took about twenty minutes to get to the house. As they entered, the doctor was still tending to Jack. The bullet had been successfully removed, the bleeding had stopped, and now it was a matter of seeing how well he would respond. He still lay unconscious, but it was from the pain medication he had been administered. When Lorraine saw McCarty enter through the back door past the broken glass, she put her arms around him and began crying softly. He held her for a long time, and then she told him the whole story of what had happened, with Kelly relating more details about the horrific encounter.

As afternoon turned to evening and then night, McCarty's mind raced as he sat waiting and hoping for Jack Sparkes to wake up. The two German agents had caused so much pain and death on this mission, and while McCarty knew he wasn't directly responsible, it weighed heavily on him, blaming himself for not stopping them sooner—for not saving those who had been lost so needlessly.

They had dealt with one of the spies, but his accomplice was still at large, and as far as McCarty was concerned, he was the more dangerous of the two by far. Replaying everything he had learned about the man and what he had been up to, McCarty tried to piece it all together.

The attempt to attack the house here on Grammer Street was amateurish at best, unnecessary, and the act of someone not in control. Or was it the act of someone who was very much in control? The dead man had likely been manipulated by Kahr, who'd appeared to be the dominant of the two when McCarty had encountered them by the church two weeks earlier. Becher had probably been needed for his technical skills, but once he was no longer an important part of the operation, perhaps he'd become expendable.

The watchman at No. 4 mine had said that he'd seen Becher coming from the direction of the cliffs by Grebes Nest. That had to be the area from which they'd mounted their operation. Perhaps there was an opening on the beach from the natural cave he had seen by the danger sign in the mine. He knew in his gut that August Kahr was going to try and blow up the No. 4 mine, and that it would happen tonight or tomorrow.

The phone rang at nine-thirty p.m. Lorraine picked up the handset and spoke into the mouthpiece. Then she turned around woodenly and held it up to McCarty.

"Bill," she said, "it's August Kahr. He wants to speak with you."

McCarty got up slowly and walked toward her. He smiled grimly and gave her hand a squeeze as she passed him the candlestick phone receiver. Patrick Kelly and two of the others, who were still present and standing guard, gathered around to listen.

McCarty didn't waste any time. "The two men at the overpass were bad enough, but dumping Hanna like that is going to cost you."

"Ha! I did not think you would find the girl so quickly! I know it is a bit cliché, but you see, she knew a little too much about me," Kahr replied. "The poor thing was like a frightened kitten at the end. Such a shame."

"If you meet me right now," McCarty offered, "I promise to kill you quickly."

"No, you wouldn't do that, because you are soft. You have rules," Kahr replied, "but I'm sure you would like to. After all, we have done some damage here on your little island. By now, I'm sure you will also have discovered the old woman my compatriot Becher stabbed. That must have angered you. She screamed you know."

"I doubt that. I would wager that old woman was a lot tougher than your little friend," McCarty said. "So much for the superior race. "

"Ah yes, my dear compatriot Kurt," Kahr said. "Did you know that the degenerate pervert thought he was in love with me? One of the few good things that Hitler has done for Germany is to exterminate homosexuals. I assume Becher is actually dead and not making deals with you?"

"Quite dead," McCarty replied. "I needn't go into details, but let us say he wasn't up to the task you set him."

Kahr laughed. "Thank you. It saves me the bullet I would have had to waste on him. So, what now, Mr. McCarty?"

"It's lieutenant actually, and now? Now I'm going to deal with a cowardly killer whose only skill is knowing how to push the plunger on a detonator from a safe distance."

"Ah, my dear Oberleutnant, if you only knew," Kahr replied. "I almost wish we could meet again in person and continue this stimulating conversation."

"We will, and I look forward to that meeting," said McCarty, "but you won't enjoy the conversation."

"That is unfortunate, but I will just have to try and struggle through. Now, while I am sorry to end our pleasant chat, I do have a few final details to attend to, so if you would please excuse me, I will say goodbye now, William." With that, Kahr hung up.

McCarty turned to the group who were waiting for him to say something.

"Lorraine," he said, "I need you to call the phone-company switchboard and find out the extension that the call came from. It will tell us where Kahr is right now."

She quickly called the switchboard, and her friend on duty confirmed that the call had come from extension 374 at the dryhouse near the entrance to No. 3 mine.

"So, he's actually at No. 3, just down the road!" Kelly exclaimed.

"We should get over there right now!" said one of the men.

"No," McCarty replied, "he'll already have left there, but it gives me an idea of how much time I have to work with. He will be on his way to No. 4. We were *meant* to check where he called from; he wants us to waste time looking for him there."

o o o

August Kahr hung up the telephone in the surface dryhouse of the No. 3 mine and got back in the company truck he had stolen from among those kept at the No. 4 yard. The afternoon had turned cloudy, and now in the evening, there was a light snow falling as Kahr drove the sturdy vehicle along the rough pathways to the cliff above Grebes Nest. For all his drinking, Kahr was in excellent physical condition and easily descended the steep, slippery pathway to the beach. He rounded the point, his feet getting wet as the tide was still ebbing, and entered the secret cave. Lighting the way with his batteried lamp, he made his way quickly to the steel-doored room.

Inside, he opened one of the wooden cases holding the gold bars. Holding one in each hand, he laughed, knowing his plan was about to be realised. When he returned to claim his prize, he would live a life of luxury that few could ever know. He was about to replace the ingots, but instead, he slowly and deliberately took each bar out of the case—each one a kilogram of .999% pure gleaming gold—and stacked them. It was a fabulous sight, and he could have sat there all night and just stared at it, but there was work to do. He would leave the ingots out, and because gold doesn't tarnish, this would be the sight that would greet him when next he came back to this hidden room after the war.

Now he went to the corner. Moving the rocks hiding the thirteenth case, he opened the lid and took out the bottle with the skull and crossbones. He lined his rucksack with the box's straw-packing material and then carefully nestled the bottle in the bag. Then he placed a rubber gas mask on top and secured it. In another small canvas sack, he placed the two sticks of special formula nitro he had put aside for tonight, along with two wired blasting caps, a roll of extra wire, and a detonator.

The last task Kahr performed before closing the heavy steel door and locking it was to set a trip wire, connected to a small concussion bomb. Kahr was taking no chances with his prize. Step in the wrong direction, and the booby trap would cause damage to internal organs or even death to anyone within the room's enclosed space. With one last fond look, Kahr closed the door and locked it.

Back down the tunnel he went, and at a safe distance from the steel door, he pushed one stick of nitro into cracks in the sandstone and slate walls on either side of the man-made shaft. He ran the wires back to about one hundred feet from the cut off to the No. 4 mine's danger sign and screwed them down to the detonator's terminals, leaving it in the ready position. He continued down the tunnel until he reached the little boat, just inside the cave entrance. Kahr looked at his Stowa watch. It was ten forty-five p.m. Time to pull the boat down to the shore and get ready to signal U-184.

o o o

On Grammer Street, McCarty heard Lorraine yell, "Dad!" and ran to Jack's room.

Jack's eyes were open, and he was slowly adjusting to his surroundings.

"Did we get him?" he croaked.

Lorraine held a glass of water to his lips.

"Oh, you got him, Sparky," said Patrick Kelly. "No doubt about it."

"Lorraine? Are you okay?"

"Dad, I'm fine; don't worry about me. How are you feeling?"

"Like I got shot," was Jack's reply, leaving no doubt that both he and his sense of humour were alive, and that he would be all right.

"Jack." McCarty reached out and held Jack's big hand.

"Kahr?"

"We don't have him yet, but I know where he is," McCarty answered.

"Listen up now, young fella. This is what I'd say to my son, or my son-in-law for that matter," Jack said with a little smile. "That fucker is evil. Take no chances, even if you have to let him go."

"Jack, remember that first day at the main office? What I said to Brenda?"

"I remember, skipper," he replied. "I remember."

"Nothing's changed, Sparky. A promise is a promise."

"I know, but sometimes I wish it wasn't."

"Me too," he said, glancing at Lorraine, "for some things, but not this."

Jack went back to sleep, and McCarty went back out to the living room where he announced that he was going out for a while. Patrick Kelly began putting on his coat to go with him.

"No," said McCarty. "I've got to do this on my own—"

"No, you don't, William McCarty!" interrupted Lorraine. "Mr. Kelly goes with you, or you don't go at all!" Her eyes were brimming with tears as she spoke.

Kelly looked at him and shrugged his shoulders.

"Okay," Bill conceded, "you're right. I just don't want to see anyone else get hurt."

"Bill," Kelly said, "we're both military men. I know the risks, so let's go get this fucker."

Giving Lorraine a last hug, McCarty went out to the truck, followed by Patrick Kelly. The other men would stay at the house and stand guard.

○ ○ ○

Without Becher, it wasn't easy manoeuvring the boat out of the cave entrance and down over the rocks to the water. But the reward! Everything was coming together just as he had imagined, even with the inconveniences he'd had to endure. He smiled as he tried to visualise Becher's last moments, and his only regret was not being able to see it for himself. Looking at his watch, he saw that it was now eleven p.m., and hopefully, a periscope was being raised to see his signal on this dark, moonless night. He flashed his light in a coded pattern and repeated the signal several times. There would not be an answering flash, as there was a chance that it would be seen from any patrols on the cliffs above—there *had* been the occasional patrol, but they were easily avoided.

Kahr had to trust that the submarine would be there as he stepped into the boat and began rowing out to meet it. As he rowed, directly away from Grebes Nest toward the northwest, he sensed rather than saw a presence. In front of him, fifty yards away, she rose slowly from the deep. Cold salt water streamed from her deck in a foamy froth. He was close enough now to see the large white "U-184" on the side of the tall grey conning tower, and at its front, a bright heraldry symbol: a white shield outlined in black with a vertical, deadly looking, spiked mace crossed by three, red, stylised lightning bolts. Kahr clambered aboard and tied the little boat to a railing stanchion. He began climbing the welded ladder rungs on the tower as he heard the hatch wheel being spun open.

Oberleutnant Ingenieur Werner Dietz appeared and greeted August Kahr. He welcomed Kahr to U-184, inviting him down below to report to Kapitanleutnant Dangschat. For only having been on combat patrol since November ninth, he still had the beginnings of the characteristic German Navy submariner's beard, as did most of the U-184's crew. Two of the eighteen-year-olds, however, showed little sign of any growth yet and were teased good-naturally about it. The crew was happy overall, and morale was good, still in the early days of their deployment.

"Why don't you cast off that funny little boat; you won't need it anymore," said Dietz. "We don't want to drag it all the way back to Germany, do we?" The man laughed a little condescendingly. "And aren't there supposed to be two of you being picked up?"

"My partner has unfortunately met with an accident, which I will detail in my report, and I will cast off the boat presently; I just need a word with the captain first," answered Kahr.

As the oberleutnant ingenieur descended the ladder, Kahr reached into his rucksack and donned the full-face gas mask, pulling the straps tight, creating a strong rubber seal that would protect his eyes, nose, and mouth. Then he took the bottle with the sarin and threw it down the open hatch as hard as he could, not waiting to see if it burst on impact. He slammed the hatch shut with a loud clang and spun the wheel tight. Kahr took the steel sprag rod he had brought and shoved it between the spokes of the hatch wheel, rendering it immovable, the same way it was used on an ore car to stop it rolling.

Right away, he could see that someone was trying to open the hatch. The sprag scraped back and forth a few inches, but the wheel could not turn. For a moment or two, Kahr could hear a dull thud from the other side of the hatch, likely someone hammering in desperation on the heavy metal door with their bare fist. The movement on the hatch, and the sound, soon stopped, and Kahr looked at his watch. He allowed fifteen minutes for the sarin to work and then added an extra five just in case.

Kapitanleutnant Gunther Dangschat was twenty-seven years old on the day he died. He and the other crew members everywhere had begun to experience eye pain and blurred vision, followed by a cough and tightness in the chest as they went into respiratory failure. In ten minutes, only a handful were still alive near each end of the boat, but their deaths too quickly followed.

○ ○ ○

Kahr checked the black dial on his Stowa. It had been twenty-one minutes since he'd dropped the bottle. He pulled out the sprag and spun the wheel on the large circular hatch. It was supposed to open easily with the help of the powerful springs, but he had to pull hard before it gave. As it opened, he heard a thud and realised that the crewman trying to open the hatch had died with his arm still in one of the spokes. The sound he'd heard was his lifeless body dropping to the deck below. Kahr checked carefully as he descended the ladder. There were two bodies there, the one that had fallen and another near the conning-tower periscope. He went down to the control-room level and looked around. Death was everywhere, and the only sound he could hear was the whine of the electric motors slowly idling.

Kahr had paid very careful attention to the workings of the U-boat that had brought them to North America and knew just how much to turn the big wheels that controlled the sea water ballast in order for the boat to sink slowly enough for him to disembark safely. One of the crew had even been kind enough to let him try it when they'd needed to dive. Looking by the control telegraph, he saw the captain laying across a padded bench. As Kahr went toward the ballast controls, he noticed a ring on the captain's right hand—a beautiful, heavy-looking gold ring depicting a submarine, with U-184 in raised lettering underneath. It came off easily enough, and he slipped it into his pocket before beginning to turn the ballast wheels.

Kahr knew that, right now, they were in one of the deepest areas of Conception Bay, with more than nine hundred and fifty feet of ocean directly below. With a maximum test depth of seven hundred and fifty feet, he hoped the boat would crush at close to a thousand, but even if it didn't, at that depth, no one would ever find out what had happened to it.

As he turned to leave, a man staggered up behind him, unheard above the noise of the electric motors. A shock went through Kahr's system and he cried out as the man began grabbing at the mask on his face. The spy pushed and kicked at the unfortunate sailor, who sank to his knees, blood coming from his eyes and nose, a final death rattle emanating from between his drooling lips.

Kahr scrambled up the ladder as if the hounds of hell were after him. Pushing the hatch closed, he spun the wheel and jammed the sprag in, just in case any more of the doomed crew were still alive and able to pursue him. The submarine was sinking as he untied his little boat and rowed quickly away, worried about being dragged under by suction as the U-boat slipped beneath the freezing water. He was about fifty yards away and pulling off his gas mask when he lost sight of the conning tower.

o o o

While Kahr knew how to make the sub take on sea water as ballast to submerge, he didn't understand the dynamics of Conception Bay and its currents, or how the submarine would be affected by the rate of descent in conjunction with its bow and stern planes. The sub might have gone straight down to over nine hundred feet, except that the captain had already ordered the planes to be pre-set to a shallow-dive position. Consequently, as the boat submerged, still idling, it drifted very slowly with the current, moving under the water in an almost straight line across from Grebes Nest. Rather than going deep to near crush depth, the boat glided on a slight downward angle toward shallower waters for the next six hours until it nosed down to within one hundred yards of Spoon Cove, along the western arm of Conception Bay, in barely ninety feet of water.

The bow drove into the mud, and the boat settled itself upright in an underwater trench carved out by the bottom of one of the icebergs that occasionally drifted into the bay on their annual southward journey. Within another ten hours, the electric motors shut down as the batteries lost power. The boat was tight and in no danger of losing its structural integrity, though the temperature dropped, which would slow the decomposition of the bodies on board.

This muddy area was not known as a good place to fish, so there was little chance of discovery due to nets being caught on the sub's rigging. Over time, the tides and currents caused the mud to shift and build up against its sides, leaving only the top of the conning tower occasionally visible, sometimes for months at a time, and at other times, completely covered, all depending on the shifting silt conditions.

When the U-boat failed to communicate further, in keeping with the earlier story, it remained listed as missing and presumed lost, having ceased communication somewhere near its previous coordinates. In fact, Germany had no idea what had become of it. What had been of such absolute importance was now moot. As August Kahr had planned from the beginning, in the Abwehr's minds the agents, the submarine and the map to the gold were lost, and while unfortunate, there were many more U-boats, as well as plenty of treasure hidden in other places, ranging from Germany to England to Ireland, as well as the eastern coast of North America.

o o o

It continued to snow lightly as McCarty and Kelly drove toward the No. 4 mine. When they reached the dryhouse near the collar entrance, they saw a night watchman standing in the doorway, silhouetted by the light behind him. He approached the truck.

McCarty showed his identification, explained briefly what had happened, and asked, "Have you noticed a man going in the entrance here?"

"No, b'y," the man replied. "I knows there's no one has gone apast me here. I was downslope a bit earlier on me rounds, so I would of seen 'im if he went by me."

"What's your name?" asked McCarty.

"I'm Dennis Power, sir."

"Thank you, Dennis," Kelly said. "Keep a sharp eye out now; there's someone around here who isn't afraid to play rough."

"All right, b'ys. You be careful too."

They heard him lock the door as he went back inside.

"What do you think, Bill?" Kelly asked.

McCarty started the truck and put it in gear. "I think we're going to drive along here until we get to Grebes Nest. Something tells me we're close. Real close."

Kahr reached shore and didn't bother hauling up the boat. He wouldn't be needing it anymore. He planned to wear a disguise and get off the island in the morning before the big explosion. He would stay right in St. John's, where he could blend in among the many nationalities living in the capitol city. He reached into his coat's inside pocket and drew out a heavy silver flask, into which he had poured the rest of the rum, and took a long pull. After the fright he'd had back on the submarine, he needed it. The alcohol warmed his stomach as he began scrambling over the slippery rocks and rubble that had fallen due to so many years of the cliff's freeze-and-thaw cycle and the never-ending waves. He entered the cave and began walking toward the danger sign and the detonator waiting there.

As Bill McCarty and Patrick Kelly approached the clifftop by Grebes Nest, they both noticed the truck parked in amongst some low fir trees and heavy brush. McCarty jumped out and felt the hood. It was cold, but no frost had formed on it yet.

"What do you think?" asked Kelly.

"This is the truck that was stolen," McCarty replied, looking at the number on the side. "It's him."

They walked near the edge of the cliff.

"Down there!" Kelly exclaimed. "Look! There's a boat!"

The low wave action kept the abandoned boat close to shore, bumping it slowly against the rocky beach.

"Pat," McCarty said, "you're not going to like this, but I need you to stay here. You're a good man, and you fought well today, but you're regular air force. This is different. I trained especially for this, and I need to go alone, quietly, and with one purpose in mind. Only one person is going to come back up that path, and if it isn't me, you're going to empty that Smith and Wesson into them, okay? Don't wait for him to shoot first. And no surrender."

Kelly looked at McCarty and ran through a dozen reasons in his head why he should stay with him, but in the end, as difficult as it was for him, he nodded in agreement.

"I knew I should have taken the Thompson instead of my revolver. If it isn't you who comes back up that cliff path, you know I won't be able to go back to Grammer Street, right?"

"But you know it's the right thing to do."

"Yeah," Kelly replied. "Doesn't make it any easier."

"Nothing about this has been, Pat." McCarty shook the man's hand and then walked toward the steep cliff pathway.

At the bottom, he made his way carefully around the point to Grebes Nest. He could see the little boat slowly making its way out from shore. Soon it would be beyond the grip of the waves that were keeping it close. McCarty could see where the boat had come in, as well as tracks in the snow going in both directions, to and from the cliff. He followed the crooked trail around rocks and other obstructions on the beach leading up to it. At first, it looked as if the tracks just ended at a blank rock face with some bushes growing in front, but going closer, he realised that the bushes were not growing out of the rocky ground. They weren't attached to it at all. He dragged them aside to reveal a low natural opening in the cliff. *This must be the other end of the cave, leading from the danger sign!*

McCarty pulled his Colt from its shoulder holster and made sure there was a round in the chamber. Then he put it back and switched on his flashlight. Ducking low, he entered the cave. Almost immediately, the surface he was standing on started to shake violently, accompanied by a roar that deafened him momentarily. It threw him to the ground. The entire cave continued to vibrate, and a huge cloud of dust and smoke obscured his vision, making him blink as particulates of matter slowly settled to the ground.

As reason returned, he understood that there had been an explosion nearby. He was getting to his feet when, through the settling dust, he saw a strong beam of light bouncing through the gloom off the sides and floor of the cave, heading in his direction. McCarty quickly switched off his light and stood in the blackness surrounding him.

When the oncoming light came within twenty feet, he spoke loudly: "August Kahr, by the authority of the Canadian, British, and Newfoundland Governments, I am arresting you on charges of espionage and murder."

The light spun crazily in a circle, then stopped abruptly as McCarty switched on his flashlight, holding it in his left hand, arm straight out from his side. In his right, he held the Colt, pointed at the ground. He clicked the thumb safety off and gripped it firmly,

"Oberleutnant McCarty!" came Kahr's cultured voice. "How nice to see you again."

"It seems as if you had a little accident," McCarty replied, hoping that Kahr's ego would lead to him telling him more about the planned blast. "I hope you didn't waste all your special nitroglycerin on that one explosion."

"So, you know about our special-formula mixture," Kahr replied. "I can assure you that the main event is still set to happen and very soon. Would you like to know where and when?"

"What makes you think I don't already know?" countered McCarty.

"Oh, come now, my friend. I would have thought better of you than that. You don't think that, after being here for over a year, we haven't made sure to cover every possibility in keeping our real target concealed?"

McCarty regretted not having gone further back than six months when he reviewed the employee list, and said, "I know it's in No. 4, and I have received the clearance to shut the mine down until we find your so-called super nitro. There will be no shift today, or any other day, until we find every last bit of it."

Kahr was silent for a long moment, and McCarty knew he had touched a nerve. *It will end soon now,* he thought.

"What's the matter?" McCarty taunted. "Is your superior German intellect at a loss for words?"

Kahr already had his gun out and quickly aimed toward the flashlight McCarty was holding. He fired three times in quick succession, the bullets missing their target, but before McCarty could raise his Colt to fire back, there was a bright muzzle flash and the sound of another loud gunshot from behind him. Spinning around, he raised his gun.

"It's me! Don't shoot!" Patrick Kelly shouted from the darkness, before switching on his own light, revealing himself.

"Jesus Christ!" McCarty replied. "I thought I told you—"

"Yeah, yeah, I know, but I heard that explosion, and the fucking ground shook so hard I nearly shit myself! Again! No one would ever need a friggin' laxative, hanging around with you, that's for sure. Besides, the more I thought about Jack and Lorraine, and having to face them if something happened to you—"

They heard a low moan coming from up ahead. In the glow of their lights, they could see August Kahr laying on his side, which was bleeding. His gun lay a few feet away, where it had fallen when he'd been hit by Kelly's bullet.

"I need medical attention," Kahr groaned. "You arrested me. I am in your custody, and you have to abide by the rules of war. I am a German soldier, and you have to help me."

"You know, Pat, that was pretty sloppy shooting, unless you were actually trying to hit him there," McCarty said, pointing and ignoring Kahr.

"Are you kidding? It's a miracle I hit him at all, for Christ's sake. I'm a lousy shot. That's why I have a machine gun."

"I am wounded. I need help, and you have to give it to me!" Kahr whined. "Get me a doctor. I demand it!"

"Would you like me to teach you how to aim better?" McCarty asked Kelly.

"Sure. After all, you're the one with all the fancy training. I'm just the guy who saved your life."

"Guess I'll never hear the end of that, huh?"

"Probably not," Kelly confirmed.

In front of them, Kahr began to cry. "I am in pain, God damn you. I need help!"

Foolishly, he tried to inch his way sideways toward the Luger. McCarty put the first one in his stomach, and Kahr let out a high-pitched scream.

"I told you we'd meet again and that you wouldn't like the conversation," McCarty said evenly.

"Help! You can't do this! You have rules! Help!" Kahr continued to yell while sobbing.

"Sorry. The rules are suspended. Help's not coming, and a promise is a promise. This is for all of them," McCarty continued quietly, "but especially for Brenda."

Kahr's last word in this realm was: "Who?"

The sound of the shot was very loud as the bullet tore into his throat, putting an end to his plans of being rich after the war. He emitted a gurgling sound, which went on just long enough for him to know what was about to happen. His body convulsed several times as McCarty looked eye to eye with him, and then he was gone.

After the sharp slap-back, reverberating off the walls, died away, Kelly remarked, "Pretty sloppy shooting yourself."

"I'll probably pay for it later, but I hit exactly what I was aiming at."

"Well, there's no way that nut was going to tell you anything anyway," Kelly rationalised.

"I know," McCarty replied, "but God help me, I would have done that even if he had."

McCarty picked up his two spent brass casings and then went over to Kahr's body, going through all his pockets for any clue as to where the explosives might have been placed. In one pocket, he found a heavy gold ring with a submarine emblem on it. Another inside pocket held a silver flask that smelled of alcohol, which Kelly pocketed with a grim smile. A rucksack lay beside him with a large sum of money, some clothes, and several magazines holding more ammunition.

Kelly picked up Kahr's Luger, and tucked it into his waistband as they walked further into the cave to investigate the explosion. They hiked all the way to the spot where the danger sign was. Just beyond it, a lot of dust still hung in the air. In the distance, some more rock fell from the roof. The area did not appear very stable.

"Looks like he blew the area farther in," Kelly said.

"Could be covering up where they planned their sabotage operations," McCarty replied. "Probably shouldn't go any farther in though. Too dangerous right now."

"No point anyway, I guess," agreed Kelly.

Neither man knew about the gold.

They trudged back toward the entrance and noticed a number of empty wooden boxes along one side, which had held the spies' concentrated nitroglycerin. Patrick Kelly let out a low whistle as both men realised how powerful the explosion from the combined contents would be.

August Kahr lay nearby, eyes staring sightlessly upward. McCarty had seen what looked like a pit behind him and shone his light down. It was roughly circular, about ten feet across, and he could hear water running somewhere far below. Tossing a rock in, it took a good two or three seconds before they heard it splash down.

"Good enough," McCarty said out loud.

"We're not going to remove the body?" Kelly asked.

"Not worth it, McCarty replied. "This entire operation stinks. I'm going to write a report concentrating on the fact that something has been left undone here. The rest may have to be a bit creative. With the proper support, we might have figured it out, but I've had it with bureaucracy. I've had it with a lot of things."

As Kahr's body rolled fittingly over the side, McCarty could still see an old woman named Bridget Kelly in her cellar, and young Hanna Martin, laying frozen in a cistern on Fourth Street. He feared he would never stop seeing them. Patrick Kelly shone his light in the pit, and they watched the body windmilling as it bounced off the walls for a moment before it disappeared into the darkness. Then there was a distant splash. McCarty took the money from the rucksack, and the rest followed Kahr into the pit. The money would be a mysterious donation to the island's churches, but McCarty knew it would never make up for letting himself give in to his dark side, however justified, and committing what amounted to cold-blooded murder, even though he would do it again, given the same circumstances,

○ ○ ○

McCarty and Kelly emerged from the cave entrance to a steady snowfall that was now beginning to blanket the beach. To discourage anyone from looking too closely at their handiwork, they took some time to block the entrance to the cave, just as Kahr and Becher had done but with more permanence in mind, using larger rocks. Then it was quite a chore getting back around the point and back up the slippery cut to the clifftop.

"We'll go back to the dryhouse and call Lorraine before we head back to Grammer Street," McCarty said, "so they aren't worried."

"Okay, but I can't imagine why they'd be concerned. It's not as if we were out here doing something dangerous," Kelly replied wryly.

Although it was meant as dark humour, neither man laughed. Kelly maintained his devil-may-care attitude on the outside, and McCarty appeared calm, but both men were changed. In the moment when he could have chosen to carry out his lawful duty, McCarty had taken on the role of righteous executioner. No one would blame him. In fact, if anyone on the island besides Kelly ever found out, they would probably shake his hand, but that wasn't the point.

The overhead wipers brushed away the snow that had accumulated on the windshield as McCarty put the truck into low gear and started back toward the mine entrance.

"I guess we can let them know where to come to pick up their truck," said Kelly, pointing at the vehicle Kahr had stolen.

"Why don't we just drive it back for them?" McCarty suggested.

"Hey, good idea," Kelly said. "I'll get it, and see you there." McCarty stopped the truck and Kelly hopped out, walking back to the abandoned vehicle.

McCarty waited until the other truck started, and right away, he heard the horn and saw Kelly flashing the headlights to get his attention as he roared up from behind, sliding to a stop just a few feet away. He didn't have time to ask what was happening before he heard Kelly yelling.

"A map! Kahr left a map!"

"What? A map of what? Show me!"

"Look!" Kelly fairly shouted, spreading out a large sheet of paper on the front seat and shining his flashlight on it.

The diagram showed a cross view of the mine with an ore car descending on an angle, approaching an object on the tracks, which had been drawn in fine detail. It was a detonator with the plunger pulled fully back. Wires leading from it were shown going up the wall to a little shelf with a bundle of five cylindrical objects wrapped together. On the wall was the number 126. From the relative height of both the car and the plunger, McCarty could plainly see what would happen when they met.

"The morning shift, Bill! He was planning to kill them all and blow up the mine down at level 126!"

"Jesus Christ, what time is it?"

"It's nearly six a.m.," replied Kelly, looking at his watch. "The shift will be travelling downslope any time!"

Without another word, both trucks made for the No. 4 mine collar as fast as they could. The snow made driving

THE SECRET OF BELL ISLAND

treacherous, and much of the distance back was spent sliding all over the slippery pathways. Reaching the dryhouse entrance, Kelly and McCarty jumped out of the vehicles and noticed only one person walking toward them. Hope arose, for a brief moment, that the men had not yet shown up for the morning shift. Then they both noticed that the heavy endless cable for the ore cars was moving.

"When did the morning shift head downslope? How long ago?" McCarty shouted.

"About ten minutes, b'y. They must be halfway down by now," the man answered, looking at the truck that had been stolen. "Why? What's going on? Where did you get that—"

Kelly cut him off. "Stop them!! The emergency stop for the cable! Stop it now, or there's going to be an explosion!"

"What? Blasting? They won't do that today—"

Kelly looked at McCarty and took out his gun. "Stop the fucking cable now, or I will shoot you."

As the man fairly ran toward the emergency stop, with Kelly pursuing, still waving his gun, McCarty saw a Royal Enfield motorcycle near the collar entrance. As he ran for it, he saw that the cable hadn't stopped. He hadn't heard or felt an explosion yet, and desperately hoped there was still time. He kicked over the machine, which started right away, and roared into the collar entrance, speeding down the slope beside the rail tracks.

Up top, Kelly yelled again, "What's wrong? Why isn't the cable stopping?"

"I don't know," the man yelled back. "I turned off the breaker, and it's supposed to stop! I don't understand!"

"Look," Kelly said, "I'm sorry about the gun, but there's a bomb that's been planted in the mine. If those cars come into contact with the detonator, everyone down there is going to die! Including my friend who's trying to stop it!"

"Oh!" the man replied, the situation now becoming clearer to him. "Is he—"

"Yes, God damn it! He's the navy fella! Now help me turn off every friggin' electrical breaker here until that cable stops! The saboteur must have rigged it somehow to keep going!"

Far below, a large group of men sat in the three-car train as it continued to descend into the mine. Some joked around, while others were more contemplative. Lunch bags were checked, and a few took a drink from the glass bottles of tea their wives had packed for them. All were ready to put in a good hard day's work in order to provide for themselves and their families. A quarter mile ahead, just past the one-mile mark, a trap lay waiting for them that could not only kill them all but rain down destruction on an unimaginable scale. No one below in any of the mines would survive, and many more above—both in the area and all around the shores of Conception Bay— would be doomed as well.

At first, the miners heard rather than saw the figure flying down the slope. Several of the men turned their heads back in the direction of the sound and saw a light bouncing crazily up and down as a motorcycle came roaring into view, going at a rate of speed that was almost guaranteed to have the driver flying off to their death at any moment. Just then, the cars they were riding in lurched to a stop. Luckily, no one decided to get out right away, as the motorcycle did not slow down, the driver like some black-haired spectre, his long coat flying behind him as he passed. Fifty feet ahead of them, the machine locked up its brakes and skidded sideways to a stop.

Now a dozen miners jumped out of the cars and ran toward the mad man on the motorcycle. Was this some crazy prank by one of their own or had someone gone completely out of their mind? If the former, it would be an immediate firing offence, and if the latter, they would subdue the berserk individual until someone in authority could be informed. And the cars! Why had they just stopped?

As they approached the man getting off the machine, he took off his coat and knelt down in between the rail tracks. Now they noticed that the man was wearing a shoulder holster housing a big pistol. He threw a little black identification folder toward them as he leaned over a device of some kind on the track. No one had yet made a sound as one man picked up the wallet and opened it.

It read: *"Royal Canadian Navy - Lieutenant William McCarty, RCN 2940M, CIC Special Operations Section."* The picture attached was definitely the man before them, and at least a couple of the men there had heard the rumours of a navy man looking around for Nazi agents, but until now, they'd thought it was just a story.

McCarty disconnected the terminal wires and traced the wiring back along the ground and up the wall. All those present understood what a detonator was and where the wires were likely to lead. He reached up overhead, to a small shelf cut in the rock, and removed the taped-together bundle of dynamite. Slowly, he removed each blasting cap and carefully placed them a short distance from the sticks of explosives.

"Sorry, men," McCarty said. "I didn't mean to interrupt your workday, but I thought you wouldn't mind too much under the circumstances."

All of the men murmured their thanks to McCarty for having removed the threat to life and limb, except for one man who had a complaint.

"Hey there, navy fella," he said loudly, "next time could you just use a bicycle? That friggin' noise with you flyin' by nearly made me spill my tea."

As usual, even in the face of possible death, the Newfoundland sense of humour prevailed, and they all laughed.

McCarty asked. "Is there a blaster I can trust with these explosives?"

"Randall Skanes here is your man for the dynamite," one of the miners replied, pointing to a big man who stepped forward.

"Okay," McCarty said. "Thanks for your patience. Better get back aboard. I'm going to get the cable started up again."

With that, McCarty walked to a nearby dryroom and called the surface. Kelly told him that Kahr had apparently bridged some wires so the cable wouldn't stop until several other breakers were also turned off. Bill told Pat that the immediate threat was averted, but McCarty knew in his heart that all the heavy nitro was still unaccounted for. He got back on the motorcycle as the cable began running again, and the men on the ore cars continued their descent to the deepest working level. As they went by him, every single man nodded their thanks.

When McCarty dropped Kelly off at his house, there was really nothing to say. Kelly held out both the silver flask and the Luger he had liberated from August Kahr toward McCarty, but he just shook his head. A silent knowing look that survivors of shipwrecks or air disasters might share would have come close to their silent farewell as they shook hands.

By the time McCarty reached Grammer Street, it was almost nine a.m., and he had been up more than twenty-four hours. The men on security watch had left after his phone call from the mine, letting them know that Kahr was finished. As he came in the door, he heard Jack's booming voice coming from his convalescent bedroom at the back of the house.

"Billy McCarty!" he bellowed. "Get yerself in here, skipper, and tell me all about it!"

As he unbuttoned his coat, Lorraine put her arms around him and just held on for several minutes. Then he walked with her to Jack's room.

"Well?" Jack asked expectantly.

"Sparky, I'm tired. I've been up all night, working hard while you've just been lazing around in bed, no doubt being waited on hand and foot by your lovely young nurse."

"Why you young—"

"Okay, okay. Short version. Kelly's all right, but no one can ever know that Kahr is dead. We found some dynamite in No. 4 that was set to explode when the morning shift started. We took care of that, and I'm convinced there's more, but there seems to be no immediate danger, so everything is safe for the time being. I have to sleep now, so goodnight . . . or morning."

"All right, b'y. Go on have yer beauty rest. Jaysus, you'd think you were after saving everyone's life or something."

With that, Jack reached for the bottle of Lamb's navy rum and a glass beside his bed.

"Doctor's orders," he said, smiling. "You know, for the horrible pain and all and since you don't drink, my son, I'll have one for you too."

McCarty turned to go. The day had been long. He had worked hard. Someone had tried to kill him. He had killed. He was in love with someone he could not be with. Many innocent lives around him had been destroyed, and to what end? For what purpose? He doubted what he was doing and where he was going. What happened next might have been the exhaustion, it might have been the combination of the events of the day, or possibly, it was pre-ordained. Meant to be. Unavoidable. He would never know.

"Just a minute," McCarty said.

He took the bottle, thinking about his alcoholic father, who had eventually died from the drink, and his own fear of experiencing the same fate. He still poured a large glass, though, and took the first drink of his life, downing it all as it burned his throat and warmed his stomach. It would help him sleep. Take the edge off. Surely just one wouldn't hurt. Lorraine said nothing, and even Jack was speechless.

McCarty went upstairs, undressed, and dropped into bed, the temporary pain-numbing effects of the rum proving the truism that alcoholics seldom know in the beginning but always find out sooner or later: *"One is too many and a thousand not enough."*

Bill McCarty stayed on for three more days, until he finished writing his report and the local authorities were satisfied that there would be no more killings. On the second day, Jack felt well enough to get out of bed and pose for a photograph in the backyard on Grammer Street, with the group of Bell Islanders who had been with him on the front line. McCarty dragged out the Nazi flag and laid it on the ground, and each man made his mark on it. After Lorraine used Jack's company camera to take the shot, he balled up the flag and handed it to Patrick Kelly, who carried it with him through the rest of the war as he flew patrols with his faithful Thompson along the east coast of Newfoundland.

Jack Sparkes and a trusted group continued quietly for years to try and find the hidden nitroglycerin, without success. Eventually, they stopped looking, and it was forgotten about.

○ ○ ○

On the morning of Wednesday, November 25, 1942, McCarty got up early and made breakfast for Jack and Lorraine for the first and only time. Then he dressed warmly, shook hands with Jack, and kissed Lorraine. She knew it was for the last time and looked questioningly towards the bedroom where his suitcase was.

He shrugged. "If I take it, that's the end. If I leave it," he paused for a moment, looking into her eyes, "then I'm just going out for a while."

As Lorraine's eyes filled with tears, Jack said, "Okay, skipper; then we'll see you for supper." Though trying to go along with the ruse, he began to choke up himself.

"Goodbye, Sparky," he said, as he continued to look at Lorraine for another moment. Then he left, walking all the way down to Beach Hill and the ferry. When it reached Portugal Cove, he made his way to Torbay and a military flight back to Halifax.

Chapter 30

Bell Island, Sunday, July 28, 2018

It was eight thirty a.m., and Jurgen Meyer wasn't answering his phone. On Hibbs Road, breakfast dishes were washed, dried, and put away. Tom Crane and the girls were raring to go, and even the "little puppy" seemed to pick up on their energy. The big Newfoundland was handing out semi-crippling leg bonks to any victim who got too close. Bev figured it was because the dog's previous day's adventure had given him renewed purpose.

Eventually, Matt decided to go over to the hotel to check on Meyer. He was beginning to worry, because in the brief time he had known the man, Jurgen Meyer did not seem like the kind of person to be late for an appointment. Kathleen offered to accompany him, pointing out that, if necessary, maybe her sister-in-law, working at the front desk, could check his room.

Kathleen and Matt drove along the former East Track, now called Steve Neary Boulevard, toward the hotel by the high school. As they arrived and he shut the motor off, he looked at her. "You're pretty cool, I guess. You know, for being a girl and all."

"What a charmer," she replied. "But you might as well know right now, you're not getting past second base unless you agree to take me to the prom."

"If what we've been doing is your idea of second base I think I might not survive third. But I've gotten kind of used to your snoring and sheet stealing," he said, leaning toward her.

As they kissed, they heard an ungodly sound next to the Tahoe, accompanied by blue and red flashing lights.

"Jesus," Kathleen said, looking at Matt, "I thought that was you for a minute."

"I can do better than that," he replied, before rolling down the window for the RCMP cruiser that had pulled up next to them.

"Hello, Officer Rideout," he said, smiling as he recognised her from the day before. "What's wrong? Can't a couple of kids do a little necking in public? I'm being good, honest."

"Not you I'm worried about," Rideout replied. "It's that Ryan girl next to you I'd be watching out for. Just in case you want to know, Mr. Hunt has come to, but he isn't talking. Got a concussion and a few broken ribs, and probably won't ever be a dog lover. I'm just about to go and check on the other man, who appears to have been with him." Then she got out of her car and entered the inn.

Meyer's rental was still parked in the hotel driveway as Matt and Kathleen walked up the steps to the front door. Kathleen convinced her sister-in-law that they were concerned enough about their friend to warrant entering his room, even though she said there was a Do Not Disturb sign on the door. When they walked upstairs, they found Constable Rideout knocking for a second time on Peter Farrell's door and getting no reply.

"I can open that for you in a minute, Jessie," said Kitty. "We're just checking on Mr. Meyer here."

Just then, they heard a muffled thump coming from Meyer's room.

Rideout walked back toward them. "Just a minute. Give me that key and step back."

"What is it? What's wrong?" asked Kathleen.

"Just stay back a minute; something's not right."

Rideout unlocked the door and opened it cautiously, with one hand hovering lightly over her service pistol. There was a scraping sound coming from the closet door. Drawing the firearm now, she pulled back the folding door and saw Jurgen Meyer struggling weakly against his bonds. The officer looked through the rest of the room and the bathroom, while Kitty called for an ambulance and Matt freed Meyer.

Although he appeared to be recovering quickly from the experience, Meyer was convinced to go to the hospital anyway for a more thorough examination and to get some IV fluids into his dehydrated body, after being trussed up in the closet for a day and night.

Meyer told them that all he knew was that some fellow guest, who he knew as Peter Farrell, had knocked on his door and jabbed him with a needle. That was the last thing he remembered. The RCMP officer went down the hall to Farrell and Hunt's rooms. To all appearances, Farrell had departed. A thorough examination of both rooms followed and anything left behind was bagged, tagged, and removed.

As Meyer was loaded into the ambulance, he grabbed Matt's arm and quickly whispered, "Matt, that man is very disturbed. I have my job to do, but I would advise you to think twice before going any further."

"Jurgen," Matt replied, "as far as I'm concerned, if it was just me, I wouldn't let that fucker scare me off. But I have to think of the girls; so right now I'm not sure. I'll be in touch though."

On the way back to Hibbs Road, Matt was silent for a while as he considered the safety of everyone involved with the crazy adventure he had found himself involved in. Finally, he told Kathleen what Meyer had said and shared some of his concerns with her.

"What do you think?" he asked finally.

"I think you have a big decision to make, but whatever you choose, I'll back you."

"Wow. Where were you all those years ago when I didn't actually want opinions but got 'em anyway?"

"I was right here, being a sweet innocent girl, just like now."

"Hmm," was his doubtful response as they arrived and parked the car.

○ ○ ○

Everyone gathered around expectantly when Kathleen and Matt came through the door. They explained what had happened to Meyer.

"I know you're not going to like this next part," Matt said, looking at Cassie and Bev and making his decision, "but I'm not willing to accept the responsibility of exposing our family to any further danger from that criminal. I'm sorry, but as long as Farrell is around, exploring the air shaft is off.

Evelyn and Tom exchanged a look that Matt didn't understand. Both Bev and Cassie walked over and hugged him.

"So, we're a family, Uncle Matt?" Cassie asked.

"Of course," he answered.

"Even me?" asked Bev.

"Especially you, Rocky," Matt answered, noticing the chunk of ore she had held earlier, now sitting on the coffee table in front of the overstuffed couch.

"Hey," Bev bragged, beaming, "I got a nickname!"

"Matt," said Tom, "we got a phone call just before you arrived from the RCMP. They say a man definitely identified as Farrell stole a motorboat down at the Front and got away toward the mainland. He's long gone."

"Beverly, shall we check our climbing gear and get it ready?" asked Cassie, in a very formal tone.

"Absolutely, Cassandra," replied Bev. "We want to make sure that everything is nice and safe, so Grandpa doesn't worry."

"Of course, Beverly. Better safe than sorry."

Matt looked at Kathleen. "Is there any woman, or dog, in this house whose little finger or giant paw I'm not wrapped around?"

"Nope," she answered simply, and gave him a kiss as Kip looked on.

"Welcome to belated parenthood, old man," said Tom, grinning.

Matt finally laughed, as Kip thumped his tail, shaking the floor.

By the time Cassie and Bev emerged from Cassie's room, Evelyn and Tom had prepared a late lunch for everyone. With that finished, and tea mug in hand, Matt spoke.

"It's after two o'clock," he said, "and it's clouding over. Jurgen needs a day to rest, so we're going to call it quits for today and get at it bright and early tomorrow instead."

There were groans from the girls.

"Agreed?" Matt asked, standing up to his full height for emphasis.

Reluctantly, Cassie and then Bev nodded affirmatively.

o o o

THE SECRET OF BELL ISLAND

After leaving Jurgen Meyer trussed up in the closet at the Inn, Peter Farrell had taken his suitcase downstairs to his rental car and driven down Beach Hill to the water on the island's south side. The boat theft, after he'd parked the car, had been easy. He'd simply paid an unsuspecting local fisherman to give him a little tour of the old ore piers, and when the man got out to secure the boat, Farrell had pushed off and throttled directly toward Portugal Cove over on the mainland, where the ferry docked. Stranded, it would take the man a good hour to report the theft. Luckily for him, Farrell had wanted to leave a witness. He'd needed someone who could identify him and tell the authorities what he looked like and exactly which way he had gone.

When Farrell had reached the marina next to the ferry landing, he'd tied the boat up at an empty berth among dozens of other small craft. Putting on a ball cap and sunglasses, he'd boldly stepped into the walk-on line for the MV *Legionnaire* ferry going right back to Bell Island.

Reaching the island side after the twenty-minute trip, he'd gotten into his compact, nondescript rental car, now sporting stolen licence plates, and begun driving to the west end of the Bell Island airstrip and a certain old air shaft where he was convinced that he would find a treasure trove of Nazi gold, hidden more than seventy-five years earlier.

It was close to six p.m. when he got out and opened the car's trunk, retrieving the backpack stored there and opening it up. He removed the Sig Sauer p226 pistol and holster from his waistband and dropped them in next to the extra magazines, and added the car's tire iron to use as a pry bar, if necessary. Finally, he grabbed a flashlight on a lanyard, which he put around his neck, and walked toward the shaft. He used the tire iron to scrape away three-quarters-of-a-century's worth of dirt and debris from around the metal grating, and then pried as hard as he could before it opened reluctantly with a metallic groan.

His light revealed nothing as he shone it into the darkness of the shaft. He tossed the iron in, just in case there was water below. He heard it clang off one of the rungs farther down and then there was a muffled thump. As he looked at the rusty rungs leading into the gloom, he frowned, regretting not buying a pair of gloves.

It was a testament to his greed and obsession that he eased over the lip of crumbling concrete, but based on Hunt's report about Matt McCarty uncovering the shaft and trying to open the hatch, it seemed to him like an ideal place to search for the hidden gold. He grabbed the first ladder rung at the top of the shaft. It felt solid enough and taking a deep breath he began to descend, the flashlight hanging from his neck showing each rung as he went further. After about twenty rungs, he stopped and shone his light below. There was still no sign of the bottom, but that did not deter him.

When Farrell neared forty-rungs deep, he began to notice some cracks in the concrete. One of them was several inches wide, and water seeped from the earth behind it, leaving a trail of greenish-brown slime that followed the trickle into the depths. There were more cracks in the cement walls as he continued, but soon, he could see the bottom of the shaft. The rungs ended about seven or eight feet from the bottom, and gauging the distance from the end of the ladder to the surface, he knew he would have to drop the last little bit to go any further. He was a tall man, strong and fit. When it was time to ascend, he knew that he could jump for the bottom rung and pull himself back up. Excitement ran through him as he let himself down the last few rungs using arm strength alone. Judging the distance he had to drop, he let go of the last rung.

Ten feet farther away from the vent, the ground was solid, but the sinkhole below the shaft was the worst place Farrell could have chosen to land. The shock to his system when his feet touched the surface and kept going down was traumatic for a person who had not experienced fear before. Instinctively, he spread out his arms as the quicksand-like mud reached his chest, otherwise he may have gone under right away.

Far above, there was a tiny pinprick of light, but right at the bottom of the shaft, there was only pitch black. He dared not risk sinking further by reaching down for his flashlight, and he could feel himself slipping an inch at a time deeper into the muck. For the first time in his life, Peter Farrell contemplated death as something real. Something tangible. Something that before this day, here and now in the blackness as he sank deeper, happened only to other people. Now, death seemed a near certainty, and he began to cry.

As the mud reached neck level, his feet touched something hard. There was a rock ledge below, and now Farrell had a solid surface to stand on. He carefully lifted his flashlight, on its lanyard around his neck, above the surface. He had to wipe the lens on his hair to remove the mud, and then he slowly shone it around him, hoping for a miracle. About five feet behind him, he could see some rusty railroad tracks, but a cautious step in that direction told him the rock ledge he stood on went no further. Trying to lunge for the track would be fatal.

Scanning the dirt and rock wall in front of him, he saw it: a chance, albeit a slim one. A few feet to his right, there was a tangle of roots protruding from the side of the earthen wall, closer than the rail track. They looked solid enough, and if he could grab hold, he might be able to pull himself out of this mess. A glimmer of hope. There was just one problem.

Feeling with his foot, he could tell the ledge he was standing on did not extend in that direction either. If he was to grab for the roots, he would have to push off the rock below him and hope the momentum would carry him far enough. The mud was thick, and it would not be easy to move through. If he didn't make it, there would be no going back. He would sink, and as the muck closed over his head, he would suffocate.

He knew fear now. It permeated his being, and his whole body began to shake. He was cold and scared, and he could taste the possibility—no, the probability—of imminent death. Just like those he had killed. Now he understood it, and not just as an abstract concept. He knew it in his soul, and he wanted to scream. He did scream. Loudly and for as long as his breath held. Then he pushed off from the ledge. His right hand came close, very close, but the roots were just a few inches beyond his reach. As he panicked, feeling his body sink, his left hand scraped the wall and felt a root extension protruding from it below the surface. He grabbed it and pulled himself along, holding his breath. With his head now submerged in the mud, he reached again blindly with his right hand, and it found purchase.

With a will to live he'd had no idea he possessed, Farrell dragged himself forward with both arms. His head broke the surface, and the muck began to release him as he worked his way hand over hand along the root system toward dry ground. Once he was free of the trap that he had unwittingly landed himself in, he lay there for twenty minutes, gathering his strength. Finally, he got to his feet and began to scrape the thick mud from his face and clothing. Shining his flashlight around, he could see a dead end farther down on the ocean side of the tunnel, but going inland, it looked clear, with the old rail tracks curving away in the distance.

Unless he could find some way of bridging the area he had just escaped from, there was no way he was going back out the way he'd come in. A small stockpile of extra rails and ties lay just ahead, giving him an idea. Being lighter weight than standard steel rails, he was able to drag a rail section down the tunnel, just past the farthest edge of the sinkhole, and placed it a couple of feet from the wall. Taking the other end, he lifted it and walked it toward the wall as well. Another rail was dragged down and placed parallel to it, four feet away.

He manhandled half a dozen six-foot-long wooden ties onto the rails, crossways on top of them, and the result was a solid bridge across the mud pit. Gingerly, he stepped up on the rig and looked at the rebar ladder. Doing a test jump, he found that he could reach the bottom rung. His spirits began to lift, knowing he now had an escape route.

Farrell picked up the tire iron, which thankfully had landed forward beyond the muddy pit, and made his way inland, carefully using the rail track as a guide, wary of falling into any more sinkholes. There were several more areas along the way that looked wet, and he shuddered at their deceptively calm surfaces, knowing that they were death traps awaiting the unwary.

After walking for another few minutes, he saw something looming on his right. It took a moment for him to realise that he was looking at a large steel door and frame set into the side of the tunnel wall. Rust had bubbled the black-painted surface, and flakes of oxidised metal littered the floor around it. This part of the shaft seemed to be mostly rock, and the frame was still firmly anchored in place, despite its cosmetic appearance. The door had a padlock on it, which may have been secure at one time but was now very corroded.

Farrell's obsession with the long-lost gold returned to him in a flash as he stood there in front of the door and looked down at the tire iron in his hands. The lock survived being struck several times before he inserted the tire iron's pointed end between the shackle and body of the device and twisted with all his might. When the lock gave way, he stared at it for a moment and then slowly reached out to remove it. Farrell then pulled hard on the handle, but the rust-frozen door would not move an inch. Trying to pry it open with the tire iron was useless. Not enough leverage.

He almost missed seeing the answer, partly buried in the dirt and rubble a few feet away: a five-foot combination pry bar and spike puller, left behind by the tunnel workers, along with more track and ties meant for the continuation of the rail line. It had some surface rust but was still quite usable, and its hooked end fit neatly between the door and frame. He threw his body weight against the flexing metal rod several times until the protesting door reluctantly opened a few inches with a loud echoing screech.

Farrell was on a roller-coaster ride of emotion as he was showered with flakes of rust and dirt that had built up over more than seventy-five years of the door's damp disuse. He dropped the spike puller and grabbed with both hands, yanking it open more, inch by creaking inch, until the squealing door was open about four feet. It would go no further, but he didn't need it to. Emanating from inside the room beyond, he felt dead, still air, warmer than the tunnel.

Holding his breath, he stepped inside the room. Straight ahead, there were a number of small wooden crates, and on top of them, he saw columns of gold bars—pure gold that didn't tarnish over time. They were as bright as they were on the evening August Kahr had stacked them there on a November Sunday in 1942. Everything came together for Peter Farrell in that moment. Ultimate pleasure. Better than sex. Better than any drug.

He stepped forward, eyes only on the prize, ready to claim what was his, almost feeling the weight and texture of the gold ingots before they were in his hands. To his right, his light revealed several shelves with various objects. He walked toward them and saw what looked like two rotted and mildewed uniforms. Above them was a scoped Mauser rifle and ammunition, as well as several other guns, all in good condition except for some surface rust and verdigris. There were more objects, but Farrell couldn't wait any longer.

He went over to the bench with the gold ingots and picked one up, feeling the heaviness of the small brick, which weighed more than two pounds. Next to the open box they had been removed from was a small sharp-ended pry bar. He quickly opened several more of the boxes stamped with the imperial German eagle clutching a wreathed Nazi swastika. Each was filled with damp, mouldy straw packing material and had twenty-four shining gold bars nestled within. As he filled his backpack with all twenty-four of the exposed gold bricks, he quickly realised it was too heavy. Reluctantly, he took out half of them. In round terms, his backpack now held about a million dollars, but after all he had been through, it was not enough.

It was midnight, but he had plenty of time to work between now and morning. He didn't know when McCarty might come looking for the gold, so there was only one chance to do this. He calculated being able to make at least four or five trips to the top and back, with every trip being worth a million dollars. If anyone showed up and interrupted his plans, there would be no talking and no mercy, just a bullet for any and all who got in his way. Hoisting the backpack onto his shoulders, he walked towards the heavy metal door.

He had been lucky when he entered the room, but luck was about to run out for Peter Farrell. With his next step, his foot came into contact with the trip wire at ankle level, and he saw the device's spring-loaded handle fly up into the air out of the corner of his eye. It took less than a second for Farrell's brain to process the incoming information and react. Just before the internal fuse detonated the device, he managed to make it just outside the door and around the corner.

As the grenade exploded, the piston of air leaving the room blew the door almost fully open, and in doing so, followed behind Farrell and propelled him several feet down the tunnel, as if riding a wave. Blood dribbled from both sides of his head as his ear drums ruptured, and his balance was compromised. The force of the blast disoriented him, and he didn't notice that his arms and legs were bleeding from small rocks, dirt, and rust flakes that had been blown against his body, with his clothing offering little protection.

He stumbled back down the tunnel toward the ventilation shaft that he would never climb. In addition to his other injuries, vital organs had been damaged by the concussive force of the grenade, and he was operating now on adrenaline while bleeding to death internally.

It was a miracle that Farrell was still ambulatory at all, but his mind began shutting down like the rest of his body as he staggered from the dry floor of the tunnel into one of the sinkholes he had so carefully avoided when approaching the treasure room. As the weight of the gold helped drag him under, for one last moment, he became dimly aware of what was happening. He tried to cry out but there was no sound as the mud entered his mouth and nose. The pit would slowly take his body and the twelve gold bars down more than one hundred and forty feet before joining the huge underground lake of mud that had existed there for thousands of years, fed from deep inside the earth.

When the mining company had first learned of the deadly sinkholes, they had kept it quiet, but it was the final nail in the coffin of the financially doomed underground-ore delivery plan. All construction ceased, and a danger sign was erected. A river of fresh water, originating from a fissure underneath Wild Duck Pond—now known as West Dam—fed into the underground lake, as did water from several other sources, and the current slowly pushed its way through the mud before eventually entering the ocean via an underground channel.

Sometime in the future, Peter Farrell's underground journey would end, but it would take many years before his body joined August Kahr's skeletal remains—or the few pieces of it that currents and sea creatures had not carried away—where the underground river joined the ocean below Grebes Nest.

Chapter 31

Bell Island, Monday, July 29, 2018

Jurgen Meyer was released from the Dr. Templeman Health Care Centre early Monday morning. After returning to his hotel room to change, he made his way to Hibbs Road in time for a late breakfast with the whole gang.

Equipment was checked, goodbyes were said, and the group—consisting of Matt, Tom, Cassie, Bev, and Jurgen Meyer—left Hibbs Road for the east end of the Bell Island airstrip, where adventure waited.

"It's been a pretty wild ride these past ten days, Ev," Kathleen said, as the house grew quiet.

"Yes. Can you imagine if I had known Matthew all those years since childhood? What would that have been like? I wonder."

"I can't begin to imagine. He seems to draw trouble like a magnet but—"

"A magnet. Irresistible?" Evelyn asked.

"Yeah, I guess," she laughed.

"Probably would have had me jumping off cliffs and crawling into caves like Cassie and Beverly," Evelyn continued.

"You would have loved it. That's why you're letting Cassie do it. He's got a way of engendering trust in people," Kathleen said.

"Yes, I s'pose. Cuppa?"
"Of course."

o o o

They parked the two vehicles by the ventilation shaft and there was an immediate concern. Getting out of the SUV, Matt noticed that the hatch on the vent was open.

"Matthew, I am worried that maybe Peter Farrell did not really leave the island, or maybe came back," Meyer said.

"Well," Matt said, "the authorities were quite sure from the eye-witness report that he headed toward the mainland."

Cassie and Bev looked at each other. They could both see where this was leading. If the men got too worried, they might not be allowed to enter the shaft. They looked pleadingly at Tom Clarke.

"Safety has to be first and foremost," Tom said. "That much is true, and that's why I borrowed a couple of Motorola two-way radios from the museum. We use them underground to talk with home base if we need to. And Mr. Meyer probably thinks I can't spot a man who's packing a pistol, but unless I miss my guess, you have a gun tucked under that left arm. Correct?"

"*Ja,* indeed I do, Thomas," confessed Meyer. "Luckily, the man Farrell didn't get into my room safe. But now I must tell you something. I want to go down and investigate below, but I am still feeling a little dizzy. I thought I would be okay, but it would serve no one for me to fall down that shaft."

Matt looked at Tom, who shrugged and shook his head. His big hands were still plenty strong, but his recurring knee problem meant that he could not go. Then he looked at the girls, who did not move or say anything, knowing instinctively that trying to influence Matt right now would be counter-productive. After a long pause, he walked over to Meyer, who reached inside his coat and handed Matt a 9mm Glock 19 pistol, with a laser sight attached. Matt depressed the release button on the side of the pistol and dropped the mag into his hand, examining it. He ensured there was a live round in the chamber then and reinserted the full magazine.

"You know guns," Meyer said, stating the obvious.

"Yes," Matt replied simply. "My only comment is that the fifteen-round magazine is illegal in Canada, but that's likely to make no difference to the charge when I go to jail, because the gun itself is prohibited here, with the short Austrian version four-inch barrel."

Meyer gave one of his rare smiles and stood waiting. Because the hatch was open, and because he was responsible for the girls' safety, Matt slipped the firearm into a pouch attached to his climbing harness and turned to face them.

"Okay, I'm going down first, and if I'm satisfied that it's safe after a good look around, you can join me. Today we use a fall-arrest rope and descend using the ladder rungs. The rope will be anchored up top, and if for some reason you fall, it will stop you."

He showed Cassie and Bev how to open the gate of a rope-grab assembly. It had a cam that would "grab" the rope and stop a fall. The other end attached to the front of their harness with a short connecting tether.

They all finished preparing for the adventure by doing a radio check, putting on climbing gloves, and checking helmet lamps and then each other's harnesses. Matt hooked onto the fall arrest then, and clicking on the portable gas sensor, swung one leg over the open shaft.

"Does everyone understand their jobs?" Matt asked. There were thumbs up all around.

"Last thing," he said. "Make sure you maintain three-point contact with hands and feet on the ladder at all times. Do not— I repeat, do *not*—get overconfident or impatient and skip a rung, or try to go too fast. Copy?"

Bev and Cassie hadn't seen the business side of the man before. Even with the rappelling and cave exploration, he had seemed less formal.

"Copy, Uncle Matt," said Cassie solemnly.

"Yes, sir," replied Bev, forgetting for a moment to call him Grandpa.

"Okay, last, last thing."

Anticipation.

"Be careful, but have fun," Matt said with a grin and a wink as he switched on his helmet lamp and Go-Pro miniature digital-video camera. This would be an adventure that needed to be preserved. Then he began descending into the dark shaft.

As Matt got down a few feet, he saw the date, 1925, framed in the concrete, confirming what Tom had said. He also noticed that dirt had recently been disturbed from the ladder rungs, and that in places, the rust had chipped away, showing brighter metal underneath. This proved what he had already been sure of: Someone had not only opened the hatch but had also descended the ladder.

He took his time, monitoring the gas sensor frequently and checking each rung carefully, especially in the areas where the concrete was cracked, showing wet earth behind it. There was some crumbling, probably due to both age and the materials used, but the overall structure appeared to be sound. Matt's headlamp had several settings, and he had it set on full-power flood, so its lithium-ion battery cut a wide swath through the darkness below. Looking down, he could now see what looked like railway ties at the bottom. The concrete got more cracked the farther down he went, and from several of them, he could see root tendrils protruding, as well as little greenish-brown rivulets of water running down the sides of the shaft. He approached bottom, disconnected the rope grab, and used the fall arrest line to carefully lower himself the short distance onto the rail ties below.

Noticing that the area beneath the ties looked wet, Matt tossed a rock in, and as he watched it disappear, he realised it was a mud sinkhole. Keying the Motorola, Matt explained to the people topside what he had encountered, and that he was going to further stabilise the landing zone, building it up for the others to be able to stay on fall arrest until they reached bottom. It took him about thirty minutes, using extra rail ties, but when he was finished, there were now steps leading up to the bottom ladder rungs, so they could easily get to the bottom and then back up.

o o o

On the surface, there were two girls trying to be patient but wanting desperately to join Matt. When he radioed in and said they were clear to follow him down, first Cassie and then Bev descended the shaft, observing the protocols and feeling excitement with just the right tinge of heathy fear. When they were both safely at the bottom, they had a little team meeting.

"Do you think the person who came down here earlier was Farrell?" Cassie asked.

"I wouldn't have thought so before, but right now, I'm not going to rule it out. Stay behind me while we go forward and watch out for any darker areas of the surface. That sinkhole at the bottom of the ladder isn't just from the water dripping down, and there could be more. We're going to walk along the rail tracks and only step on the wooden ties as we go."

Matt let his hand casually hover over the pouch holding the Glock as they ventured further into the tunnel. The combined light of all three adventurers quickly showed them a number of roughly rounded darker areas on the surface. First Bev and then Cassie tossed rocks in, and they vanished in seconds.

As they got further into the tunnel, Tom called them on the radio.

"How are you making out down there, people? Check in please."

"We're good. How's Jurgen?"

"I am fine, Matthew. Have you found anything yet?"

"Nothing yet," Matt replied. "We just. . . ."

"What? Are you alright?" Meyer asked.

"Yes, stand by," Matt replied. "Okay, I see something up ahead. I'll get back to you in five."

On their right was a fair-sized sinkhole. On the ground leading up to it, they could see a trail of some reddish substance.

"Is that—" started Cassie.

"Looks like it," offered Bev.

Matt touched a droplet with his glove and looked closely.

"It's blood, and it's fairly fresh," he announced. "The trail leads further back that way."

"No," said Cassie, realising what it meant. "It came *from* that way," she said, pointing farther into the shaft. "It stops right at the edge of that sinkhole."

"Ooh," murmured Bev, "do you think. . . ?"

"You're right, Cassie, and it doesn't look good," said Matt.

"Grandpa, I see something up there on the right. Look!" Bev exclaimed.

"Oh, Uncle Matt, that looks like a door!" Cassie added.

Just then, Tom called again on the radio. "Matt, Jurgen went to have a look around the area, and he's found Peter Farrell's car! It has different license plates on it, but he's positive. He recognises it from being at the hotel."

"That doesn't surprise me now," Matt replied. "We've seen some evidence that someone has been down here recently and may have been hurt. I have to check on something, and I'll get back to you. Don't make any report yet about finding that car."

"Copy. Be careful!"

Nearby was another stack of fifteen-foot-long sections of steel rail and six-foot wooden ties. With their powerful helmet lamps, they could see where the track and excavation had ended, about another hundred feet in at a blank wall of earth and rock. A rusting ore car left behind was held in place on the track with a sprag inserted in one of its wheels. Ahead on the right, as Cassie had exclaimed, there was a large open door. They approached warily, looking around in case Farrell had laid some sort of trap for them. Soon they were level with the entrance, and while the memories they later recalled of that moment varied a bit from person to person, the video would show exactly what they saw as they stood on the threshold.

The room was a mess but there had been nothing inside delicate enough to be badly damaged by the blast. A bench had blown over, and the extra Luger pistols had landed on the ground, but what really caught their attention was a dozen shiny yellow objects scattered around.

"Wait!" Matt exclaimed, detecting the smell of cordite in the still air. The girls froze as he looked around the corner into the room and did a careful sweep of the interior with his light. Looking down, he could see a tangle of thin cable and a classic-looking grenade pin attached to it.

"Okay, I think it's fine now," he said.

"Was there an explosion in here?" Bev asked, sniffing the air and looking around.

"Must have been a booby trap set for anyone walking into the room," Matt replied. "Unless you were looking for it, you probably wouldn't notice the wire. The residue smells fresh, so it must have been tripped not long ago."

Their attention was drawn back to the gold bars.

After examining the room carefully a second time for any more surprises, Matt said, "Go ahead, pick one up for the camera."

Bev and Cassie each picked up a gold ingot and posed for the video camera. All three were a bit dazed by the discovery, especially when they saw eleven more of the small wooden crates, some opened, stamped with the eagle clutching the Nazi swastika. The opened boxes each showed twenty-four gold bars nestled in straw. It could have been an occasion for celebration, but instead, all three became quite solemn.

"We learned about this in school, Uncle Matt," said Cassie. "This is all gold that was stolen from prisoners in the camps and the countries that were invaded, and even from their own citizens. Isn't it?"

"Yes, I'm pretty sure that's where this all came from," Matt replied. "It's a very sad story, and it's unfortunate that we can't change what happened in the past. But that's where people like Jurgen Meyer come in. He can help repatriate a lot of this wealth. One thing the Nazis were good at was keeping meticulous records, and Jurgen has access to them all."

"Let's radio up and tell him what we found!" exclaimed Bev.

"We could do that," Matt said, "or . . . we could make this sad history lesson a bit brighter with a little surprise."

They all smiled.

"Deal," said Cassie.

After radioing up that all was well, and pretending they were taking a break to eat, the group did a careful inventory. After prying open all the boxes, they found two hundred and seventy-six kilograms of gold.

"If every crate held twenty-four ingots," Cassie said, "that means twelve are missing from that first box."

"I think I know what happened to them, and Peter Farrell," Bev said quietly, as she thought about the trail of blood that she had seen leading to the mud pit.

"I think we all do," Cassie replied, looking at Matt, who nodded in agreement.

After a moment's contemplative pause, Bev asked, "Should we bring anything from here back up with us?"

"I don't think so," Matt replied. "Jurgen can have his surprise by looking at the video, but right now, I think we're obliged to leave everything in place, so we can report the find. Then it will be up to the government to work with the German authorities to assist with the repatriation process."

"Agreed," said Cassie.

With that, they left the room and swung shut the heavy but now freely moving door.

"I'm getting hungry for real now," announced Matt. "Anyone else?"

Both girls agreed and began discussing what they would have for lunch.

Matt smiled, thinking how resilient these young people were. He was very proud of the way they'd behaved and was impressed with their empathy toward those affected by the horrors of the past.

"Hey, Bev," Cassie said excitedly as a thought suddenly occurred to her. "Once we go back to school, we'll have to do our first English assignment of the year as a joint project."

"Huh?"

"Can't you just see it?" continued Cassie. "Every year, the same boring, predictable assignment. But not this year. This year is gonna be a lot different when we write, 'How We Spent Our Summer Vacation'."

"Holy shit! Yeah!" Bev exclaimed.

"Language, Beverly," Matt admonished.

"What?"

"Just kidding, Rocky."

o   o   o

Back on top, the three managed to give a defeated look to Tom and Meyer. When Jurgen asked if they had found anything, Matt said, "We looked really carefully, but besides signs of the previous construction, the only other thing we found was this."

As Matt got the room section of the video cued up to view, Meyer said, "It's okay. I had hoped for success, as this assignment has been personal for me. I wish I could have joined you down there either way."

"What do you mean it's been personal?" asked Cassie.

He began, "I told you the night we met that the people in my group are descendants either from families who were brutalised by the Nazis or those who were responsible for that brutality. How we came together is a miracle of healing, and a commitment to learn from this tragic past. This case was personal for me because my grandfather was an SS colonel. Finding the gold wouldn't have made up for the loss in terms of human suffering, but it might have helped others in need, and for me, maybe restored a little family honour."

The three explorers looked at each other.

"Well, Jurgen," Matt said, "I'm a bit sorry now that we had you on, but hopefully we can make up for it by showing you this."

As the video rolled, even on the small screen at the back of the GoPro camera, Meyer could see what they had discovered, from the girls holding up the two gold ingots to the inventory they had done of every shining yellow bar. He nodded as the heavy door was closed, and looked up with tears in his eyes.

"Thank you," he said simply. "This means. . . ."

"It's okay," Cassie said, and reached out to touch him on the shoulder.

Matt told Meyer and Tom their theory about what had likely befallen Peter Farrell, as Tom Clarke, being practical minded as usual, began rooting through the abundance of tools in the back of his pickup. Finding what he was looking for, he carried his portable torch kit to the grating.

"Anybody need anything from in here before I weld 'er up?" he asked. "Best not to leave it open, you know, for safety." He winked.

"Thank you, Thomas. That would be good," said Meyer, now smiling.

Bev reached up and patted the gold hunter on his shoulder. "Lovely fellow," she said.

As Tom Clarke spot welded the ventilator hatch shut, Matt voiced a concern: "Jurgen, we have to inform the authorities of the find. How can we make certain that this treasure doesn't just get taken away and not repatriated to where it should be going?"

Meyer reached into his pocket and produced a German diplomatic passport and a letter of introduction from the German Consulate General in Ottawa.

Matt studied it. "Is this . . . um . . . ?"

Meyer gave a rare laugh. "Yes, Matthew, this is very real. When I report the discovery, the Canadian Government will be very cooperative in assisting to get it back to Germany."

"The gun?" Matt asked, handing the firearm back to Meyer.

"Special diplomatic license, completely legal."

"Well," Matt said, "in that case, there's only one thing left to do."

"Go home and eat?" Bev asked hopefully.

"You got it. I'm starving," he replied.

"Me too," said Cassie.

"Me three," added Meyer, looking at them expectantly.

"Keep workin' on it, buddy," said Tom.

They all laughed, and after packing up, they left for Hibbs Road.

o o o

Kathleen had a large-screen TV at her house, so after a meal at Evelyn's, they all trooped to her place to watch the video. There were a few gasps along the way from Evelyn, while at times, Kathleen's eyes got a little wider as she tried not to appear too concerned about the more dangerous aspects of the day's adventure. She held Matt's hand throughout, at times squeezing hard enough to make him wince as Cassie and Bev looked at him and each other, grinning from ear to ear.

"What was your favourite part?" Cassie asked the group when it finished.

"You and Beverly holding up the gold bars," answered Kathleen.

"Seeing two strong young team members have a once-in-a-lifetime opportunity to take part in an operation that will change a lot of people's lives," said Matt.

"Hanging out with my uncle," Cassie said.

"Literally *hanging* out with my grandpa," Bev added.

"Honestly?" Evelyn answered. "My favourite part was when Tom welded that hatch shut."

"Impressing your sister with my welding skills," Tom said, looking at Matt. "Maybe I'm finally going to get lucky after all these years."

Evelyn turned red as both girls covered their ears and loudly cried, *"NO!!"*

Jurgen Meyer just looked at them all and really had no words.

"So, taking into account the missing twelve ingots," Tom said, "how much do you think you'll be able to give back to the people on your list?"

"What is the current market value for an ounce of pure gold?" Kathleen asked.

"Roughly $2,500 in Canadian dollars," Meyer answered.

Cassie looked up for a moment.

"There she goes," said Bev, marvelling at Cassie's mental gymnastics.

"Twenty-four-and-a-half million Canadian dollars, or approximately sixteen million Euros," Cassie offered.

"Gee, can't you be more specific?" Bev kidded.

"You have all been so hospitable and willing to help the cause," Meyer said. "I don't think I can ever repay you."

"Happy to help; just get that stuff where it needs to go, and we'll call it even. This has been an adventure I would have paid to be on," said Matt.

With that, Jurgen Meyer departed to go and report the discovery.

"What do you say we all take a walk down by the Number Two Cove," Kathleen suggested.

"Fresh air would be good after being underground all day," Matt agreed.

"I'll go get the little puppy to come along," said Cassie.

Soon, they were all walking toward the cliffs and enjoying the smell of the salt air in the late afternoon sun, while listening to the waves curling in to the shore and foaming over the slabs of rock that slanted down from the land into the sea. Matt couldn't have known that he was looking at the exact spot where his father had gotten into a dory seventy-six years earlier to go looking for the saboteurs who had left the treasure they'd found in the underground room with the steel door.

Chapter 32

Ottawa, Tuesday, July 30, 2018

Colonel Robert Bowdring had come to the Canadian Intelligence Corps from the air force. Originally a fighter pilot flying CF-188 Hornets, he was found to have an aptitude for intelligence work at the end of his exemplary flight career. Now forty-two, he was known as a fixer. His job was to investigate potentially dangerous matters of a military nature affecting the safety and security of the nation.

Checking his daily list of flagged items, he saw that a former naval lieutenant had recently died and had likely left behind some reference to an operation he had been part of during World War Two, which had initiated an internet search for more information about it by his son. However, the file from the operation in question had been classified "Secret," and until eventually becoming declassified, the contents should not see the light of day. Many such files existed from that time, although most would be considered moot after so many years. When Bowdring read through this file, however, it set off his internal alarm bell and initiated immediate action.

He realised that a terrible mistake might have been made in 1942, regarding the outcome of "Operation Red Iron." The assigned field agent, Lieutenant William McCarty, had

THE SECRET OF BELL ISLAND

submitted a scathing post-operation report, and not surprisingly, had spent the rest of the war sitting behind a desk. Bowdring's experience and gut told him that the report had been intentionally buried, likely due to the potential embarrassment of a superior officer who'd ignored McCarty's earlier warnings. It should have been obvious that the operation had been left incomplete, and that there could still be a ticking time bomb lurking even now underneath Bell Island, Newfoundland.

By the field agent's calculation, from finding twelve empty high-yield nitroglycerin boxes, the result could produce almost two and a half tons of explosive force. Bowdring made a phone call and spoke with a contact at the Department of Energy, Mines, and Resources. They said if that nitro was still in the mines, especially at a lower level, and it exploded, it was possible that the tunnels in all of the adjacent ore beds could collapse and about fifteen square miles of the north side bottom of Conception Bay could drop between thirty and forty two feet all at once. If that happened, it would create a tsunami and even Bell Island's high cliffs would not protect it. The devastation to the rest of Conception Bay would be massive, likely destroying anything within a half mile of shore. Knowing full well the shit show that was about to happen, and knowing there was no choice, Bowdring made the first of many phone calls that day.

The team was assembled according to a pre-arranged emergency plan. It consisted of hazmat and explosives specialists, lidar technicians, deep water and submerged cavern divers, as well as full technical support. A C-130 Hercules aircraft was fuelled and readied by the 17th Wing Winnipeg and flown to Ottawa to pick up personnel and supplies. A CH-147F Chinook helicopter flew to St. John's from a base in Gander. It would airlift people and supplies from the airport in Torbay to Bell Island, because the small airstrip there was too short for the huge transport plane.

Bowdring reached for his always ready go-bag and met his driver at the front door by the unmarked Suburban. Soon he was heading toward Ottawa's Canadian Forces Support Unit Uplands site. It wasn't widely advertised, but after the air base had officially closed military operations there in the 1990s, a few special units of the Canadian Intelligence Corps continued to maintain a presence, along with a warehouse stockpiled with supplies for any anticipated operation from rescue to invasion. The normally covert truck sped through traffic with emergency strobe lights flashing and soon reached the airport.

o o o

When Jurgen Meyer reported in to his contact at the consulate in Ottawa, a phone call was then placed from there to the Canadian Minister of Foreign Affairs, who made several other calls. By the time he was halfway to Newfoundland in the Hercules, Bowdring already knew the general details of the discovery of a cache of gold left behind, possibly by the same spies who'd sought to destroy iron-ore production on Bell Island during the war. He was now prepared for the next in-coming phone call, introducing him to Jurgen Meyer.

"Colonel Bowdring, I assume you have been briefed generally in regards to the situation here on Bell Island?" Meyer inquired.

"Yes, and you must know I have questions," the colonel replied. "Your cover is the not-for-profit gold-hunter group?"

"Cover? I don't know what you mean."

"Meyer, we're on a secure line, so let's talk straight. I've done a little research. You are with the BND, right? German

Federal Intelligence Service. It stands to reason that they would have at least one of you working in secret with a group like that to keep things honest. No harm in that; it's a good idea."

"Very well, Colonel," Meyer replied. "You are correct, but as it happens, I do actually have a very personal connection with this particular operation. Just a short while ago, when I reached out to my connection in Ottawa, asking for assistance in recovering German property that has been found buried on Canadian soil, I was told that we can now piggyback that objective on another operation here. I believe you are sending personnel to do an evaluation of a potential threat left over from the war?"

"Yes, from the same people who hid your gold. That's why I'm in the air on the way to Bell Island as we speak," he replied. "I should be landing in St. John's soon, and then taking the ferry, with people and equipment, to the island. Let's get together and have a longer conversation. I also want to talk to this Matthew McCarty, who with one quick internet search has possibly triggered the biggest and most expensive recovery operation in Canada for the last twenty years. Do you know where he is staying?"

"Of course, Colonel, and I think you will enjoy meeting Matt and his interesting family," Meyer replied. "They take some getting used to, but I find them both amusing and likeable."

"All right," Bowdring said with a chuckle. "Now, instead of Colonel, why don't you just call me Bob, and instead of Major Jurgen Eckhart Meyer of the Bundesnachrichtendienst, I will just call you Jurgen. Agreed?"

"Ahh, you have done your research, Bob! Yes. Agreed. Please call me Jurgen. I look forward to seeing you in person."

"Auf Wiedersehen," Bowdring replied, and disconnected.

MIKE PHELAN

St. John's YYT, Tuesday, July 30, 2018

It was evening when the heavy Hercules circled east over the Atlantic and then came in low over Logy Bay, touching down with a puff of smoke from its tires on the main eighty-five-hundred-foot runway at YYT St. John's International. The big cargo and troop plane taxied to an area of the airport reserved for the Royal Canadian Air Force transient-servicing unit. The big tandem-rotor Chinook helicopter was already on site, and the loadmasters of both aircraft took over, supervising the transfer of vehicles and equipment. It would take two trips to move men and gear to Bell Island by helicopter the next day.

In the meantime, quarters were secured for personnel at the Canadian Forces Station, a short drive away on the north shore of Quidi Vidi Lake. The facility was newer, and besides being a naval support facility for Maritime Forces Atlantic, it was also home to the Royal Newfoundland Regiment's Museum. The famous RNR had a rich, storied history, its predecessor units dating back to 1795. After distinguishing itself in many conflicts and both World Wars, it became a unit of the Canadian Army in 1949, when Newfoundland joined Canada as its tenth province, or as described locally, when Canada joined Newfoundland.

Chapter 33

Bell Island, Wednesday, July 31, 2018

While the marine scientific team began preparations for an all-out assault on the mines and the surrounding waters of Conception Bay, Bowdring got in his Suburban and drove himself to Portugal Cove, where he boarded the MV *Flanders* ferry to Bell Island.

Hearing about the history of the island was one thing, but seeing the beauty of the cliffs in the morning sunshine made him smile with admiration at some of mother nature's best work. Soon he was driving off the ferry and up Bell Island's winding Beach Hill Road. Bowdring had arranged to meet Jurgen Meyer at the inn where he was staying, and before long, he pulled up to the quaint former convent turned hotel. Meyer was sitting at his usual table in the restaurant, with his back to the wall, right where Bowdring would have chosen.

He walked over and introduced himself. "Hi, Jurgen. I'm Bob."

Meyer stood up and shook his hand. Taking Bowdring's measure, he said, *"Guten morgen,* Bob. Coffee?"

They both ordered a full breakfast and then talked over more coffee. Both were in agreement that the saboteur's work from the war was still far from over. Meyer made sure to let Bowdring know about Peter Farrell and his sidekick.

Bowdring, in his limited interactions with Farrell, would never have suspected that he was anything but a dedicated and loyal employee.

"I asked Matthew to wait where he is staying so you can meet him," Meyer said. "He knows that you are assisting with the gold retrieval, but nothing more yet. He also knows his father was assigned to find the spies during the war but very little else."

"Okay," replied Bowdring. "Let me check him out. If I like what I see, maybe I can help fill in some blanks."

They got in the Suburban and headed over to Hibbs Road. As they pulled up in front of number 23, they could see Matt and an attractive woman in a field behind the house, walking up from a cliff with a couple of teenage girls wearing full climbing gear, along with the biggest dog Bowdring had ever seen, followed by a couple of cats.

He started laughing as he and Meyer got out of the truck and had to force himself to stop before he got to the odd group. As Evelyn arrived with a large pot of tea and a platter of sandwiches, he was introduced to everyone by Meyer, and they all made ready to sit around a big outdoor picnic table behind Kathleen's house. Kip and the cat posse first circled the newcomer a couple of times, and after a tentative bonk on the leg, Bowdring was allowed to sit.

He took out an identification wallet and tossed it on the table. Matt opened it to reveal a very official-looking shield and plastic holographic picture ID card with the colonel's name, rank, and serial number. It was passed around to everyone and then went back in his pocket.

"Colonel—"

"Please, Matt, call me Bob. I just needed to get the identification formality out of the way. I understand you and your family have had some interesting adventures since you began your visit."

"To put it mildly, yes."

"I know you have managed to figure out that your father had considerably more involvement in the war than you may have previously thought, but I imagine you still have more questions than answers."

"Truer words, Bob," Matt replied. "But why are you actually here? I'm guessing they didn't send you personally just to assist in removing the gold from that old tunnel."

"Correct," Bowdring confirmed, "but with all due respect, I'm reluctant to discuss the details fully right now, as it is a matter that is both delicate, and at the same time, could cause—"

"You mean the explosives that might still be down in No. 4 mine?" Bev interrupted.

"If you find out the nitroglycerin is there, do you think it's still dangerous?" asked Cassie.

"You'll have to drain the mine to remove it," Bev added. "Probably drain all the mines too, 'cause they're connected in places. Right, Cass?"

Cassie looked off for a moment. "Yup, can be done. Get a powerful pump or two in the right place in the deepest part of the mine. Then it's just a matter of time."

"Who wants tea?" asked Evelyn.

Kip placed his massive head on Bowdring's leg for an ear scratch, and one of the cats jumped on the dog's back, making itself at home.

Matt just smiled and watched as Bowdring turned to Evelyn blankly. "Yes, please, or preferably something a lot stronger."

"You haven't had her tea yet. Better wait. You might not need anything stronger," replied Meyer.

"A Disney movie," Bowdring mused to no one in particular. "I'm stuck in the middle of a Disney movie."

"Bob," Matt began, "let me help you right out of the gate with something that I've learned here. Bell Islanders are more than just a hardy bunch. They're smart. If you use that, and just play everything as open as you can with them, you'll not only get a group that doesn't scare easily but you'll also have a lot of expert help at your disposal."

"Even the kids?" he asked, looking at Cassie and Bev.

"Especially them. Even if they drive you to an early grave, as they will likely do to me. They'll probably be running the show before you leave."

Both girls looked at the colonel, and he stifled a shiver as they smiled innocently at him.

Bev said, "Aww, Grandpa, that's so sweet."

"Oh, Uncle Matt," added Cassie.

Bowdring thought it best not to try and figure out the complicated familial affiliations, while at the same time wondering if the two young women were really looking at him as if he were some sort of prey.

"You've had dealings with Peter Farrell? And his accomplice?" Bowdring asked.

"I had a conversation with Farrell, yes. Right now, we have reason to suspect that, despite the authorities thinking he escaped to the mainland, he's actually still here on the island and very dead. I imagine you've got people who can confirm that once they take a little trip down a certain ventilator shaft. As for Delbert Hunt, he had the misfortune of attacking the girls and finding out how protective Newfoundland dogs are with their family. Right, Kip?"

It must have been his imagination, but for a moment, Bowdring thought the animal stood a little taller.

"That's not a dog," he countered. "I've seen smaller horses. Tell you what. Today would be a good time to relax and then get a good night's sleep, because tomorrow morning there's going to be a lot of activity, and I'll need help from you and Jurgen. And I suspect that, after the mad scientists finish their calculations, they're going to tell us to do what young Beverly and Cassandra have already suggested: drain the Bell Island mines. I don't know how you'd get hoses and pumps down there, two or three miles through the water, but that's not my problem."

"The ventilator shaft," Cassie said.

"What about it?" Bowdring asked.

"Gives me an idea. One thing we do a lot of in Newfoundland is oil exploration. What if you used smaller drilling rigs above the mines and drilled straight down to the deep part at sixteen hundred feet, and pumped out the water that way? Bet it wouldn't take a super long time."

Bowdring looked at Cassie and then Matt, who shrugged his shoulders, not having to say, *"I told you so."*

Then he looked around the table, settled on Bev, and feeling like he needed to reassert himself somehow, finally said, "I can fly fighter jets, you know."

"Hmm," she mused, "sounds intriguing. Tell me more, Colonel Bob. How's the view up there, and how would one apply for that job?"

o o o

For the rest of the day, people, equipment, portable living spaces, and vehicles were transported by helicopter and ferry to Bell Island, with the MV *Legionnaire* and MV *Flanders* laying on extra trips to accommodate everything. A base of operations was set up at the east end of the airstrip, encompassing the No. 4 mine and surrounding area.

Uncharacteristically for the government, things moved pretty quickly after that. A newer form of underwater 3D cave mapping was done, using a new approach employing a stereo video camera mounted on a remotely operated vehicle, which gave an accurate image of the mine, as though you were actually travelling in it downslope.

The general findings were further refined, and the exact location of every stick of nitroglycerin was mapped using latest-generation nano-sensors that detected minute amounts of off-gassing and confirming that the explosives were still in an active state. The engineers calculated that an explosion of the anticipated magnitude in the support pillars of the No. 4 mine would indeed trigger a catastrophic event.

Because remote retrieval of the material was not practical, the decision was made that the mine first had to be drained before removing the explosives. Sure enough, as Cassie had suggested, the method chosen was to use mini-platforms designed for use on fields of smaller oil and gas reserves. Two of them would be utilised and anchored on the north side of the island over the lowest ore beds. With newer high-capacity axial-flow pumps, it was estimated that it would take about sixty days to drain the mines. The nitro removal could begin to take place before that, as it was not at the lowest levels.

o o o

Matthew McCarty and Jurgen Meyer led the way to the underground room where the gold was stored. Meyer got to experience what Matt and the girls had felt when they'd first made the discovery, and it was an especially poignant moment for him. There was no comment as Matt and Jurgen picked up the Nazi uniforms and the weapons left behind by the saboteurs in 1942, and walked with them to the mud pit, unceremoniously dumping them in and giving a silent cheer as they went to meet Peter Farrell amid a few bubbles coming from beneath the surface. Forensics would later determine, from blood and fingerprints, that it was almost certain he had met his fate there.

The technicians were also able to determine the depth of the shaft of mud, and the scope of its underlying lake area. They recommended that, once the valuables had been removed and the area fully mapped, it be sealed off, as it would continue to be a dangerous and potentially unstable area. After they made their final ascent from the shaft, they watched as the gold bullion, packed in its original wooden cases, made its way to the surface. To move the cargo from the room to the bottom of the ventilation shaft, they had oiled up and utilised the old ore car, which was only fitting.

"So, Matthew, it is time now to part company. I will be sorry to leave, but may I keep in touch with you?" Meyer asked.

"Of course, Jurgen, after all you're part of our crazy family now, right?" Matt replied.

"Yes, of course," he agreed. After hesitating a moment, he said, "My friend, something puzzles me. You and Cassandra and Beverly were directly responsible for finding nearly twenty-five million dollars worth of gold, but you have not suggested or even hinted about a possible reward or percentage of the find in return."

"Jurgen, I can't place a value on what this whole experience has meant. I'm not rich by any means, but I've managed to save a little, so money doesn't mean much to me. It's the girls I'm proud of. Cassie and Bev both want to go to university, and it will be difficult for them financially, but they know where the proceeds of the discovery are going, and they wouldn't ask for a penny. Just wouldn't be the way of it, here on the island."

"I see," said Meyer. "Well, it's too bad, but unfortunately we do have strict rules about where the proceeds go. Matthew, I am going to accompany the cargo from here to the St. John's airport now, and then fly directly to Germany with it. I won't be able to see anyone else, and I'm not good with goodbyes anyway, but please give them my thanks and let them know that I wish them every good fortune."

"I understand, Jurgen. It has been a pleasure to meet and work with you, and please do stay in touch."

They parted with a handshake and no further words.

Meyer boarded the big Chinook helicopter and took off from the east end of the airstrip, near the old ventilator shaft.

o o o

The plan to drain the mines necessitated a full underwater mapping, using the latest technology, of the entire north side of Conception Bay as well as where the mini rigs would be towed and anchored. Along with known wrecks in the area, others were now discovered. Over the years, many vessels in this vicinity had either sunk, been scuttled on purpose, or had just gone missing. Quite a few of them were found, putting an end to any number of mysteries and providing some amazing opportunities for underwater recreational diving and scholarly exploration by Ocean Quest Adventures and The Shipwreck Preservation Society of Newfoundland & Labrador. The most unusual object discovered, however, was a metallic cylindrical shape over two hundred and fifty feet long and twenty-two feet wide, sitting upright on the bottom in only ninety feet of water just off Spoon Cove. The object was odd enough that a dive team was dispatched to investigate.

The submarine was partly buried in mud, but appeared to still be watertight after seventy-six years. Its designation, "U-184," could be made out on the conning tower, and visible on the mast was the heraldic outline of an upright, black-spiked mace on a white shield, crossed by three red, stylised lightning bolts. In time, the submarine would be raised and the desiccated remains of its entire crew respectfully repatriated to their homeland, thereby effecting long-awaited closure for the families of the sailors on the submarine that history said was lying crushed, over a mile deep, three hundred and fifty miles away, north of the Flemish Cap.

When Matt heard of the discovery, the mystery of the gold ring was finally solved. Subsequent autopsies performed on crewmen would reveal trace amounts of sarin, and combined with non-public knowledge about Kahr and Becher's secret mission, a tentative explanation for the fate of U-184 was proposed, whereby one or both of the saboteurs in 1942 had concocted a plan to keep all the gold for themselves and to kill all those aboard the boat and sink it in order to hide the plot.

The discovery of the submarine had intrigued Fran's friend Stewart Luffman so much that she'd said the hell with it, let's go visit, and that's how Fran and Evelyn became close friends. It was quite a sight the day she pulled up outside the Clarke home driving a '57 T-Bird convertible, and soon, while Stewart was talking to Matt and Tom out back, all the girls piled into the car and went joy riding around the island. Matt left the gold ring with Luffman, and he promised to research Gunther Dangschat's family and try to determine if there was a living relative to give it to.

MIKE PHELAN

○ ○ ○

Matt visited Patrick Kelly to let him know that they were finally dealing with the danger in the No. 4 mine. Kelly listened attentively while Matt spoke, and when he told the old pilot about the gold, Kelly actually gave a small laugh and nodded, almost as if the information solved some long-held puzzle for him. The pilot had nothing to say after that and seemed to fall asleep. Later in the evening, having turned ninety-nine just a few days before, Patrick Kelly died. The next day, Emma Rees called to say that she had a note from the man, dated the day of Matt's first visit, leaving the framed picture on his wall to him upon his death, along with a small wooden box. Matt was grateful that Kelly must have had a lucid moment and was happy to have the photo memento from his father's war days. He was surprised when he picked both items up and read the scrawled note in an accompanying sealed envelope:

> "Matthew," it began, "today is a good day, so I better do this quick. I have to take a guess and hope you are half the man your father was. I wish I could have been a teetotaller like him, and then maybe all my days would be good ones, ha ha. You are now going to learn some things about the past that I will have to trust in your good judgement to let stay there. Everything you need to know is in the picture.
>
> Captain Patrick Kelly, RCAF, ret."

Matt was sorry the old pilot had died but laughed at the idea of his father having been a teetotaller in the distant past. It was later that night, as Matt tried to figure out what the old man had meant in his note, that he looked at the picture and read his words again: *"Everything you need to know is in the picture."* He picked it up, noting that it was heavier than he would have thought, and shook it. Grinning, he turned it over and carefully pried off the back. Dated December 1, 1942, in Kelly's precise (and at one time), neat handwriting, with the fountain-pen ink unfaded by exposure to light, was a complete account of his involvement in the wartime "Operation Red Iron," including all the time he'd spent with Lieutenant William McCarty, down to the last uncensored detail.

By the time an incredulous Matt finished reading the last of many pages, he would have a better understanding of not only his father but himself as well. When Matt opened the wooden box, inside was a tarnished silver flask and a German Luger, still loaded but minus three rounds.

o o o

It was almost a full month after the discovery of the gold, and nearly time for Cassie and Bev to start their last year of high school. The whole gang had come together for a little birthday celebration for Tom Crane when a courier arrived at number 23 Hibbs Road. In a heavy German accent, he asked if this was the residence of Cassandra Clarke. As Cass came to the door and accepted the package, the man looked past her.

"And you must be Beverly," he said. Then, one by one, he pointed at each person now crowding around the front door and correctly named them all. Lastly, a lumbering presence pushed its way through the small crowd, and the man looked down. "And you are Kip!" he exclaimed, "who likes to be scratched behind the ears and gives ferry-boat rides to cats."

Then he looked at them for a moment and just said, "Thank you from all of us," and walked away.

Unusual for the group, they were all at a loss for words. Cassie saw that the package had a German diplomatic seal and was addressed to her and Beverly Adams. The girls looked at Matt.

"Probably not a bomb," he said, smiling and shrugging his shoulders. "Go ahead and open it."

Kathleen poked him as Bev ran to get the scissors.

Inside was a brief note. It just said, *"With gratitude for a job well done. This did not come from the gold, ha-ha – JM"*

The large volume of paperwork included official documents, in each young woman's name, for unlimited scholarships to any higher-learning institution they chose after successfully completing high school, as well as trust accounts for living and other expenses to the age of twenty-five. All documents had been signed and countersigned by senior representatives of the German and Canadian Governments.

Cassie and Evelyn cried. Tom, wearing his paper birthday hat, patted them both on the shoulder while Kathleen and Matt smiled at each other. Kip gave a short baritone woof, and Bev said, "That lovely fuckin' fellow. Oops, sorry Grandma."

"Go put that damned kettle on, and we'll call it even," Evelyn replied, laughing now.

○ ○ ○

Later, as Matt and Kathleen went for a walk after supper, she asked, "Will you be leaving soon?"

"Depends," he answered.

"On?" She was smiling.

"Well, first I need to know something," he said, "and let me get this straight: You're smart, beautiful, have a great sense of humour, and you aren't interested in trying to change me, right?"

"Agreed," she answered, with an exaggerated toss of her rich chestnut hair.

"Are you sure you're not an axe murderer or maybe have some weird thing for really old guys?"

"Are you sure you want to know?" she countered.

"I guess it doesn't matter. Either way, I'd go happy."

They turned off Hibbs Road and continued walking east along Backview Street past the Adams house. Then Matt stopped in front of a small, well-kept white bungalow with dark trim. Behind the house, as at Kathleen's, there was an open field leading to the cliff beyond. The three-rail wooden fence around it needed a bit of upkeep, but overall, it looked very cosy. He took her hand and led her up the short walk to the door. As Kathleen's eyes began to widen, he took out his key ring, which had not only a shiny new key on it but also two recently added small, round, brass miner's tokens.

"To answer your question," he said, "I'd need to go back to the West Coast to clean up some things first, and get what little bit of my former life I care about shipped out here, but—"

"WHAT!? WHEN? You bought this? You sneaky—!"

"Yup. Now, I don't want to be presumptuous, but I'm in a position to offer you sleepover privileges and a drawer or two at my place, as well as your very own space in my toothbrush holder, not to mention being privy to long drawn-out stories about my fabulous, exciting life after leaving the Rock a million years ago. I might even tell you about how, once upon a time in my rock and roll days, I almost used to be famous."

"I guess I can handle it," Kathleen replied, (after feigning careful consideration), "but you'll have to be prepared to listen to stories of my exciting Bell Island life in return."

"Agreed. I'll bet it's a long, interesting story."

"Years long," she replied. "Now take me inside your lair and kiss me and stuff."

He did.

Chapter 34

Bell island, One year later

The mines were all pumped dry and the nitroglycerin safely and successfully removed. Even though modern mining methods would likely be able to take advantage of the billions of tons of ore still available deep under Conception Bay, and despite some romanticised memories of its past glories, it was not likely that Bell Island would once again become an iron-ore producer. While not yet official, it was very likely however that the mine museum would be expanded to utilise some of the areas that were now to be kept dry, for overnight camping adventures underground and for scholarly studies, including recording and cataloguing hundreds of now-exposed mine artefacts. There was even talk of reopening the No. 3 and No. 6 mine entrances and repurposing them. The beach entrance and the man-made shaft where the gold had been found were left accessible for official use but heavily gated and locked for the safety of the general public.

o o o

Kip had passed in the spring after a long, faithful, and happy life. Cassie's "little puppy" rested in a place of honour in the field out back where he had taken down Delbert Hunt, who was serving a very long sentence as a prisoner in Ontario's Millhaven Institution, where even with protective segregation—due to his reputation for having committed the type of crimes he had—he feared for his life on a daily basis. Kip's area continued to be a meeting place for the girls and was visited often by the neighbourhood cats, who sunned themselves on the big red rock next to him and seemed to stand guard over Kipawo's final port of call.

Friday, July 26, 2019

The tourists had all left the island's east-end lighthouse area for the day, while at the adjacent Keeper's Cafe, Matt and Kathleen were just finishing their usual Friday night house-special: codfish cakes and a salad. Evelyn and Tom, keeping each other's company more and more these days, were up dancing, along with a house full of other Bell Islanders, to a rousing old Harry Hibbs tune being played by the Friday Night House Jam Band. Many friends, old and new were in attendance. Bev's parents, Sharyn from the Cottages with Joanne from the Rolling Pin Bakery were there, and even Fran had come over with Stewart Luffman from St. John's for a visit.

Cassie and Bev were talking about their plans for the fall, which for Cassie would include working toward a degree in Newfoundland Studies at Memorial University. She would focus on the history of mining on Bell Island and the plans for its future, which she would be in a unique position to actually help shape.

Bev, much to the sorrow of her boyfriend Selby Gosse, would be leaving the island to attend a military college in

Ontario in preparation for a career as an Air Combat Systems Officer. Her dream was to be a fighter jet pilot in the Royal Canadian Air Force, and whether he wanted to or not, for the next several years, Colonel Robert Bowdring would become her mentor. Knowing that, with her, resistance was futile, he'd agreed . . . as long as she didn't start calling him "Grandpa." She replied that there was only one of those, and besides, he was "Colonel Bob," and didn't he already know that b'y?

As the song finished, regular emcee Peter Doyle strode up to the microphone and called out, "Cassie Clarke and Matt McCarty, get your arses up here and give us a tune."

In a now trademarked move, they both shook their fists at him as they walked up onto the tiny stage to the cheers and laughter of the audience. Matt picked up his acoustic guitar and Cassie her violin. As they prepared to play, Doyle continued speaking.

Raising his hands for silence he began. "Ladies and gentleman, now that Matthew McCarty here has been back home on the island for a full year after his long absence—and why he left to begin with I still don't understand, although I've heard it said it was to go to Vancouver to become a hippie . . ." He paused to let the rousing laughter die down. "It's time to declare him a born-again official Bell Islander, because otherwise, we wouldn't stand for a mainlander coming in here and stealing one of our women."

As the audience roared again, another man stood up. "Tis the other way 'round, Peter!" he laughed. "It's the first time I ever seen a codfish jig itself."

"Then I'm a happy cod," Matt yelled back, laughing.

One more person in the crowd called out, "You got lucky with that Ryan girl, my son; she's some pretty."

"Oh, believe me, she knows it," Matt informed the room.

"Hey!" came from Kathleen's direction.

Finally, as the room settled down and got quiet, Cassie leaned into the mic and said, "This is Lorraine's song."

Matt nodded and looked around, before saying, "Wherever you are, Lorraine, and no matter what it takes, we'll never give up until we find you."

Little did he know then that Lorraine Sparkes story was far from over.

Cassie started with the violin and then Matt joined her on his guitar, while in her sweet voice, she sang,

> *"Take nothing for granted, honour your friends,*
> *Rejoice every morning,*
> *When you're wrong, make amends.*
> *Be honest and faithful, to your own self be true,*
> *And don't be afraid to say,*
> *'I love you'."*

Epilogue

When Lieutenant William McCarty reached Halifax and submitted his report in December of 1942, he was perfunctorily congratulated on a job well done and summarily ignored regarding his continued concerns. He sat at a desk for the rest of the war, which suited his new bride and her family. McCarty became a functional alcoholic and remained haunted for the rest of his life by what he had seen and done in the war. A daughter, Heather, was born in 1946, and a son, Matthew, followed four years later. As much as he wanted to, he wasn't able to be a family man, and when his wife was diagnosed with mental illness, he retreated even further from those around him.

When the opportunity to return to Bell Island came about in 1955, he brightened for a while, and seeing Lorraine again brought him a time of brief happiness. However, that time was fleeting and soon coloured with regret, when one day she simply vanished without any explanation. When the letter from her finally came, six years later, he stared at it, imagining her now probably happily married with a family and enjoying everything he had once hoped to share with her. Once every year after lonely year, he would take the letter out. Not being able to bring himself to open it, he would always put it back again in the old cigar box, unread.

MIKE PHELAN

St. John's, July 2018

When Hunt came for him, it was a welcome relief. For a moment, he was back on Grammer Street, and Sparky was introducing him to his beautiful red-haired daughter. As her emerald-green eyes met his, they both knew. . . .

And then he was at peace.

Author's Note

While everything the characters on the preceding pages do and say is entirely fictional, at least half of their names are drawn with the greatest respect from a list of actual miners who gave their lives chasing the red rock from the early days all the way to the end. I did this as a way of keeping their memories alive, and of course, I made sure all of them were "good guys."

When I started writing this book I wanted to create and enclose a map to make it easier to follow the activities of the characters from 1942 and 2018, but considering the challenges of including both timelines it was not possible to do the task justice. If you want to have a closer look at the many actual streets and locations I describe in the novel I recommend checking your favoured web based map for both regular and satellite views. For instance, if you 'zoom' in, a satellite view past the north-east end of the Bell Island airstrip will lead you to an aerial view of a white tube shape which is the entrance to the book's famous No. 4 mine. Near the cliff is the very real Grebes Nest and east of that is the network of early tunnels that emerge on the beach as a result of the surface mining from the late 1890s. Cruise the streets and see if you can find where Lorraine lived in 1942 and where Cassie's "little puppy" lived on Hibbs Road . . .

Acknowledgements

To say this book couldn't have been written without the kind assistance of Bell Islanders would be the epitome of understatement. As the author, I gratefully acknowledge the help of the many who patiently answered my persistent questions about every facet and detail regarding Bell Island life from the pre-mining days before 1895 up to World War Two, the years after until the last mine finally shut down in 1966, and following that up to the present day. While there never was a proposed underground ore delivery system from the mines to the loading piers, the rest of the mining information in this book is as historically accurate as I could make it based on their help, my own Bell Island memories and hundreds of hours of research.

Special thanks to Mayor Gary Gosine and the Wabana Town Council, Radio Bell Island CJBI 93.9 FM, Teresita McCarthy and Ed Fitzgerald from the Bell Island Community Museum, as well as Henry Clarke and his talented crew from The Theatre of the Mine. Of particular assistance was Gail Hussey-Weir, author of *The Miners of Wabana* (Breakwater Books).

If you would like to browse a fabulous wealth of information on all things historical about Bell Island and the mines including hundreds of photographs please visit my friend Gail's website at historic-wabana.com.

I would also be remiss if I didn't mention "Dicks" on the beach, who really have had the best fish and chips with stuffing and gravy since they opened in 1950.

Mike Phelan
2021

PS: Better late than never, Kipawo is pronounced Kip'-ah-wah . . .

CPSIA information can be obtained
at www.ICGtesting.com
Printed in the USA
BVHW040244100622
638844BV00004B/2